Praise for Loree Lough
and her novels

"Loree Lough's *An Accidental Mom*
is a tender romance."
—*RT Book Reviews*

"Well-defined characters with a
believable conflict highlight *His Healing Touch*
by Loree Lough."
—*RT Book Reviews*

"Loree Lough comes up with a new and
interesting twist to this charming baby story."
—*RT Book Reviews* on *Suddenly Mommy*

"Splendidly written, this uplifting romance
is head and shoulders above the
usual marriage of convenience and
definitely not to be missed!"
—*RT Book Reviews* on *Suddenly Married*

LOREE LOUGH
An Accidental Hero

&

An Accidental Mom

Love Inspired

LOVE INSPIRED BOOKS

ISBN-13: 978-0-373-65146-7

AN ACCIDENTAL HERO AND AN ACCIDENTAL MOM

AN ACCIDENTAL HERO
Copyright © 2003 by Loree Lough

AN ACCIDENTAL MOM
Copyright © 2003 by Loree Lough

Printed in U.S.A.

CONTENTS

AN ACCIDENTAL HERO   7

AN ACCIDENTAL MOM   263

Books by Loree Lough

Love Inspired

Suddenly Daddy
Suddenly Mommy
Suddenly Married
Suddenly Reunited
Suddenly Home
His Healing Touch
Out of the Shadows
†*An Accidental Hero*
†*An Accidental Mom*

*Suddenly!
†Accidental Blessings

LOREE LOUGH

A full-time writer for many years, Loree Lough has produced more than two thousand articles, dozens of short stories and novels for the young (and young at heart), and all have been published here and abroad. She is also an award-winning author of more than thirty-five romances.

A comedic teacher and conference speaker, Loree loves sharing in classroom settings what she's learned the hard way. The mother of two grown daughters, she lives in Maryland with her husband.

AN ACCIDENTAL HERO

Wait on the Lord, and He shall save thee.
—*Proverbs* 20:22

To my family,
whose loving support gives me courage, and to the
heroes who save us from all manner of danger
without a second thought for themselves,
for *that* is true courage.

Chapter One

Cammi Carlisle had been heading east on Route 40 since dawn, doing her level best to keep her mind on the road rather than the reasons she'd left Los Angeles. It would take Herculean strength and the courage of Job, too, to tell her father everything she'd done since moving away from Texas….

Sighing, she looked away from the rain-streaked windshield long enough to glance at the blue-green numerals on her dashboard clock. Fifteen minutes, tops, and she'd be home. Dread settled over her like an itchy blanket.

Her dad would never come right out and voice his disapproval of her decisions. Instead, he'd shake his head and say, "It's your life…but I think you'll be sorry…."

He'd said it when she signed up for Art instead of Bookkeeping in high school, when she traded her scholarship to Texas U. for acting lessons at the community college, when she announced her plans to move to Hollywood and try her hand at acting.

Cammi sighed, wondering how old she'd have to be before her dad no longer made her feel like a knobby-kneed, silly little—

From out of nowhere, came the angry blare of a car horn, the *whoosh-hiss* of tires skidding on rain-slicked pavement, the deafening impact of metal smashing into metal…. Then came an instant of utter stillness, punctuated by the soft tinkling of broken glass peppering the blacktop.

Cammi loosened her grip on the steering wheel and took stock. She'd been traveling north, but her fifteen-year-old coupe now faced south in the intersection of Amarillo's Western Avenue and Plains Boulevard—the very corner where, thirteen years earlier, on a rainy night much like this one, her mother had died in a fiery car wreck.

Still reeling from the shock of the impact, Cammi stepped shakily onto the pavement. She didn't seem to be hurt, and prayed whoever was in the other car had been as fortunate. Not much hope of that, though—the vehicle reminded her more of a modern-art sculpture than a pickup.

The truck's side window had shattered on impact, making it impossible to see the driver. Gently, she rapped on the crystallized glass. "Hello…hello? Are you all right in there?"

"I'm fine, no thanks to you," came the gruff reply.

The door slowly opened with a loud, protesting groan. One pointy-toed cowboy boot thumped to the ground, immediately followed by the other.

"Are you *crazy?*" the driver demanded as he stood and faced her.

Pedestrians had gathered on the street corners as the drivers of other vehicles leaned out of their car windows: "Anyone hurt?" one woman asked.

"Doesn't appear so," a male voice answered, "but I'm gonna be late, thanks to these idiots…."

Good grief, Cammi thought. As if her reasons for coming home weren't bad enough, now she'd have to add "caused a car crash, smack-dab in the middle of town" to the already too-long list. Suddenly, she felt light-headed and grabbed the gnarled fender of the cowboy's pickup for support. He waved back the small crowd that had gathered, and steadied her, two strong hands gripping her upper arms. Crouching slightly, he squinted and stared into her eyes.

"You okay? Should I call 911?"

The dizziness passed as quickly as it had descended. Cammi shook her head. "No. I'm okay." And to prove it, she stepped away from his truck and smiled.

He thumbed his Stetson to the back of his head and looked her over from head to toe. Satisfied Cammi was indeed all right, he nodded and crossed both arms over his chest. "Did you even *see* that red light?"

Blinking as the cold October rain sheeted down her cheeks, she stared, slack-jawed and silent, as her gaze slid from his dark, frowning eyebrows to his full-lipped, scolding mouth. Not a bump or bruise, Cammi noted, not so much as a split lip. Thank God for that! "I-I'm sorry. I don't know what was…"

He ignored her just as surely as he ignored the quickly

thinning crowd. Muttering under his breath, he began pacing circles around what was left of their vehicles. *"Is she blind?"* he said, throwing both hands into the air. "Where'd she get her driver's license, in a bubble gum machine?"

Unlike her sisters and so many of her friends, Cammi had earned her license on the first try, and hadn't been involved in so much as a fender bender since. "I can see perfectly well, thank you," she snapped, "and there isn't a thing wrong with my hearing, either."

He looked up suddenly. Scrubbing both hands over his face, he expelled a deep sigh, then slid a cell phone from his jacket pocket. "Well," he said, flipping it open and punching the keys with his forefinger, "at least you're not hurt." Frowning, he gave her a second once-over.

If Cammi didn't know better, she'd have to say he looked downright concerned.

"You *are* all right, right?"

Except for that brief dizzy spell.—and Cammi thought she knew what was to blame for *that*—she'd come through the accident unharmed. A quick nod was her answer.

Facing the intersection, he spoke quietly into the phone, shaking his head. He reminded her a bit of her father, what with his frustrated gestures and matter-of-fact reporting of the facts. He probably outweighed her dad by twenty pounds, all of it muscle, she decided, remembering the way his strong hands had steadied her moments earlier. The similarities made Cammi swallow, hard, knowing that the reprimand this cowboy gave her would pale when compared to the look of disapproval she'd see in her father's eyes once she got home. It would've been tough enough, bringing him up to speed on the reasons she'd left L.A.—*without* this mess. Especially one so similar to the wreck that killed her mother. Especially considering that in his mind, this too, like so many other things, had been her fault.

Stubborn determination, she knew, was the only thing that stood between her and tears. But there'd be plenty of time for self-pity later, after she'd told her father about Rusty, about the—

"Tow trucks are on the way," he said, interrupting her reverie. He snapped his phone shut, dropped it back into his pocket. "You look a little green around the gills," he added, wrapping those big fingers around her upper arm yet again. "Soakin' wet, too," he continued, leading her toward Georgia's Diner. And in a voice she couldn't describe as anything but tender, he added, "What-say you wait inside, where it's warm and dry, while I take care of things out here."

She hated to admit it, but she *did* feel a bit dazed and confused. Why else would she have so quickly and willingly followed his instructions?

As he reached for the door handle, Cammi considered the possibility that he was one of those multiple person-ality types…raging mad one minute, sweet as honey the next. What if he'd just robbed a bank, and the accident had interfered with his getaway?

He held the door open and smiled. "Order me a cup of coffee, will ya?" He nodded toward the intersection. "I have a feeling I'm gonna need it once that mess is cleaned up."

Like a windup doll, Cammi went where he'd aimed her, wondering yet again why she was being so agreeable. It wasn't like her to let others tell her what to do. She chalked it up to the welcoming comfort of being in the restaurant where, as a teenager, she'd spent hundreds of hours, earning spending money for movies and mascara and the myriad of other things high school girls need.

"Hey, Georgia," Cammi said, stepping behind the counter to grab the coffeepot. "Mind if I help myself?"

"Well, as I live and breathe!" Cammi's former boss tossed her cleaning rag aside to add, "Look what the wind blew in!" Georgia wrapped Cammi in a warm hug, then held her at arm's length. "You sure are a sight for sore eyes, honey. Are y'home for a little visit? I'll bet your dad is just thrilled outta his socks. Every time that man comes in here, it's 'Cammi this' and 'Cammi that.'"

It stunned her a bit, hearing her father had spoken well of her. But Lamont London had never been one to air his dirty laundry in public. She waited for Georgia to take a breath. "I'm home to stay," she managed to say between hugs. "Had a little accident out there in the intersection, and that's why I'm—"

"Accident? You okay, honey?" Georgia pressed chubby palms to Cammi's cheeks. "Let's have a look at you…."

Cammi gave Georgia a one-armed hug, mindful of the hot coffee sloshing in the egg-shaped pot she held in her other hand. "I'm fine, but my car isn't. And neither is that cowboy's pickup truck." She took a step back and pointed toward the intersection. "I was told to wait in here while he 'took care of business.'"

"Well, now, will wonders never cease. A real-live gentleman, in this day and age!" Georgia walked toward the customer who'd just seated himself at the counter. "Glad to have you home, honey," she said, winking at Cammi. "You know where ever'thing is, so go right ahead and help yourself."

Cammi filled two mugs with coffee and carried them to a booth near the window wall. The overhead lights glinted from the narrow gold band on the third finger of her left hand. Sighing, she stared through the diner's window, watching the cowboy "taking care of things" out there. For all she knew, he could be arranging to steal her car and everything in it. Why had she so casually handed over control of the situation, when usually, *she* demanded to be in charge of her life?

Cammi groaned softly, knowing that wasn't even remotely true. No one in charge of her own life could have messed things up as badly as she had this time!

Maybe his soothing DJ-deep voice was the reason she'd obeyed like a well-programmed robot, or was it those greener-than-emeralds eyes? Or that slanted half smile? Or his soft Texas drawl…?

Fingernails drumming quietly on the tabletop, she sipped black coffee, watching as he talked with yellow-slickered police officers, as he scribbled on the tow truck drivers' clipboards, as he collected business cards. He pointed and gestured, nodded in a way she could only term *efficient*. No, she corrected, the better word was definitely *manly*.

Once both tow trucks drove off with their loads, he headed for the diner, big shoulders hunched and hands pocketed as he plowed through wind and driving rain. It suddenly dawned on her that the coffee she'd poured for him would be cold by now. Cammi hurried to the counter for a hot refill, and was just settling back into the booth when he walked through the door.

He shook rain from his hat and denim jacket and hung them on the pole attached to the seat back, then slid onto the bench across from her. "I, uh, owe you an apology."

Not a word about the trouble he'd gone to out there, about being drenched by the cold rain, about being without his truck for who knows how long…thanks to her. Cammi blinked and, smiling a bit, held up one hand. "Wait, let me get this straight…*I* ran the red light, totaled your truck, and *you're* apologizing?"

His cheeks reddened and his brow furrowed. "Yeah, well, I went overboard. *Way* overboard." He wrapped both hands around his mug, then met her eyes. "Wasn't any need for me to get that hot under the collar."

She'd had plenty of time, sitting there alone, to toss a few ideas around in her head. His truck hadn't been a new model, and his clothes, though clean and neatly pressed, had a timeworn look to them. Which told her that, without his pickup he'd likely be hard-pressed for a way to get to work. No wonder he'd given her such a dressing-down! Now his quiet, grating voice and the haunted look in his eyes made her believe something far more serious than property damage had inspired his former grumpy mood.

"Let's make a deal," she suggested. "If the mechanic can get your truck back on the road in a day or two, *then* you can apologize for blowing things out of proportion." She grinned. "But I have a feeling that apology isn't going to be necessary, don't you?"

His smile never quite made it to his eyes, Cammi noted.

For an instant, she considered asking about that. Instead, she slid a paper napkin toward him. Earlier, she'd jotted her insurance agent's name and number and her own cell phone number on it. "Better drink up while it's hot," she said, pointing to his mug. Before he could agree or object, she tacked on, "I want to assure you the accident won't cost you a dime. It was my fault, completely, so if you need a rental car until your pickup is repaired, or if—"

His mouth formed a thin line when he interrupted. "Thanks, but I'll manage." He held out one hand and cleared his throat. "Name's Reid, by the way. Reid Alexander."

She wondered if his skin was naturally this warm, or had the hot coffee cup heated it? "Cammi Carlisle," she said. It still seemed strange, saying "Carlisle" instead of "London." Deep down, she admitted her new last name wouldn't upset her dad half as much as the rest of what she would have to tell—

"If you have a pen," Reid was saying, "I'll give you my phone number, too, in case your insurance agent needs it."

Cammi fished the felt-tip pen from her purse and watched as he plucked a napkin from the chrome stand-up holder on the windowsill. She liked the strong, sure lines of his handwriting, the firm way he gripped the pen. He had a nice face, too, open and honest, with look-straight-at-you green eyes that told her he was a good, decent man.

But then, she'd believed that about Rusty Carlisle, too…at first.

"Hungry?" he asked as she tucked his phone number into her purse.

She didn't think she'd ever seen thicker, darker lashes on a man. "As a matter of fact, I haven't had a bite all day."

He raised an arm and waved. "Hey, Georgia," he called, grinning. "How 'bout a couple menus over here."

The husky redhead shot a "you've gotta be kidding" look his way, and propped a fist on an ample hip. "I don't remember seeing you come in here on crutches, honey, so unless your leg is broken, come get 'em yourself." To Cammi, she mouthed *Men!* and went back stacking clean plates behind the counter.

Reid chuckled. "Be right back," he whispered. "Wouldn't want to rile the cook."

"Right," Cammi agreed, "'cause y'never know *what* might end up on your plate."

She liked the way he walked…like a man who knew who he was and where he was going in life. He leaned over the counter and grabbed two plastic-coated menus and exchanged a few words with Georgia. The good-natured tone of their banter told Cammi they knew one another well. Funny that Cammi didn't know him, too; she'd only been away from Amarillo two years, after all.

Only. A silent, bitter laugh echoed in her head. The past twenty-four months seemed like a lifetime now....

When he returned, Reid slid into the booth, handed her one menu, flattened the other on the table in front of him. "So, what can I order you?"

Georgia made the best burgers in Texas and Cammi had been craving one of her specialties for weeks. "I'll have a bacon cheeseburger and fries, on one condition."

He met her gaze. "Condition?"

There was no mistaking the suspicion and mistrust written on his handsome face. Cammi wondered what— or *who*—had caused it. "I'm buying," she announced, holding up a hand to forestall his argument. "You'd be home now, safe and sound and chowing down something home-cooked, no doubt, if I hadn't plowed through that red light. Buying your supper is the least I can do, and I won't take no for an answer."

That teasing look on his face made Cammi's stomach lurch. Was he *flirting* with her? Under normal circumstances, she might have been flattered. But these were hardly normal circumstances.

"There isn't a nickel's worth of fight left in me. So okay, you'll buy, this time."

This time?

Cammi got to her feet. What better way to hide from her reaction than to put on her "efficient waitress" face? "A lifetime ago," she explained, "I worked here at Georgia's. Maybe I can pull a few strings, get you some extra fries or a free slice of pie." She wiggled her eyebrows. "Georgia bakes it herself, you know."

Laughing, Reid said, "Yeah, I know." Then he added, "I'll have whatever you're having."

Cammi hurried to the counter, and came back carrying silverware in one hand and a pitcher of ice water in the other. She was about to leave again, to get glasses and straws, when he grabbed her wrist.

"Thanks," he said, giving it a little squeeze. "This is right nice of you, especially after the way I behaved out there."

The bright fluorescent light had turned his eyes greener still. "You behaved like any normal person would under those conditions." She eased free of his grasp. "This is the least I can do."

She puttered behind the counter and caught up with Georgia as the diner owner slapped burgers onto the grill and dumped frozen fries into the deep fryer. She couldn't help wondering as she watched her former boss poke the meat patties with a corner of a metal spatula, why she hadn't experienced any of these heart-stopping, stomach lurching "first meeting" feelings with Rusty. Cammi shook her head.

But honestly! What business did she have feeling *anything!* Cammi blamed the long drive, the accident, the reasons she'd been forced to leave L.A. for her strong reaction to Reid. Finding out she was going to be a mother on the very day she'd become a widow would make any woman behave strangely, right?

When Cammi finally slid the food-laden tray onto

their table, Reid gave an admiring nod. "It's like riding a bike," she said, dismissing his unspoken compliment, "you never forget how to balance." *If only balancing my life were as easy as balancing this tray,* she thought.

He waited until she was seated to say, "I owe you more than an apology, I owe you an explanation. All that bellowing and…" He shook his head. "Well, it was just plain uncalled for. This is a flimsy excuse, I know, but I had a similar experience some years back, and *that* accident…" He took a deep breath, exhaled. "Let's just say I'm downright sorry for behaving like a mule-headed fool."

His admission conjured a memory, one so strong Cammi didn't trust her voice. The boy who'd been driving the truck the night her mother died…*his* name had been Reid. One and the same? Or a queer coincidence?

She didn't realize how intently she'd been staring until he shifted uncomfortably in the seat. If he was *that* Reid….

"Did you know that cold fries cause indigestion?" she asked.

His expression said, *Huh?*

Using a French fry as a pointer, Cammi explained: "It has something to do with the way cooking oils mix with stomach acids. I think. Something like that." She was rambling and knew it, but better to have him think she was a babbling idiot than to press him for details… and find out she might be sitting face to face with the guy who'd killed her mother.

She'd been horrified to learn how her danger-hungry

stuntman husband had died, but his death only served to underscore what she'd realized on their wedding night—they hadn't married for love. The cold hard fact was, they'd been friends with one thing in common: a tendency to act on impulse.

So jumping to conclusions about Reid didn't seem the smartest thing to do at the moment. Besides, she recognized Reid's far-off expression as an attempt to hide from the miseries of his past. She recognized it because she felt exactly the same way. Cammi wanted to comfort him, if only for this brief moment in time, and gave in to the urge to blanket his fidgeting hands with hers.

Then, suddenly, for a reason she couldn't explain, Cammi found herself biting back tears, found herself feeling guilty for harboring so much anger toward Rusty. It would be hard, very hard, getting past the *way* her husband had died…and with whom. Still, on the day he'd been buried, Cammi had promised herself that Rusty's child would never know those awful details.

Reid eased his hands from beneath hers and broke the uneasy silence. "So, you live 'round these parts?"

She hadn't realized until that moment exactly how much she'd missed hearing a good old-fashioned Texas drawl, how much she'd missed Amarillo, how good it felt to be on familiar turf. "Actually," she said, shrugging, "my dad lives not too far from here." She sipped her soda. "And you?"

It seemed as if a shadow crossed his face, darkening his features.

Reid cleared his throat. "Once, I was a…" He took a

deep breath and started over. "Well, I'm a ranch hand now."

He said "now" as if it were "the end," and she wondered for a moment why. But Cammi wouldn't ask that question, either, because crashing into his life had already caused enough damage, without rousing bad memories as well. From now on, she'd keep the conversation light, carefree, noncommittal.

Cammi looked out the window, gestured toward the bustling street. "I grew up in Amarillo, but I've been away a few years."

He smiled. "Lemme guess…you're married with kids, and your husband's job took you away from home."

"No." She stared into her mug, saw the overhead lights glimmering on the surface of the glossy black coffee. She could tell him about Rusty, about the rush wedding, but then she'd have to admit what an addle-brained twit she'd been, running off without a thought or a prayer to marry a man for no reason other than that he'd asked her to. "No husband, no kids." She pressed a palm to her stomach. *At least, no kids yet,* she thought. "I've been in California, trying to become an actress," she finished in a singsong voice.

Usually when she said that, people chuckled at her admission, rolled their eyes, smiled condescendingly. Cammi waited for one of the typical responses. It surprised her when instead, Reid said in a soft, raspy drawl, "Well, you're sure pretty enough to be a movie star."

Everything, from his smile to his tone to the sparkle in his eyes told her Reid was interested in her. If they'd met at another time, under different circumstances…

But even if Cammi trusted her judgment—and considering the gravity and multitude of her mistakes, she most definitely did not—what man in his right mind would consciously get involved with a pregnant widow?

"So, what happened?" Reid asked.

"Happened?"

"To your acting career."

Thankfully, he hadn't asked about the *rest* of her life.

While she'd inherited her mother's dark eyes and hair, the acting-talent gene hadn't been passed down. Cammi had given it her all out there in L.A., but she'd had less luck pleasing directors than she'd had pleasing her dad. "Guess I just wasn't cut out for Hollywood," she said.

It was true, after all, in more ways than one. And when this pleasant little meal and friendly conversation ended, she'd have to go home and admit that fact—and a few more—to her father and sisters.

Home.

She glanced at her watch. "I'd better see about getting a taxi. My dad was expecting me over an hour ago. Don't want to worry him."

"I'd drive you, but…" He extended his hands in helpless supplication.

Cammi took no offense at the reference to his destroyed pickup because there hadn't been a trace of sarcasm in his voice. "You oughta smile more often." One brow lifted in response to her compliment, making him look even more handsome. Cammi felt the heat of a blush color her cheeks. "I like your smile, is all," she said, and started digging in her purse.

Reid leaned forward. "What're you looking for?"

The rummaging had been a good excuse to avert her gaze. "Change, for the pay phone." A half-truth was better than an outright lie, right? "My cell phone's dead." Cammi glanced toward the booth on the far wall and made a move to get up, but Reid held up a hand to stop her.

"Here," he said, passing her his cell phone. "I never use up all the minutes on my plan, anyway."

He sent her a lopsided grin that made her heart beat double time. She had no business reacting to this man. For one thing, he might well be partly responsible for her mother's death. For another, she was newly widowed… and with child.

"While you're at it, ask the dispatcher to send two cabs."

She flipped the phone open. "You wouldn't happen to have the number of the taxi company programmed into this thing, would you?"

"Never had any use for cabs, myself." On his feet, he added, "But I can duck into the phone booth over there and look one up." He grabbed the cell phone. "Might as well call 'em myself, long as I'm in there, anyway."

She watched him walk away. Reid was different from just about every man she'd met in California. Oh, he was good-looking enough to join the parade of those pounding the pavement in search of leading man roles—more than attractive enough to land a few, too. Which is why it seemed so strange that everything about him, from the leather of his cowboy boots to the top of his dark-haired head screamed "genuine."

Careful, Cammi, she warned. *The man doesn't need any more trouble in his life.*

And neither did she, for that matter.

Chapter Two

If he'd had the sense God gave a goose, Reid would have ordered Georgia's pie for dessert, or another cup of strong, diner coffee. He would have pretended that a ravenous appetite required yet another burger. Something, *any*thing to keep Cammi with him a little while longer. But once he'd called for the taxis, there was no stopping time, and Reid had to satisfy himself with hanging around as they waited for their drivers. For several minutes after hers drove off, he found himself staring as the taillights turned into glowing red pinpricks before disappearing into the rainy black night.

"Where's your truck?" Billy asked half an hour later, nodding toward the taxi that had delivered Reid to the Rockin' C Ranch.

He flung his jacket onto the hall tree. "Had a crack-up in town."

His friend's face crinkled with concern. "You okay?" he asked, one hand on Reid's shoulder.

"Yeah." Physically, he was fine. But something had

happened to his head, to his heart, sitting with Cammi at Georgia's. She looked awfully familiar, but he couldn't for the life of him remember where, or if, they'd ever met. Something he'd have to think about long and hard before he saw her again.

"Whose fault was it?"

Reid heard the caution in Billy's question; his friend didn't want to wake any sleeping ghosts, and Reid appreciated that. "Hers."

Nodding, Billy headed down the hall toward the kitchen. "Put on a pot of decaf couple minutes ago. Martina made apple pie for dessert tonight. Join me?"

Though he'd wolfed down his burger and fries before downing two cups of coffee at Georgia's Diner, Reid said, "Hard to say no to anything Martina whips up."

While Billy sliced pie, Reid filled a mug for each of them. "Li'l gal ran a red light," he explained, grabbing two forks from the silverware drawer, "and I broadsided her."

Wincing, Billy whistled. He didn't say more. Didn't have to. He'd been there *that* night, too.

"Really, son, you okay?"

Reid nodded. "Yeah." Okay as the likes of him deserved to be, anyway.

"Just remember, this one wasn't your fault, either."

Billy had talked "fault" after meeting then fourteen-year-old Reid at the E.R. "I talked to the cops," he'd said on the drive back to the Rockin' C, "and they told me three eyewitnesses stated for the record that Rose London ran the red light." Then he'd reached across the front seat and grabbed Reid's sleeve. "Quit fiddlin' with the bandage, son, or you'll wear a scar on your forehead the rest of your days."

Reid half smiled at the memory, because ironically, the scar he wore now, in almost exactly the same spot, had been inflicted by a raging Brahma bull, not a car accident.

"Stop lookin' so glum," Billy was saying. "Just remember, the accident wasn't your fault."

He'd said pretty much the same thing all those years ago: *"You're not to blame for what happened to the London woman."*

True enough—Mrs. Lamont London had run a red light, same as Cammi Carlisle, and he'd plowed into the side of *her* car, too. However, assigning fault did nothing to ease Reid's guilt. Not then, not now. And Billy had bigger problems to worry about than traffic accidents, present or past, since his doctor's prognosis.

"Georgia says 'hey,'" Reid said, changing the subject. "Said she misses seeing you and Martina."

The fork hung loose in Billy's big hand. Absent-mindedly, he shoved an apple slice around on his plate. "Gettin' harder and harder to drag my weary bones into town," he said on a heavy sigh. "Gettin' hard to drag 'em anywhere."

Reid knew Billy had never been one to wallow in self-pity, so it didn't surprise him when his longtime friend sat up straighter, as if regretting the admission, and cleared his throat.

"That list I gave you this morning was longer'n my forearm," Billy said. "When did you have time to stop at Georgia's?"

So much for changing the subject, Reid thought. "Accident happened in front of her diner." Cammi's pretty, smiling face flashed in Reid's mind. "We, uh, the other driver and I got all the particulars out of the way over burgers and fries."

Billy chuckled. "Ain't that just like you, to buy the kid a meal after she cracks up your only means of transportation."

Kid? He nearly laughed out loud, because Cammi Carlisle was more woman than any he'd seen since returning to Amarillo. More woman, in fact, than the dozens who routinely followed him around the rodeo circuit. Right now, she was the one sunny spot in his otherwise gloomy life. He was about to admit *she'd* insisted on paying for the food when Billy spoke.

"Amanda called." Using his chin as a pointer, he added, "I wrote her number over there, on the pad beside the phone."

Reid groaned inwardly at being forced to recall his last day with the tall willowy blonde who, despite his arm's-length interest in her, seemed determined to change his mind about "the two of them."

He thought of the afternoon, more than six months ago, when the surgeon gave Reid permission to leave the Albuquerque hospital. Amanda had been there... *again*. He hadn't wanted to hurt her, so he blamed his sour mood on the months of physical therapy that lay ahead of him. "Isn't fair to string you along while I recuperate," he'd said. "I need time, to make some hard choices about the future."

He realized now that his evasiveness had given her

hope that, at the end of his "alone time," she'd be part of that future.

Reid strode across the room, saw from the area code that Amanda had been near Amarillo when she'd called. Shaking his head, he groaned again, this time aloud. First thing in the morning, he'd call her, invite her to breakfast, and set things straight.

"Well," Billy interrupted, getting to his feet with obvious difficulty. "Guess I'll drag my ol' bones up to bed." He started clearing the table.

"I'll take care of these."

Chuckling, Billy winked. "I was hopin' you'd say that." He limped toward the door, stopping in the hallway. "Don't be up all night, now, frettin' about that accident, y'hear? I know it roused some ugly memories, but thinkin' it to death won't change anything."

True enough. Still… "I'll turn in soon."

The look on Billy's face said he knew a fib when he heard one. "Don't forget, the new ranch hands start at first light."

Reid only nodded.

"G'night, son."

Billy had been the closest thing to a father Reid would ever know. Watching him suffer, watching him die, as he was now doing, was about the hardest thing Reid had ever done in his life. A tight knot of regret formed in Reid's throat, all but choking off his gruff "'Night."

He listened as Billy shuffled slowly up the steps. If he could trade his own robust health to get Billy's back, he'd do it in a heartbeat, because what did *he* have to live for, to look forward to? Sadly, life wasn't like that.

Reid would have to be satisfied with doing everything humanly possible to make Billy as comfortable as possible during the time he had left.

Standing woodenly, Reid gathered up the dishes and added them to the already full dishwasher. The fact that Martina hadn't turned it on told him that she'd known her husband and "adopted" son would share a late-night snack. The thought made him smile a bit, despite the dark thoughts pricking at his memory.

The drone of the dishwasher's motor harmonized with the ticking clock and the pinging of water in the baseboard heaters. It wasn't really furnace weather just yet, but because of Billy's steadily declining condition, Martina had set the thermostat at seventy degrees and left it there. The mere thought made Reid wince. When his hot-tempered stepfather was diagnosed with cancer, it hadn't hurt like this—hearing the news about Billy's condition had been painful and terrifying. It didn't take a membership in Mensa to figure out why; almost from the moment Reid set foot on Rockin' C soil, Billy had scolded him for not doing his all-out best on chores, helped with homework, convinced Reid he *was* good enough to ask the prettiest girl on the cheerleading squad to the homecoming dance.

One palm resting on either side of the sink, Reid stared out the kitchen window, watching raindrops snake down the glass as wind buffeted Martina's butterfly bushes. She often stood here, overlooking the wildlife that visited her gardens. She'd probably been standing on this spot when she'd called him a couple months back to tell him about Billy's prognosis.

After they hung up, Reid threw everything he owned into his duffle bag and drove straight through, arriving in Amarillo the very next day. He'd moved into the same room he'd occupied when his mom was the Rockin' C housekeeper and his stepdad the foreman.

Hanging his head, Reid wondered if he would've been so quick to come back and help out if his injuries hadn't already ended his rodeo career.

Just one more thing to feel guilty about.

Well, he was here now. Determined to do everything in his power to help Billy and Martina, in any way he could, for as long as they needed him.

The grandfather clock in the hall struck one, reminding him that Billy was right: The rooster crowed mighty early at the Rockin' C. If Reid knew what was good for him, he'd try to catch some shut-eye, starting now. He flicked off the kitchen's overhead light and quietly climbed the wide, wooden stairs, skipping the third and the tenth so the predictable *squeak* wouldn't wake Billy or Martina.

Two hours later, he lay on his back, fingers linked beneath his head, still staring at the darkened ceiling. The rain had stopped, but the wind blew harder than ever, rattling the panes in his French doors.

He wondered if Cammi had made it home safely, if her homecoming had been warm and welcoming. She hadn't seemed at all that enthused about being back in Amarillo. Brokenhearted because she hadn't "made it" in Hollywood? Reid didn't think so. Cammi seemed too down-to-earth, too levelheaded for pie-in-the-sky dreams of stardom. No, her reluctance, he believed, was more likely due to a falling-out with some wanna-be actor in L.A. Or maybe she'd come home for the same reason he had…to help an ailing sibling or parent.

It got Reid to thinking about his own father, who'd taken off for parts unknown the moment his mom said "We're going to have a baby." And his mother? Well, for all her good intentions, she had a talent for choosing no-account men. The promise of a leak-proof roof and a steady supply of whiskey was enough for her. In exchange, she promised forty hours' worth of work each week…from her young son.

She had already put four ex-husbands behind her when she said "I do" to Boots Randolph. Grudgingly, Reid had to admit that Boots had taught him plenty about ranching. And while he'd been the best provider, he also had a hair-trigger temper, and Reid still bore the scars to prove it.

Had Cammi run off to California to escape a father like Boots?

The very thought made Reid clench his jaw so hard that his teeth ached, because it wouldn't take much of a blow to break someone that fragile.

No, not fragile. Cammi's demeanor—right down to that model-runway walk of hers—made it clear she was anything but delicate. He liked her "tell it like it is" way of talking, admired how she looked him dead in the eye and admitted the accident had been her fault—no excuses, no explanations.

She was agile, as evidenced by the way she'd balanced that tray of diner food on one tiny palm. Quick-witted, too, so he couldn't imagine what had distracted her enough to run that red light.

Picturing their vehicles again, gnarled and bent, made Reid cringe. It could have been worse. So much worse, as he knew all too well. Miraculously, they'd both walked away from the wreck without so much as a hangnail. "Thank God," he whispered, though even as he said it, he knew God had nothing to do with their good fortune. If the so-called Almighty had any control over things like that, Rose London wouldn't be dead, her husband wouldn't be a widower and her four daughters wouldn't have grown up without a mama.

He forced his mind away from that night. Far easier to picture Cammi, smiling, laughing, gesturing with dainty hands. Once she'd locked onto him with those mesmerizing eyes of hers, he'd been a goner. She'd looked so familiar that he'd thought at first he'd met her somewhere before. But Reid quickly dismissed the idea, because he'd never seen bigger, browner eyes. If he met a girl who looked like that, it wasn't likely he'd forget!

Reid sensed Cammi was nothing like the women who'd dogged his heels from rodeo town to rodeo town. How he could be so sure of that after spending forty-five minutes in her presence, Reid didn't know. Still, it was a good thing, in and of itself, because it had been a long time since he'd felt anything but guilt.

Guilt at being born out of wedlock. Guilt that taking care of him had made life a constant struggle for his mother. Guilt that though he'd turned himself inside-out to please his parade of stepdads, he'd never measured up.

Guilt that, while rodeoing was by its nature a business for the wreckless, his devil-may-care attitude had cost him his career. And the biggest, naggin'est guilt of all... that one rainy night a decade and a half ago, he'd been behind the wheel of the pickup that killed a young wife and mother.

He tossed the covers aside, threw his legs over the edge of the bed and leaned forward, elbows balanced on knees. Head down, he closed his eyes. When he opened them, Reid stared through the French doors, deep into the quiet night. Self-pity, he believed, was one of the ugliest of human emotions. He had no business feeling sorry for himself; he'd been given a lot more than some he could name. He had his health back, for starters, a good home and a steady job, thanks to Martina and Billy. If not for this confounded disease of Billy's, he'd have the pair of them, too, for decades to come.

He'd taught himself to dwell on the positives at times like this, to get a handle on his feelings—remorse, shame, regret, whatever—because to do otherwise was like a slow, painful death. Billy and Martina needed him, and he owed it to them to get a grip.

A well-worn Bible sat on the top shelf of the bookcase across the room. Martina had put it there, years ago, when he'd come back to Amarillo for his mother's funeral. "Whether you realize it or not," she'd said, "Boots did you a favor, beating you until you'd memorized it, cover to cover."

"How do you figure that?" he'd griped.

She had smiled, hands folded over her flowered

apron. "Anything you need is in those pages. That's why folks call it 'The Good Book'!"

She'd been so sure of herself that Reid had almost been tempted to believe her. But blind faith had been the reason his mother had married badly…five times. If she hadn't taught him anything else, she'd shown him by example what a mind-set like that could cost a person!

Three or four steps, and he'd have Martina's Good Book in his hands. Two or three minutes, thanks to Boots's cruel and relentless lessons, and he'd locate a verse that promised solace, peace, forgiveness. A grating chuckle escaped him. *Just 'cause it's in there don't make it so,* he thought bitterly.

In all his life, he'd known just two people who were as good as their word, and both of them were fast asleep down the hall. He loved Billy and Martina more than if they'd been his flesh-and-bone parents, because they'd *chosen* to take a confused, resentful boy into their home and love him, guide him, nurture him as if he were their own. Though he'd given them plenty of reason to, they'd never thrown up their hands in exasperation.

And he wouldn't give up on them now.

Suddenly, he felt a flicker of hope. Again, Reid considered crossing the room, taking the Bible from its shelf. Maybe Martina had a point. She and Billy had made God the center of their lives for decades, and they seemed happier, more content—despite Billy's terminal illness—than anyone he'd ever known. Maybe he should at least give her advice a try.

He stood in front of the bookcase and slid the Bible

halfway out from where it stood among paperback novels, Billy's comics collection and Martina's photo albums. A moment, then two, ticked silently by....

"Nah," Reid grumbled, shoving the book back into place. He remembered, as he slid between the bedcovers, how often he'd overheard Martina's heartfelt prayers for Billy's healing.

But the healing never came. Instead, Billy's condition worsened, almost by the hour. If God could turn a deaf ear to Martina, who believed with a heart as big as her head, why would He listen to a no-account like Reid!

Staring up at the ceiling again, he shook his head. There was no denying that Martina believed God had been the glue that held the decades-long marriage together. Once, during a visit to the Rockin' C a few years back, Reid had encountered a deep-in-prayer Martina in the living room. Glowing like a schoolgirl, she'd sung the Almighty's praises. "You talk as if He hung the moon," Reid had said, incredulous. She'd affectionately cuffed the back of his head. "He *did,* you silly goose!"

*Some*thing otherworldly was certainly responsible for their contentment and happiness. Scalp still tingling from Martina's smack, Reid had wondered if he'd live long enough to find a love like that.

"You're only twenty-seven, son. Give the Father time to lead you to the one He intends you to share your life with." As Reid opened his mouth to object, she'd added, "Think about it, you stubborn boy! If He could hang the moon, surely He can help you find your soul mate!"

Soul mate, Reid thought now. Did such a thing even exist anywhere other than in romance novels?

Romance. The word made him think of Cammi. Pretty, petite, sweet as cotton candy. When his gaze was drawn again to the gilded script on the Bible's spine, he stubbornly turned away, closed his eyes.

As he drifted off to sleep, it was Cammi's smiling face he focused on.

A few hours earlier...

"Wow, lady," the cabbie said. "This is some place you've got here."

"Isn't mine," Cammi corrected. "River Valley is my dad's."

He nodded. "Still, mighty impressive all the same."

She couldn't deny it. Anyone who'd ever seen the ranch had been impressed, if not by the three-story stone house, then by the two-lane wooden bridge leading to the circular drive, or the waterfall, hissing and gurgling beneath it. Everything had been the result of her father's design...and his own hardworking hands.

The tall double doors swung wide even before Cammi stepped out of the cab. Bright golden light spilled from the enormous foyer, painting the wraparound porch and curved flagstone walkway with a butter-yellow glow and casting her father's burly form in silhouette. A booming "Camelia, you're home!" floated to her on the damp Texas breeze. Then, his deep voice suddenly laced with concern, Lamont added, "What's with the taxi? Did you have car trouble?"

Cammi grinned at the understatement. "You could say that."

"You should've called," he said. "I'd have come for you."

Could have, should have, would have. How many times had she heard *that* before leaving home?

Lamont held out his arms and Cammi melted into them. Plenty of time to tell him about the accident—and everything else—later. For the moment, wrapped in the warmth of his embrace, she put aside the reasons she'd left home. Forgot his "you'll be sorry" speech. Forgot how determined she'd been to prove him wrong, for no reason other than that for once in her life, she'd wanted to make him proud.

Proud? So much for that! Cammi thought.

"Good to have you home, sweetie."

My, but that sounded good. Sounded right. This was where she wanted…no, where she *needed* to be. And if the length or strength of Lamont's embrace was any indicator, her father felt the same way. At least, for now. "Good to *be* home," Cammi admitted.

He released her and went for his wallet.

"Dad," she started, "I can pay the—"

But Lamont had already peeled off a fifty. "That'll cover it, right, son?" he asked, shoving the bill into the driver's hand.

"Yessir, it sure will!" Eyes wide, he waited for permission to pocket the bill.

"Keep the change," Lamont said, grabbing Cammi's bag.

The man beamed. "Sayin' 'thanks' seems lame after a tip like this!"

Grinning, Lamont saluted, then slung his arm over

Cammi's shoulder. "Drive safely, m'boy," he said, guiding her toward the house. He hadn't closed the front door behind them before asking, "Where's the rest of your gear?"

"I shipped some boxes a couple of days ago. They'll be delivered tomorrow, Monday at the latest." She tugged the strap of her oversized purse, now resting firmly against his rock-hard shoulder. "Meanwhile, I have the essentials right here."

"Meanwhile," he echoed, frowning as he assessed her rain-dampened hair and still-wet clothes, "you're soaked to the skin." He nudged her closer to the wide, mahogany staircase. "Get on upstairs and take a hot shower. After you've changed into something warm and dry, meet me in the kitchen. Meantime, I'll put on a pot of decaf."

In other words, Cammi deducted, despite the late hour, he expected her to fill in the blanks—some of them, anyway—left by her long absence; she hadn't been particularly communicative by phone or letter while she'd been gone, with good reason, and she was thankful Lamont hadn't pressed her for details. Now the time had come to pay the proverbial piper. "Warm and dry sounds wonderful," she said, more because it was true than to erase the past two years from her mind.

"Everything is exactly as you left it."

How like him to keep things as they were. Though her mother had been gone thirteen years when Cammi headed west, the only things Lamont had replaced were the linens, and even those were duplicates of the originals. Something told her it was love of the purest possible kind that kept him so stubbornly attached to his beloved Rose. The fact that her dad had held on to memories about *her,* too, inspired a flood of loving warmth. "I'll just be a few minutes," Cammi said, standing on tiptoe to kiss his cheek. Almost as an afterthought, she added, "Love you, Dad."

"Love you, too."

At least for now you do, Cammi thought.

Suddenly, the prospect of being in her old room, surrounded by familiar things, rejuvenated her, and she took the steps two at a time, half listening for his oh-so-familiar warning:

"You're liable to fall flat on your face and chip a tooth, bolting up those stairs like a runaway yearling."

He'd said the same thing, dozens of times, when Cammi and her sisters were children. She stopped on the landing and smiled. "I'll be careful, Dad," she said, pressing a hand to her stomach, "I promise." He had no way of knowing she had a new and very important reason to keep that promise.

Cammi blew him a kiss and hurried to her room. The sooner she got back downstairs, the sooner she'd know if this amiable welcome was the real deal…or a temporary truce.

Real, she hoped, because she would need his emotional support these next few months, even if it might come at the price of seeing his disappointment yet again. How would she tell him that, in yet another characteristically impulsive move, she'd exchanged "I do's" with a movie stuntman in a gaudy Vegas wedding chapel?

And it wouldn't just be the non-Christian ceremony he'd disapprove of.

When Reid had asked earlier if she had a husband and children, her heart had skipped a beat. For a reason she couldn't explain, it mattered what Reid thought of her. Mattered very much. So much so, in fact, that though she'd enjoyed his company, she'd rather never see him again than risk having him discover the truth about her. And if a stranger's opinion mattered that greatly, how much more difficult would it be to live with her dad's reaction!

For the past four months, since learning of Rusty's death and the baby's existence, Cammi had spent hours thinking up ways to break the news to her father. She'd hoped an idea would come to her during the long, quiet drive from California to Texas. Sadly, she still didn't have a clue how to tell him that in just five short months, his first grandchild would be born.

Lamont would be a terrific grandfather, what with his natural storytelling ability and his gentle demeanor. If only he could learn he was about to become a grandpa in the traditional way, instead of being clubbed over the head with the news.

What Cammi needed was a buffer, someone who'd distract him, temporarily, anyway, from asking questions that had no good answers. "Hey, Dad," she called from the top step, "where's Lily? I sort of expected *she'd* be the one bounding down the front walk when I got home…with some critter wrapped around her neck."

"Matter of fact, she's in the barn, nursing one of those critters right now."

Lily was the only London daughter who'd never left home. A math whiz and avid animal lover, the twenty-four-year-old more or less ran River Valley Ranch. "As much time as she spends with her animals," Cammi said, "I'll understand how she manages to keep your ledger books straight."

"That makes two of us," Lamont said, laughing.

She ducked into her room, telling herself that if she survived coffee with her dad, she'd pay Lily and her critter a little visit. Maybe her kid sister would drop a hint or two that would help Cammi find a good way to tell them…*everything*.

A shiver snaked up her spine when she admitted there *was* no good way.

Lamont's back was to her when she rounded the corner a short while later, reminding Cammi of that night so many years ago, when she'd padded downstairs in pajamas and fuzzy slippers. "Dad," she'd whimpered, rubbing her eyes toddlerlike despite being twelve years old, "I can't sleep."

When he'd turned from the kitchen sink, his red-rimmed eyes were proof that he hadn't been able to sleep, either, that he'd been crying, too. "C'mere, sweetie," he'd said, arms extended as he settled onto the caned seat of a ladder-back chair.

She'd ignored the self-imposed rule that said a soon-to-be teenager was too old to climb into her daddy's lap, and snuggled close, cheek resting on the soft, warm flannel of his blue plaid shirt, and closed her eyes, inhaling the crisp spicy scent of his manly aftershave.

Even now, all grown up and carrying a child of her own, she remembered how safe she'd always felt when those big arms wrapped around her, how soothing it was when his thick, clumsy fingers combed through her curls. Her unborn baby deserved to feel safe and protected that way, too; had her impulsive lifestyle made that impossible? Could Lamont accept what she'd done, at least enough not to hold it against his grandchild?

It hadn't been hard to read his mind that night, the eve of Rose's funeral. What was going through his mind now? Cammi wondered. Had looking through the rain-streaked window at his long-deceased wife's autumn-yellowed hydrangeas conjured a painful memory? Had the moon, which painted a shimmering silver border around each slate-gray cloud, reminded him how much the mother of his children had always enjoyed thunderstorms?

She wouldn't tell him about Rusty and the baby tonight. Tomorrow or the next day would be more than soon enough to add to his sadness. There's a time and a place for everything, she told herself. And sensing he'd be embarrassed if she walked in and caught him woolgathering, Cammi backed up a few steps, cleared her throat and made a noisy entrance.

"Hey, Dad," she said brightly, shuffling into the kitchen on white-socked feet. "Coffee ready?"

He masked his melancholy well, she thought as he turned and smiled.

"Sure is," Lamont said. "Still drink it straight-n-plain?"

"Yessir."

"We Londons are tough, so save the milk and sugar for kindergarten kids!" they said in unison.

Laughing, father and daughter sat across from one another at the table. A moment passed, then two, before Cammi said, "So how've you been, Dad?"

"Fine, fine." He nodded, then reached across the table, blanketed her hand with his. "Question is, how're *you?*"

She looked into gray eyes that glittered with fatherly love and concern. There were a few more lines around them than she remembered, but then, worrying about her had probably put every one of them there. Cammi felt overwhelmed by guilt. He'd worked so hard to provide for his girls, all while doing his level best to be both mother and father to them. He deserved far better than what she'd always given him.

"I'd hoped to accomplish something out there—" she blurted. "Something that would make you really proud of—"

"You've always made me proud," Lamont interrupted, "just being you. You know that."

She didn't know anything of the kind, especially since her mother's accident, but it still felt good, real good, to hear him say it. Suddenly, she found herself fighting tears.

Lamont gave her hand an affectionate squeeze. "I told you before you left home that those Tinsel Town phonies didn't have enough accumulated brain matter to power a lightbulb."

He'd said that and then some!

"So how'd you expect dunderheads like that to have

enough sense to see what a great li'l gal you are!" He patted her hand, then added, "I know you gave it your all, sweetie. If your best wasn't good enough for 'em, well…" He lifted his chin a notch. "Well, that's their loss."

So he thought her failure to land any decent roles in L.A. was responsible for her dour mood. Cammi was about to set the record straight when Lamont said, "You did the right thing, coming home. You have any idea what you'll do now that you're back?"

Lamont's question implied she was home to stay, and he was right. This baby growing steadily inside her deserved a stable home, deserved to be raised in a house where it would be treasured, and protected and nurtured by a big loving family. It didn't matter one whit what was good for *her*; from the moment she'd learned of its existence, Cammi had put the baby first, always, and that meant giving up her crazy ideas of stardom. She'd earned a degree in Childhood Development, had spent nearly three years teaching four- and five-year-olds before heading for L.A.

She ran a fingertip around the rim of her mug. "I made arrangements to meet with the Board of Ed first thing tomorrow. There are some openings in the Amarillo School District."

"Good plan." He slid his chair back and got to his feet. "Baked an apple pie today…."

"Baked a pie? You?" Cammi laughed. "What's this world coming to!"

"If you call following directions on the box 'baking,' then I baked a pie." He chuckled. "It was Patti's day

off, see, and I got a hankering for something sweet."
Unceremoniously, he plopped the dessert on the table.
"Care for a slice?"

Cammi went around to his side of the table, gently
shoved him back into his chair. "You tore open the package and put it in the oven, all without your housekeeper's
help, I might add. Least I can do is serve it up."

She wasn't surprised, as she rummaged in the cup-
boards for plates, silverware and napkins, to find everything right where her mother had kept them. "More
coffee?"

Lamont held out his mug, and, smiling, she topped
it off.

"Did I tell you it's good to have you home?"

She folded a paper napkin and laid it beside his mug.
"Yes, you did." Bending at the waist, Cammi kissed his
cheek. "Did I tell you it's good to *be* home?"

Cammi didn't miss the slight hitch in his voice when
he echoed her response. "Yes, you did." She slid a wedge
of pie onto a plate. As he speared an apple with one tine
of his fork, he added, "I sure have missed you."

She looked at him, smiling nervously, blinking. What
was going on here? Her stoic, keep-your-feelings-to-
yourself dad, admitting a thing like that? "Heard from
Ivy or Vi lately?" she asked carefully.

"Your sisters will be here for a welcome-home celebration as soon as we can arrange it. Patti will be whipping up a special dinner for us."

Cammi had been fairly sure that, like most everything
else in her life these days, her homecoming would be a
fiasco. In fact, she'd been dreading the whole miserable

scene so much that she'd been distracted and run the red light in Amarillo.

Memory of the accident brought Reid Alexander to mind yet again. Cammi pictured the handsome, tortured face. She knew precisely what event from her past haunted *her,* but what had painted the edgy, troubled look on his—

"So, what happened to your car?"

Cammi gave a dismissive little wave. "Little fender bender in town is all. No big deal."

Thanking God yet again that no one had been hurt, she remembered the napkin, tucked into the front pocket of her purse, that Reid had given to her in the diner. "The mechanic will call you with an estimate," he'd said, looking as if he'd been the one responsible for the damage.

Cammi braced herself, waiting for her dad to ask whose fault the accident had been, waiting for the safety lecture that would surely follow once she admitted she'd been one hundred percent to blame.

Instead, Lamont said, "Important thing is, you're home now, safe and sound."

And so is your grandchild, she thought, thanking the Almighty again.

He shoved his empty pie plate to the center of the table. "Not bad for store-bought and frozen, eh?"

Not bad at all, Cammi thought, looking into his loving face. Not bad at all.

And pie had nothing to do with the sentiment.

As she made her way up to bed around 2:00 a.m. after having a heart-to-heart with her sister Lily in the barn, Cammi's mind drifted back to Reid. His voice and manly stance, and the bright green of his eyes set her heart to pounding, as if she were a teenage girl in the throes of a first crush.

She dreaded going to bed because she knew she wouldn't be having a peaceful night's sleep.

More than likely, she'd have nightmares induced by worries about her condition—and how Lamont would react to the same news.

Chapter Three

Reid stood beside his rumpled bed, staring at the napkin bearing Cammi's name and phone number. Thinking about her had kept him up most of the night. Shaking his head, he slapped the napkin onto the nightstand, because there didn't seem to be a single legitimate reason to call her.

Couldn't use the car repairs as an excuse, because he'd already told her the mechanic wouldn't have time to assess the damage until Monday, at the earliest. Couldn't say the tow truck driver needed information, because she already knew their vehicles had been delivered to Wilson's Garage.

What was wrong with honesty? he wondered. Why not just tell her he enjoyed her company and wanted to see her again. He could suggest a movie, or a quiet dinner, someplace where he could get to know her better.

Reid held the receiver in one hand, the napkin in the other, then noticed that his alarm clock said five-thirty. Groaning, he blew a stream of air through his teeth. What was he thinking? Not everyone got up with the cock's crow! She'd driven all the way from L.A. to Amarillo and had had a car wreck, all in one day. Surely she'd be sawing logs at this hour.

Still, he thought, palming the napkin once more, hadn't she said this was her cell phone number? More than likely, it was turned off and recharging. He could leave a message, and if she didn't return the call, he could tell himself it had somehow been lost in cyberspace….

Holding his breath, Reid punched in the digits. After three interminably long rings, her lyrical voice said, "Hi. This is Cammi."

He could almost see her, smiling, bobbing her head, big eyes flashing as she recorded the message. The mental picture distracted him so much that he didn't hear the *beep*. "Uh, hey, Cammi. It's Reid. Reid Alexander. From last night, and, uh, y'know, the accident?" He looked at his watch. "It's just past five-thirty, Saturday morning and, well, I was just wondering if…"

What if he suggested a date and she rejected him? "…if there's anything I forgot. Y'know, phone numbers, or…whatever. So, call if you need anything." He rattled off his cell phone number, even though he had seen her tuck the napkin he'd written it on into the front pocket of her purse. Reid glanced at his watch again. "I hope you're okay, 'cause, well, I've heard that sometimes a person doesn't feel the afteraffects of an accident till the next day, or even the day after that." He rubbed his face and winced. "I hear-tell aspirin is good for what ails you." *Shut up, you idiot!* he told himself. "Anyway, I hope you're all right. Thanks and—"

"You're welcome. And I'm fine. How're you?"

He felt like a colossal birdbrain, a jerk, a sappy block-headed schoolboy. He could only hope Cammi didn't agree. "I, uh, thought I was leaving a message." No wonder he hadn't heard a *beep!*

"I got into the habit of answering the phone that way, so I'd sound in demand in case a producer ever called."

When she giggled, Reid's heart beat double time.

"I guess since I'm no longer in demand, I can start saying a simple 'hello' like everybody else, huh?"

Another merry giggle tickled his ear. He wanted to say, *First of all, you're not like everybody else.* Instead, Reid said, "You're very much in demand, at least by one beat-up cowboy."

Her tiny gasp made him grin. Would she be sitting there, wide-eyed, one hand over her mouth? he wondered.

"You're up awfully early."

"Early? Should've been up and out half an hour ago," he said, glad she hadn't hung up despite his long-winded "message" and his blatant flirtation. "But what're you doing up at this hour, if you don't mind my asking?"

Her sigh filtered through the wires, kissing his eardrum. Reid shivered involuntarily.

"No specific reason," Cammi said. "I just have… There's a lot to be done today."

Was that sadness he heard in her voice? Reid hoped not, because something told him that if anybody had earned the right to be happy, it was Cammi. "Well, I won't keep you, then. Just wanted you to know you can call, any time, if I forgot anything."

"You didn't forget anything, but if I remember something you might have forgotten, I'll be sure and call." After a long pause, she added, "And I hope you know you can do the same."

He nodded, then shook his head and chuckled under his breath, because of course she couldn't *see* him nodding. "Sure. Right. I'll do that." Reid cleared his throat. "Well, you take it easy, y'hear?"

"I will. You, too."

"Catch you later, then."

"Have a good one!"

If one of them didn't put a stop to this, they'd go on "ending" the conversation till sundown. Much as he'd enjoy spending the day with her, even by phone, he took the bull by the horns: "Bye, Cammi. Glad to hear you're still feeling fine."

"Thanks. Glad you're all right, too. I'll call if I hear anything from the insurance company or the mechanic."

"I'll do the same."

He put the phone back into its cradle, wondering why the room felt colder and darker.

Reid remembered that earlier, he'd pocketed Billy's note, the one with Amanda's hotel and room number. Grimacing, he fished it out. The sooner he got things cleaned up, the better. She answered on the first ring.

"Hey," he said, "I got your message and—"

"Reid, *dar*ling!" she shrieked. "How *are* you! Why haven't you *called!* I've been so *wor*ried about you!"

He sighed. "Will you be free in about an hour? I know it's early, but—"

"Oh, Reid," she cooed. "I'm *never* too busy for *you.*"

He stifled a sigh of frustration. Amanda's tendency to overemphasize even the simplest words was but one in a long list of reasons that it could never work out between them.

"When did you get into town?"

"Why, *yes*terday, of course. I called the *minute* I settled in, so we could get together and talk about *us.*"

He could tell her, here and now, that there never had been and never would be an *us,* but Reid didn't believe in taking the easy way out. The night he'd won the Silver Buckle award, Amanda had tearfully admitted she didn't have a ride home. And because Martina and Billy had drummed into his head that gentlemen treated women like ladies whether or not they deserved it, he agreed to drive her. He should have immediately put the brakes on her intense thank-you kiss in the hall outside her apartment. If he had, he wouldn't have paid for his thoughtfulness every day since.

"I didn't leave my room *once,*" Amanda was saying. "I'd just *die* if you called while I was out!"

"Mmm-hmm," he said distractedly. He had tried, over and over since that first night, to explain that one kiss doesn't seal *any* deal, least of all of the relationship kind. Her sobs had made him decide to explain things another day, when she wasn't so…emotional. *And today's that day.*

"I can hardly wait to *see* you, Reid! Did you miss me as much as I missed *you?*"

In place of a response, he said, "How 'bout I pick you up at eight, buy you some breakfa—?"

"Oh, Reid! I'd just *love* that!"

"See you at eight."

Reid felt strangely guilty after hanging up, not for severing the connection with Amanda, not for what he was about to tell her, but because it seemed this meeting with Amanda was tantamount to cheating on Cammi. He couldn't help but chuckle at that, because wouldn't it be a bitter irony if Cammi was home right now, rehearsing the same speech for him that he was about to make to Amanda!

Amusement faded fast as he imagined her, hemming and hawing as she sought a compassionate way to deliver her message. It would hurt worse than a fall from a saddle bronc, no matter what words she chose or how kindly she spoke them.

"Ridiculous," he muttered. "Face it, man…you barely know the woman!"

Still, admitting how it would sting if Cammi rejected him started a 'what goes around, comes around' mantra swirling in his head. It made him decide to set Amanda straight gently. Very gently…just in case. He half ran down the stairs, anxious to get it over with, once and for all. If he didn't waste any time, he could get the new ranch hands squared away before heading into town….

The moment he stepped into Martina's big sunny kitchen, he saw that she'd set the table. The scent of fresh-brewed coffee permeated the air, and pots and pans promising a full country breakfast were steaming on the stove.

"Good grief," he said, looking around. "What time did you get up?"

Martina handed him a glass of juice. "Never you mind. Just sit down and eat before everything gets cold."

Billy only shrugged, so Reid did as he was told; might be a lot easier for Amanda to take his "I'm not good for you" speech if he wasn't wolfing down bacon and eggs while he made it.

"I want you to have a healthy meal in your belly," Martina told her husband, "before we start out for Fort Worth."

It wasn't like Billy to comply so quickly, without so much as a teasing retort or a sly wink. Reid blamed it on nerves; Billy had never liked long drives or sleeping in hotel beds, and liked doctors' exams even less. This trip to the latest in a long list of specialists would require both.

Martina handed each man a plate piled high with link sausages, over-easy eggs, crisp golden hash browns, and buttered toast. She filled their coffee cups, then joined them at the table. Spreading homemade raspberry jam on her bread, she asked, "You okay this morning, Reid?"

He looked up, more than a little surprised at the question. Later today, she'd drive her husband all the way to Fort Worth for who-knows-what kind of prognosis. "I'm fine. How 'bout you?"

From the day Reid's mom brought him and his beat-up cardboard suitcase into this house, Martina had taken Reid under her wing, treated him like the son she'd never had. He couldn't love her more if she were his mother. A guilty thought rapped at the edges of his mind: Reid did love her more than his own mother. But then, Martina had *earned* that love.

"Never mind about me."

"I'm fine," he said again.

Her left brow rose, the way it always did when she thought he was holding something back. "You're not all stiff and sore? After that collision last night?"

He reached past the Eiffel Tower saltshaker and the Big Ben pepper mill to grab her hand. "Nope."

She still didn't believe him, and the proof was that in addition to raising her brow, Martina had tucked in one corner of her mouth.

God knows the poor woman had enough on her slender shoulders, what with all she did around the house and helping Billy with Rockin' C business. And now this mind-numbing death sentence…. "Honest," he added in a voice much too bright for his mood, "I'm right as rain. Fit as a fiddle. Sound as a dollar."

Billy chuckled as Martina sighed and shook her head. "Well, all right. If you say so. But there's a bottle of aspirin in the medicine cabinet, just in case."

Reid couldn't help but smile around a bite of spicy sausage, because truth was, his neck did feel a speck creaky, and a cramp in his lower back had nagged at him several times during the night. He blamed the long, sleepless hours for his minor discomforts; seemed every time he closed his eyes, he saw Cammi, smiling that *smile* of hers…brown eyes flashing, dimple deepening, musical voice reminding him of the wind chimes outside Martina's kitchen window. How was a man supposed to get any shut-eye when—

"What in thunder did you put in those sausages?" Billy asked his wife.

Her brow furrowed.

He used his butter knife as a pointer. "You can see for yourself the boy's off in la-la land."

Reid stopped chewing and smiled nervously under their scrutiny. He looked from Martina to Billy and back again. "What?"

The couple exchanged a knowing glance, and Martina giggled.

He put down his fork. "C'mon guys. Cut it out. You're gonna give me a complex."

"This girl who ran into you," Martina began, "is she pretty?"

Reid felt his cheeks flush. Because Billy and Martina were on to him? Or because Martina's question gave him yet another mental picture of Cammi? "She's okay," he said, though *pretty* didn't begin to describe her.

"What's her name?" Martina asked.

"Cammi Carlisle."

"Carlisle," Billy said out loud. "Don't know the name."

"Must be new in town," his wife told him.

Reid helped himself to another sausage. "She was on

her way home from spending a couple years in California when we, uh, met. Said she'd lived here all her life before that."

Billy and Martina looked puzzled.

"Maybe Carlisle is her married name. Maybe her parents are divorced and—"

Reid didn't hear Billy's explanation, because his mind had locked on the word *married*. Unconsciously, his fingers tightened around his fork handle. Heart thundering as his ears grew hot, he remembered asking Cammi if her husband's job had taken her away from Amarillo. The only word he could come up with to describe how she'd looked was *sad*. Even now, he heard the sorrowful note in her voice when she'd answered. Her reaction conjured more questions than answers.

Maybe Cammi had followed some guy to California. Maybe they'd tied the knot while they were out there, and things went sour, so she'd come home to put an end to it. That sure would explain why her mind hadn't been on the road when she ran the red light.

Then again, maybe there hadn't been a husband at all, and she'd come home for no reason other than that she couldn't cut it in Hollywood.

The real question was, what did he care?

At that moment, all Reid wanted was to get off by himself. It would take half an hour to drive to Amanda's hotel. He'd have plenty of time to roll those notions around in his head a time or two on the way over, see if he could figure out why the idea of a man in Cammi's life nagged at him like the aftereffects of a bug bite.

Reid scooted his chair back and got to his feet. "Great

meal, Martina, as usual." He carried his plate and silverware to the sink, grabbed his jean jacket from the wall peg and opened the back door.

He was half in, half out when she said, "Where are you going in such an all-fired hurry?"

"Got those new guys starting work today, remember. Don't want them lollygaggin', 'specially not on their first day." He nodded toward the outbuildings. "Might as well put them right to work on that fence."

Billy was leaning back in his chair, preparing to agree, when Martina said, "Before you go, I have a favor to ask you."

Reid stepped back into the kitchen. "I'll do it."

Her brows rose. "But you don't even know what it is yet!"

"Can't think of anything I'd refuse you."

She smiled, then folded her hands in front of her. "Well, you know how terrible I am with directions." She bit her lower lip, glancing quickly at her husband before meeting Reid's eyes. "And you know Billy can't drive anymore, so I was wonder—"

"Say no more," he interrupted. "What time were the two of you planning to hit the road?"

"Right after lunch," Billy said.

Reid put his hands in his pockets and nodded. More than enough time to get this nasty business with Amanda *and* the new ranch hands taken care of. "I'll just get the boys started, make sure they have enough to keep them occupied till we get back. I have a, uh, errand in town, but I'll be back by noon. We can head out whenever you're ready."

Martina gave a relieved sigh. "I had a feeling we could count on you." She brightened to add, "I took the liberty of booking a room for you at our hotel."

The long drive before and after the doctor's appointment would wear Billy to a frazzle, so despite the fact that he hated hotels, Reid would stay the night.

"All I can say," Billy put in, "is *this* doc better be worth the trip." He gave Martina a stern yet loving look. "Those last four quacks weren't worth their weight in feathers. You've run me all over, looking for a—"

"A miracle. Yes, that's right," she finished for him. Tears filled her dark eyes. Suddenly, she gripped her husband's hand, gave it a little shake. "I have faith, mister, and I won't rest until we've exhausted every possible option!"

On his feet now, Billy gathered her close and nuzzled her neck. "Aw, now, honeypot, don't get all weepy on me." He pressed an affectionate kiss to her cheek. "Don't pay me any mind. Y'know I love you to pieces for all you're doin' to save my ornery hide, right?"

Eyes closed, Martina nodded and pressed her freshly kissed cheek against his knuckles. If Reid hadn't already known how absolutely devoted she was to Billy, this scene would have made it obvious.

Her wavering breath pulsed in the quiet room.

So as not to disturb them, Reid slipped out the door, feeling like an interloper for eavesdropping on this very private, very loving moment.

Something nagged at the periphery of his consciousness.

He'd never been one to envy what others had…
but it sure would be nice to know a love like that
before he met his Maker.

After giving the ranch hands their orders, Reid drove
to Amanda's hotel and found her waiting for him outside
the entrance. "I *figured* you'd be driving some kind of
monster truck," she said, giggling when she opened the
passenger door, "so I wore *blue* jeans."

She sidled up, intent on planting a kiss right on his
lips. He gave her his cheek instead, and pretended not
to notice the disappointment that registered on her face.
She recovered quickly, though—he had to give her that.
After a second or two of silence, she snuggled close.

"I hate to sound like an old codger," he began, pointing at the passenger seat, "but you need to slide right
back over there and buckle your seat belt." He stared
straight ahead. If Rose London had been wearing her
seat belt thirteen years ago, she might have survived the
accident. Since that night, he'd been a stickler when it
came to road safety.

But Amanda had no way of knowing that, and her
wide-eyed expression proved it. "Had a fender bender
last night," he added, "so it's making me more cautious
than usual."

"How sweet," was her breathy reply.

Amanda chattered about turbulence during her flight
as Reid drove to Georgia's Diner and parked in the lot,
babbled about too few towels in her hotel room as they
walked inside, yammered about Amarillo's gray skies
and chilly temperatures as they scanned menus. "You

look *won*derful," she said, once the gum-snapping wait-ress had left with their order.

Reid knew she expected him to return the compliment, but to say anything flattering right now would only make his speech that much harder to deliver. *No point putting off till tomorrow what you can do today,* he silently quoted Billy. Taking a deep breath, he plunged in, saying it was all his fault that she'd come to believe they had a future as anything but friends. To spare her feelings, he called himself a fool, a self-centered jerk, a boor.

To his amazement, Amanda didn't resort to tears, didn't disagree. In fact, she said nothing, nothing at all. Instead, she simply stood and gathered her things before walking woodenly out the door. Groaning inwardly, Reid put a twenty on the table to cover the cost of the food they'd ordered, and followed her. He caught up to her on the entrance to the parking lot.

"Amanda," he began, "don't go away mad. There's no need—"

She threw herself into his arms and held on tight. Reid looked up, as if the answer to this problem was written on the underside of a rain cloud. He was about to offer to drive her back to the hotel when movement across the street caught his eye.

Cammi—in tiny black shoes and a bright white sweater—mouth agape and eyes wide, looking directly at him.

It was as if the world had come to a dead halt. Cammi no longer heard the steady din of traffic, didn't see sparrows flitting to and fro, pecking the sidewalk in search of food scraps dropped by hurrying pedestrians, couldn't feel the biting blast of autumn wind against her cheeks. She wasn't even feeling the rush of satisfaction from the successful interview she'd just come from with the principal of Puttman Elementary that had resulted in a teaching position. Instead, she was aware only of Reid, locked in an intimate embrace with a tall, striking blonde.

It made no sense why jealousy reared its ugly head, started her heart beating faster.

Reid hadn't mentioned a woman last night in Georgia's Diner. But then, why would he? He certainly didn't owe her any explanations. The sight of him, face half buried in the blonde's long, gleaming tresses, made her fumble-footed, and she tripped over a protruding blob of hard tar, squeezed into a crack in the curb.

Tires skidded, horns honked, brakes squealed as she landed on hands and knees in the road. She felt ridiculous, crawling around in a small circle, grabbing up the tube of lipstick and ballpoint pens that had spilled from her purse.

She had no idea when Reid had crossed the street, or when he'd knelt beside her. But there he was, lips a fraction of an inch from hers, smiling as she stuffed a rat-tail comb, a pack of tissues and a quarter into her bag.

"We've gotta quit meetin' this way," he drawled. Cammi giggled nervously, despite the dull ache in her lower back, despite the burning, bloody scrapes on her knees and the palms of her hands.

As they neared the curb, a wave of nausea and dizziness staggered her. But, just as he had the night before, Reid steadied her.

"You okay?" he asked, voice laced with concern.

She was about to answer, when the blonde he'd been hugging so tightly flounced up. "Well," she huffed, "at least *now* I understand why you wanted to *end* things." She blinked mascara-blackened lashes at Cammi. "I hope you'll be *very* happy, following your rodeo *cowboy* from town to town." Glaring at Reid through narrowed eyes, she added, "I feel it only fair to warn you, you *won't* be the only one!" With that, she spun on her stiletto heels and click-clacked off. "And don't you even *think* about following me, Reid Alexander," she tossed over her shoulder.

Reid seemed torn between helping Cammi and fixing things with the angry woman. "I'm okay," Cammi assured him. "Really. Now hurry, or she'll get—"

He met Cammi's eyes. "Trust me, Amanda is fine. She's like a cat...always lands on her feet." Then his eyebrows knitted with worry. "Wish I could say the same for you," he added, inspecting her scraped palms. He led her to the bus stop bench and sat her down. "Here, let's have a look at you, see if anything else is bleeding or—"

"I'm fine, honest." She nodded toward the blonde. "But she isn't. You'd better go after her, before—"

Reid tugged a neatly pressed blue bandanna from his back pocket and gently brushed road grit from her hands. "You've done a pretty good job of scratching yourself up."

But Cammi barely heard him as she watched Amanda step into a taxi and slam the door, hard. "Oh, wow. Oh, man. Just look what I've gone and done this time." Hanging her head, she sighed. "I'm so sorry," she stammered. "If I wasn't such a clumsy oaf—"

"Now, cut that out," he ordered. "You don't have a thing to be sorry for."

Cammi studied his handsome, caring face. She'd never seen that much concern on Rusty's face, not in all the months she'd known him. She pointed to the cab. "She's leaving, and—"

"You can't end what never began."

"Maybe I hit my head when I fell," she said, rubbing her temples, "and addled my brains even more than usual, because that makes no sense whatsoever."

Chuckling, Reid slid an arm around her waist and pulled her to her feet. "Let me buy you a cup of coffee, and I'll explain." He paused. "You were headed for Georgia's, right?"

She nodded. "Yes. I was in town interviewing for a teaching position at Puttman Elementary and thought I'd go into Georgia's for a cup of tea."

"How did the interview go?"

"I got the job." She smiled. "I'll be teaching fourth graders."

"Congratulations!" Reid said. "How about I keep you company at Georgia's, but what-say we cross with the traffic light this time."

"Okay, but it's not nearly as adventurous…."

She liked the sound of his laugh and wished there

was a way she could hear a lot more of it. But in her condition…

Reid chose the same table they'd shared last night, ordered coffee for himself and asked the waitress to bring Cammi a cup of herbal tea. "Something to soothe your nerves," he explained when the girl left. "You might want to make an appointment with an eye doctor."

"Eye doctor?"

"You had a dizzy spell last night, too, as I recall." He shook his head. "Maybe you need glasses or something."

Cammi took a deep breath, let it out slowly. Might as well just get it out in the open, she thought. "I don't need glasses, Reid. I need a bassinet."

Reid grinned, then snickered, then frowned. "A…a *what?*"

"Uh-huh. You heard right. A bassinet." She nodded as she saw understanding dawn on his face. "I'm four months pregnant."

His gaze went immediately to the third finger of her left hand, where the thin gold wedding band gleamed in the fluorescent light. "But…but—" He licked his lips. "But I thought… You said… You told me you weren't married," he stammered.

"My husband died four months ago. In an accident." No point spilling *all* the beans, Cammi thought, remembering the shame of hearing who Rusty's passenger had been. She'd save the "how" and "with whom" for a later conversation. If there *was* a later conversation.

Reid grabbed her hands and leaned forward. "Good grief, Cammi, why didn't you tell me about this last night?" He slapped one hand over his eyes. "I feel like a monster, bellowing at you the way I did." When he came out of hiding, he said softly, "I'm sorry."

Shaking her head, Cammi retrieved her hands, tucked them into her lap. "Nothing for you to be sorry about. I—"

"I kept asking myself," he interrupted, "what could distract a smart woman like you enough to run a red light." Reid ran a hand through his hair. "A widow just four months, and having a…" He blinked. "Having a baby, yet. I'm such a heel!"

She abruptly changed the subject.

"So who was the blonde?" she asked.

"Started following me around the rodeo circuit a couple years ago. I tried to tell her I wasn't what she was looking for, but—"

"Reid Alexander?" she blurted. "You're *that* Reid Alexander! Now I know why your name sounded so familiar. Wow. Can I have your autograph? You've probably earned more buckles than any cowboy in the history of the rodeo!"

When he blushed, Cammi's heart skipped a beat. "Tell me all about it," she said, sipping her tea.

She loved the deep, gravelly sound of his voice, the way his left brow rose now and then, and the way only one side of his mouth turned up with each grin. His green eyes flashed when he talked about the competitions, darkened when he spoke of the shoulder injury that ended his career, dulled when he told her about his friend Billy's terminal illness.

"We're heading to Fort Worth later today," he said

in conclusion, "to see if this specialist has a miracle cure."

"I'll pray for him," Cammi said. "And for a safe trip there and back, too."

She didn't understand why, but suddenly he seemed angry. Had she said something wrong?

Suddenly, pain like none she'd experienced sliced through her midsection. Biting her lower lip, she grimaced.

He was on his feet and beside her in a heartbeat. "What's the matter?"

Try as she might, Cammi couldn't find her voice. Squinting her eyes shut, she gripped her stomach and prayed, *Not the baby, Lord. Please don't let it be the baby.*

Reid slid into the booth beside her, draped an arm over her shoulders. "Is there anything I can do to hel—" He leaned back, eyes focused on the red vinyl seat. "Cammi," he said slowly, deliberately, quietly, "you're… you're bleeding."

Cammi looked down as tears filled her eyes. "Oh, no," she whispered, "no…."

"Georgia," Reid bellowed, scooping Cammi up in his powerful arms, "call the emergency room. Tell them we're on the way!"

Ordinarily, the feisty older woman would have balked at being ordered about that way. But one look at Cammi, and Georgia nodded. "You bet," she said, grabbing the phone.

"By the time an ambulance could get here," he told

Cammi, backing out the door, "we'll be halfway to the hospital."

Somehow, he managed to get the pickup truck's passenger door opened with one hand, then gently deposited her inside. "Don't look so scared, pretty lady," he said, buckling her seat belt, "everything will be all right."

Leaning against the headrest, she closed her eyes. *Stay calm,* she told herself. *Steady breaths, take it easy...because the Father is with you....*

Reid turned on the headlights and the hazard lights and put the truck in gear. "It'll be all right," he said again as the tires squealed onto the road.

"I hope so," she admitted. But already, she'd bled another puddle on the truck's bench seat. "Miscarriage," she sighed.

Reid reached across the seat to squeeze her hand. "Keep a good thought, okay?"

Tears streamed down her cheeks. "Pray, Reid," she managed to say. "Please, pray for me..."

Chapter Four

If he thought for a minute it would do a lick of good, Reid would ask the Good Lord to halt all the other traffic between here and the hospital. Would ask to be delivered directly to the emergency room.

The childish wish quickly faded when he took a look at Cammi and saw her lovely face contorted with pain and fear. He couldn't even put his arms around her, hold her close and promise to stave off anything and everything that might harm her...not if he wanted to get her safely to the E.R. as fast as humanly possible.

Reid patted her hand, feeling like an idiot each time he repeated "Don't worry" and "It'll be all right." She needed solid support, not empty assurances. If he had the power, he'd move heaven and earth to spare her this torment.

Anger made him squeeze the steering wheel tighter. *He* didn't have that kind of power, but *God* did. Didn't the Good Book say "Ask and ye shall receive"? Cammi had asked, no, *pleaded* was more like it, for Him to spare her baby. Yet, as the seconds turned into minutes and the minutes steadily mounted, she grew paler and weaker…and still her precious Lord hadn't acted.

Barely half an hour had passed since she'd sat across from him in Georgia's Diner, sipping tea and calmly telling him how four months ago, in the space of a few hours, she'd become a widow and learned about the baby. He didn't think it strange that she'd glossed over the particulars of the accident that killed her husband; Reid had never been the type to dwell on the gory details, either. But she'd been downright happy to talk about the baby. "This kid changed my whole life for the better," she'd said, joy in her voice and glittering from her dancing brown eyes. "I can hardly wait to meet him…or her!"

Though Cammi had hardly made a sound since they'd left the diner, he knew she was in pain—physical and emotional. Rather than cry out, instead of whimpering, she sat quietly, alternately holding her breath and panting—something else they had in common: he'd handled the broken bones, muscle pulls and torn ligaments in exactly the same way. Reid didn't think for a minute that she'd adopted her stoic demeanor just for his benefit. Her behavior last night—taking full blame for the accident—told him she was made of sturdy stuff, the "no point cryin' over spilt milk," "grin and bear it" type. Just one more reason to respect and admire her.

"It'll be all right," he said yet again, wishing he could turn back the clock to a time when she had reason to grin.

Last time he'd spoken those words, Cammi had

whispered, "I hope so." She obviously hadn't intended him to hear her greatest fear, whispered on the heels of what appeared to be another severe cramp: "Miscarriage…" Much as he hated to admit it, he thought so, too.

Seemed unfair, comparing a li'l gal as gorgeous as Cammi to a pregnant mare, but it was the only parallel he could draw from. He'd spent years around the stables, and knew the signs when he saw them: Cammi was losing her baby, if she hadn't already. He'd succeeded in saving a few foals in his day…and had failed a time or two as well. It had been hard, mighty hard, watching the mamas nuzzle limp, leggy newborns, determined to bring them 'round with soft, loving snorts and whispery whinnies. He'd risked being stomped more times than he could count, going into the stalls to carry the lifeless critters away. But the "out of sight, out of mind" theory, he'd learned, didn't heal the hurtin' any quicker in the four-legged world than in the two-legged kind.

Most times, thankfully, after a few rough days of searching for their young'uns, the fillies came to grips with the cold, cruel facts. But sometimes, the heartbroken mothers were never the same again. Cammi seemed strong enough to survive her loss, but then, every mare that gave up after the death of a foal had surprised him….

Cammi's raspy, trembling voice broke into his thoughts. "Reid. Please…pray for me?"

Pray? he thought. To the God who had let her husband die, who had let *this* happen to her—all in the space of a couple of months? Reid couldn't believe his ears. He blamed her blood loss, delirium, panic…what else could make her spout such gibberish?

He chanced a peek at her, at the tears glistening on her long dark lashes, at the hope emanating from her big frightened eyes, and realized she'd meant it, right down to the last syllable. Foolish as it seemed, Reid couldn't refuse her anything, especially at a time like this. If prayer would bring Cammi even one moment's comfort…

Reid cleared his throat, tried to remember something—anything—Martina had taught him, tried to conjure any of the hundreds of passages he'd memorized under his stepfather's brutal hand. Isaiah 49:13 seemed as good as any: "'Sing, O heavens; and be joyful, O earth; and break forth into singing, O mountains,'" he recited, "'for the Lord hath comforted his people, and will have mercy upon his afflicted.'"

Eyes closed, Cammi heaved a shaky sigh as Reid continued with Revelation 7:17. "'For the Lamb which is in the midst of the throne shall feed them, and shall lead them unto living fountains of waters: and God shall wipe away all tears from their eyes.'"

He saw her slowly nod as a peaceful smile kissed the corners of her mouth. "Perfect," she said softly. "And now, will you pray?"

The breath caught in his throat. If chapter and verse wasn't praying, what was?

But even as he asked the question, Reid knew that what Cammi wanted, what she needed from him now: A heartfelt, plainspoken plea, not for herself, but for her baby.

He felt like a hypocrite for giving so much as half a thought to the idea of asking *God* for help. A lifetime of unanswered prayers and bitter disappointments had taught him that the Lord, if He even existed, had turned His turn back on Reid, on Martina and Billy, on so many good people Reid had known.

Still, the Bible verses had definitely calmed her, as evidenced by her now regular, shallow breaths. He'd heard enough from-the-heart-pleas in his stepfather's fire-and-brimstone church to know how it should be done. Wouldn't help, he thought again, but what could it hurt?

"Lord," he began, "You taught us that with faith, nothing is impossible, so bless Your daughter, Cammi, now." She'd need strength of the superhuman kind, Reid acknowledged silently, to accept what the E.R. doctors would say about her pregnancy. "She believes You'll help her, believes You'll keep her baby safe and sound, right up to the moment You've chosen to bring it into this world."

It was hard to continue, because when she squeezed his hand, a tiny sob issued from her, causing a hard lump to form in his throat. Oh, what he wouldn't do to keep her safe and sound! "And Lord," he added, "keep *Cammi* safe and sound. We ask these things in Your name…."

Together, they uttered a quiet "Amen."

One second, then two, ticked silently by before she said, "Thank you, Reid," and nodded off.

Dread wrapped around him like a cold wet wind.

"Only a few more minutes," he said, squeezing her small hand. "I can see the E.R. entrance sign."

It reminded him of the last time he'd been to this hospital, when he'd visited his mother. She lay pale and gaunt against flowery bedsheets provided by the nice hospice ladies. He'd barely stuck a boot tip into her room when she ordered him to leave, to stay away until after she'd gone to meet her Maker. "I don't want you to remember me this way," she'd whimpered, turning her face to the wall. Fiery rage had burned inside him, because he'd childishly—foolishly—expected medical science to do what God had refused to do. Despite the torturous treatments they'd put her through, the cancer continued to grow, until one day, mercifully, she slipped into a coma.

That's when he went back to the rodeo, and he didn't return again until Martina called to say Billy had arranged everything—the wake, the funeral, the headstone. Reid was alone at his mother's grave when he swore the next time he set foot in a hospital, it would be feetfirst—with a tag wrapped around his big toe.

Unfortunately, he'd seen the inside of too many hospitals across the country. The risks he took riding savage, untamed beasts told the rodeo world that Reid Alexander, "All-Around Cowboy," had no fear. In truth, he flat-out didn't give a hoot what happened to him. How ironic, he thought, that having nothing to live for had made him a star.

At the moment, though, Reid cared very much, because this small, helpless woman beside him *needed* him to care. He stomped the truck's brakes outside the

E.R.'s double-wide entry, leaped from the cab without bothering to close the driver's side door, and bolted into the hospital. "I've got a woman out there," he bellowed, pointing frantically, "and she's had a miscarriage. She's bleeding badly, and—"

The nearest nurse looked up from her clipboard, peered over black half glasses at his shirt and blue jeans. He followed her gaze. Until that moment, Reid hadn't realized how much of Cammi's blood had soaked into his own clothes.

"Bring her inside and take a seat," the nurse droned, pointing at two empty chairs in the waiting room.

Eyes narrowed and lips thinned by fear and frustration, he took a step closer, thumped a forefinger on the form she'd been filling out. "Sprained ankles and upset stomachs can wait," he growled. With each word, his voice escalated in volume and vehemence. "But the lady outside *can't.*"

She must have heard hundreds of similar speeches. Shrugging, she went back to her scribbling. "Like I said, take a seat and we'll get to you when we—"

Reid spotted a gurney behind her and, stomping toward it, he snarled, "When I get back in here, there had better be a doctor standing where you are." He didn't wait for her to protest, didn't tell her what he'd do if his order wasn't carried out. Instead, Reid blasted the wheeled cot through the doors and parked it alongside Billy's pickup.

One look at Cammi, slumped against the window, was enough to turn his red-hot rage into ice-blue fear. She'd been pale as a ghost when he'd left her mere moments ago; in the short time he'd been inside, she'd gone whiter still.

"Cammi, honey," he said softly, "we're goin' inside now, okay?" He eased his arms under her, tenderly lifted her from the passenger seat and lay her on the gurney. Reid draped his jean jacket over her, then hurried toward the E.R. entrance, taking care to avoid cracks in the sidewalk that might jar her.

"Hey, buddy," an orderly said, "you can't leave your truck there. We need that space for the ambulances when—"

He tossed the man his keys. "Be my guest," he snapped. "I'm kinda busy right now."

"Easy, Reid…" Cammi whispered.

Was he hearing things?

"…unless you want the E.R. docs to admit you, too, after you've had a stroke—or someone punches your lights out."

That she'd be concerned about *him* at a time like this said a mouthful about the kind of human being she was. From the instant their eyes met last night, he'd felt compelled to protect her from anything and everything that could harm her. What she'd said just now made him want that even more.

He was about to say something comforting, something consoling, when he spotted a man in a white lab coat. "Doc!" he shouted. "Hey, Doc!"

Brows raised, the fellow pointed to himself.

"Yeah, you," Reid hollered, pushing the gurney toward him. "This li'l gal is having a miscarriage. She's lost a lot of blood and—"

One look was all it took. Immediately, the doctor took control, barking orders to nurses and aides as he steered the gurney through the "Staff Only" doors to the emergency room. "Did you see the gal with the clipboard?"

Reid ran alongside him. "Nurse Ratchet, y'mean?"

The doctor grinned slightly. "Tell her I said you're to provide whatever info she needs on this patient."

Cammi could barely keep her eyes open. Who would defend her if he wasn't with her?

"Do it *now*," he insisted. "Name's Lucas. Brandon Lucas."

Reid grasped Cammi's hand, brought it to his lips. "I'll be right back, promise."

She nodded weakly, and in a barely audible voice said, "I know. I'll be fine...."

"'Course you will." She *had* to be, because—

"The nurse?" Lucas reminded him, then snapped shut the curtains surrounding Cammi's cubicle.

Reid stood there a second, unable to decide whether to burst in, or to do what the doctor ordered.

"Sooner you get it done, buddy," Lucas said through the pastel-striped material, "the sooner you can come back and hold her hand."

He pictured her, weak and alone, small and vulnerable, and realized there was no place on earth he'd rather be. But Lucas was right—the sooner he provided that nurse with whatever facts might help in treating Cammi, the sooner he'd be with her, making sure no one overlooked a single detail.

Lord, he prayed as he ran to the waiting room, *watch over her.*

* * *

Cammi hadn't so much as moaned through the tests and procedures. Watching the way she endured it all reminded him of the wild filly Billy had brought home from auction a decade or so ago—uncomplaining, no matter what paces they put her through. It made him chuckle to himself, realizing that twice, now, he'd compared Cammi to a horse. Ridiculous for a lot of reasons, starting with how petite she was.

He sat beside her as he had in the E.R., as he had while they prepped her for surgery, as he had in post-op…right arm resting on her hospital bed, fingers linked with hers. Now and then, when she shifted, the dim overhead night-light glinted from her wedding band. It was a cold, hard reminder of her connection to another life, another love. He knew, even as jealousy surged inside him, that he had no reason—no right—to feel this way. *You barely know the woman,* he reminded himself.

But that wasn't true. For a reason he couldn't explain, Reid felt as if he'd known Cammi all his life, as if some higher power had deliberately caused their paths to cross.

Better, smarter, safer, he decided, to focus on the small stuff, like the fact that she rested more peacefully when he wrapped his hand around hers.

Reid ignored the ache in his shoulder, already weakened by the punishing fall he'd taken from Ruthless, that monstrous-mean Brahman. He concentrated on how he'd rolled from the bull's sharp hooves just in time to keep from being trampled, instead of remembering that

Ruthless had ended his rodeo career. The discomfort of sitting in this position was secondary to what Cammi needed. Besides, she'd survived so much in these past few months that it made Reid feel good, being the one to provide this small solace for her now.

Almost as though she'd read his mind, Cammi turned toward him, her face less wan now, her eyes a bit brighter. "You don't have to stay, Reid. I'm fine. Honest."

He shook his head, gave her hand a slight squeeze. No way he'd leave. For one thing, she would need someone with her when the surgeon came in to tell her about the baby. "Until your dad or one of your sisters takes my place, I'm stayin' put." With his free hand, he tucked a dark curl behind her ear. "Who do you want me to call first?"

She gasped quietly and covered her mouth with the fingertips of one hand.

"What? Are you in pain? Want me to get a doctor in here?"

"No—at least, not the physical kind."

He didn't understand, and said so.

"Your clothes. Look what I've done to your clothes! I've ruined them."

Only then did he remember the deep maroon stains covering his entire midsection. "Work duds," he said, sloughing it off. "Don't give it another thought." He didn't like the tiny worry furrow that had formed on her brow. In an attempt to erase it, he said, "So, who can I call for you?"

Cammi stared at the ceiling and bit her lower lip. "My dad," she said after a while, "I suppose."

She reminded him of someone, but for the life of him, Reid couldn't think who. He was far more interested in why she sounded so apprehensive at the mention of her father. He tried again to change the subject, flipping open his cell phone and doing his best to imitate a nasal-voiced operator. "May I have your number please…."

Grinning, Cammi recited it while Reid dialed. "Don't give him too many details," she said. Almost as an after-thought, she added, "No point making him worry."

Nodding, Reid counted the rings.

"Lamont London," answered a deep, gravelly voice.

London? *Now* he knew why Cammi looked so famil-iar: She was the spitting image of Rose London—the woman he'd hit with his pickup…the woman who'd died that rainy night so many years ago! Reid swallowed, hard. Maybe he'd be lucky and there were two Lamont Londons in Amarillo, because if *this* one was—

"I don't have all day," the man griped. "Who is this?"

He'd recognize that angry Texas drawl in a shoulder-to-shoulder crowd at New York's Penn Station. And why wouldn't he, when he'd been hearing it in his nightmares for years. "I, uh, I'm calling about your daughter, sir," he said. "Cammi wants you to know she's fine, but she needs you to—"

"Cammi? Where is she? And if she's fine, why can't she talk to me herself?" Lamont demanded.

Reid could almost picture him, big and broad as a grizzly and every bit as threatening. "She's kinda groggy right now."

"Groggy?" Concern hardened his tone even more. "Groggy from what? Confound it, boy, I want some answers, and I want 'em *now!*"

"Then, you'd best get yourself over here and talk to her doctor." Reid told Lamont the name of the hospital, rattled off Cammi's room number and snapped the phone shut. He felt a mite guilty, ending the conversation so abruptly. After what Lamont had gone through on the night of his wife's death, being summoned to a hospital this way would surely awaken bad memories.

It awakened a few haunting memories for Reid, too, and the hairs on the back of his neck stood at attention as he remembered that night—Lamont's menacing glare, the hostile accusations he'd hurled outside the O.R.

Even at fourteen, Reid understood why Lamont blamed him for the accident that had clearly been Rose's fault. Grief and sorrow had stolen the man's ability to reason things out, erased rational thought from his mind. Years later, Reid understood it all even better. If *he* had spent years sharing life, love and children with the girl of his dreams, and a pickup-driving boy had ended it all, well, in Lamont's boots, Reid would have been a hundred times harder on that knock-kneed young'un!

Images of the scene shook him more than he cared to admit. But Cammi needed his calm reassurances now, so he shoved the black thoughts to the back of his mind. He pocketed the phone.

"I expect your dad will be here in..." He searched for a phrase, something that would convince Cammi her father would soon be here for her. Martina was fond of saying "quick as a bunny," so he tried it on for size. The moment the silly, feminine-sounding words were out of his mouth, Reid cringed.

It was so good to see her smile that he couldn't help mirroring her expression. "What're you grinning about?"

"You're a very sweet man, Reid Alexander."

Sweet? He'd been called a lot of things in his day, but "sweet" wasn't one of them.

"Because something tells me 'quick as a bunny' isn't part of your usual cowboy vocabulary." She paused to lick her dry lips, then added a sleepy "So, thanks."

Thanks? For what? he wondered, holding a straw to her mouth. "Slow an' easy, now," he said as she sipped. After returning the mint-green cup to the night table, he finger-combed dark bangs from her forehead. "What-say you close your eyes, try and catch a few winks before your dad gets here."

She tilted her head, making him want to gather her close, hold her so long and so tight that nothing could ever get close enough to hurt her again.

"Thanks," she repeated.

This time he asked his question aloud. "Thanks for what?"

"Oh, just…" Cammi shrugged. "I don't know what I would have done if you hadn't been there for me today, that's what."

Her voice still hadn't regained its lyrical quality and her lower lip trembled when she spoke, he noticed. Had she overheard the doctors and nurses discussing her case? Did she already know she'd lost the baby, or merely sense it?

"I have a lot of explaining to do once my dad gets here," she said on the heels of a ragged sigh.

He continued stroking her hair, amazed by its silky texture, trying to count the many shades of brown that gleamed among the satiny tresses. "Explaining?"

Another sigh. "I never got around to telling him about the wedding, so he has no idea I was married, let alone that I'm a widow."

Reid wondered why Cammi had eloped, especially considering it was common knowledge that long ago, Lamont had earned his title as one of the wealthiest men in Texas. He couldn't help feeling sorry for the big guy, because not even all his money could buy him out of hearing about the secret wedding, the death of a son-in-law he'd never met, the loss of a grandchild he knew nothing about—all in one fell swoop.

She met his eyes. "Uh-huh. I see by the shocked look on your face that you're beginning to get the picture."

Having been on the receiving end of Lamont's wrath, he saw far more than she realized. Reid frowned. "You're safe. What else could matter to the man?"

As if she hadn't heard him, Cammi said, "He'll be so disappointed in me." Tears formed in the corners of her dark eyes. "Not that he isn't used to that after all these years of being my father. Just once, I'd like to do something right…something he'd be proud of!"

Reid lifted her hand to his lips and gently kissed each slender finger. "You're safe and sound," he said again, more forcefully this time. "He loves you, I'm sure, so that's all he's gonna care about."

"From your lips to God's ear."

He bit back the urge to say, *What's God got to do with it?* If the Almighty had been doing His job up there, Reid thought, Cammi wouldn't be lying here now, worrying how her father would take the news. "Get some sleep," he said instead. "You're lookin' a mite pasty-faced."

"My, but you're good for a girl's ego."

Smiling, Reid used the palm of his hand to gently close her eyes. "Shh," he whispered, kissing her forehead. He hadn't noticed till now all the faint freckles that dotted the bridge of her nose. "Say another word and I'll be forced to take drastic measures."

Her delicately arched brows rose slightly.

"I'll have to sing you to sleep," he explained, "and believe me, my lullabies sound scarier'n a coyote's howl."

"Oh, I don't know," she whispered. "After all you've done for me today, anything that comes out of your handsome mouth will be music to my years." Cammi sighed. "I'll go to sleep, but only to spare the ears of the patients down the hall, mind you."

Cammi was fast asleep before Reid finished tucking the covers under her chin. He sat back, glanced at his wristwatch. Any minute now, Lamont London would arrive, no doubt carrying a full head of steam—and finding Reid Alexander in his daughter's room would do nothing to improve his mood. And Cammi sure didn't need to witness the angry scene, especially not in her condition.

Besides, Reid had promised to drive Billy and Martina to Fort Worth later. He'd called several times to report on Cammi's condition, and they'd rescheduled Billy's appointment for that evening. "I'll check on you soon," he promised, pressing a soft kiss to her temple.

He couldn't help but wonder about the affectionate little gestures he'd been doling out to Cammi, almost from the moment they'd met. He had never been physically demonstrative, not even with people he knew well and loved with all his heart.

In the doorway, he stopped for one last glance. She looked like a vision, thick black lashes dusting her lightly freckled cheeks, satiny hair spilling across her pillow like a mahogany halo. He could think of only one word to describe her: *Beautiful*...inside and out. She was everything he'd ever wanted in a woman. On the rare occasions when he allowed himself to dream of a wife and a houseful of kids, it was a woman like Cammi he pictured at his side, sharing life's ups and downs.

He wished he could be here, holding her hand, when the doc came back to deliver the sorry news about the baby. But Reid had a far bigger regret than that.

Soon she'd put two and two together, and when she realized *he'd* been the other driver in the accident that killed her mother, he'd be lucky if she didn't hate him.

"Sweet dreams, pretty lady," he whispered sadly. "God knows you deserve them."

One thing was certain...*his* dreams tonight sure wouldn't be sweet.

* * *

Cammi didn't know how much time had passed since Reid brought her to the hospital. She only knew it felt as if she'd gone thirteen rounds in a boxing match. Blindfolded. With her hands tied behind her back.

Everything ached, from the soles of her feet to her scalp. Squinting, she rested a palm on her stomach. *Father,* she quietly prayed with a lump in her throat, *watch over us and protect us.* Despite her fervent prayer, deep down she feared her baby was already lost to her.

Reid had watched over them, Cammi admitted. She'd always taken pride at not being the clingy, needy type, but she didn't remember needing anyone more than she'd needed Reid today. If she hadn't been so exhausted, she could thank him now for all he'd done. But she'd gone and fallen asleep, and while she was off in dreamland, he'd taken her at her word, and left.

She'd roused enough, there at the end of his visit, to remember the way he'd said goodbye. His tone had confused her, because he'd sounded as if he'd never see her again. Not that she could blame him, all things considered. *Big handsome guy like that,* Cammi thought, *deserves better than the likes of me.*

Even the simple act of running a hand through her hair reminded her of him, of how he'd gently tucked a curl behind her ears, brushed the bangs from her eyes. She stared at her left hand, thinking of the way he'd kissed each knuckle…all but her ring finger, that is. And was it any wonder? What man in his right mind would deliberately saddle himself with a woman who carried such heavy burdens.

Dr. Lucas walked into the room just then, white lab coat flapping behind him, stethoscope clacking against the pen in his lapel pocket. "Mrs. Carlisle," he said, kindly extending his hand. "Remember me?"

She'd been pretty out of it when he introduced himself before surgery, but yes, she had a vague recollection. Cammi nodded and shook his hand. "Thanks for stopping by, Doctor. I was just wondering about…things."

He dragged the chair beside her bed closer, spun it around and sat, forearms resting on its back. "How much do you recall of what I told you outside the operating room?" he asked, laying her chart on the night table.

"Not much, I'm afraid."

Lucas nodded. "Well, let me go over it again. For starters, everything looks fine. Your D-and-C went very well and—"

"D-and-C?" Cammi's heartbeat quickened. She grabbed the bed controls, pushed the raise backrest button. "So, it's true, then?" Tears stung her eyes. "I lost the baby?"

Nodding gravely, Lucas said, "I'm afraid so." He leaned forward. "But there wasn't a thing you could have done to prevent it. Most people have no idea how common miscarriages are. It's no consolation, I know, but it might help some to know that ten percent of all pregnancies end sometime between the seventh and twelfth week."

He'd been right. The information did absolutely nothing to console her. "But I fell this morning, and last night I was involved in a minor traffic accident…."

"Fact is, by the time a miscarriage begins, the baby has already been lost for quite some time." Shaking his head, Lucas added, "Neither your fall nor your accident is responsible for this. One of the hardest things about miscarriage is that most of the time, there's no clue as to the cause."

He grabbed her file, flipped to the second page. "We ran the whole battery of tests on you, starting with a transvaginal ultrasound and HCG to confirm you were, indeed, pregnant, CBC to determine the amount of blood loss, WBC to rule out potential infections. The D-and-C was mostly precautionary, because remaining tissue can cause infection."

Lucas turned to another page, then met her eyes. "Everything looks completely normal, so I can assure you there's no reason you can't have another child… when you're ready, of course." He tapped a fingertip on the clipboard. "And let me stress that there is *no* reason to expect anything like this might happen again."

Another baby? Cammi hadn't even come to grips yet with losing this one. At the moment, she wanted nothing more than to be alone, to think and pray about…about *every*thing.

"Mind if I ask you a personal question?"

Unable to trust her voice, Cammi shook her head.

"That guy who brought you in—is he your husband?"

Another head shake. "Friend," she said. "He's just…a friend."

"Has anyone notified your husband?"

She took a deep breath, released it slowly. "My husband died in a car accident four months ago. In California."

Lucas's eyes widened. "I'm so sorry, very sorry." Standing, he put the chair back where he'd found it, tucked her file under his arm. "Is there anyone I can call for you? Anything I can do?"

"Nothing, thanks. My father is on his way." He should be here by now. He must be stuck in traffic.

He dug around the oversize pocket on his lab coat, withdrew a business card. "If there's anything, anything at all I can do to help…"

Cammi accepted the card, knowing even before he released it that she wouldn't call. "Thanks," she said again.

"Have they brought you anything to eat?"

She answered with a question of her own. "Will you be signing release forms now?"

"In the morning. I want to keep you overnight for observation."

"Whatever you say, Doctor."

He made a note on her file and recapped his pen. "You're to take it real easy for a week or so. I mean it. Nothing strenuous. That means no laundry, no vacuuming, no lifting anything heavier than a five-pound bag of sugar." Lucas started for the door. "And have someone go to the pharmacy," he said over his shoulder, "to pick you up some iron tablets. You lost a lot of blood and need to build yourself up again."

"Okay."

"And no stairs. At least for the first few days."

"But my room is—"

His wagging forefinger reminded Cammi of a metronome. "Uh-uh-uh. 'No stairs' means *no stairs*. Camp out on the couch until Wednesday or Thursday."

Then she remembered the school, and Principal Gardner. "I'm supposed to start a new job on Monday!"

"Out of the question. Do that, and you'll be right back in here by lunchtime, needing a transfusion…or worse."

Feelings of helpless frustration overcame her.

"I'll want to see you in two weeks," Lucas said, half in, half out of the room. "I'll have my nurse give you a call to schedule an appointment."

What else could go wrong? she wondered as the doctor disappeared around the corner.

He hadn't been gone a full minute when her father clomped into the room on well-worn cowboy boots. "What in tarnation is going on around here?" he said, tossing his dusty Stetson onto the foot of her bed.

Careful what you ask for, Cammi thought wryly, *'cause you might just get it.*

Halfway into the seven-hour trip to Fort Worth, Billy yawned and stretched. Digging in the sack of treats Reid had brought, he pulled out a candy bar and clucked his tongue. "You drive like an old man, you know that, son?"

Reid glanced at the dashboard, noted he'd been traveling at exactly the posted limit. *Should've seen me a couple of hours ago,* Reid thought, remembering his trip to the hospital, when he discovered the pickup could actually go the hundred twenty miles per hour promised by the speedometer. "If obeying the law makes me an old man, I've been old since I was fourteen."

"Hmm," Billy teased around a mouthful of chocolate. "That reminds me—the west fields need some fertilizer...." He laughed, then added, "You can't kid a kidder, kid. I remember the way you used to drive that ancient green tractor of mine. Why, even the chickens knew to head for the henhouse when you climbed onto the seat of that monster!"

"True enough," Reid said, chuckling, "but that was different. I never drove the tractor on the highway."

"Speaking of highways, how far is it to Fort Worth, anyway?"

"Three hundred fifty miles, give or take." He glanced at the dashboard clock. "I reckon we'll roll into town just in the nick of time for your appointment."

Billy blew a stream of air through his teeth. "Seven and a half hours on the road, and for what?" he grumbled.

"God willing," Martina said from the back seat, "for a new medication or treatment that will save your life. Or, as you're so fond of saying, 'to save your ornery hide.'"

Turning to face her, he winked. "Guess I could at least *act* a mite grateful, eh?"

In the rearview mirror, Reid saw her blow Billy a kiss, saw the love beaming from her eyes. The sight made him smile, despite the traumatic morning, despite the long trip ahead...and the reason for this outing, because this couple was proof positive that happy marriages did exist. "I'd like to see a reporter from one of those women's magazines interview you guys," he said offhandedly.

"Interview us?" Billy faced front, eyes widened in disbelief. "What in thunderation for?"

Martina clucked her tongue. "William, please watch your language," she said, gently tapping his shoulder with the blunt end of a knitting needle. To Reid, she said, "It's a good question, though—why would a reporter want to interview *us?*"

Reid shrugged. "You've been married—what, a hundred fifty years, yet you're still billing and cooing like young lovebirds."

"Thirty-five years," Martina corrected.

"Only *seems* like a hundred fifty," Billy put in.

She gave him another light rap on the shoulder.

"Jiminy Cricket," he said, laughing. "You didn't let me finish. I was about to add, 'living with me.'"

She giggled quietly. "Lies paint a dark spot on our souls, you know."

"Oh, I don't mind," Billy said. "The Good Lord already knows I'm a tad dotty.'"

Reid frowned. "Is that in the Bible?"

Martina lifted her chin. "No, it isn't. But since my beloved granny said it, and my wonderful mama repeated it, there must be some truth to it." She paused, then changed the subject. "Hard to believe we've been together that long, and most of them happy years, at that."

"Most?" Billy put in, heaving a huge fake sigh.

She leaned forward to muss his hair. "Yes, 'most.'

Because *mostly,* you're willing to compromise, to talk things out, to negotiate. That's why marriage to you has been easy. Mostly."

"No, it's been easy because you're wonderful."

She giggled again. "No, because *you're* wonderful."

Reid had heard it all before, enough times to know that once they got the old "who's best" ball rolling, it could go on and on. "This meeting of the Mutual Admiration Society has concluded," he droned. He didn't put any stock in Martina's notions about lies darkening the soul, but he sure did hope there was truth to the reasons she'd listed for their successful marriage. He'd always considered himself fair-minded and reasonable, so if he ever found the right girl…

If he found the right girl? Reid believed he *had* found her. Didn't make sense, being so sure about something that important in such a short time. But it would take a miracle to get "the right girl" to forgive him for her mother's death.

What would Cammi be doing right now? he wondered. Sleeping peacefully, he hoped. If she were his wife, she wouldn't need for anything, ever. He'd take two jobs, three if he had to, to provide anything her heart desired. He had a feeling it wouldn't be hard… meeting her heart's desires. She had an easy way about her that told him she'd be happy and satisfied with only the barest of necessities, provided her loved ones' needs were being met. She didn't seem the type to be impressed by mansions, imported furniture or fancy sports cars.

Imagine how good it would feel, he thought, being

greeted by the likes of that smile after a long, hard day. He pictured Cammi, taking his arm, leading him to his favorite easy chair, where she'd snuggle into his lap to hear about his day. He could tell by the way she'd leaned into the conversation at Georgia's the night of the accident for her, listening was a fine-honed skill.

Frowning, Reid pursed his lips. He'd never gone boots-over-Stetson for a woman before, not even the most gorgeous and willing of them—and there had been plenty, like Amanda, who'd dogged his heels around the rodeo circuit. So why did he feel this way about Cammi, a woman he'd only just met?

No similarity between her and his own mother, whose loud, boisterous behavior so often shamed and humiliated him. In many ways she seemed more like Martina.

You're an idiot, Alexander, he chided himself. Her husband had only been gone a few months, and—

Husband. It surprised him, the way his fingers tightened on the steering wheel and his jaw clenched at the very thought of her sharing any portion of her life with another man. He tried to shake off the unthinkable thought. *Mind on the road,* he told himself. *Mind on the road…*

"What's going through that handsome head of yours?" Martina asked.

He met her eyes in the rearview mirror and forced a grin. "Just concentrating on the drive, is all."

"Nonsense," she countered. "A man doesn't grind down his molars and grimace because he's reading road signs and avoiding potholes."

Billy chuckled. "Well, I'll give you my two cents' worth. He's buildin' castles in the air about that li'l gal he crashed into."

Reid feigned a look of exasperation. "Two cents is about all that theory is worth. Here's an idea—go on back to sleep and save talk like that for—"

Billy laughed. "What's that old saying? 'Methinketh the cowboy protesteth too mucheth.'"

"Good thing there isn't a law against butchering Shakespeare," Reid pointed out, "'cause you just massacred that line."

Martina leaned forward, excited about some wildflower or other growing alongside the road. Thankfully, Billy seemed interested in the scenery, too, pointing out tree species and shrubbery the state had planted in the last "Beautify Texas" campaign.

Reid had managed to sidetrack them—this time— but he knew he'd better be more careful about where he did his daydreaming from now on, especially when it involved Cammi Carlisle.

Which might be tricky, considering how often and how deeply she filled his thoughts.

Reid would have given anything to hear the same silly banter going home as he'd endured on the drive to Fort Worth, even if it meant putting up with talk of his having a "thing" for Cammi Carlisle. But the specialist who'd examined Billy last night agreed with all the others:

Billy had Amyotrophic Lateral Sclerosis.

ALS.

And there was no known cure.

When the doctor in Amarillo first diagnosed the illness, Reid wanted to learn about the disease that might kill his best friend, his father figure, his mentor. Trips to the library and hours searching Internet Web sites made him yearn for those days when his only knowledge of ALS was that it had taken the life of baseball great Lou Gehrig.

In a horribly predictable fashion, the slight muscle weakness that sent Billy to the doctor in the first place quickly progressed, stealing finger dexterity and making it impossible for him to continue stringing the colorful, long-plumed fishing lures he'd been creating for years at the request of friends and neighbors.

Thanks to ALS, there'd be no more going off at dawn, fishing all by himself; twitching limbs and muscle spasms could cause him to lose his balance and topple out of his one-man johnboat.

Things would worsen gradually over these next few months, sapping Billy's strength and dignity until, one by one, every major organ stopped doing its job.

Now, as Billy leaned against the passenger window pretending to be asleep, as Martina's knitting needles click-clacked fast enough to create sparks, Reid wished he could reach out to them, wished there was something he could do or say to bring them comfort. But since the one thing they needed to hear—"cure"—was an impossibility, he held his silence.

For a reason he couldn't explain, he wanted Cammi near. It made no sense, and he felt selfish for so much as thinking that she could comfort *him,* especially after all she'd been through. Still, something told him if she knew the details about Billy's illness, if she knew how much the man meant to Reid, she'd shelve her own troubles to help him bear up under his.

On the other hand, being a devout Christian, Cammi would likely ply him with a list of Bible verses and prayers. He didn't cotton to getting into a verbal sparring match with a good, churchgoing gal about the existence of God *or* His presence in their day-to-day lives.

It would be hours yet, before he delivered Billy and Martina back to the Rockin' C Ranch, and since dawn had just broken it was too early to call Cammi. He'd barely slept a wink, lying on that too-soft hotel mattress, wondering how she was doing, wondering if her doctor had released her from the hospital and how she'd taken the news of the miscarriage. He could only hope that whatever was wrong between her and Lamont could be set aside until Cammi was her strong, healthy self again.

He wanted to hear her voice. No, *needed* to hear it, if for no other reason than to prove she'd made it through the night all right. As soon as he got the hands started on their next chore, he'd take five minutes and give her a call. He'd start out by apologizing for not being there when she woke up, for not being there to hold her hand when the doctor came in.

Reasonable or not, for the first time in his life, he intended to do what felt *right,* rather than what made sense. That meant 'fessing up, admitting he'd been the one driving the pickup that awful night. If she didn't slap him silly, maybe there was hope for them.

Maybe.

He knew this: He had to *try*.

Chapter Five

"I promise to tell you everything," Cammi said, "the minute we get home."

By the time Lamont had arrived at the hospital the day before, she'd been sleeping comfortably, thanks to the mild sedative the nurse had given her. She'd given the hospital staff strict instructions not to reveal anything to her father about her condition so Lamont had no choice but to go home and wait till this morning to find out why she'd been hospitalized.

Lamont's brow furrowed, a sure sign his patience was wearing thin. "You think I can't handle some ugly news?" He tossed the plastic bag he'd been carrying onto her tray table.

"It's not about what you can handle, Dad, it's—"

He took his hat from the foot of her bed and, holding it by the brim, spun it round and round like a disconnected steering wheel. "It's no secret that hospitals give me the heebie-jeebies."

True enough. He'd gone through a mighty rough spell

after Rose's death. While he holed up in his den with a bottle of whiskey, Cammi took charge. She started by gathering the ranch hands to explain that they hadn't been paid because her dad was "under the weather." Handing the foreman the ranch checkbook, she instructed him to do what her father would…until Lamont was ready to do it himself.

She'd helped her mother enough to know how everything else should be done. And so she did it, from packing lunches and readying her sisters to catch the school bus, to monitoring their homework. It had been her fault, after all, that Rose had been out that night in the first place; if Cammi hadn't needed a new dress to wear for her solo in the Harvest Days show at her school, Rose would have been home, safe and sound, that terrible, rainy night.

So Cammi didn't complain when her friends went to the mall or to the movies on weekends while she cleaned, did laundry, cooked suppers that could be frozen and heated in the oven on weeknights. Nothing pleased her more than when she was able to coax her bleary-eyed father to eat a few bites of something healthy every evening. Because if it hadn't been for her silly girlish vanity, if she'd been satisfied wearing one of the dozens of dresses already in her closet, he'd still have had his beloved Rose.

When the food supply ran low, Cammi scoured the house for loose change and dollar bills and, stash in hand, phoned Rose's best friend. Nadine did more than deliver staples that day; she sat Lamont down and reminded him what Rose would have expected of him.

From that day forward, he'd done his duty—and then some. But his aversion to hospitals hadn't changed one whit. Cammi could use a bit of Nadine's commonsense wisdom right about now.

"If something is wrong with you, I want to hear about it," Lamont said, sliding a forefinger round and round under his suede hatband.

"There's nothing wrong with me...." She hoped and prayed that was true, because someday, she wanted a houseful of children.

"Person doesn't wind up in a place like this if nothing's wrong."

"I know, I know. And I promise to tell you everything once we're home. For now, let's just say it's nothing serious. Okay?"

Lamont sat the hat on the foot of her bed again. "Let's have a look at you...." He lifted her chin on a bent forefinger. Grinning, he said, "Good golly, Miss Molly. You look like something the dog drug in."

"Then, it's a good thing I'm not thinking of entering the Miss Texas pageant, eh?"

"Hogwash. You'd win, hands down, even after..." He paused. "...after whatever put you in this rotten place."

He handed her the plastic bag. "Thought you might need a change of clothes. Hope I did okay, putting an outfit together."

Cammi peeked inside, where a neatly folded sweatsuit lay nestled on her underthings. She had a hard time blinking back tears of gratitude. "It's perfect," she told him, climbing out of bed.

Lamont nodded. "I'll just wait in the hall while you get out of that foul thing they call a hospital gown."

"So you can be closer to the main entrance?"

He grinned slightly. "Main *exit* is more like it."

Despite every effort to stay awake during the half-hour drive back to River Valley, Cammi dozed off half a dozen times. Finally, though, the magnificent ranch house appeared on the horizon.

"Home never looked better," she said, mostly to herself.

He parked the truck out front, and asked as he unlocked the front door, "So what'll you have, coffee or tea?"

One of the nurses had said dehydration went hand in hand with hemorrhaging. "Nice tall glass of water would be great. The air is so dry in that place."

Closing the door behind them, Lamont threw his keys into the burled wooden bowl on the foyer table. Hands on her shoulders, he inspected her face. "You're lookin' mighty pale. Head on into the den and put your feet up. I'll be in soon as I fetch our drinks." He turned her around, gave her a gentle shove toward the doorway.

Cammi started forward, then changed her mind. What she was about to tell him would break his heart, would become one more item on his long "Ways Cammi Has Disappointed Me" list. She might not get a chance to tell him, once the truth was out, how dear he was to her, how very hard she'd been trying these past few months to live in a way that would make him proud, to make up for being the reason Rose was out that night.

She spun on her heels and threw her arms around him. "I love you, Dad. So much that sometimes—"

He kissed the top of her head. "And I love you, too, sweetie, more than words could ever say." Tilting his head back, he gave her another once-over. "Now get on in there," he said, tousling her hair, "and sit down before you fall down."

Nodding, Cammi did as she was told, choosing the end of the deep blue leather couch nearest his favorite chair. Feet resting on the glass-topped coffee table, and huddled under a fringed afghan, she closed her eyes. She didn't know how much time had passed before Lamont walked into the room, carrying a steaming mug of coffee for himself and a glass of ice water for her.

He put the mug on his end table, handed her the tumbler. "You sure you're up to this?" he asked. The black leather of his recliner squeaked in protest as he settled his bulk onto its ample seat. "We can put off… whatever…until later."

Nodding, she sipped the water. The old mantel clock above the fireplace ticked off the seconds as Lamont rested a booted ankle on his knee. Fingers drumming on the chair's worn armrest, he heaved a sigh.

Cammi sat up straighter, put the glass on a soapstone coaster beside the sofa. "There's really no way to ease into this."

Fingers steepled under his chin, Lamont nodded. "Just start at the beginning, sweetie."

She could see by the tired expression on his face that he'd prepared himself for the worst. True to form, she wouldn't disappoint him. And wasn't *that* a bitter irony, she thought; in every way imaginable, she'd let him down, time and time again, but this time…

Clearing her throat, she did as he suggested and started at the beginning, explaining how she'd met Rusty on a movie set. "I'd been hired to play an extra," she said, "and he was a stuntman." She told Lamont how it had been love at first sight—or so she'd thought; how much they seemed to have in common; how much fun they'd had together. "He wasn't a Christian," she continued, "and I knew you wouldn't like that. So I decided to work hard, to pray hard, and when he accepted Jesus as his Lord and Savior, *then* I'd tell you about him and… everything."

Cammi slid past the buying of the marriage license, the ceremony, the honeymoon. It wasn't like Lamont to sit there so quietly. Since Cammi didn't know what to make of it, she plunged on.

"Didn't take long to figure out he'd hardened his heart to the Word." She began fiddling with the afghan's fringe, nervously wrapping it first around one finger, then another. "Then, there were rumors…." She had to stop for a moment, because remembering how humiliating it had been to hear about Rusty's secret life threatened her precarious hold on self-control. "Turned out they weren't rumors, after all."

She took another sip of water, hoping Lamont wouldn't recognize it as a stall tactic, nothing more. "He'd been gone four straight nights when…when a policeman woke me at three in the morning. He drove me to the morgue, where they showed me…"

Cammi ran both hands through her hair. "He'd

crashed his convertible into a tree, impaling himself on the steering column…and injuring his…date."

Lamont's eyebrows lifted as his hands gripped the chair's armrest. "His *date?*"

Cammi nodded. "Weird, huh? Some people think it's perfectly acceptable to have a wife *and* a girlfriend."

Lamont sat on the edge of his chair, elbows resting on his knees. He clasped his hands together and said, "Something tells me there's more…."

"Yes," she whispered, "there's more." *Just say it,* she thought. "Later that same day, my doctor called to say—" Cammi met her father's eyes "—to say I was pregnant."

He hung his head. "I sorta thought that's what you'd say."

He stared at the floor and didn't speak for what seemed to Cammi like an hour. Then he got to his feet and sat beside her on the couch.

"C'mere," Lamont said, drawing her into a hug.

The floodgates opened, releasing all the misery and sadness, all the regret and recrimination she'd been bottling up since that horrible day. It surprised her, when she'd cried it all out, to see tears in her father's eyes, too.

"I'm so sorry, Dad. I hate being such a disappointment to—"

He laid a finger over her lips to silence her. "Shh," he said. "Don't talk that way. You've never been anything but a joy." Holding her at arm's length, he gave her a gentle shake. "You're the spittin' image of your mama, and I'd love you for that alone. God forgive me for saying it, but you're twice the woman she was, twice as smart, twice as thoughtful."

Using the pads of his thumbs, he dried her tears. "Do you know what she was doing the night she died?"

Cammi nodded. "Shopping for a new dress for me."

"She forgot your dress, darlin'. That was her excuse when she left here that night, but it wasn't in the car after—" He took a deep breath. "I told her not to go out in that weather, but would she listen? *No-o-o.* 'There's a sale at Gizmo's,' she said. 'If I wait till tomorrow, I'll miss all the latest styles!' she said."

He sat back, pulled Cammi with him. "The cops gave me everything they found in her car—cassette tapes, keys, her purse…and four dress boxes from Gizmo's." He held her at arm's length to add, "Did Gizmo's ever sell girls' clothes?"

Cammi shook her head.

"I've been telling you for years the accident wasn't your fault. If I'd known *why* you blamed yourself…" Lamont ran a hand through his hair. "Maybe if I'd been a better father, I would have asked."

"Dad, you—"

"You didn't hold it against me, did you?"

"Hold what against you? You've been the best father a girl could ask for!"

"Y'know," he said, kissing her temple, "I believe you mean that. Which is just one of a thousand reasons I love you like I do. You never gave it a thought, did you, that if I hadn't been so wrapped up in my own self-pity, I might have asked—"

"Dad, really. Stop saying things like—"

"And look at you now, not an hour out of the hospital and trying to excuse my bad behavior. You're something else, you know that? You'd never put your life at risk for something so trivial as a sale on dresses, and the proof is the way you handled things after your mama's funeral."

She remembered only too well that at first, he'd held it together. It was later, after the friends stopped dropping by and the in-laws stopped calling, when the casserole dishes had been reclaimed and the flowers had all dried up, that he'd let grief and despair claim him….

"If she'd died for any other reason, I could have handled it. It would've hurt like mad, but…*dresses?* Pretty clothes were more important to her than staying safe for her family?" He gave Cammi another gentle shake. "Don't you see, sweetie? I'll love her till the day I die, but I can't forgive her for making you girls motherless, for making me a widower. I've never been disappointed in you—it's *her* I'm disappointed in!" One last shake before he let her go. "And let's not forget that if you hadn't stepped in, run things while I was havin' myself a pity party, we might've lost everything. You saved our bacon, Camelia."

Cammi tried to take it all in.

"Well," Lamont said on a heavy sigh, "at least it's all out in the open now."

"No, not all of it, Dad. There's one more thing…."

"I know. You lost the baby."

His voice was flat, unemotional, when he said it, as if he couldn't bear to say it any other way.

She felt the tears begin to well up again. Unable to trust herself to speak, Cammi nodded. When she found her voice, she said, "I didn't love Rusty, not the way a wife should love her husband, but I wanted this baby. Wanted it very much." The reasons poured out even faster than her tears—how the child had turned her from a dreamy-eyed girl to a feet-on-the-ground woman, how she'd made solid, rational decisions for the first time in her life for no reason other than that she *had* to behave responsibly from now on, for the baby's sake.

She didn't tell her father about the handsome cowboy she'd met, who'd been her hero in every sense of the word, who'd somehow managed to steal her heart in just a few days. Admitting she was falling in love with him, already, was the same as admitting every other good thing she'd done lately had been a mistake. Besides, there didn't seem to be much point in telling him about Reid, because what chance did she have for a future with the man who she suspected had been driving the other car that night!

"You've been making responsible decisions since you were twelve, sweetie. And you'll go right on making them. God has blessed you with—"

Cammi didn't hear anything after *God*. Anger deafened her, rage blinded her. She was suddenly keenly aware that God had let her down, big time. She'd done it all by the book, right down to keeping her promise to remain a virgin until her wedding night…and in a city like Hollywood, no less! She'd started every day with a devotional, ended each by reading His Word. It hadn't been easy, what with her wacky waitress schedule, but she'd found a church and hadn't missed a single Sunday service. Despite the ugly rumors that surfaced after Rusty's death, she hadn't given in to the temptation to hate him. Rather, she'd decided early on to tell the baby nothing but good things about its daddy. She'd never asked the Almighty for anything but the strength to do His Will, and yet He'd taken the baby. He'd—

"Sweetie," Lamont was saying, "what's wrong? You're white as a bedsheet."

"I'm fine. Just a little tired, maybe."

"Why not go up to bed and take a nap, then, while I rustle us up something to eat."

"Can't. Doc says I'm not to use the stairs for a few days," she muttered. "Need some iron tablets, too, and I can't start my new job for at least a week."

"New job?"

With everything that had happened, Cammi hadn't found time to tell him about her new teaching position. "Puttman Elementary. Fourth grade," she said dully. "I was supposed to start on Monday."

"Well, I'm sure the principal will understand."

No doubt he would. Mr. Garner had seemed like a nice enough fellow. Which wasn't the point at all. Having something to do would help put the miscarriage to the back of her mind, would keep her occupied.

"I'll scrounge up some bed linens," Lamont said, standing. "You'll sleep right here till your doctor gives you the green light."

Cammi nodded.

"Mind telling me who it was that called me from the hospital?"

"As it turns out, he's the guy I crashed into last night. I ran into him again in town, after my meeting with the Puttman principal, when…" She remembered Amanda, remembered losing her footing on the corner, tumbling into the street, Reid's big strong arms steadying her. "He was there when…"

"Good, you have his name and address, then. I need to thank him for getting you to the hospital safely, for staying with you till he knew I was on my way."

Cammi knew a gift wouldn't be necessary or expected, not with a man like Reid, and said so.

"Reid?"

"Reid Alexander. He used to be an award-winning rodeo cowboy, and now he works as the Rockin' C foreman."

Lamont put his back to her. "I know perfectly well who he is." The hard edge to his voice told her Reid was indeed the boy who'd been driving that night.

As if he'd read her mind, Lamont said, "Besides, he's a cowboy, and cowboys are trouble. I oughta know." He looked over his shoulder. "When this accident mess is cleaned up, I want you to keep your distance from him."

Hearing those words hurt.

"Trust me," Lamont added. "I know what I'm talking about. Stay away from the likes of him."

For a moment after he left the room, she asked herself what had happened to give him such a negative mind-set toward all cowboys. He had a few kinks in his armor, but self-righteousness and judgmentalism weren't among them. Especially considering he himself had been a cowboy all his life!

Maybe Lily knew the answer to that question. And maybe Cammi's little sister would gather up some old movies—comedies, preferably, and novels, too… books with plots that had nothing whatsoever to do with love and marriage and babies. Because if she didn't find something to occupy her mind while she recuperated, she'd end up feeling sorry for herself. And that was the last thing she wanted, or could afford, to do.

Weird the way the mind works, Cammi thought, because the mere mention of love and marriage and babies made her think of Reid. *Again.* He'd said he had to drive his boss to see a specialist about controlling Billy's ALS. He'd probably be halfway home by now, hopefully with good news. Maybe after her nap, she'd give Reid a call, see how things turned out.

And maybe you won't, she thought.

Lily sat on the arm of the sofa and held out the phone. "Some guy wants to talk to you."

"Mechanic, probably," Cammi said, putting the receiver to her ear. She felt much better after her long nap. "Hello?"

"Cammi, hi. It's Reid. Just thought I'd call to see how you were doing."

She felt herself blush and tried to turn away so Lily wouldn't see it. "I'm…I'm fine. And your boss? How's he?"

There was a considerable pause before he said, "Not so hot."

Another pause, then, "How 'bout I buy you a cup of coffee in town?"

"Sorry, I'm confined to quarters for the better part of a week. I'd invite you to come here, but…"

Before she had a chance to make up an excuse, Reid interrupted with "Maybe some other time, then."

"Maybe."

"So, what did your doctor say?"

Cammi filled him in, spelling out the doctor's orders while being careful not to mention the miscarriage; she hadn't had a chance to fill Lily in yet.

"Wish I'd been there when Dr. Lucas told you about… you know, the uh…"

It touched her that he was having a hard time saying "miscarriage." "I wish you'd been there, too." He had no idea how much she'd wished it! But it was probably for the best that he'd left before the doctor showed up. Reid already had more than enough reason to avoid her without witnessing the blue funk she'd slipped into after hearing the news.

"Well, guess I'll let you go. You need your rest."

"Right." A couple of days ago, she'd have said "I'll pray for your boss." Well, a lot of things were different now. "Good luck to your boss."

"He's been more like a father to me than a boss," Reid said, "but I appreciate the sentiment, anyway." And then he chuckled.

"What."

"You surprised me, that's all."

"How?"

"I thought for sure you'd say something like 'I'll keep him in my prayers.'"

Cammi harrumphed. "Why would I do a silly thing like that? It isn't like He hears anything I say, anyway."

Silence. Then Reid said, "'Course He hears you, Cammi. Why would you say such a thing?"

"Because it's true, that's why." She didn't like the turn of the conversation. Didn't like the angry feelings swirling in her gut...where her baby used to be. "Well, I appreciate your call," she said, hoping he'd take the hint and hang up.

"No problem. Mind if I check in on you again soon?"

"It's a free country." *Get a grip, Cammi,* she told herself. It's *God* you're mad at, so why take it out on Reid?

"Get some rest," he said again. "Talk to you later."

She had barely hung up when Lily said, "Who was *that?*"

Cammi pretended to be engrossed in adjusting the hem of her pajama top. "The guy from the other night."

Lily grinned. "Car Crash Cowboy, y'mean?"

"None other."

"Care to explain why I didn't hear any talk about insurance companies or mechanics or body shops?"

She was wiggling her eyebrows when Cammi looked up. Might as well get it over with, she thought. "Have a seat, kiddo," she said, patting the cushion beside her. "I have a story to tell you."

"Is this the one about the husband named Rusty who died in a convertible with his girlfriend?"

Cammi couldn't believe her ears.

"Close your mouth, big sister. We don't need a fly-catcher."

She snapped her teeth together. "There are no flies in Texas this time of year, anyway." She slapped the couch again. "Now, have a seat and tell me how you know so much."

"Oh, let's just say a little bird told me."

Lamont wasn't the type who would have told her, so—

"Stop trying so hard to figure it out." Lily giggled. "I can almost see the smoke comin' out of your ears!"

Cammi gasped, feigned shock. "You were *eavesdropping!* Shame on you, Lily!"

Her cheeks flushed. "No, I wasn't," she said. "At least, not at first. I was diddy-boppin' down the hall when I heard voices. By the time I figured out who was talking…and about what…it was too late to backtrack. Sounded so serious, so important that I didn't want to interrupt."

Cammi sighed. "Well, it's actually a relief. I didn't relish having to repeat it all, anyway."

Lily scooted closer, slung an arm over Cammi's shoulder. "Sorry you had to go through that, sis. Honest. That Rusty was a bum. A no-good, low-down—"

"Wasn't all his fault. I had a part in that mess, too, you know."

"You didn't cheat on your spouse. Worst thing you did was take the word of that stinking—"

"Lily, really…"

"Well," she said, giving Cammi a sideways hug, "I can't help it. For the past few hours I've been stewing over what that jerk did to you." She balled up a fist and shook it in the air. "If he wasn't already dead, I'd hunt him down and kill him myself!"

Cammi turned to face her. "Whoa. Are you sure you're my baby sister? The one who mothers orphaned calves and rescues critters that would otherwise become roadkill? The same sweet girl who nursed a hawk until it was well enough to fly away home? The gentle soul who cringes when Dad mashes a spider?"

"This is different," she huffed. "We're talkin' *family* here." She jabbed a thumb into her chest. "Anybody messes with my kin whilst I'm around," she said in her thickest Texas drawl, "has got Lily London to answer to!"

Cammi hugged her. "I love you, too, kiddo."

"So what's all this anti-God stuff? Never thought I'd see the day when Camelia London would blaspheme the Lord."

"Wasn't blasphemy," Cammi defended. "I only said… I'm just sick to death of looking to heaven for help and getting nothing but dust in my eye."

Lily blinked, swallowed and licked her lips. "Good grief, Cammi, what would Dad say if he heard you talking this way!"

"I have too much respect for him to talk this way in his presence."

"Well, don't you worry…I'm sure not gonna tell him. I like all my parts right where God put 'em, thank you!"

She coughed. "Sorry for the *God* reference, what with you bein' *mad* at Him and all."

"Yeah, I'm mad. Don't I have a right to be? I wanted that baby, even if it did come by way of a low-down, no-good, stinking, cheating jerk! I prayed myself hoarse, trying to make the right decisions for our future. Why, I'll bet there are calluses on my knees, I spent so much time praying for it to be healthy, and happy, and well loved, and cared for, and everything else a baby deserves to be! And what did God do? Nothing, that's what. So yeah, I'm mad. Good and mad. Because what have I ever done in my life that would make Him—"

"Cammi," Lily said softly, "stop it. You're supposed to be resting. You want the bleeding to start up again?"

She took a deep breath, let it out again. "No, of course not," she said, shaking her head.

"You have to give yourself some time, Cammi. Time to let this all sink in. In a couple of days, you're going to feel completely differently about everything. You'll feel—"

"No, I won't. I'll feel exactly the same in a couple of days, in a couple of months. I'll feel that God let me down, is what I'll feel! I'll feel that way because it's true. I wanted this baby, wanted it so very much. And oh, Lily, it breaks my heart that He took it. I miss it, miss it so…."

Until a tear splashed on the back of her hand, Cammi hadn't realized she'd been crying.

Lily gathered her close, patting her back as she whispered, "Hush, now. It's okay. I understand."

But Cammi knew Lily didn't understand. How could

she, when she'd never carried a child inside her, never looked forward to feeding time and nursery rhymes and even diaper changing. She'd never planned a nursery, right down to which Mother Goose character would dominate the decorating theme, never held her breath as she anticipated feeling those first fluttering little kicks.

She hoped Lily would never know the fear that wraps around a mother's heart when the brutal cramping begins, or the terror that goes with seeing your life's blood—and that of your unborn child—pouring out like water from a tap. Hopefully, Lily would never know the heartache of hearing the word *miscarriage*.

Cammi cried until spent, feeling foolish and childish and weak-willed. Which made things all the worse, because she didn't like behaving this way—especially not in front of her youngest sister. What kind of example was that!

She didn't understand it, because she'd never been one to give in to tears, had always controlled her emotions, not the other way around. All her life, she'd looked down her nose at girls and women who got weepy when things didn't go their way. After her mother's death, when her dad fell apart before her eyes, Cammi vowed to be strong, to be in command of herself at all times. She owed him that much.

Were these tears a wake-up call? A lesson in humility from on high? *What do You hope to teach me, Lord,* she demanded silently, *that the poor choices and stupid decisions I've made all my life have been my own unique brand of boo-hooing?*

Anger, she decided, was even more self-destructive than self-pity. She had to get hold of herself, right now, for her own sake as well as for Lily's, for her father's.

Cammi sat up and grabbed a tissue from the dispenser on the coffee table. Blotting her eyes, she said, "Sorry, Lily. Didn't mean to fall apart like that."

"Hey, everybody needs a good cry now and then. It's human. Why else would God have given us…" Lily bit her lip.

"Don't worry, I don't expect you to share my views on You-Know-Who," she said, aiming a thumb at the ceiling.

Lily got to her feet. "Time to feed Elmer the calf. Anything I can get you before I head out to the barn?"

Cammi shook her head. "Nah. I've got everything I need right here." She smiled. "But thanks, kiddo. I love ya."

Lily's "love you, too" echoed in Cammi's mind long after her sister left the room.

Funny, she thought, how this being angry with God seemed to invigorate her. She needed to think about that, figure out why—

The phone's insistent ring interrupted her reverie. She lifted the receiver. "Hello?"

"Cammi. It's me, Reid."

"Again?" she teased.

"Yeah, I had to ask you…are you really okay? You sounded a little strange when I called before."

"My sister was with me. I didn't want her hearing about the—" She straightened her back and lifted her chin, determined not to wallow in self-pity

"—miscarriage secondhand." She laughed, a little too long and a little too hard, but what did she care? Reid had already formed his opinions about her—negative ones, no doubt. "Turns out she'd heard the whole story while standing in the hallway as I spelled it out for my dad."

He didn't say anything right away. When he did speak, Reid's deep voice sounded concerned. "So, you're okay, then?"

Mad as a wet hen, but healthy as a horse, she thought. Odd, but Dr. Lucas hadn't warned her that thinking in clichés was a result of miscarriage.

There, she'd said it again. And she hadn't fallen apart saying it. Trick is, she realized, not to avoid it, but to say it over and over and over. *Miscarriage, miscarriage, miscarriage…*

Nope. That wasn't going to work. And the proof was the hard knot that had formed in her throat.

"Cammi?"

She took a sip of water. "I'm here."

"I sure would like to see you."

You would? But why?

"Soon as you're up to it, I want to take you to dinner. Someplace nice, where we can talk."

It was too soon after Rusty's demise to think of it as an official date. And her father had flat-out forbidden her to see Reid—romantically, she presumed. But there was no reason under the sun they couldn't be friends, right?

"Tell you what," Reid was saying. "When you're feeling better, give me a call and we'll set it up."

He'd been so easy to lean on yesterday. If only he knew how easy.

"Cammi?"

"Sorry," she said, free hand rubbing her temple. "Sounds like a plan to me." She couldn't imagine calling him to "set things up," but being rude to the guy hardly seemed necessary. Like Lily said, time would pass, and as it did, Reid would forget he'd made the offer.

"Talk to you soon, then?"

"Yeah, soon."

Not, she thought, hanging up. Reid was a great guy. Too great. In just a few days, he'd succeeded in making her fall for him, like some silly schoolgirl with a crush on her high school's quarterback. Well, she was too old and too wise to go down that road again. If Rusty hadn't taught her anything else, he'd taught her that!

Suddenly, Cammi felt sleepy again. Lying back among the pillows Lamont had brought her, she closed her eyes.

And despite all her tough talk, Reid's handsome face carried her off to dreamland, where they sat side by side on a wide, covered porch, rocking a child in the cradle between them….

That evening Reid lay on his back, fingers linked behind his neck, staring at the shadowy blades of the ceiling fan above his head. Something hadn't set well with him about that phone call to Cammi. He'd come to expect a certain melodious quality to play in her voice. Surely everything that had happened would tone the music down some—but that much?

He'd been tossing and turning for hours now, wondering about it. Had he been wrong about her being spunky and tough? Was she an average woman, after all, with no special ability to roll with the punches, take life on the chin? He didn't think so. He'd met her under nerve-racking circumstances, and if what she'd gone through earlier didn't count as "stressful," Reid didn't know what did.

It was that reference to God, more than anything else, that got him to wondering, because she'd seemed to him a rock-solid believer, a live-life-by-the-Good-Book kind of gal. He felt that way in part because she'd said things like "I'll pray for Billy" and "Pray with me, Reid," and in part because he didn't think a person was born resilient, and Cammi was one of the most iron-willed people he'd ever met. Stuff like that didn't fall out of the sky; it was built into a body by dint of hard work, and prayer, and, yes, faith.

Hearing her talk like that about the Almighty, well, it rattled him. *He* didn't have faith because God had never answered a single prayer he'd prayed. Maybe, like one of the Old Testament verses said, he was paying for the sins of his parents, neither of whom had lived a model Christian life. And maybe, he simply hadn't earned God's attention. Cammi, on the other hand, *had* earned it. Virtue all but glowed in her big brown eyes. He took comfort in the fact that people like Martina and Billy—and Cammi—had developed lasting relationships with the Almighty; it gave him hope that someday, if he kept his nose to the grindstone long enough, even the likes of him could have God's ear!

Besides, Cammi seemed to take such comfort from believing the Lord actually listened to her prayers. That knowledge gave her the confidence to be wide open and accepting, to be fearless. It's what made her happier, more grounded than most, and—

At a horrible thought, Reid sat upright in bed. Now that she'd put his name together with the rodeo, could she have found out what kind of life he'd led on the circuit? Had she seen him for the many-flawed man that he was? Had she judged him too big a sinner to be worthy of her time?

No, Cammi didn't strike him as self-righteous. He'd only known her for a few days, but Reid already felt as if he knew her well. If the eyes are the windows to the soul, he thought, Cammi was good to the bone. And he ought to know; he'd spent hours looking into those chocolate-brown eyes. Even now, the memory of them made his stomach flip.

Something else had to explain her mood….

Then he remembered the despair that drove many a good mare mad. Depression would explain the dullness in her voice, explain her anger at God, too. And who had more reason to slump into a blue mood than Cammi, who'd so recently become a widow, who'd just lost her first child?

On his feet now, Reid began pacing. He kept it up for a minute or two, then stopped midstep. Hadn't she said the doctor ordered a week's worth of R and R? And hadn't she told him "no stairs allowed"?

Reid got dressed in the dark and hurried down the stairs, carrying his boots in one hand, his Stetson in the other. In the kitchen, he dashed off a quick note to let Martina and Billy know where they could find him— and headed for River Valley Ranch.

Chapter Six

Reid pressed his forehead to a pane in the French doors and watched as Cammi put down her magazine and grabbed the remote. She wore a white terry-cloth robe with bright blue butterflies on the pockets, and slippers to match. He smiled, thinking she looked adorable with her thick dark hair gathered up in a swingy ponytail—like a high school girl at a slumber party.

She flicked through the stations twice before settling on a black-and-white movie featuring Humphrey Bogart and Ingrid Bergman. Strange, Reid thought, how he'd seen five minutes of that film here, ten minutes there, without ever watching it from beginning to end. He was wondering if Cammi would settle in to enjoy the whole thing, when she lifted her arms overhead and stretched, reminding him of the cougar he'd seen while traveling with the rodeo, its sleek, well-toned body reaching high on the trunk of a scrub pine to work out the kinks in its back and signal competitors that she was a beast to be reckoned with. It was quite a sight to behold. And *Cammi* was a sight to behold, too.

The day before, they'd shared something few people have, something that forever changed their relationship from whatever it *had been* to… He shrugged. He didn't know how to define what they'd been, what they were now to one another, but he knew this: He wanted her in his life from now on.

Woolgathering like that had been what prompted him to get out of bed, throw on some clothes and head to River Valley Ranch in the middle of the night. During the drive over, he'd argued with himself: Would he be sorry for dropping by unannounced? Or would things turn out as he hoped? Well, he was here now, gawking into her den like a peeping Tom; might as well go for broke, find out once and for all what they meant to each other.

Not wanting to scare her, Reid pecked his fingernails lightly on the glass. Immediately, she hit the remote's mute button and sat up, searching out the source of the sound. After a second or two, she looked over her shoulder and directly at him. Or so it seemed. He shivered involuntarily, though he knew she couldn't possibly see him with the backdrop of night having turned the interior windows into black mirrors.

"You really *are* obnoxious," she said, flinging the door open.

"Sorry," he whispered hoarsely, "didn't mean to wake you."

"I wasn't sleeping." Cammi tightened the belt of her

robe, tugged at its wide collar. "I thought you were the dog."

"You wouldn't be the first li'l gal to call me that," he said, grinning.

Apparently, Cammi didn't appreciate his middle-of-the-night attempt at humor. She stared hard at him for a long moment. "How long have you been out there?" she said at last.

"Minute or two, I reckon." He rubbed his hands together. "Mind if I come in, take the chill off?"

She hesitated, then nodded, and Reid stepped inside. It didn't escape his notice that, before closing the door behind him, she checked the mantel clock. He was wondering how long it would be before she mentioned the time as she perched on the sofa arm.

"Whatever were you thinking, coming here at this hour?"

He felt even more ridiculous now than he had standing on the deck, staring through the slats in the window blinds. "I, uh…" Reid held out his hands, palms up. "I needed to see for myself that you were okay." He could have said concern for her had kept Cammi on his mind since he'd left the hospital, but the truth was, she'd dominated his thoughts from the moment she'd plowed into him in front of Georgia's Diner.

"I'm fine." She lifted her chin to add, "Wasn't expecting company at this hour, but…"

Then she pursed her lips, and he read it as a sign she didn't want to talk about the miscarriage. At least, not here and now. Best way he knew to change the subject was with small talk, but he'd never been much good at that. "Nice place," he said, nodding as he glanced around.

He expected her to agree, to point out one of the den's burled-wood antiques, or the massive stone fireplace that dominated an entire wall. Instead, she stood and said, "I was just about to fix myself a cup of tea."

She hadn't invited him to join her, he noted. Just as well, because her doctor had ordered her some serious R and R. "I thought you were supposed to be taking it easy."

Laughing softly, Cammi gestured for him to follow. "Brewing tea isn't exactly heavy labor," she said, padding down a long hall toward the kitchen. She flipped a switch, flooding the room with a pale yellow light. "Regular or herbal?" she added, firing up the teakettle.

He'd lap water from a mud puddle if it allowed him to spend a few more minutes in her company. "Regular. But only if you let me—"

She shot him a you-must-be-kidding look and grabbed two mugs from an overhead cabinet. "Thanks, but since I know where things are, it makes more sense if I do it myself."

Nodding, Reid sat at the white-tiled table and hung an arm over the back of a ladder-backed chair. "Where's your father?"

"Upstairs, asleep."

He'd decided halfway between the Rockin' C and River Valley that not even the risk of a confrontation with Lamont London could keep him away. Memories of that night in the E.R. still echoed loudly in his head, almost as loudly as they had in his dreams. It was a relief to know he wouldn't have to worry about that tonight. At least, he hoped not. "You're not afraid all this gabbing will wake him?"

She dismissed his concern with a wave of her hand. "You're safe…." Grinning mischievously, Cammi tilted her head. "Unless you do something to make me scream."

He'd cut off his own arm before doing anything that would frighten or hurt her! "Don't worry," he said, laughing. "I might be obnoxious, but I'm not dangerous."

She winced at the reminder she'd called him a dog. "Sorry about that," Cammi said, filling their mugs with steaming water. After dropping tea bags into each, she added, "I honestly thought you were Dad's dog…and he really did name the pup Obnoxious, by the way."

It surprised him to learn that Lamont had a sense of humor.

She handed him a mug and a spoon, then pointed out the sugar bowl, nestled on a lazy Susan amid napkins, salt and pepper shakers, Tabasco and steak sauce. "Milk?"

"Nah. I'm a high-test man, all the way."

"I like my coffee black, but put sugar in my tea." She shrugged. "Don't know why."

"Why do you need a reason?"

She studied his face, and he squirmed a bit under her scrutiny. "Dunno," she said after a bit.

Time to change the subject…again. "So, how're you feeling?"

"Déjà vu?"

Her answer didn't make a lick of sense, and he said so.

She said, "You asked me that in the den."

She looked adorable, standing there frowning, arms crossed over her chest, tiny slippered foot tapping on the shiny linoleum. "Guess I did, at that." He took a gulp of tea and decided not to take her bad-tempered mood personally. She'd been through a lot these past few days…these past few *months.* "No need to apologize for bein' cranky. I understand perfectly what—"

Eyes wide, she gasped. "Cranky?"

If he'd given it a minute's thought, he could've chosen a better word. "Well, not *cranky,* exactly," he began. "Maybe just—"

Clucking her tongue, Cammi rolled her eyes. "Sorry. Didn't realize I sounded so…so…prickly."

"I'm sure if I came callin' at a respectable hour, you'd be your usual good-spirited self."

"So how's your father figure-slash-mentor-slash-boss?"

He had to hand it to her; she'd changed the subject far more smoothly than he had. Pity was, she'd chosen a subject he'd just as soon avoid. It was hard enough knowing Billy wouldn't be with them much longer, without being asked to admit it out loud. "Poorly, to put it mildly."

"Sorry to hear that."

And he knew she meant it because sympathy glowed in her dark eyes, echoed in her voice. Reid could have kissed her for that. *All in good time,* he cautioned.

"At first, the docs thought it would take a couple of

years for the ALS to…" He couldn't bring himself to say *kill him*. "Billy's provin' 'em wrong at every turn, 'cause every day, he's twice as bad as the day before."

"Before I left for the rodeo circuit, I used to see him and Martina fairly often at church services and socials. The kids used to call him Gentle Ben, because hard as he tried to act like a tough old bird, he could never quite pull it off. The things he did for the Children's Center are proof he has a heart even bigger than the Rockin' C." Cammi shook her head and sighed. "How's he handling it?"

He remembered how, not so long ago, Billy could heft bales of hay and bags of feed as if they'd been featherlight. And if Reid had trouble watching him struggle with even the simplest tasks like buttoning his shirt and feeding himself, how much harder must it be for the once-proud and self-sufficient Billy?

"He's doing okay, I reckon, all things considered." Reid ran a fingertip around the rim of his mug. "He wouldn't admit it in a million years, but he's scared."

"And who can blame him?"

"Wish there was something I could do to make life more bearable for him, until…" Though he suspected the end wasn't all that far off, Reid couldn't finish the sentence.

Cammi blinked, sandwiching his hand between her own. "You're already doing it, just by being there for him when he needs you."

She withdrew her hand and stirred her tea. "Must be awfully hard on Martina, too. Those two are like newlyweds, even after all these years together."

My, but she had gorgeous eyes, especially when they got all misty that way. "Mind if I ask you a question?"

"Something tells me I couldn't stop you if I tried."

Chuckling, he shook his head. He loved her sense of humor, her tendency to put aside her own troubles to focus on the needs of others. There she sat, newly widowed and recuperating from a miscarriage, sincerely concerned about Billy and Martina. "You're something else, Cammi Carlisle, you know that?"

She wrapped both hands around her cup. Did she realize that when she looked down that way, her eyelashes hid the entire top half of her cheek? Or that when she bobbed her head in response to a compliment, it only made him want to pay her another?

The truth started spilling out, things he'd been thinking since the moment they'd met. "Seems I've known you my whole life, as if you've been here, right beside me, for decades. Now tell me, does that make a lick of sense?"

'Course it didn't make sense. Nothing did anymore. Take, for example, the way he couldn't seem to keep his big yap shut in her presence.

She grinned, exposing a deep dimple in her right cheek. Funny, why hadn't he noticed it before? He suppressed an urge to touch it.

"You're pretty easy to be around, too," she said.

Not exactly the response he'd hoped for, but it would do…for now. "So, can I ask you a question?"

"I thought you just did."

He mirrored her grin. "All right, so let me ask another one, then."

She tilted her head, waiting.

"Do you miss him much?"

Again with the big blinkin' brown eyes! If she kept that up, he wouldn't have any choice but to go over there, take her in his arms and—

"Who?"

"Your husband."

Frowning now, Cammi stared at the tabletop again. "I'd rather not talk about Rusty."

Rusty. Moronic name for a grown man, Reid thought. But what he said was "Still hurts pretty bad, huh?"

She shrugged one shoulder. "Only my ego."

He didn't understand, and said so.

"I guess I didn't tell you that Rusty died behind the wheel of a vintage convertible…with a blond starlet at his side. They'd been drinking and carousing for days. Who knows where they were headed when he lost control of the car?" She sighed. "Steering column impaled him, and the impact threw his date forty feet from the car. Last I heard, she was still in traction."

She tried to sound so matter-of-fact, so distanced, so emotionless. But she hadn't fooled him; the facts surrounding the accident had hurt her almost as much as losing Rusty. *And what makes you think* you're *the man to help her get through it?* he asked himself. Because he knew better than anyone that hadn't been the first time she'd lost someone in a car crash.

In his opinion, ol' Rusty must have been plum loco; if *Reid* had had the good fortune to marry a woman like Cammi, he sure wouldn't be chasin' skirts!

"Whirlwind romances are doomed from the start," she added in that same dull, soft-spoken voice.

Sorry to hear that, pretty lady, he thought. Because what he felt for her could be described exactly that way.

"We barely knew one another," Cammi continued. "Had absolutely *no* business getting married."

She must have loved the big idiot; why else would she have said "I do"?

"Thought I loved him," she said, as if reading his mind. He watched her pick at a nub on her place mat. "I thought wrong."

Evidently, there had been enough of *something* between them to make her believe she could start a family with the guy.

She looked up to say "Only good thing to come of that marriage was the baby." Cammi stared into space, blinking. "And now…"

And now she didn't even have that. Seeing her so sad, on the verge of tears, made his heart ache, made him want to bundle her up in a big hug and apologize for asking about What's His Name.

Definitely time to change the subject. He searched his mind for something upbeat to talk about. No one was more surprised than Reid when he said, "My timing couldn't be worse, considering the circumstances, but I don't want to let you slip away. So when you're ready…" Now that he'd started, he couldn't very well back out of this. Well, he *could,* but then he'd never know if she felt the same way. If maybe someday she *might* feel the same way. "…I was wonderin' if we could get to know one another better."

Feeling like a stuttering, blithering idiot, Reid clamped his jaws together. He got up, walked around to her side of the table, took her hands in his and stood her up. Oh, but she felt good in his arms! So good, he regretted not having done it sooner. A *lot* sooner. Cammi all but melted against him. Could it mean that, despite all she'd said about whirlwind romances being doomed, she felt the same way? *Well, a guy can hope.*

"You're something else," he said again.

She'd wrapped her arms around him, almost automatically, he noticed, pressing her dimpled cheek into his shirt. Now Cammi looked up, stared into his eyes. He could see that what he'd said had confused her. She looked over his shoulder, as if her response was written on the wall behind him. Her voice trembled when she said, "Reid, I—"

Fingertips to her lips, he shushed her. He didn't want to hear anything logical right now. Didn't want to hear that it was too soon after Rusty's death, too soon after the miscarriage, too soon after they'd met. Just because her reasons made sense didn't mean he had to like them!

"What's past is past," he said. And cradling her lovely face in his hands, he kissed the tip of her nose, her forehead, her chin, wishing with each kiss he could erase her every worry and doubt, her grief and sorrow. "I'm sorry as I can be that you lost your baby, but I want you to know that even if you hadn't, it wouldn't have mattered to me. I would gladly have helped you raise that young'un." Though he hadn't consciously given the matter any thought, Reid meant every word.

The look on her face told him Cammi thought that when she'd opened those French doors she'd let a crazy man inside. And he couldn't very well deny it, because he *was* crazy…crazy about her!

He'd never experienced anything like this in his life. Maybe he ought to take things easy, slow down, find out if this was an infatuation or the genuine article.

One look into her lovely face erased all doubt. He was pushin' thirty, and falling in love for the very first time! He pulled her closer, lifted her face and kissed her. He'd held plenty of women this way, kissed them, but never had he felt like *this*. His brain must have short-circuited, because he didn't know if he liked the wacky thoughts tumbling in his head, in his heart…or hated them. He thought he'd survived every "first time" experience a man could have, but this? Not even as a teenager had he felt so out of control.

He took a step back, hoping to get some perspective, hoping Cammi wouldn't notice that her kiss had left him as breathless as a moony-eyed boy. But one look into her gorgeous face added another first to his list: Always before, *Reid* had been the protector, the nurturer in his relationships. This time, he felt safe, knowing Cammi would look out for him as fiercely as a mama lion watches over her cubs. His heart, his feelings, his needs would always be safe in her care—somehow, Cammi sensed that she was the reason he felt unguarded and helpless in the first place!

At rodeo-sponsored charity auctions, bids for a date

with Reid outdid the others. He'd been voted Rodeo Bachelor of the Year three times over. His cowboy cronies good-naturedly named him "The Filly Magnet." And thanks to his talent for smooth-talking, women he'd romanced dubbed him "Slick." Reid almost chuckled aloud at the irony, because he couldn't recall a single one of those carefully rehearsed "lines" when he was with Cammi.

Maybe that's because he knew that with her, he could have things some men take for granted—home and hearth, complete with a wife, a couple of kids, a loyal family dog. He'd think of a better name than Obnoxious, but the picture would be just as pretty.

Before Cammi, he'd known there'd come a day when he'd return to the rodeo, despite his shoulder injury, even if it meant permanently disabling himself…or worse. Because what *else* was he to do with his life?

He had an answer to that question now, thanks to Cammi.

Reid tucked her hair behind her ears, stroked the pads of his thumbs across her cheeks. "Good to see some pink in your face again."

He thought she looked cute as all get-out, blushing that way. Suddenly overcome with emotion, he clutched her to him. What would it take, he wondered, to make her his own? Whatever it was, he'd do it!

But first things first. He had to 'fess up, tell her everything—that it had been *him* behind the wheel of the other car on that dreadful night. The sooner she knew the truth about him, the better.

He held her at arm's length, hoping with every breath

that she wouldn't hate him. "Cammi, there's something you need to know about me. I—"

Creaking from above interrupted him, and he looked at the ceiling.

"Dad's room," she explained. "I can hardly believe he's still up." Biting her lower lip and wincing slightly, she backpedaled to open the door. "Maybe you'd better go. He'll be furious if he finds you here at this hour."

He wondered what she'd say if he told her that her dad already had plenty of reason to raise the roof if he found Reid here, and not just because of the time. In Lamont's book, Reid surmised, there would never be a good time to find Reid in his kitchen, alone with his daughter.

On a brighter note, the disruption bought him one more day before he'd have to come clean, before he'd have to deal with her reaction to the news. One more chance to show her his good side, to try to win her over.

Reid reached out, snagged her slender wrist and pulled her to him. He pressed his mouth to hers, putting everything he had into the kiss, because it had to say everything he couldn't. "I've been dreaming of finding a girl like you most of my adult life."

His words had touched her, as evidenced by her blushing smile and the bashful tilt of her head. She bit her lower lip, then whispered a shy "Good night, Reid."

Walking away from her was perhaps the hardest thing he'd ever done. From the top step of the porch, he said, "Lock up tight after I leave, y'hear?"

Cammi nodded. "And you drive safely."

Two long strides put him back inside, where he drew her close yet again. "One more for the road," he said, kissing her. "I'll call you tomorrow," he added when the delicious moment ended.

He winced when she closed and bolted the door, because a little part of him hoped she'd throw herself into his arms, tell him to stay. "You've been eavesdropping on too many of Martina's chick flicks," he told himself, descending the porch steps.

A black-and-white long-haired dog bounded up to him just then. "My guess is, you're Obnoxious," Reid said, crouching to tousle the animal's fur. "Do you know how lucky you are, living under the same roof with a gal as wonderful as Cammi?"

Obnoxious answered with a bark, then disappeared around the corner of the house. When the kitchen light went out, Reid stood and put his hands in his pockets. "G'night, pretty lady," he said. "Sweet dreams…."

The steady *clop-clop* of Lamont's cowboy boots on the hardwood floor announced his entrance. Obnoxious left the warmth of Cammi's arms, climbed off the couch and trotted up to his master, oblivious of the man's messy hair or the sheet wrinkles crisscrossing his left cheek. Lamont bent to ruffle the dog's fur.

"I thought I heard voices," Lamont told Cammi. He stood and snugged the belt of his buffalo plaid robe.

Cammi considered evading the question, but decided against it. "The man I crashed into—the one who took me to the hospital…?" She swallowed, not knowing what to make of his deepening frown. "He stopped by to see if I was all right."

Lamont didn't move, but narrowed his eyes. "At this hour? That boy never did have a lick of sense!"

"He didn't want to wake everyone by calling, so—"

"Fool. He should've waited till morning." His mouth formed a thin, taut line. "Then I coulda poked a finger into his chest, made sure he got the message loud and clear when I told him to take a hike."

Maybe Reid had been right, maybe she *was* cranky, because her dad's unreasonable attitude grated on her nerves. "What do you have against cowboys all of a sudden?" She posed the question in the most respectful voice she could muster, but just in case she missed the mark, she smiled—as camouflage. "*You're* a cowboy, let's not forget."

"True enough." He crossed both arms over his chest as Obnoxious sat beside him. "But *this* cowboy never killed anybody."

She sat up straighter.

"You heard me."

Smoothing the bangs back from her face, Cammi shook her head.

He stomped across the room and flopped onto the seat of his recliner, and the dog joined him. "I don't have anything against cowboys. It's just one in particular I don't cotton to. The boy did a good deed, driving you to the E.R., staying with you till I got there. I'll give him that. So we'll send him a box of cigars, some beef jerky, apples for his horse. Doesn't matter *what,* long as we show our appreciation." He aimed his pointer finger at Cammi. "When you get the last of this accident mess cleaned up, you'll be done with him, once and for all."

Done with him? Dad had issued an order, no question about it. Cammi was about to start listing Reid's better qualities when her father said, "Reid Alexander is the polecat who killed your mother."

Cammi couldn't admit that she'd already figured that out. Lamont had always been big on family loyalty; he'd see her defense of Reid as a betrayal.

"*He* was the lowlife who was driving the other car that night."

"Why didn't you ever tell me this before?" Cammi responded.

Scowling, he shook his head. "Didn't want to say his name, for one thing. Didn't want you girls havin' to deal with more facts than necessary. It was hard enough on the lot of you, just grappling with…" Sighing, he ended with a flick of his hand.

"But half a dozen eyewitnesses said Mom ran the red light, said it wasn't Reid's fault. I overheard at the funeral that the other driver had been cleared of all charges, right there on the scene."

Lamont only shook his head. "I don't care *what* the law said. That fool boy had no more business being out in weather like that than your mother did. What kind of parents let a fourteen-year-old boy drive, anyway?"

"I went to school with a boy who had special permission to drive at fourteen because his father was an invalid. Maybe something similar happened to Reid."

But wait…hadn't Reid called Billy his father figure?

Hadn't he said that Martina had been more a mom to him than his own mother had? Cammi wondered what had happened to his mom and dad. Why had this kindly couple stepped in to parent him?

Then something dawned on her. "Driving without a license is against the law, so he would have been issued a ticket for *that* the night of Mom's accident, right?"

Lamont waved the question away. "His mama and her drunken bum of a husband were working as hired hands at the Rockin' C in those days. 'Bout that time, Billy took a spill from the barn loft, busted up his leg pretty bad. The sheriff had taken the stepfather's license away for drunk driving. So Billy arranged for the kid to get one of those 'special permission' licenses you talked about, paid him to run into town for supplies and whatnot. Way I hear it, he was on his way to the pharmacy, to pick up Billy's painkillers, when…"

Cammi realized now what Reid had been trying to tell her earlier, when the squeaking from the floor above warned them her father could thunder down the stairs at any minute. She folded her hands. "If he was driving legally and the accident wasn't his fault, then why do you hold Reid respon—"

"Because for starters," he interrupted, "he had no business being in that king-size pickup. And because no boy of fourteen has the horse sense or the coordination to react to a situation like that. 'Specially not in the middle of a wicked storm."

Lamont got to his feet, clomped across the floor and stopped in the doorway, the dog close on his heels. "Get some sleep, Cammi. You need your rest." He hesitated, then added, "And get any fool notions of starting up with that fella out of your mind!"

She didn't disagree. Didn't agree, either. Cammi would wait until she was back on her feet to talk this out with Reid, face-to-face. Only then would she decide whether or not to "start up with that fella." "G'night, Dad," she said.

"See you in the morning. Patti will be here tomorrow, so brew up an appetite."

Food was the last thing on her mind right now. But Cammi smiled and nodded. "It's been a long time since I had one of her big country breakfasts."

"Violet and Ivy will be here the day after tomorrow. Sort of a welcome-home dinner."

It had been a long time since she'd spent time with her sisters. Too long. "I can't wait to see them," she said, meaning it.

"Sorry if I seemed a mite gruff."

Grinning, she quoted Reid. *"Seemed?"*

Chuckling, Lamont threw her a kiss and headed upstairs, Obnoxious close on his heels.

Cammi turned out the light and snuggled under the covers, wondering how long before he sent the dog packing. Wondering if the dog would cuddle up with her again, or beg to be let outside.

Wondering how she was going to broach the subject of her mother's death next time she talked to Reid....

Chapter Seven

The doorbell rang at precisely eleven o'clock the next day. It was too late to be the mailman and too early to be the pizza guy Lily often called at lunchtime. Thankfully, Cammi had showered and changed into a white sweatsuit and sneakers, because at least she wouldn't have to explain being in a robe and slippers at this hour of the morning.

Cammi peered out the etched-glass window beside the front door and immediately recognized the lady who'd come calling. "Martina!" she said, smiling as she threw open the door.

"Good to see you, Cammi."

Martina balanced a plate of cookies in one hand, a potted plant in the other, as Cammi wrapped her in a warm hug.

Draping an arm across the woman's slender shoulders, Cammi led her into the foyer and closed the door. "Goodness, what's it been—two years since I've seen you? What brings you out this way?"

Martina stood near the staircase, dark eyes sparkling in the sunlight that filtered in through the windows. "I'm on my way back from town. Had to pick up some medicine for Billy—"

Gently, Cammi ushered her toward the kitchen. "I heard about his illness," she said. And seeing the sadness on the older woman's face, Cammi took her elbow. "Let's get caught up over coffee and cookies."

In the kitchen, Martina held out the English ivy plant. "Brought you this," she said. "It's a cutting from one I've had since before Billy and I were married."

"It's beautiful." Cammi put it on the kitchen windowsill. "Perfect," she said, standing back to admire the way sunshine gleamed from the deep green leaves.

"It was the least I could do after Reid told me what happened to you. I thought maybe it would cheer you up some."

She pursed her lips. "I don't know him well, but I think Reid sometimes talks too much."

Martina put the cookies on the table. "Baked these just this morning. I remember that your father has a weakness for chocolate chips." She took a seat at the table, watching as Cammi poured them each a cup of coffee. "You're wrong about Reid, by the way," she said, as Cammi removed the clear-plastic cover from the plate. "Usually, he's more tight-lipped than a turtle. No one was more surprised than me when he came home last night—" Martina laughed softly "—or should I say this morning, and told me where he'd been until all hours—and why."

Cammi sat across from her, slid the sugar bowl and

creamer closer to Martina. "It was quite a ways for him to come, just to see how I was holding up. Especially when he could've accomplished the same thing with a phone call."

"Not at that hour." Martina looked right, then left. "Where's Lamont?"

"He went into town, some kind of business at the bank." She paused, taking in the woman's uneasy expression. "Why?"

"Well," she said, relaxing some, "next to my Billy, Reid is the bravest man I know. I wouldn't say he's *afraid* of your dad, exactly. Let's just say whenever the name Lamont London comes up, the boy gets a tad… nervous."

Obviously, a lot more had happened on the night her mother died—and since then—than Cammi knew.

"No one blames Lamont for the way he behaved, for the things he said that night," Martina continued, "least of all Reid. We all understood that your daddy loved your mama so much, he just couldn't help himself. Grief made him do and say…" She pressed her lips together as if she couldn't bear to repeat any of it. After stirring a spoonful of sugar into her coffee, Martina added a dollop of milk. "I wasn't there, mind you, but Billy told me about it after he brought the boy home." Sighing, Martina shook her head. "Lamont was hard on Reid, mighty hard."

Cammi's heart ached, for the pain her dad had gone through that night, for the way he'd taken it out on Reid. She'd heard bits of gossip over the years, but never enough to fill in the missing pieces. And since her questions about that night were always answered with a stern "You'll have to ask your father about that," Cammi and her sisters had never heard the whole, unadulterated truth. "Please, tell me what happened."

"He called Reid a murderer—one of the kinder things he said, I might add," Martina began. "He said Reid deserved to spend the rest of his days in prison for killing his Rose, for taking her from her girls, from *him*." A frown of disapproval creased her brow as she stirred her coffee. "As I said, I wasn't there, and I thank God for it every time I see that worried look come across Reid's face. I'm so *glad* I didn't have to be there to hear…." She shook her head. "Wasn't a pretty sight, I don't imagine."

Cammi nodded. "Must have been awfully hard on Reid."

"Oh, yes. Very hard." She sighed, looked wistful. "He was such a happy-go-lucky boy before that night. Since then…" She lifted her cup, blew softly across the surface of her coffee. "Now he's an odd mix of somber and serious and devil-may-care. He looks carefree on the surface, but I know better. I know because I remember the risks he took during his rodeo days." Martina clucked her tongue. "And if you had seen some of those li'l gals he dated…" Her frown deepened and she shook her head, harder this time. "Seemed to me he took those ridiculous awards far too seriously."

Something told her Martina wasn't referring to rodeo buckles, earned for outlasting other cowboys on the backs of wild stallions and raging bulls. "Awards?"

"Bachelor of the Year, for starters." She waved her

hand as if shooing an annoying fly. "Not one of those women could be called a lady, not in my opinion, anyway, considering how they threw themselves at him." Martina fanned her face with the fingertips of one hand, then slapped the tabletop. "He'd never admit it, of course, but I think he became a daredevil because he just plain didn't care whether he lived or died. I always believed he took chances hoping he *would* die in a fall."

Cammi pictured him, Stetson at a cocky angle above his brow, western-style shirt hugging his broad chest, dusty jeans clinging to his muscular thighs as he aimed a knock-'em-dead smile at his gaggle of cloying, clinging girl groupies. Unable to explain the surge of jealous anger that pulsed through her, she helped herself to a cookie, proceeded to break it in half.

"Why did he leave the rodeo?"

"Took a nasty spill from a Brahman bull by the name of Ruthless. The fall shattered his shoulder, and the trampling tore muscles, pulled ligaments and tendons. He was at death's door, I tell you! Spent weeks in the hospital and months in physical therapy afterward. His right shoulder hasn't been the same since, which means he couldn't hold his own in competitions, not in the saddle, not with a rope." Martina leaned forward and whispered, "And every chance I get, I say a prayer for ol' Ruthless, 'cause he might just have saved Reid's hide!"

Cammi's puzzled expression prompted the woman to go on.

"See, the accidents were happening closer and closer together, each a little more serious than the last." She sat back. "Only the Good Lord knows if Reid would've survived the next one."

The image of Reid, hobbling and helpless, made her stomach lurch. She wondered who had taken care of him, prepared his meals, changed his bandages, massaged the ache from bruised muscles as he recovered. Surely not one of the floozies who'd chased after him. She took a sip of coffee, hoping to wash away the bitter taste *that* picture had left in her mouth.

"So how's Billy?"

Immediately, Martina's bright eyes dulled with pain and regret. "Oh, Cammi, he's not well. Not well at all. My Billy isn't long for this old world, I'm afraid."

Cammi reached out, covered Martina's hands with her own. "I'm so sorry. If there's anything I can do, anything at all, just name it. Even if it's only to lend an ear now and then, when things get…difficult."

She slid one hand out, used it to pat Cammi's wrist. "Even as a girl, you were big-hearted and sweet. Remember the time you gave your choir robe to Sally Olsen and pretended to have laryngitis so she could sing the solo at the Christmas service?" Martina grabbed a cookie and took a bite.

Ah, Cammi thought, *the good old days*…when Martina played the organ at the Church of the Resurrection, and Cammi held the lofty position of being the youth choir's soloist. She'd always believed Sally had the prettier, better voice, and routinely said so. But the choir master and Sally's dad had been embroiled in a long-standing feud…which ended the day Cammi pretended she couldn't sing and Mr. O'Dell gave Sally the lead.

Martina sat up straighter. "And I think you know if *you* need to talk, I'm here for you, too."

She took that to mean Reid had filled Martina in on what she'd been through since leaving Amarillo for L.A., and since returning to Texas. "Isn't it strange," she said to change the subject, "that Reid and I lived in the same town all those years, yet we never met."

"No. Not strange at all. There are miles and miles between our ranch and yours. We're in different school districts." She harrumphed softly. "Besides, Billy and I never ran in the same social circles as your mom and dad."

Cammi recalled the fancy parties her parents threw several times a year, recalled that Martina and Billy hadn't been invited to a single one. "But our families have attended the same church for as long as I can remember."

Martina shook her head. "Reid was never allowed to come to church with Billy and me. Not while his mama was married to that horrible man, anyway. He'd drink himself into a stupor every night of the week, then drag her and Reid to his church on Sunday morning." She wrinkled her nose with disgust. "It was one of those metal outbuildings on the edge of town, where the preacher spewed fire-and-brimstone sermons."

Martina leaned in to share another secret. "Folks say that man used poisonous snakes to test his followers' faith!" she whispered hoarsely, wide-eyed, one hand pressed to her chest. Martina sat back, added in a voice of disapproval, "Sadly, Reid was long gone when the cancer took his mama, and by then, he'd been nursing a grudge against the Lord for years."

A grudge against the Lord...

Martina looked at Cammi from the corner of her eye. "You'll be good for him," she said, standing. "It's about time he settled down. I thank the Almighty that this time, he chose well. You're the answer to my prayers. Billy's, too."

It was a lot to absorb in such a short time, and Cammi didn't know how to react.

"Reid deserves some happiness." Martina pushed in her chair. "Lord knows he's had enough sorrow in his life."

Of course he deserved happiness, Cammi agreed, but what on earth made the woman think *she* could help him find it?

"Hate to eat and run," Martina said, heading back toward the foyer, "but I have to get home with that medicine. Billy had enough of it to last a few more days, but I'm not one to take chances. What if there's a storm? What if I forget to gas up the car?" She gave a nervous laugh. "Like Reverend Johnstone says, 'Trust in the Lord but lock your car!'"

Smiling, Cammi opened the front door. Giving Martina a goodbye hug, she added, "Thanks for stopping by. You've brightened my whole day. Dad's too, once he sees those cookies!"

"See you at church on Sunday?"

Cammi stiffened. Her own grudge against God made her want to shout that she had no intention of attending services, this Sunday or any other, for that matter. But out of respect to this gentle woman who'd always been devout, Cammi said, "If I'm feeling up to it, you might see me there."

"I'll pray for you," she said, squeezing Cammi's hands. "And Billy and I could use your prayers, too."

She couldn't promise to pray, but couldn't bring herself to say she wouldn't, either. So Cammi nodded and said, "Thanks again for stopping by. It was great seeing you."

"You take care of yourself, now, you hear?" And hands clasped under her chin, she said, "It's so amazing."

"What is?"

"How much you look like your mama." She laughed. "But I expect you're bored to tears, hearing what a beautiful woman Rose London was."

She'd heard it all her life, it seemed. "No, I love hearing about her."

"Well, I'll be on my way. I'll be sure to give Reid your love."

Cammi wanted to say, *No! Don't do that!* But her spunky visitor was down the steps and halfway to her car before she could form the sentence. Grinning, Cammi waved, thinking she'd like to be a speck on the wall when Martina delivered that message, because wouldn't it be interesting to see how the Bachelor of the Year reacted to *that*.

Weeks after Reid's return to Texas, Billy had met with his lawyer, and when the dark-suited man left the Rockin' C, Billy had handed Reid a legal-looking document.

"Makes perfect sense," Billy had said when Reid protested the power of attorney.

"I don't want any part of the paperwork," Martina agreed. "You're the son we never had. Surely you don't expect us to turn to strangers at a time like this."

He couldn't have refused them, even if it hadn't been "a time like this."

From that day on, Reid had taken care of all official ranch business. He made a point of discussing everything with Billy first, of course, because he sensed Billy would leave this old world easier, knowing the spread he'd spent a lifetime building was in good hands.

He'd just deposited a hefty check—money that had come from the sale of a prize-winning calf—when he heard a familiar voice behind him. Reid didn't need to turn around to know it was Lamont London, having a conversation with the next person in line. With any luck, he could duck out of the bank without being seen.

Under ordinary circumstances, he would have waited until he got outside to put on his hat and sunglasses. But no meeting with this bear of a man could be called "ordinary circumstances."

Reid strode purposefully to the door, feigning interest in the deposit slip as a way to avoid eye contact. Experience had taught him that the very sight of him brought it all back to Lamont: whose fault the accident had been didn't change the ugly fact that Rose London died that night. Rather than stirring up trouble, Reid made it a point to avoid Lamont whenever he could.

But this wasn't to be one of those times.

Lamont stepped halfway out of the teller's line. "You're up mighty early for a fella who comes callin' in the middle of the night."

Reid had two choices: Keep walking—and appear disrespectful and guilty—or face the man.

He stopped dead in his tracks, removed his hat and shades, and looked Lamont in the eye. "Didn't want to wake the whole house by phoning. I was worried about Cammi."

Lamont's bitter chuckle echoed in the high-ceilinged, marble-floored building. "Decent man would have waited till morning."

The implication was clear. "Duly noted," Reid said, nodding.

He'd barely got his hat back on when Lamont added, "In the future, you'd be wise to avoid my spread…and my daughter."

He looked into the man's face, saw years of anger and resentment, grief and regret written in every crease. This was neither the time nor the place for an all-out confrontation, but one thing needed to be said. "Cammi's a full-grown woman, capable of making up her own mind about…things." He paused to give his words a moment to sink in. "I give you my word—I'll honor any decision she makes."

His eyes mere slits now, Lamont said, "If my girl is so much as considering spending time in your company, then she's lost her cotton-pickin' mind."

Reid stood as tall as his six-foot frame would allow

and squared his shoulders. "Maybe so," he said, donning the sunglasses, "and maybe not."

He walked toward the double glass doors and stepped outside. Despite the bright sunshine, Reid felt the chill of Lamont's icy glare. If they'd been living in the days of Billy the Kid or Wyatt Earp, what he'd said to Cammi's father just now would've been dubbed "fightin' words." Who was he kidding? It didn't matter that the calendar said "Twenty-first Century"; Lamont London still lived by 1800s principles.

He'd stay away from River Valley Ranch out of respect for the man, but it would take an act of Congress to keep him from Cammi. As soon as she was able, he'd take her out for a night on the town. Afterward, he'd get her alone someplace and spill his guts, tell her the truth, that is, if Lamont hadn't spilled the beans already. If she decided it'd be too hard, living life with the man who'd killed her mother, well, it would hurt to the bone, but he'd accept it.

Behind the wheel of Billy's pickup now, he poked the key into the ignition. He sat for a moment after cranking up the truck's motor, staring straight ahead, seeing nothing. Life would be tough enough without Billy, but Reid believed he could stomach it, with Cammi by his side. Without her, though...

"Lord," he whispered through clenched teeth, "if You're up there, I sure would appreciate a hand up, here."

Reid finished up his business in town, then headed straight home. He was tempted to take the turn-off that led to Cammi's place, but the scene in the bank made him decide against it. No telling how long before Lamont returned to the ranch, and Cammi was in no condition to witness a brawl between her father and him.

About a mile before the Rockin' C drive, a shiny black SUV with black-tinted windows barreled down the road, leaving a wake of road grit and dust in its wake. He recognized its stern-faced driver instantly. Reid knew there was nothing—not a store or restaurant, not even a gas station—between here and River Valley Ranch to bring Lamont so far out of his way.

Nothing except Reid himself, that is. Maybe, in that spirit of the Old West, Lamont had decided to call Reid out, insist on a showdown at sundown, a duel at dawn.

A foul mood descended upon him as he wondered how long he'd have to slink around, avoiding the Londons, skirting their ranch. When would they accept that he'd simply been in the wrong place at the wrong time and stop hating him for what had happened that night?

Something told him "never" answered all three questions, and his already dark mood deepened. *Quit feelin' sorry for yourself, Alexander,* he thought. *It's your own fault, after all.*

He should've listened to Billy when he tried to talk Reid out of going to the cemetery on the morning of Rose's funeral. But Reid had been certain it was the right thing to do. He'd prayed on it, he'd insisted, and he had to do what he felt the Lord wanted him to do.

Turned out the visit only made matters worse. Far worse. If he'd known what would happen when he

borrowed a white shirt and tie from Billy, when he got
Martina to press a sharp crease into his blue jeans, when
he hitched a ride into town, then hid in the stand of pines
behind Rose's grave, waiting for her family and friends
to pay their last respects…

As the last mourners led the teary-eyed London girls
to a waiting black limo, Reid made his way across the
velvety lawn to where Lamont stood, stiff and silent,
one hand over his eyes, the other on Rose's casket.

"Mr. London?"

Slowly, he faced Reid. "What're *you* doing here?"

Back then, Lamont stood head and shoulders taller
than the fourteen-year-old boy and outweighed him by
fifty pounds. Still, Reid stuck by his "do the right thing"
decision. Stiffening his back, he said, "There's somethin' I need to say."

Lamont went back to staring at the coffin. "Well,
don't that just beat all," he said, mostly to himself. "The
boy needs to say something." He cast a surly glance at
Reid. "I don't care what you need. Now get yourself on
home. You're foulin' the air, just by standin' there."

Reid picked at a hangnail on his thumb. Picked so
hard he started it bleeding. Stuffing it into his jeans
pocket, he cleared his throat. "I came here to say…I'm
sorry, sir, mighty sorry about what happened the other
night—"

Shoulders hunched and fists doubled up at his sides,
Lamont whirled to face Reid again. "Are you deaf, boy?"
His eyes all but shut in a fierce frown, he snarled, "Not
just deaf, but dumb, too. Didn't I make myself clear at

the hospital the other night? I pray to God I never lay eyes on you again!"

Reid took a step back and winced, prepared to take a hard right to the chin—or worse. He could have turned tail and run, but the way Reid saw it, he had a beating coming. That, and then some! Because although everyone—the police, witnesses on the scene, doctors and nurses in the E.R., Martina and Billy—insisted the accident hadn't been his fault, Reid hadn't swallowed a word of it. It was Lamont's hateful speech outside the O.R. that rang true in his young mind: He'd killed a wife and mother. Maybe Lamont was right—maybe there *had* been something Reid could've done to prevent the crash. He'd likely never know for sure, but if whalin' the tar out of Reid would make Lamont feel better, well, he owed the man that much.

He'd opened his eyes when Lamont said, "Don't worry, boy. I won't sully myself by layin' a hand on the likes of *you*."

It had taken quite a while to figure out what that meant. Even now, the knowledge created a hard knot in Reid's gut. It would have done his conscience a world of good if Lamont *had* thrashed him back then in the graveyard.

He steered the pickup into the Rockin' C drive, parked it beside the detached garage and stomped into the house, where Martina stood at the stove, stirring something in a deep pot. "What was Lamont London doing here?" he asked, hanging his jacket on the wall peg.

She sighed. "Looking for you."

"Me?"

She nodded somberly. "You, and answers. Why you paid his daughter a call last night, what kind of relationship you have with her, what your intentions are—"

"Who'd he talk to, you or Billy?"

"Billy, mostly."

Reid grit his teeth. Billy was in no shape to be dealing with that man. "If he riled him, I'll—"

She sent him a confident smile. "If anyone got riled, it was Lamont." She went back to stirring the contents of her pot. "I'm afraid he didn't get what he came for."

"What *did* he come for, if not answers to his questions?"

Martina laid the ladle in a bright rooster-shaped spoon rest. "To lay down the law, to deliver a list of do's and don'ts to you." Grinning, she winked. "But Billy set him straight."

The scent of spicy tomato sauce wafted in the air, and she closed her eyes to inhale a whiff. "Mmm. I haven't made spaghetti sauce in ages. Lunch'll be ready in half an hour or so," she announced, sliding another pot from the cabinet. "You have plenty of time to get cleaned up." The noodle kettle sat in the sink basin under the tap water. Martina stuck her forefinger into the hissing stream and added, "Time for a quick nap, even." She shot a maternal glance over her shoulder. "I imagine you could use one, seeing as how you didn't get much sleep last night."

"I'm wide awake," he admitted. Running into Lamont at the bank, seeing him again on the road, learning he'd been here, had jarred Reid enough that he'd probably have trouble falling asleep even hours from now.

After supper that evening, Reid put Billy to bed, then helped Martina with the dishes. When the last pot was dried and put away, she kissed him good-night. "Don't stay up too long," she said, mussing his hair.

"Don't worry, I'm just gonna watch the TV news for a spell, then I'll come up." At the foot of the stairs, he wished her sweet dreams and headed for the family room.

The telephone on the end table beckoned him. He lifted the receiver, then glanced at the clock. Only nine, he thought. Too late to call her?

Only one way to find out...

He dialed her number, holding his breath, hoping she'd answer, or that her youngest sister would pick up.

"Lamont London."

He gave a sigh of frustration. "Reid Alexander," he said matter-of-factly. "I'd like to talk to Cammi."

There was a long pause before Lamont said, "I need to talk to you, Alexander. Can you meet me at Georgia's Diner?"

"When?"

"Now."

Reid swallowed. "I reckon I can be there in half an hour."

"Fine."

Reid stared at the buzzing earpiece, wondering what Lamont London wanted with him. Well, he'd find out soon enough, wouldn't he? Reid dashed off a note and propped it against the salt and pepper shakers in Martina's spotless kitchen. *"Went to Georgia's for a confab with Lamont London,"* he wrote. *"If I'm not back by morning, send in the S.W.A.T. team."* And he signed it, *"Love, Reid."*

He drove slightly more than the speed limit, hoping to establish some kind of home-turf advantage by arriving first. Unfortunately, Lamont must have had the same notion, for when Reid pulled into the parking lot, he saw the man, backside leaning against the fender of the enormous black SUV, arms folded over his chest and gray Stetson riding low on his forehead. The instant he saw Reid, he uncrossed his booted ankles and stood, feet shoulder-width apart.

"Evenin'," Reid said, walking toward him.

Lamont gave a halfhearted salute and one nod of his head. "Evenin'." He started for the diner's entrance. "Thanks for agreeing to meet me."

"No problem," Reid said, opening the door. He stood aside as the older man entered. "You made good time getting here."

Lamont removed his hat. "There wasn't any traffic." He led the way to a table in the rear of the restaurant and pulled out a chair. "Coffee?" he asked when the waitress came over.

Reid nodded at the girl. "No cream, no sugar."

"Ditto," Lamont agreed.

She scribbled on her pad and left them alone with their frowns. A minute of complete silence passed before she delivered the coffee and moved on to take another order.

Lamont spoke first. "Guess you're wondering why I asked you to meet me here."

Reid began making an accordion out of a paper napkin. "You could say that."

"About...the accident..." Lamont cleared his throat, coughed into a weathered fist. "Just wanted to say... maybe I was a mite hard on you back then."

Lamont was a proud, stubborn man. This apology hadn't come easy. Reid saw no point dragging things out, making him grovel. "I'd have done the same in your shoes," he admitted. "Or worse."

Lamont met Reid's eyes, held his gaze for what seemed an eternity before saying, "I'll admit, it still doesn't set well—your courtin' my girl, that is."

Courting. Reid took a long, slow sip of his coffee, thinking Lamont would have fit in real well back in the Wild, Wild West days. "I wouldn't worry too awful much about me courtin' Cammi if I were you." He unfolded, then refolded the paper accordion. "I haven't told her yet that it was me behind the wheel of that truck." Reid took a deep breath, exhaled. "She'll likely send me packing when she finds out."

A strange expression darkened Lamont's face, and it puzzled Reid.

"I just wanted to clear the air in case..." Lamont winced. "I want Cammi to be happy, is what I'm tryin' to say."

"She's been through a lot lately," Reid agreed. He shook his head. "I know it sounds squirrelly, me talkin' this way so soon after meeting her, but I'm crazy about that girl of yours. If she'll have me, if she can find it in her heart to forgive me for…" Reid didn't think he needed to spell out why, not to Lamont of all people. "If she'll have me," he said again, "I swear, I'll do right by her."

Lamont drained his mug, put it back onto the table with a *thud*. He tipped it this way and that, watching the remaining drops of coffee swirl around in the bottom of the cup before saying, "Then I reckon as long as we're in agreement on that, you 'n' me don't need to be best friends, now, do we?"

"No. I reckon we don't."

So they'd come to an understanding. Cammi's happiness was more important than what either of them wanted. Lamont had as much as agreed to give his blessing—*if* his daughter wanted Reid. *Mighty big "if,"* he said to himself.

"Well, guess that about says it all," Lamont said, standing. He unceremoniously threw a five-dollar bill on the table and pressed the Stetson into place on his head, then extended his right hand. "I don't know if I would have come here, in your shoes, so thanks for meeting me."

Reid gave his meaty hand one hearty shake. "No, sir," he said. "Thank *you*."

Lamont's brows knitted in the center of his forehead. "Thank me? For what?"

Releasing his hand, Reid said, "Let's just say if I'm ever lucky enough to have young'uns of my own, I hope I can love 'em as unselfishly as you love yours."

Drawing his head back slightly, Lamont blinked several times. "Well, I…uh, well—"

The shadow cast by Lamont's hat brim made it impossible to know for sure, but Reid had a feeling the man was blushing. "Guess we oughta be hittin' the road," he said, saving him. "Sunup comes mighty early, and Billy's new ranch hands haven't learned the ropes yet."

This time Lamont held the diner door open. "He didn't look so hot when I saw him today," he said as Reid passed by.

"The docs figure he has six months, tops."

The men walked side by side to Lamont's truck. "That's a sorry shame. I always liked old Billy…."

"Can't think of a soul who doesn't."

Again, Lamont nodded. Then he opened his driver's door and climbed into the SUV's cab. "Be seein' you," he said, slamming the door.

Reid answered with a two-fingered salute to his hat brim. *Yeah,* he thought, *I reckon you will.*

At least, he hoped so.

It depended entirely on how Cammi would take it when he told her…everything.

Chapter Eight

Dinner the following night with the family was everything Cammi expected it to be—and then some.

For every delicious morsel of food Lamont's housekeeper served up, Violet and Ivy dished out unwanted advice. Like blond stereo speakers, the twins voiced shock that their eldest sister had secretly married a near stranger, had been carrying his child when he died. They were harsh and disappointed that Cammi had kept her hardships to herself these past few months.

Lily, usually the most likely to take up for the underdog, didn't participate in the heated discussion. She sat, sullenly poking at her food, too preoccupied to join either side of the debate. Cammi made a mental note to seek her out later, find out what had caused the uncharacteristically gloomy mood. Hopefully, nothing had happened to one of Lily's beloved animals.

Lamont finally put an end to the twins' carping criticisms. "Give it a rest, girls," he scolded, throwing down his napkin. "I thought we put this kind of squabbling behind when you left kindergarten."

He meant well, Cammi knew. And the Good Lord knew the man deserved one peaceful meal, after all she'd put him through these past few days…these past few *years*. But he had no idea that his fatherly refereeing always caused more harm than good; inevitably, it widened the gap separating Cammi from Violet and Ivy.

As if to prove her theory, the twins traded "I told you so" glances, a silent signal that Cammi read to mean, *the prodigal returneth*. She loved her sisters dearly, but at times like these, it was very difficult to *like* them.

Maybe if she could steer them away from her mistakes…

"So, how's the boutique, Ivy?" The shop had been Ivy's lifeblood ever since her fiancé left her at the altar.

The youngest twin's blue eyes brightened. "Wonderful!" she said smiling. "I'm expecting a shipment of turquoise jewelry. You'll have to stop by and pick out a pair of earrings—my welcome-home gift to you."

Cammi patted Ivy's hand. "You're a peach, kiddo." And turning to Vi, she said, "And the dance studio? How goes it?"

"Oh, it's tap-tap-tapping along." Vi gave a proud smile. "I have nearly two hundred students this year."

"I'm so proud of you, Vi! Any shows on the calendar?"

She nodded enthusiastically. "I'll get you tickets.

You'll love the Thanksgiving performance. We're dancing to numbers from *Phantom*."

Cammi thought Vi spent entirely too much time at her school, but who was she to talk when she'd just blown two whole years trying to make it as an actress. As for Vi's love life, well, Cammi knew better than to bring *that* up. She couldn't think of a single boy Vi had brought home who hadn't riled Lamont. But then, in all fairness to Vi, she couldn't name a guy *any* of them had brought home that he'd approved of.

And Reid Alexander would prove to be the source of his biggest disapproval yet. Which was a shame, because she sensed that beneath Reid's ladies' man facade lived a good old-fashioned hero. Cammi remembered the soft warmth of his lips, the steady beat of his heart against her as he tenderly wrapped her in his muscular arms. She wondered what it might have been like if Lamont didn't already know Reid's history. "Dad," she'd say, striking a game-show hostess pose, *"this is Reid, the fella who killed Mom...."*

Immediately, what started out as a halfhearted joke backfired. For the thousandth time, she pictured that life-altering night, when lightning crackled, slicing through the storm-black sky. She imagined rain, sheeting over the horribly misshapen station wagon, where inside her mother lay bleeding and helpless and—

"Good grief, Cammi," Lily said, her brow furrowed with concern, "you're pale as a ghost. Why don't you go into the den and stretch out on the couch for a while? Ivy and Vi will help me with the dishes."

The twins exchanged another secret glance, making

Cammi wish that just once, she shared their talent for each knowing what the other was thinking.

For the past half hour, Cammi had been trying to ignore the fact that she'd been feeling light-headed. No surprise, really, considering that only a few days ago—

"She's right," Lamont agreed, mistaking Cammi's hesitation for reluctance to do as Lily suggested. "Take a nap or something while we clean things up in here." He smiled at Lily, then at Vi and Ivy in turn, his not-so-veiled hint inspiring them to nod their agreement. They reminded Cammi of those doggies people liked to perch in the rear windows of their cars.

"I just hate to miss out on dessert," she teased, standing on wobbly legs.

"We promise to save you a slice of pie," Lily said, reaching out to steady her. "Now, get on out of here. How do you expect us to bad-mouth you behind your back if you're right here facing us!"

Laughing, Cammi held up her hands in mock surrender. "All right. I give up." She headed for the family room, grateful to have a family who loved and cared about her despite the stupid mistakes she'd made. A dizzy spell stopped her halfway down the hall, and Cammi grabbed the wall's chair rail for support.

"I'm really worried about her, Dad," she heard Lily whisper. "How much blood did she lose, anyway!"

"I don't know" was his answer. "I wasn't there."

"You weren't?" That voice belonged to Vi, Cammi realized. "If you weren't there, how'd she get to the hospital?"

Lily said, "The guy she crashed into the other night drove her."

"Crash!" said Ivy. "What crash?"

Cammi heard Lily's impatient sigh. "Do you *ever* hear a word anyone says," she droned, "if it isn't about *you?* I told you on the phone—Cammi had an accident coming into town, and she met up with the other driver the very next day. Started having her miscarriage right before his very eyes, and he drove her to the E.R."

"If he hadn't been there for her," Lamont put in, "God only knows what might have happened to Cammi."

She'd had the same thought, dozens of times. Reid truly had saved her, in every sense of the word. But she never would have guessed her dad could be open-minded enough to admit it!

"So who *is* this guy?" Ivy asked. "Do I know him?"

Lily cleared her throat. "Ever hear of Reid Alexander?"

Silence, then Violet said, "Not the rodeo cowboy whose name is always in the gossip columns…."

Leave it to Vi, Cammi thought, *to point out the most negative thing about him.*

"One and the same," Lily said.

"I've seen pictures of him in all sorts of magazines and newspapers," Vi added, "and let me tell you, he's one good-lookin' dude!"

"Now, girls…" Lamont said. Cammi recognized it as a warning to change the course of the conversation, now.

Evidently, all three of her sisters caught the admonition, too; she heard the unmistakable sounds of plates being stacked, silverware being gathered, tumblers being collected. "We'll take care of these, Dad," Ivy said. "Go on into the den and keep Cammi company. We'll all have pie in there together when the dishes are done."

Cammi heard the feet of his chair scrape across the thick Persian rug that blanketed the polished dining room hardwood. "Think I'll take you up on that offer," he said. And chuckling, he added, "I wouldn't complain if a cup of coffee came with my pie."

She craned her ears, trying to figure out what had caused the sudden, complete silence.

"How 'bout you, Cammi," Lamont called, his voice a tad louder. "Should the girls bring you a cup, too, when they deliver your pie?"

Not even as kids had his daughters been able to get anything past him. What made her think she could pull the wool over Lamont's eyes now that he'd had a decade or more to hone his parenting skills? He had her, dead to rights; no point now in pretending she'd been heading back toward the dining room from her perch on the family room couch.

"Sounds great," she muttered.

Vi sounded genuinely surprised when she said, "Dad, how'd you know Cammi was standing there?"

"My lips are sealed," he drawled.

The girls' giggling voices faded as they moved into the kitchen. Cammi waited, and when Lamont caught up to her, he grinned and slung an arm around her. "So, heard any good gossip lately?"

Red-faced and shaking her head, Cammi sighed.

"Well, I guess you're a shoo-in for the Best Ears in Texas award."

He ushered her into the family room, and as she settled onto the couch, he rubbed his chin. "Best Ears award, eh?"

What he'd said about Reid echoed in her mind. "You're up for Father of the Year, too."

He slouched into his recliner. "And why's that?"

"What you said about Reid…" She shrugged. "It was a nice thing to say, that's all."

A shadow crossed his face, and the merry grin and twinkling eyes were replaced by a dour expression. Cammi would have asked what happened to change his mood…if she hadn't been so afraid of the answer.

With Lamont having turned in earlier than usual, and Lily in the barn tending her critters, Cammi had the darkened house all to herself. She slid the napkin bearing Reid's phone number from her pocket, where she'd tucked it earlier.

The mantel clock counted out the eight o'clock hour as she lifted the receiver from its cradle. Too late to call, given Billy's condition? Hopefully not, she thought, pressing the numbers.

For the next few minutes, Cammi and Martina exchanged pleasantries. Then the older woman said, "Why do I get the feeling you didn't call just to talk to me?"

Cammi heard the smile in her voice and was about to admit she'd called for Reid when Martina laughed.

"He's right in the next room, watching a baseball game with Billy. I'll get him."

Because of the ALS, Reid's time with his old friend was limited, she knew. "No, don't interrupt them," she said. "Can you have him—" She heard the phone hit a hard surface, then the *thud* of slant-heeled cowboy boots nearing the phone.

"Hey, there, pretty lady. What can I do for you?" Reid said cheerfully.

The imperious tones of the twins' voices still ringing in her ears, she needed to hear his voice. "Just wondering if you'd heard from the mechanic, is all."

"Nope. Guess that means you haven't either, right?"

"Hard to tell when we'll get our wheels back."

"*If,* y'mean," he said, chuckling. "So…where's your dad?"

"Upstairs, asleep probably."

He paused. "Think it's safe for me to stop by?"

Cammi coiled the phone cord around her forefinger, trying to come up with a legitimate reason to say yes.

"I won't stay long, I promise."

She wished Lamont hadn't confirmed her suspicions about Reid's involvement in her mother's accident. Cammi didn't know how she'd behave face-to-face with him.

"There's something I have to tell you, and…"

He's said as much last night, in the same dreary tone of voice. Cammi realized Reid wanted her to hear from *him* that he'd been driving the other car that night. "And what?" she urged.

"…and something I need to ask you."

She couldn't imagine what he might want to ask her. But last night, while tossing and turning on the pillowy leather sofa in Lamont's den, Cammi had made a decision, and Reid had a right to know what conclusions she'd come to.

"Okay," she said. "But park at the back end of the drive, and I'll meet you in the barn."

"No way! You're supposed to stay off your feet, remember?"

"It's just a short walk from the house, and I'll take it easy. Once I'm out there, I'll put my feet up on a hay bale or something, I promise."

"I dunno. Goes against my better judgment. Maybe I should wait until—"

"I hate to sound cranky," she interrupted, reminding him what he'd said last night, "but it isn't your call."

Another pause, then he said, "I don't think you're strong enough yet."

"Let me be the judge of that, will you?" When he didn't respond, she added, "We'll have more privacy out there than in the house."

After a moment, Reid said, "Look, what I have to say can wait until you're on your feet. It's nothing urgent, nothing that's worth putting your health in jeopar—"

"Don't patronize me, Reid. I know my own limits."

He heaved a heavy sigh. "Anybody ever tell you you're mule-headed?"

She heard the teasing in his voice. "Oh, I've been told so a time or two."

"Yeah, well, I can be stubborn, too, y'know."

Which meant he could simply refuse to come over. Disappointment nagged at her, compelled her to say, "So you don't want to see me, then."

Another sigh. "Aw, Cammi, you disappoint me."

"Why?"

"I never figured you for someone who'd fight dirty."

"Curiosity killed the cat, they say."

"Okay, I give up. What does *that* mean?"

"I'm itching to find out what you want to tell me. And what you want to ask me. The sooner I find out, the sooner I'll be able to relax!"

"Stubborn," he said, chuckling, "and tricky, too."

"See you in half an hour!" Fifteen minutes later, Cammi went searching for a tablet and pen. Finding them in the end table drawer beside her father's recliner, she wrote, *"Dad—back soon. I'm visiting with Lily. Don't worry, I'm being careful. Love, Cammi."* There was a roll of cellophane tape in the drawer, too. Snapping off a piece, she used it to secure the note to his recliner's headrest.

Flinging an afghan over one shoulder, she carefully and quietly unlocked the French doors and tiptoed across the deck. If she took it easy, as she'd promised Reid, the two-minute hike from the house to the barn would be a cakewalk.

And it would have been, too…if the moon hadn't slid behind a cloud, darkening the path, causing her to catch the toe of her sneaker on a tree root.

Twenty-five minutes into the ride, it was all Reid could do to keep from stomping on the gas and speeding the whole way to River Valley Ranch. Because the sooner he got there, the sooner he could lay his cards on the table.

"And the sooner she can boot you out the door," he said to himself.

Twin lights up ahead caught his attention. Reid recognized them as the lampposts perched atop flagstone columns flanking River Valley's entrance. He passed between scalloped wrought-iron gates and coasted down the long asphalt drive ribboning from the highway to the ranch house. Though he'd seen it half a dozen times, it was hard not to be awestruck by the enormous structure. It seemed oddly out of character for a man like Lamont—hard, intimidating, and stern—to design and build a place so welcoming, right down to the many-paned windows that glowed with warm amber light. So out of sync, in fact, that Reid wondered how involved Rose had been in creating the architectural plan.

Reid didn't turn onto the wide wooden bridge that would lead him to the semicircular drive, but followed the gravel cutoff instead, and parked the pickup beside the massive red barn, just as Cammi had asked him to do. Not even the thick cloak of darkness could hide its perfection. Lamont didn't do anything halfway, as evidenced by the perfectly plumb doors to the crisp-edged white trim.

Leaving Billy's keys in the ignition, he eased the driver's door shut and headed toward the outbuilding. He half expected Cammi to be outside, waiting for him, but breathed a sigh of relief that she wasn't; she needed her rest if she hoped to recuperate quickly.

Reid knocked softly on the door, then pulled it open. *"Pssst,"* he whispered, "Cammi…"

"Nobody in here but us chickens."

He didn't recognize the voice, but remembered Cammi saying that her sister spent more time in the barn than in the house. As he tried to recall her name, a younger, smaller version of Cammi leaned out from behind a stall door. "Can I help you?"

"You must be Lily," he said, smiling as he walked toward her.

Grinning as if she'd just run into an old chum, she met him halfway. "And you must be Reid," she said, extending a hand.

Like Cammi, Lily had a firm, no-nonsense grasp.

"If you're looking for my big sister, she isn't here."

Puzzled, he said, "She told me to meet her here in half an hour."

Lily's brow furrowed. "How long ago was that?"

He glanced at his wristwatch. "Little over half an hour ago."

Her frown deepened. "Isn't like her not to follow through. Not like her to be late, either." Suddenly, she bolted to the door.

Her fear was contagious; since Reid had longer, stronger legs, he passed her without even trying.

"She would've followed that path," Lily called from behind. "The one just to your left, there."

Silhouetted by the back porch light, Cammi lay curled on her side next to the walk. "Cammi…" he said, getting down on one knee. Cradling her close, he stroked her hair. "Aw, Cammi, what have you gone and done to yourself this time?"

She lifted a hand to her forehead, wincing when she smoothed back the bangs. "Clumsy me," she said, a half smile on her face. "Caught my toe on a tree root."

Lily ran up and knelt beside them. "What happened, Cammi? Are you crazy? What're you doing out here? You're supposed to be resting." She cringed at the sight of the bruised lump on her sister's forehead. "Oh, would you look at *that!*" She met Reid's eyes. "You think it's a concussion?" Focusing on Cammi, she added, "You okay? Should we call 911?"

Cammi's giggles started slow and quiet, escalating to a hearty laugh. "Easy, kiddo," she said, breathless, "I'm fine. Just got the wind knocked out of me, that's all."

"Let's get you into the house," Reid said, picking her up.

Cammi slipped her arms around his neck, rested a cheek on his shoulder. "I can make it under my own steam, you know."

He pressed a kiss to her temple. "Yeah, I'm sure you can. But humor me, will ya?" He walked a few steps before saying, "You gave us quite a scare."

"Sorry."

Lily walked backward in front of them. "How long do you think she was out?"

"Hard to tell." He pressed his cheek to Cammi's. "She doesn't feel cold, so at least shock hasn't set in."

"Still, maybe we should—"

"Hello-o," Cammi teased, waving one hand. "I'm right *here.*"

"Oh, I don't know about that," Lily protested, tapping her temple. "If you were all *here,* you wouldn't be outside. Not in your condition. Especially not without telling anyone where you were going."

"I left Dad a note in case he woke up and came downstairs for a bedtime snack."

"Fat lot of good that would have done if…" Lily rolled her eyes. "You should've called the barn. Why do you think Dad had a phone installed down there?"

Reid didn't like this turn of events, and decided Cammi didn't need any more upset. "It's mostly my fault she's out here. I should have insisted on meeting her at the house." He clamped his teeth together. "Better still, should've waited till she was better."

Cammi laid a finger over his lips, effectively silencing him. As he carried her up the back porch steps, Lily dashed around him and held the door open.

"You get her settled in the den," she suggested, "and I'll get an ice pack for that nasty bump on her head." And when all three stepped inside, Lily closed the door. "I think we should call someone."

Cammi groaned. "Who?"

"If not 911, then Doc Albert, at least."

"No," Cammi said.

"We should drive you to the hospital, then." Lily ran alongside Reid as he carried Cammi down the hall.

"No need for that," Cammi insisted. "I'm fine."

Lily tagged Reid's heels into the den. "But you could have a concussion!"

"Lily," Cammi said, as Reid gently deposited her on the sofa, "I love you for caring, but I'm okay. Honest. Now relax, will you?"

Reid grabbed an afghan from the back of the couch, shook it out and draped it over Cammi's legs. "She's right, Lily. Sort of."

"Sort of?"

Cammi said, "Lily, doesn't Elmer need a feeding?"

Reid laughed. "Elmer? Who's Elmer?"

Cammi cupped a hand beside her mouth and whispered, "She's playing mama cow to an orphaned calf."

"Hello-o," Lily mimicked Cammi. "I'm right *here*."

"Elmer's the calf?" he asked.

Pocketing her hands, Lily nodded.

"Go on and feed him, then. I'll stay with Cammi."

"But…but what—"

"I've seen a couple hundred concussions in my day, thanks to the rodeo. I know the signs. First hint of anything more serious than a headache, I'll drive her to the hospital. You've got my word on it."

She mulled that over a bit. "Dad's gonna have a fit if he comes downstairs and finds you here again."

Despite their recent meeting at the diner, the idea of facing Lamont on his own turf unsettled Reid more than he cared to admit. He pictured the man's blazing gray eyes, the firm set of his chin. "I can handle him."

Lily said to Cammi. "Your boyfriend here has a great sense of humor. He thinks 'cause he rode Brahman bulls and wild stallions, he can handle Dad." She punctuated her statement with a merry giggle.

Cammi's eyes widened and her cheeks turned bright pink. "Lily, what a thing to say." She clucked her tongue. "Reid isn't my— He's not my *boyfriend*."

"Whatever you say." She giggled again. "I'll be right back with that ice," Lily added, disappearing around the corner.

Boyfriend, Reid thought, harrumphing under his breath. He'd never much cared for the term, so why had Cammi's remark stung like a cold slap?

He barely had time to form the question before Lily was back, towel-wrapped ice pack in hand. "If you need me," Lily said, handing it to Reid, "just pick up the phone and dial 55 to ring the barn."

She didn't wait for him to agree, and he didn't wait for her to leave before tenderly holding the cold pack against Cammi's bruised forehead. "Where do you keep the aspirins in this mausoleum?" he asked, grinning.

She held the ice pack in place with one hand, pointed toward the hall with the other. "Powder room, third door on your right."

He got to his feet. "Drinking glasses?"

"Kitchen, cupboard above the dishwasher."

From the hall, he said, "Any suggestions, in case I run into your dad on the way?"

Squinting one eye, she focused on the ceiling for an instant. "Run like crazy?"

Reid laughed. "You believe in the power of prayer." Thumb aiming heavenward, he said, "Have a word or two with The Big Guy for me, will ya?"

He couldn't help but notice how her eyes darkened and her smile dimmed. Made no sense, considering the state of his own soul, but it bothered Reid that she seemed to have lost faith in God. He made a mental note to talk with her about it…later.

She'd dozed off by the time he got back with aspirins and cool water to wash them down with. "Cammi," he said quietly, nudging her shoulder.

Her long-lashed eyes fluttered open, then zeroed in on him. "Hi," she said, her voice soft and sleep-husky. Levering herself up on one elbow, she held out a hand so he could give her the aspirin.

One by one, she swallowed them, then drained the glass of water. "Thanks," she said, lying back on the pillow. A slow, half smile brightened her face. "Once again, it's Reid Alexander to my rescue."

He adjusted the ice pack, then tidied her covers. When she'd called him her hero at the hospital, he'd shrugged it off. She'd only been kidding, he told himself; no point taking it seriously. He couldn't pretend she was teasing now. Not while she looked at him as if he'd hung the moon.

"You're gonna have a big ol' goose egg this time tomorrow," he said to change the subject. He couldn't afford to get too used to the idea that she thought of him that way, because as soon as he'd told his story, chances were better than fifty-fifty that she'd change her mind.

"So what's on your mind? You said you wanted to come over here to tell me something."

As if he needed the reminder!

"And that you wanted to ask me something."

Nodding, Reid shoved aside a stack of hardcover

books and sat beside her on the couch. Clasping his hands together, he faced her, prepared to tell her everything. And God willing, this time he wouldn't be interrupted.

"The night we met," he began, "I kept asking myself why you looked so familiar. Wasn't until I heard your dad say his name when I called him from the hospital that I knew the answer."

She turned onto her side, crooked an arm under her pillow to raise her head slightly. No question about it, Reid told himself, he had her full attention.

He slid the battered leather wallet from his back pocket and removed the laminated obituary he'd carried for more than thirteen years.

"What is it?" she asked when he handed it to her.

"See for yourself."

Cammi sat up a little, adjusted the light so she could read it. He watched as she bit her lip, as her gorgeous eyes filled with unshed tears, heard her sharp intake of air when she got to the part that said, *"Rose London is survived by her husband of fourteen years and four young daughters."*

Her hand was shaking when she gave it back to him. "Why do you carry that with you?"

Should he tell her that, when awards and fawning women and the admiration of his rodeo pals threatened to turn him cocky, he'd take out the article and make himself read it—a reminder of just how ordinary and rife with human frailties he truly was? What better way to answer her truthfully? And so he spelled it out, leaving out just one detail.

She sat up and planted both sneakered feet on the floor. Hands folded primly in her lap, she met his eyes. "Why are you telling *me* these things?"

He took a deep breath, held it a second, then released it slowly. There was no easy way to say it, so Reid simply said it.

"Said in the obit that your mama died in a car accident, and…"

She licked her lips, eyes wider than ever.

"…and it was me behind the wheel of that other car."

Cammi looked away, focused on something on the floor, then stared up at the ceiling. "I know."

She'd whispered it, so maybe he'd heard her wrong. Reid leaned forward, heart pounding. "You *know?*"

Then, boring into his eyes with hers, she sighed, "Yes. I've known for quite a while."

He hung his head, slapped a palm to the back of his neck. "How long have you known?"

"I figured it out not long after we met. And then, Dad added more details after you left the other night."

Reid stared at her empty water glass, wishing she'd left one swallow in the bottom of it, because he didn't remember his throat ever feeling so dry, not even after hours of driving cattle over dusty fields. What did she intend to do, keep him waiting all night for her reaction? Why didn't she just point at the door, tell him to get out and be done with it already!

"I also know that it wasn't your fault."

Why did he feel there was a *but* at the end of that sentence? Dread closed in around him like thick, choking smoke, forcing him to hold his breath. If he'd been a praying man, he'd have asked the Almighty to intercede on his behalf, change her mind, open her heart.

But if he'd been a betting man, he'd have wagered there'd be no help from heaven for the likes of him....

So Reid did the only thing he could do, and told the truth. "Just don't hate me, Cammi," he said, hoping she hadn't heard the remorse and self-loathing in his voice, the guilt he'd bottled up for years. Though common sense and evidence said he had nothing to feel guilty about.

She bent forward enough to softly lay a hand on his forearm. "How could I ever hate you?"

Good question, he thought. So why did he get the feeling an answer hovered, right behind it?

Whatever made him think he had so much as half a chance with Cammi!

With other women, he hadn't given a thought to marriage. He'd watched his mother hop from man to man, each a worse life mate than the last (though she claimed every time that *"This one is my Mr. Right, Reid, honey!"*). Well, "Reid honey" had no intention of repeating her mistakes. He'd made a point of shootin' straight with his girlfriends, never promising what he couldn't deliver. When they demanded to know why he refused to make a long-term commitment, he blamed the hectic rodeo schedule, the danger of his profession…and wished them well without telling any of them the truth: If he and some li'l gal had a couple of kids together, and she wasn't the *right* li'l gal for him… *No young'un of mine is gonna live the way I did!* he had vowed.

Reid had lived by his self-imposed "flyin' solo" code for years, because it protected everyone involved from the pain and humiliation of a broken heart.

So why had he allowed himself to be vulnerable this time?

The answer was surprisingly simple: Cammi was everything he'd ever wanted in a woman, everything he'd ever dreamed of in a life partner.

Reid would never have admitted it to his cowboy cronies, but when he had trouble sleeping in one of the generic, rubber-stamped hotel rooms of the tours, he'd think of men who'd left the rodeo to spend more time with their wives and kids. On those dark and lonely nights, Reid pictured himself with a family to go home to: a tidy little bungalow with a bright red door that would bang open when he pulled into the driveway; a couple of giggling, rosy-cheeked kids who would thunder onto the porch yelling, "Look, Mama, Daddy's home!" He'd added a scene to the dream in the last few days: In the doorway, hands buried in the pockets of a ruffled apron, wearing a "for his eyes only" smile, stood their mother, his wife…Cammi.

He'd already told her how he felt he'd known her all his life, how he'd been dreaming of her for…for*ever*. Would it do more harm than good to repeat it now?

Big, silvery tears squeezed from her eyes, telling Reid she knew exactly how he felt—and that maybe she couldn't bring herself to tell him she didn't feel the same way.

It wasn't a suspicion, this knowledge that Cammi

wanted to protect him from harm, from hurt; he knew it with whole-souled certainty.

Which only made him want her all the more.

With the back of her hand, Cammi dried her cheeks. "You said you had something to tell me..."

Yes, and he'd already told her.

"...and something to ask me."

He hadn't been afraid when settling onto the back of raving-mad wild stallions, had braved the wrath of enormous snorting, stomping bulls. But here he sat, adrenaline pumping and heart knocking against his ribs, too scared to ask this five-foot-two-inch slip of a thing, who couldn't weigh a hundred pounds soaking wet, to be his girl!

Clenching first one fist, then the other, Reid said, "You oughta lie back down, get some rest." He cleared his throat. "It's been a hectic couple of days."

She surprised him, getting up off the couch and settling on his lap, so much so that he nearly lost the tight control he'd been holding on his emotions. Relief coursed through him, pulsing in every fingertip, as she put her small, smooth hand into his, leaned her head on his shoulder. His arms slid automatically around her as his lips were drawn to her temple as if he'd been programmed.

"I feel like a crazy woman," she began, the fingers of her free hand playing with the hair at the nape of his neck, "for so much as considering a relationship with you." One dainty shoulder lifted in a ladylike shrug. "God help me, I am."

If a heart could sing, as the poets claimed, his was belting out a ballad now!

"But you've suffered enough," she continued, "blaming yourself for an accident that wasn't your fault. I don't want to put you through anything more."

His singing heart went silent. All his life he'd heard the adage "what goes around, comes around." Something told him he was about to be on the receiving end of the speech he'd made to women so many times. If he could trust his voice, he would tell her to spare him the gory details.

"Since I found out about..." She shrugged again. "Every time I see you now, I think about that night." She closed her eyes so tightly, the lids all but swallowed up her lashes. "And I get these pictures." A tremor passed through her, shaking her from chin to ankles. Cammi stood and walked a few steps away from him, hunching her shoulders and cupping her elbows.

Didn't take a genius to figure out what she'd meant: The very sight of him made Cammi envision the accident, and because she didn't like looking at the ugly images, she didn't like looking at *him*.

Reid glanced toward the door, gave a thought or two to leaving. No, *escaping* was more like it. Because out there, he wouldn't have to look into those big, innocent eyes—eyes that saw him as the guy who killed her mother.

"No one's to blame," she said, finally.

But lost in his own misery, Reid had tuned her out. Much as he wanted to hit the road and never look back, he'd promised to look after her until Lily finished feeding her calf.

He glanced at the phone. If he punched the number five two times, he'd be free.

No, he'd only spend the rest of the night worrying, because while Lily knew plenty about critters, she didn't know diddly about concussions. He'd stay and keep an eye on Cammi until he had proof that she'd be okay.

"Cammi, do me a favor."

She looked over her shoulder and sent him a small, sad smile. "Sure. Anything."

She'd agreed without hesitation, he noted, and without having a clue what he might ask of her. Heart aching, and wanting her for his own even more, Reid pulled back the afghan and patted the sofa cushion. "Lie down before you fall down, will ya?"

For just a moment, she paused, then she crossed the room and stretched out on the couch. Reid helped her settle the afghan over herself, and flopped onto the nearest chair. He waited until she closed her eyes before leaning his head against the pillowy backrest.

Then he closed his own eyes and did something he hadn't done in years.

He prayed.

Chapter Nine

Cammi woke with a start.

It took a minute to get her bearings, but a quick look around the room calmed her, for there sat Reid, fast asleep and slumped in her father's big chair, one long muscular leg outstretched, the other bent at the knee.

Cammi eased up off the couch. Gently, she draped her afghan over Reid, then sat on the edge of the sofa cushion and simply looked at him. At boots whose brown leather soles had walked the floor of many a barn and slid into hundreds of stirrups; at faded jeans that hugged calves and thighs made thick and hard by hours of heavy work. His biceps strained against the blue flannel of his snap-front western shirt, and his hands—one partially shading his eyes, the other, fingers splayed across his flat stomach—were further proof he'd given his all to every task. And those shoulders, nearly as wide as the backrest of her father's enormous chair...

Martina had said he'd injured the right one, hurt it so badly, in fact, that he'd been forced to give up rodeoing for good. If leaving L.A. had been hard on her, when she hadn't come close to "making it" out there, how much more devastating must it have been for Reid to give up a profession that had earned him awards?

Still, it seemed he'd taken it in stride. All part of his uncomplaining, take-it-on-the-chin demeanor, she acknowledged, now studying his face. Black-lashed eyes closed and a lock of raven hair falling over his forehead, he looked like an innocent boy. But Reid was more man than any she'd known, even with his angular chin resting on that damaged shoulder. It was good to see him this way—quiet and at peace, his big chest rising and falling with every soft, steady breath.

From the moment he'd stepped out of the pickup that cold rainy night, Cammi had thought he was as good-looking as any movie star. Not even his stern, no-nonsense expression could camouflage the high cheekbones, the square jaw, the strong nose and full, kissable lips.

Unconsciously, Cammi put her fingers to her own lips, remembering the way it felt when he'd pressed that very manly mouth to hers. *Swoon* wasn't a much-used word these days, but it explained perfectly how his kisses had made her feel.

She slouched, feeling more than a little defeated. In every way possible, Reid Alexander seemed perfect. *Make that perfect for me,* she thought. Because he was more than raw masculinity cloaked in plaid flannel and worn denim; somewhere deep in that barrel chest beat the heart of a good and decent man, one who'd overcome adversity and challenges and heartaches, all without turning bitter or spiteful.

Proof he was a Christian?

Once upon a time, she wouldn't have made a move without first consulting the Almighty. She'd prayed about everything, from which courses to take in school, to boyfriends, to whether or not to move to California. Well, that wasn't entirely true, Cammi admitted; she hadn't asked God's opinion about Rusty.

But shouldn't her past good behavior have counted for something? Yes, she'd messed up, stumbled, taken the wrong path a time or two. Still, didn't she have a right to think the Lord would stick by her, guide her, despite—or maybe because of—her missteps? Didn't the Good Book promise the Father would love and protect His children, *no matter what?*

"Guess not," she muttered.

"Wha-a-a?"

She crossed one leg over the other and clapped a hand over her mouth, sorry as she could be that her thoughtlessness had awakened him.

Reid stirred, wincing as he worked the kinks out of his neck and shoulders. The moment those sea-green eyes opened, they locked on her. Cammi shivered a bit under his penetrating stare. He couldn't have been asleep more than ten minutes. And she ought to know, because every fifteen minutes since Lily headed for the barn, he'd shaken her awake.

"Nice nap?" she asked, hoping the tremor that shot through her wasn't evident in her voice.

He sat up, rubbed the back of his neck, then yawned and allowed himself a full-fledged stretch. "Not bad," he said when he finished. "How 'bout you?"

She couldn't help but grin. "Not bad," she echoed, "considering *some*one woke me every couple of minutes to shine a flashlight in my eyes."

"Sorry, but it's the only way to know for sure if—"

"I know, I know." Grinning, she waved the apology away. "You explained it every time you roused me: 'If your pupils don't dilate properly, it's a sign you might have a concussion,'" she said in the deepest voice she could muster. "I read someplace you're to check every hour, not every—"

"I read someplace that you can't be too careful," he interrupted, knuckling his eyes. When his stomach growled, he tucked in one corner of his mouth. "Sorry."

"Hungry?"

He glanced at the clock. "I shouldn't be. Hasn't been that long since I wolfed down two heaping plates of Martina's spaghetti and meatballs."

Cammi got to her feet. "How 'bout I fry us up a couple of eggs?"

He stood in front of her and, hands on her shoulders, said, "I know it'll take longer for you to show me where things are than to do it myself, but you've *got* to start taking things easy." Reid gave her a gentle shake. "You're never gonna get back on your feet if you keep pushing yourself this way."

She liked being this close to him, liked inhaling the manly scent of fresh hay and bath soap clinging to every inch of him, liked his tough-yet-tender take-charge attitude, too. "You make me sound like a twenty-pound weakling." She reached out, played with a pearlized snap on the front of his shirt. "I'm no award-winning rodeo cowboy, but I can take care of myself pretty well, y'know."

Chuckling, he tucked her hair behind her ears. "Humor me," he said again. "How 'bout letting me take care of you—for tonight, anyway?" His stomach growled again, as if to punctuate his question.

She tidied his collar, then stepped away from him. "We'd better do *something* about that noise before my dad mistakes it for a grizzly and comes down here brandishing his trusty shotgun."

"That picture," he said, feigning a shiver, "is a nightmare in the making." He led the way to the kitchen. "Maybe you can talk him into bringing the old .12-gauge over to the Rockin' C and clearing out that nest of rattlers one of the boys found out behind the barn."

"Rattlesnakes at this time of year?"

"They love this weather we've been having."

"The rattlers aren't the only ones."

"Well, you've got an 'in' with You-Know-Who. See about getting me some protection—from snakes *and* your daddy, will ya?"

He'd asked for that favor before, in much the same way. What made him think *she* had God's ear? "Ask Him yourself," Cammi said, putting a frying pan on a front burner.

Reid opened the fridge and stuck his head inside. When he came out, an egg carton, a package of link sausages, butter and a loaf of bread were balanced in his big palms. "I've never been on very good terms with

The Big Guy," he said, depositing the food beside the stove.

Cammi turned on the flame under the frying pan. "And what makes you think I have?"

Reid shrugged. "I dunno. You just seem the peaceful, contented type."

She rolled her eyes. "You make me sound like a cow out to pasture!"

"Hardly!" he said, laughing. "But seriously, you have a solid grip on reality, a way of handling the tough stuff life dishes out. I figured your faith made you that way."

"What made *you* that way, if not faith?"

"Me?"

He laughed again, and she took it to mean he didn't feel he'd handled hardship well at all. "You've survived a few setbacks in your life, and didn't come out too much the worse for wear. How'd you cope?"

Reid took her hand and led her to the table, pulled out a chair and gently shoved her into it. "We had a deal, remember? You'll take it easy and I'll do what it takes to keep my gut quiet." He grabbed a napkin from the holder on the table, flapped it open and tucked it under her chin. "You're in for a treat, m'lady," he said, bowing with a flourish, "because few people have ever experienced a four-star Reid Alexander omelette."

He found a smaller frying pan in a low cabinet, arranged the link sausages in it and turned up the heat. Then, opening and closing cabinet doors until he found a deep-bottomed bowl, Reid added, "I learned a few tricks under the tutelage of my second stepfather, who claimed to have been a cook in the army." After cracking four eggs like a master chef, he let their contents ooze into the bowl and tossed the shells into the trash can. He rooted through every drawer until he found the one holding silverware, and, holding the bowl against his chest, he beat the eggs with a fork. "For all his other faults, old Henry wasn't a half-bad teacher."

"Real good egg, eh?" she teased as he whipped the yolks and whites into a thick froth.

"Rotten egg is more like it."

There was no mistaking the ire in his voice.

"So what's your specialty—or is breakfast the only meal you can cook?"

"You haven't lived till you've eaten one of my grilled-cheese sandwiches. And I make the best boiled hot dogs on the planet."

"I see your stepfather was a practical man."

"Yeah. Practical."

"How many stepfathers did you have?"

"Four. Each one meaner and more cantankerous than the other. Thank God for Billy is all I can say." He grabbed a knife from the silverware drawer, sliced off a pat of butter and dropped it into the skillet. As it sizzled and bubbled, he tipped the pan this way and that to coat its bottom. "Your dad might not be the cuddliest codger in town, but he's rock-solid and dependable in the father department."

She heard the admiration and respect in his voice. "True. We London girls have been luckier than most."

He poured the egg mixture into the frying pan, then looked over his shoulder to say, "It's good you know it."

Then, almost as an afterthought, he added, "I expect Lamont knows it, too."

As he dug around in the refrigerator's cheese drawer, she said, "We make sure he knows it, every chance we get."

Slicing off a few chunks of sharp cheddar, he nodded approvingly. "Guess he's the reason you girls are such devout Christians."

Were devout, she corrected mentally. "I can't speak for my sisters."

Reid dropped bread into the toaster and pushed the button until all four slices disappeared. He grabbed two small glasses from the drain board beside the sink and filled each with orange juice. "So you're saying you're not devout anymore?"

She didn't know what she was saying. Didn't know what difference the state of her soul made to him. "Let's just say I'm not quite as easily fooled these days as I used to be."

Once he'd set out butter knives, forks, napkins and the juice tumblers, he stirred the omelette. "That explains it, then."

She turned in the chair to see him better. "Explains what?"

"The fact that you're not as happy as you used to be."

"And this coming from a guy who's known me— what?—three days?" she said under her breath.

"Four, but who's counting," he answered, buttering the toast. He shrugged. "The night we met, there was a..." He stared off into space, the tip of his knife drawing tiny circles in the air as he searched for the right phrase. "There was a certain glow about you. A light in your eyes. An attitude that said 'Gimme all you got, World, 'cause I can take it!'" Reid took plates from the cabinet, put two slices of toast onto each.

"Let's see you bury a husband and lose a baby in a four-month time span and come out of it grinning like a hyena." Cammi vowed never to mention either again, ever!

"Don't know if 'grinned like a hyena' describes how I took it," he said, adding eggs and sausage to each plate, "but I've seen a few loved ones planted six feet under in my day. Never even knew my daddy."

He might have been saying "pass the salt" or "what time is it?" for all the emotion in his admission.

"Ketchup?" he asked, handing her a food-laden plate.

She shook her head. "No ketchup, thanks."

"Eat up," he instructed, sitting across from her, "before it gets cold." He downed his juice in one swallow. "Nothin' worse than cold eggs."

"Funny," Cammi said, peppering her food, "but I never would've pegged *you* as a believer."

He stopped chewing and gawked at her, green eyes flashing. "I look that much like a heathen, do I?"

"Well, no. No, of course not." She felt her cheeks going hot. "It's just…well, everyone knows that rodeo cowboys have terrible reputations."

"Oh, do they, now?" He raised his eyebrows. "What kind of reputations?"

"As girl-hungry skirt-chasers. As ladies' men, as—"

He chuckled and, using his fork as a pointer, said, "Y'know what they say."

"No, but I have a feeling you're going to tell me."

"'Never judge a book by its cover.'" Using the side of his fork, he sliced a sausage, then speared it.

"So you're saying you're a Bible-thumping, Sunday-go-to-meetin', card-carrying Christian?"

His smile diminished, and the light in his eyes dimmed. "No. I'm not saying that. I honestly can't remember the last time I saw the inside of a church." He paused. "No, that's a lie. I remember it exactly. It was the day of my mother's funeral."

Cammi took a bite of toast, washed it down with a sip of juice. "How long ago did you lose her?"

He tucked in one side of his mouth and stared into his plate. "Long time ago" was his quiet reply.

"How'd you lose her?"

"Cancer."

"Sorry."

"Don't be."

"Well, looks like we have one more thing in common."

He met her eyes again. "One more thing?"

She didn't want to get into a discussion about their mutual grief. At least, not now. Maybe in a month, or in several months, after she'd had a chance to put some distance between her and Rusty, between her and the miscarriage. Maybe then she'd be able to bare her soul and revisit the subject of "us" as it related to Reid and herself.

"Better eat up," she quoted him. "Nothin' worse than cold eggs."

"One thing's worse."

She didn't know him well enough yet to interpret what that hard-edged note in his voice meant. It went against her better judgment to ask, but she did, anyway. "What's worse?"

"A person who blames God for what's wrong with her life. 'Specially a person who loves Him with all her heart, a person who misses having Him in her life."

On the heels of a deep breath, Cammi shook her head. "And I suppose that 'person' would be me."

He quirked an eyebrow. "If the shoe fits," he said nonchalantly.

What riled her most was that Reid had hit the old nail square on its head. She *did* miss having the Lord to turn to, and she *did* love Him with all her heart. But how could this cowboy who seemed estranged from the Father know a thing like that?

"It's just something to chew on," he added, winking, "when you're finished eating this fantastic meal, that is."

She *would* think about everything he'd said, the very first moment she had to herself. And Cammi intended to square things with the Almighty. She smiled at him. "You're very full of yourself, aren't you."

And waving his fork like a white flag, Reid smiled right back. "Don't mention it," he said. "I was more'n happy to help."

"Let's see if you still feel that way when it comes time to clean up these dishes," she said, giving his elbow a playful shove.

It had taken nearly half an hour after they'd cleaned up the kitchen to convince Reid he could go home. The only reason he'd agreed was that she'd dialed the barn and asked Lily to come up to the house. Once he'd left, it took another half hour to assure her sister the danger of concussion had passed.

Now, as the first purple rays of morning began to shimmer outside the family room's French doors, Cammi continued to toss and turn, unable to put what Reid had said about God out of her mind. About the time the mantel clock struck four, she'd given up on sleep. Blaming the heavy meal for her fidgeting worked for only a little while.

Cammi knew well the reason for her restlessness, knew the way to calm it wasn't with TV or a fashion magazine.

She grabbed her mother's Bible from the bookshelf beside the fireplace and selected a verse in exactly the way her mother had taught her, letting the Good Book fall open to a random page. *"Let the Lord Jesus show you what He wants to teach you today,"* her mama would say.

Closing her eyes, her mother's well-manicured hand would guide her little girl's pointer finger, drawing circles in the air and getting closer and closer until it came to rest on a gilt-edged page. Tonight, Cammi's random selection was Isaiah 44:22.

"'I have blotted out, as a thick cloud, thy transgressions,'" Cammi whispered, "'and, as a cloud, thy sins; return to me; for I have redeemed thee.'"

Perfect, Cammi thought, smiling. It reminded her of something she'd pushed aside: that the Father understands and forgives and loves His children…even when they behave like spoiled brats. She'd made a lot of mistakes these past months. Life-altering mistakes, the biggest of which had been blaming God for the tragedies she'd suffered. None as large and grievous as feeling responsible for her mother's accident.

As a twelve year old, it made perfect sense to blame herself; as Cammi matured, common sense told her it wasn't her fault that a grown woman had put her life at risk for something as frivolous as a pretty dress, especially not a married woman with four young daughters.

Now that Cammi allowed herself to reflect on the true circumstances that led her mother to drive out into the rain that night, self-recrimination melted away. And for the first time since her mother's death, Cammi finally felt free, forgiven, blameless. It felt so good, being "right" with the Lord, that tears filled her eyes. Humbled and grateful, she bowed her head and prayed, knowing as she did that if it hadn't been for Reid's gentle persuasion, she might not have turned to the Good Book tonight.

Lord Jesus, thank You for sending a hero in cowboy boots to show me the way back Home.

Later, she'd call and thank him. Cammi snuggled into the couch and pulled the afghan over her. Reid's manly scent still clung to it, and she closed her eyes and breathed it in. The serenity it inspired was almost as reassuring as Reid's tender embrace.

Almost…

Cammi eased into drowsiness. The reservations she'd had about the right or wrong of a future with Reid faded. She had the Lord's approval, right? Why *else* would He have chosen Reid as His messenger?

Someday, Reid thought as he opened one eye, he'd put a muzzle on that loud-mouthed rooster. Rolling onto his back, he stared at the still-black ceiling.

He threw his legs over the side of the bed and yawned. Then, padding on bare feet across the hand-knotted braid rug, he scratched his chin, shoved the hair off his forehead, rubbed his eyes. Grabbing a towel from the cabinet under the sink, he frowned, remembering the way Cammi had sent him home.

Oh, she'd been nice enough. Reid didn't think she had it in her to be anything *but*. Smiling nervously, she'd clasped her tiny hands in front of her chest and apologized, four or five times, for behaving like a—what had she called herself?—a dim-witted little twit who didn't know her own mind.

He slid open the glass shower door just enough to reach the faucets and wiggle his fingers under the spray. Maybe he *had* met her only a few days ago, but in that time they'd spent countless hours together. Reid had learned a lot about her. She knew her mind better than anyone he could name. So all that hemming and hawing had been to spare his feelings, to salve his ego.

He stood at the window and parted the curtains. The tidy backyard was visible because of the spotlight he'd hooked up months ago so Martina could keep an eye on her rabbit hutch. The last of her summer flowers bobbed on the chilly morning breeze.

Movement off to the left caught his eye, and Reid leaned in for a better look. Steam from the shower had begun to fog the glass, so he used the outside of his fist to clear a saucer-size peephole. Before he could determine what had parted the grass in a three-inch wide swath, the window steamed up again. Quickly, he squeegeed it clean once more, thinking that no field mouse he'd ever seen could do that. Only one of God's critters could leave a trail like that, and it had fangs at one end and a rattle at the other.

Just yesterday, one of the hands said he'd found a nest of rattlesnakes in the pit that once housed the barn's old well pump.

It was rare for a rattler to hole up so near human activity, rarer still to see one stick its head outside at this time of day. Unable to survive any extremes of temperature, it had to be careful about when to hunt for food; early morning in October wasn't the warmest part of the day. Maybe a hare had scurried by—too tempting a treat to pass up, even in the chill of predawn.

Rattlers were common in this part of Texas, and Reid and Billy had exterminated their fair share of the potentially deadly snakes over the years. Soon as he'd had his shower, he'd grab the shotgun and a shovel and get rid of this bunch, too. They were a threat to the livestock and the ranch hands alike.

* * *

"What could it hurt?" Billy was asking Martina when Reid walked through the back door. She didn't have a chance to answer, because the man aimed another question, this one at Reid. "What was all the hollerin' and shootin' about, son?"

"Rattlers," Reid said evenly. "One of the new boys found a nest of 'em out back." He hung up his jacket and headed for the sink. "We got 'em taken care of," he added, washing his hands.

"Oh. Is that all. Well, good. Did you get 'em all?"

"Yeah, I believe we did. Didn't notice any of them slitherin' off, anyway."

"Well," Billy repeated, "good." Attention on his wife once more, he picked up where he'd left off: "It's warmer than usual outside. When am I going to have another chance to sit in the sunshine?"

Martina's stern expression told Reid that whatever Billy had requested didn't set well with her. "What's this crusty ol' pest want?" he asked, joining them at the table. "A day at the beach?"

Fist propped on her hip, she shook her head. "He wants me to set the chaise lounge out in the yard so he can—" she rolled her eyes "—'catch some rays.'" Shaking her head, she grinned at her husband. "Honestly. Sometimes you sound like a teenager."

The three shared a moment of lighthearted laughter before Reid promised Martina he'd set up the lawn chair, get Billy comfortable and check on him every fifteen minutes or so.

"Well," she said thoughtfully, fingertip tapping her chin, "I do have housework to do…."

Billy groaned. "If I live to be a hundred, I'll never understand you."

Neither Reid nor Martina commented, because both knew Billy wouldn't live to see his sixtieth birthday, let alone his hundredth.

"I might be shiftless right now, but I set aside some money in my day. Why don't you hire someone to do the dusting and vacuuming for you?"

"Because I'm way too finicky" was her explanation.

But Reid knew better. She'd always taken pride in creating a cozy home for her man, and now, more than ever, she needed something to focus on besides Billy's illness, something to do other than hover over him. A dozen times in these past few months, he'd caught her standing alone in a room, eyes closed and fingertips pressed to her lips, as if praying for busywork.

Reid ended the tense moment by clapping his hands together. "So, it's all set, then. First thing after lunch, I'll dust off the old lawn chair and—"

"Why after lunch? Why not now?"

"Because, dear, impatient Billy," Martina said, patting his hand, "it'll make your day less boring that way. Besides, the sun won't be—"

Scowling, he snatched his hand back. "Don't take that tone with me, woman. I'm not totally addle-brained and helpless…*yet!*"

Martina's dark eyes widened. "I wasn't—"

"Yes, you were. Ever since we found out about this

confounded death sentence, you've been walking on eggshells, treating me like I'm made of spun glass. Well, I'm tired of it, do you hear? Tired of being made to feel like a useless old—"

She ran from the room, one hand over her mouth, the other trying to keep them from seeing her tears.

Reid helped himself to a spoonful of oatmeal. "You have about as much tact as a charging rhinoceros...and I don't mean one with a credit card, either."

Billy's rasping sigh echoed in the big, country kitchen. "I know, I know. I'd slap myself in the head—if I could make my arm work.... Maybe one of you can do it for me."

Reid saw the twinkle in Billy's eye and knew the storm had passed. "Nobody wants to slap you in the head." He winked. "Nice swift kick to the backside might be in order, though."

Billy chuckled. "Help this old fool get to his easy chair, will you, son?"

It was heartbreaking to hear the dreary note of acceptance in Billy's voice, to watch this once hale and hearty rancher wither away like Martina's summer flowers. *If God is merciful,* Reid thought yet again, lifting Billy from the chair, *He'll take Billy quick, so he won't suffer.* Because the damage ALS was doing to the man's ego was far worse than what it was doing to his body.

Sated after a hot, nourishing lunch, Billy lay back on the blue-and-white webbed aluminum chaise longue.

Within easy reach on a folding tray beside the chair, Martina had set a battery-operated radio to his favorite country-and-western station. She'd put a tall tumbler of iced tea and a plate of homemade cookies on a blue-striped dish towel, and in his lap, several favorite fishing magazines.

After covering him with an old quilt, she'd insisted he protect his head from the sun, and plopped his battered Texas Rangers baseball cap onto his balding dome. Her final touch was a pair of wraparound sunglasses she'd dug out of his pickup's glove box.

Man couldn't ask for much more, Billy thought, smiling to himself. *Well, a man could ask for a long, healthy life.* But short of a miracle, that wasn't going to happen.

He wouldn't mind the whole dying thing so much if it didn't mean leaving Martina. Seeing as they'd never had children of their own, the idea of her being alone scared him a whole heap more than meeting his Maker. Because didn't the Good Book say that every physical ailment a man brought into Paradise would disappear in the twinkling of an eye? Or something along those lines, anyway.

After more than half a century of living the hard rancher's life, using both brain and brawn had grown routine. So routine he'd more or less taken for granted that if he wanted to heft a hay bale or add a row of numbers in the Rockin' C ledger book, he could, and with very little effort, at that. But these past few months, as the disease ate away at his pride, his dignity, his manhood, he'd learned to appreciate the smallest things, like being able to pick up a potato chip and put it into his mouth, chew it and swallow it.

Wouldn't be long, now, he knew, before Martina was forced to stick him in one of those old fogey homes, where they'd turn him into a pincushion, running tubes every which-way.

Billy sighed and shook his head. He'd made up his mind to enjoy this day as if it were his last, because according to the weather report, it might well be the final warm day of the season.

Sunshine beat down, warming him to the core, as Willie Nelson crooned in harmony with that tenor fella from the opera. Birds chirped in a nearby tree, and the quiet hum of Martina's vacuum cleaner whirred from the house—upstairs back bedroom, he guessed.

All was right with his world.

At least for now.

Thoroughly content, he closed his eyes and relaxed completely, let his arm slide off the chair until his knuckles rested among sun-warmed blades of grass. A fishing magazine slipped from the stack on his lap, but he never noticed, and it landed with a quiet *slap* beside his hand.

Billy had no way of knowing that one rattler had escaped near death this morning as Reid and the ranch hands invaded its nest. Couldn't have known it had slithered away, seeking a safe place to hide, or that later, it had decided to coil up under Billy's chair, partly shaded from the sun, yet able to bask in its warmth. How could he have known that a magazine, falling suddenly from out of nowhere, would startle the snake so badly that instinct would make it strike out…and sink its deadly fangs into Billy's hand.

Chapter Ten

Since Martina had volunteered for the first half hour of what she'd dubbed "Billy Watch," Reid went about his duties as usual.

He'd replaced a hinge on the corral gate and was about to repair the latch on one of the barn stalls when something made him stop cold, nearly stabbing the back of his hand with a Phillips screwdriver.

Sticking the tool into his back pocket, he straightened, listening for a sound that didn't belong, looking for something that seemed out of place. He heard the lowing of cows in the south field, the occasionally whinnying of stallions that trotted around the paddock. Now and then, a ranch hand's voice would call out, alerting his cohorts that the hay skid was full and it was okay to roll in another.

He stood perhaps fifty yards from where Martina had set up Billy's "sunshine event," as she called it, and from this distance, Reid could hear the strains of an old Willie Nelson hit.

Here, a bird chirp; there, a dog bark—punctuated by the quiet *bawk-bawk-bawk* of the pecking hens. Everything was as it should be—or so it appeared—so why couldn't he shake the nagging sensation that something was wrong?

Maybe it was lack of sleep, or the cold oatmeal he'd wolfed down at breakfast, or the ugly scene between Martina and Billy that made the world seem it was wobbling out of balance.

It wasn't like Billy to lose his temper that way, even more unlike him to speak harshly to Martina. But then, what man behaves normally when he knows there's a noose around his neck?

Reid couldn't dismiss the notion that the whole "Cammi thing" was causing the nagging sensations, however. If the truth be told, nothing had felt right side up since they'd met. If he needed a reason to run the other way, the list was surely long enough! Reid could neither explain nor understand why it didn't matter to him that she'd been married, that her bum of a husband made a widow of her, or that she'd lost the child conceived as a result of their union. He loved her. It was just that simple, even though he'd met her days ago, even though none of it made a lick of sense.

He chuckled to himself. Maybe the reason it felt his world had spun out of control was because it *had!*

But who was he fooling? One argument between old married people hadn't inspired this gnawing notion that something was wrong, real wrong out there. Neither had his own petty matters of the heart, for that matter. He'd lived a rancher's life long enough to trust his gut instincts, and right now, the signals were as strong as those Custer likely had sent on that fateful day. Experience had taught him if he didn't want to end up like the General, he'd better heed the warning.

Never one to panic, Reid sauntered toward the house, figuring he could look in on Billy as he checked things out. The closer he got, the more intense his belief grew that things weren't as peaceful around the Rockin' C as they seemed.

At least Billy was getting some much-needed R and R, Reid thought as he approached the lawn chair. The man hadn't budged, hadn't moved so much as an inch since Reid had started over. He was about to veer right, straight toward the house, when he realized that though he appeared to be asleep, Billy's eyes were open.

Reid covered those last steps in record time. "Billy," he said, grabbing the man's biceps. "Billy, what's wrong, man?"

Billy tried to talk, but could only manage a few unintelligible guttural sounds. Tremors wracked his body, even as perspiration beaded on his forehead. His eyes darted back and forth in their sockets, looking from Reid's face to the ground beside the chair—where nearly melted ice cubes and Billy's glass lay on the lawn, beside the radio that played a Reba McEntire song as if nothing was wrong.

And then Reid saw it—two bloody puncture wounds on the back of Billy's hand.

He met his friend's eyes. "Rattler."

Billy closed his eyes, and Reid took it to mean yes. "How long ago?"

If Billy knew, he couldn't say. Swelling and numbness had already set in, and so had the muscle spasms. Under normal circumstances, the snake bite would probably not be fatal. But these weren't normal circumstances. ALS had already weakened Billy's nervous and circulatory systems—the very things rattlesnake venom attacked.

Reid lifted Billy as gently as he could, and, hoisting him onto one shoulder, hotfooted it to the house. "Martina!" he bellowed. "Martina!"

As he entered the kitchen, he heard the vacuum cleaner roaring over the carpeting in the bedroom above.

No time to wait for her to finish the job, to run upstairs and pull the plug on the appliance. Under normal circumstances, he thought yet again, a person had four, maybe five hours to get help after a rattler bite. But as he'd already determined, these weren't normal circumstances; in Billy's already-weakened condition, only God knew how much time he had.

And Reid didn't intend to waste a single precious second.

He grabbed Martina's cell phone from the counter and headed straight back out the door to load Billy into the pickup. He wished he'd thought to grab the quilt Martina had draped over Billy out there in the yard, because if he remembered right, he was supposed to keep the man warm. Supposed to keep the bite site lower than the heart, too, he thought dialing 911. No way that was possible. Not unless he'd stuffed Billy into the bed of the pickup instead of the passenger seat.

He alerted the emergency room staff that a snakebite

victim was on the way, added that the victim had ALS, then dialed the ranch to tell Martina where he'd taken Billy. The phone rang and rang, and he cursed under his breath as the answering machine clicked on. Reid took a deep breath in a desperate attempt to keep the panic and fear out of his voice as he left his message. "Get one of the hands to drive you into town," he said before hanging up.

Because the poor woman sure wouldn't be in any shape to make the thirty-minute drive from the Rockin' C to Amarillo on her own.

Cammi had put off making the call long enough. She owed him an apology, owed him a sincere thank you, too. Dressed and showered, she felt a little more like her old self. It would take time, she knew, for the pain of losing the baby to diminish, but she had faith to get her through it now...thanks to Reid.

Was she giving him too much credit? Cammi wondered as she dialed the Rockin' C number. Would she have come to her senses on her own, in time?

Probably, she admitted as the number connected. But what if she'd made yet another mistake in the meantime, and it separated her even further from the Father?

"Martina? What's wrong?" she asked when her friend answered.

The woman sobbed hysterically. Near as Cammi could make out, someone had been bitten by a rattlesnake. Martina had mentioned Reid and Billy in quick succession. Her mouth went dry. "You need a ride to the hospital?"

Something about a ranch hand taking her burbled out, before Martina hung up.

Growing up on a Texas ranch means learning a thing or two about rattlers—where they like to hide, how they hunt prey, how to protect against a bite. Death was rare, very rare, Cammi knew. Reid was strong and healthy and would probably survive, even if treatment wasn't administered right after a snakebite. But Billy...

Cammi didn't want to think what might happen to a man already weakened by a terminal illness.

Lily slammed in through the back door and grabbed a cup of coffee. "What's up?"

"Can you drive me to the hospital?"

Lily's eyes widened. "Why? What's wrong with you?"

"Nothing's wrong with me. I'm fine." She grabbed a jacket from the small closet beside the back door. "It's Billy. Or Reid."

Lily grimaced. "Maybe you should've let us take you to the E.R. last night, because you're not making a lick of—"

"I just talked to Martina," Cammi interrupted, scribbling a note to her father. "She was too hysterical to make much sense, but near as I can tell, a rattler bit one of them."

Scooping her car keys from the counter, Lily opened the back door. "Let's make tracks, sis!"

They barely said a word during the drive from River Valley to Amarillo. "Hasn't been long since you were a patient here, yourself. Think the E.R. staff will recognize you?" Lily said, parking the car.

"I doubt it. But I'd wager they'd recognize Reid. He's a real rabble-rouser when things don't go his way."

"What do you mean?" Lily asked as they hurried toward the E.R. entrance.

Cammi explained how he'd barked orders like a drill sergeant the day she'd had her miscarriage.

They'd just crossed into the lobby when Lily said, "I like that guy. You let this one get away, you're crazy."

She might have agreed, if she hadn't seen Martina, huddled and trembling in a chair near the "Staff Only" doors. In seconds, the woman was flanked by London daughters.

"How is he?" Cammi started, hating herself even as she hoped it wasn't Reid who'd been bitten.

Slump-shouldered and red-eyed, Martina seemed cried out. Her voice was still sob-thick when she said, "Reid's in there with him. He wanted a minute alone with his boy."

Lily slid an arm around her shoulder. "Can I get you anything? Cup of coffee? Orange juice?"

Patting the younger woman's hand, Martina shook her head. "I'm just fine, dear, but thank you." She met Cammi's eyes, then grasped her hand. "Will you do something for me, Cammi?"

"'Course I will. Anything. Just name it." And she meant every word.

"Will you go back there, be with him...Reid, I mean?" She bit her lip as the tears welled up again, and daubed at her eyes with a wrinkled tissue. "I can't watch Billy—" she bit her lower lip before continuing "—and Reid shouldn't have to, at least, not all alone."

Cammi sat, slack-jawed and holding her breath. She was about to say, of course, she'd stay with Reid, for as long as he needed her, when Martina interrupted with "My Billy is dying. I've already said goodbye. The stubborn old fool doesn't want me to remember him this way." She smiled a little. "God love him." Sniffing, she added, "He wanted Reid, and nothing anyone said could change his mind."

Cammi's heart went out to Reid. Of course he'd grant Billy's last request, and be with him at the end. But it would be hard on him, so very hard….

"I can see by your face that you understand," Martina was saying. "I knew you were the right girl for Reid." A tear slid down her cheek and she brushed it away. "I've been praying for someone like you to come into his life, and I thank God for hearing my prayer!"

How like Martina to think of Reid at a time like this, instead of focusing on herself. Cammi could only hope she was made of that same sturdy, unselfish stuff, so that when loved ones needed *her*—

"Go to him, Cammi," Martina said. "He loves Billy like a father. They've been best friends for so long, it's hard to remember a time when they weren't part of one another's lives." She released Cammi's hand, waved her away. "He doesn't know it yet, but he needs you. Needs you more than he's ever needed anyone."

Cammi got to her feet and backed away. She met Lily's damp eyes. "Go on," her sister said. "I'll stay right here." She gave Martina a sideways hug. "Maybe we'll walk down to the chapel, sit in the quiet for a while."

Another sideways hug, then, "And maybe we'll get some coffee in the cafeteria."

When Martina nodded, Cammi left them and walked woodenly toward the "Staff Only" entrance. Her hands were trembling when the doors opened, her legs wobbly as she moved into the E.R. When she spotted Reid, Cammi took a deep breath and stood up straight, determined to look the part, at least, of someone who'd shown up to lend support. She stepped up behind him. For several moments, she stood stock-still, trying to decide how to let him know she was there. A touch? A word?

Without turning, he found her hand and gripped it tight, telling her he'd known all along that she was behind him. It moved her, and she expressed it by squeezing back.

"...not one for purty words," Billy struggled to say, "...but you're...like a son."

Reid swallowed. "Pretty syrupy stuff," he said, "for a guy who's not into sweet talk."

Billy's faint smile proved he got the joke. "Martina... she's gonna need you, son...."

He cleared his throat. "Don't worry, I won't let you down."

"I know...you never have. The ranch...you'll take care of—"

"You know I will, as if it's my own."

"Is."

"What?"

"Yours."

Cammi felt Reid's hand tense, felt the heat radiating from his palm to hers. He let go of her, but only long enough to slide an arm around her waist and pull her close to his side.

"What kind of drugs are they giving you?" he said on a dry, grating laugh. "You're spoutin' nonsense."

Billy gave one weak shake of his head and said, "No."

Reid shook his head, too. "But Billy, what about Martina? She's put as much of herself into that place as you ha—"

"Her idea." A shudder went through him before he continued. "Mexico…"

"She wants to go back to Mexico?"

One slight nod, then, "Mama, sisters…big ol' loving Hispanic family…"

Reid hung his head. "Billy," he said, grabbing the man's hand, "I—"

"Y'always did talk too much." Somehow, he found the strength to chuckle quietly, to open one eye and look at Reid. "Love you, son."

Reid pressed both hands on the mattress beside Billy's frail body, then balled them into fists. Cammi blanketed the nearest one with her hand, slipped an arm around his waist. Was her being here making this harder for him, she wondered, or easier? What would he be doing if she hadn't come?

"Love you, too, y'ornery ol' codger."

Billy laughed softly. "Told you—call me 'old' again, I'd take…take the strap to your—"

A moment passed while Billy closed his eyes— resting, it seemed. Reid smoothed a strand of hair over his friend's bald head. It was such a sweet, loving gesture that it brought tears to Cammi's eyes.

"That the li'l gal?" Billy rasped.

"This is Cammi," Reid said.

Billy lifted his head from the pillow and looked directly at her, both blue eyes blazing with determination. "Take care of him," he said. He lay back, spent by his short speech. One half of his mouth lifted in a mischievous grin. "Won't be easy, but…"

Another moment passed, with nothing but the *blip* and *bleep* of the monitors and Billy's labored breathing to disturb the absolute silence.

The older man lifted his head again, found Cammi's eyes. "Be good to him, girl." And then Billy slept.

Cammi stood silently by Reid's side, knowing that when words were necessary, God would tell her what he needed to hear. Meanwhile, she moved a little closer.

He pulled away from her long enough to press a kiss to Billy's forehead. "Rest well, y'old bear of a man," he said, voice thick with a pent-up sob.

Then he turned to Cammi and said, "Come to the chapel with me?"

Chapter Eleven

If Reid had ever doubted the power of prayer before, he didn't doubt it now! The congregation started a prayer chain for Billy's healing, and even the doctors couldn't explain his miraculous recovery.

Nearly a month after Billy got home from the hospital, Martina packed up, intent on moving them into her widowed sister's house, permanently.

Grateful as he was to have his old friend back, hale and hearty, Reid's heart ached. "I can't believe you're doing this," he said, staring at his hands.

Billy and Martina flanked him in black bucket seats at the airport's departure gate. "Billy and I discussed this long before he got sick," she explained. "We want you to have the Rockin' C, because we've always thought of you as our son. Besides, you worked it as if it was your own."

He wanted to ask how they'd get along, down in Acapulco, so far from church friends.

"We saved up for years, just for a day like this. We're

thinking of it as an adventure, so stop looking so sad! We're not rocketing to another planet, you know." She pinched his cheek. "We'll come visit every chance we get, and so will you."

The ticket agent's nasal monotone voice announced their flight.

She wrapped Reid in a long, motherly hug. "I'll miss you, too." Standing, Billy grabbed their carry-on bag. "Well, I guess this is it," he said. "We'll call every week."

Wagging a maternal finger under his nose, Martina added, "The phone works both ways, don't forget!"

Reid nodded.

"Now go on home." Billy gave Reid's shoulder a fatherly squeeze.

He watched them move up in the line, and grinned when they turned to wave a final goodbye before disappearing into the tunnel that would lead them to the Mexico-bound 747.

Home she'd said. The Rockin' C wouldn't be the same without her and Billy and Martina, and neither would the big old house. Reid doubted he'd ever think of it as home, or the ranch as his.

He'd always been a loner, so it surprised Reid to learn he'd developed a dislike for being alone. That first week without Billy, without Martina, seemed longer than a lifetime.

Much as he'd wanted to, he hadn't called Cammi. When he saw her again, Reid wanted to be certain he was feeling more like himself.

It had been nearly three weeks since he'd set eyes on her. She had her car back, and his truck hadn't been damaged as badly as they'd both assumed. But she hadn't driven to the Rockin' C, and he hadn't made the trip to River Valley Ranch. It had been three of the longest weeks he'd ever spent. If anyone had told him it was possible to miss anyone this much, he would have said they'd gone haywire. Finally, he gave in to the never-ending yearning and dialed her number.

"So how's school?" he asked when she answered.

"It's just what the doctor ordered."

Hearing her voice was just what he needed. "Why's that?"

"Kids are so energetic, so enthusiastic, so full of life." She paused. "Puts things in perspective, you know?"

He took it to mean she missed the baby less, thanks to the distractions of being a busy teacher. Reid could almost picture her, smiling thoughtfully as she played with the phone cord. "So you like kids?"

"Like 'em?" Cammi laughed. "I absolutely *love* them."

With a personality like hers, she had to be great with kids. The elementary schoolers who called her Mrs. Carlisle probably gathered 'round her as if she were the Pied Piper. Then, from out of nowhere, the image of her sitting in a big wooden rocker with a baby at her breast flit through his mind. With a heart like hers, she'd be a terrific mother, he knew.

Suddenly, an overwhelming desire to tell her so filled him to overflowing. "I know it's last minute, but how 'bout letting me buy you dinner tonight?" He'd take her someplace where the lights were low and the waiters slung white towels over their tuxedo sleeves, where the music wafted quietly, and reflected candlelight would glitter in her big doe eyes.

She didn't answer soon enough to suit him. He hoped it was because she had papers to grade, a lesson plan to adjust. He didn't know if he could stand to hear anything else.

"I can't have dinner," she said at last, "but I'd like to see you."

There was a certain hesitancy, and the music he'd come to recognize as her voice, well, it wasn't quite as melodic as he remembered. Reid hoped it was temporary, that once she fully adjusted to being a widow, to losing her baby...

"I can pick you up in half an hour."

Another pause. If he didn't know better, Reid would've thought he'd dialed the wrong number.

"How about if I meet you in the park across from Georgia's Diner? I can be there in, oh, forty-five minutes."

The park? At this hour? "You're sure I can't treat you to dinner?"

"No, really." She sighed. "I appreciate it, but I have thirty-odd book reports and math quizzes to grade before I turn in tonight."

He breathed a sigh of relief. "Still, it's kinda chilly to be meeting in the park, don't you think?"

A second ticked by, then two, before she said, "Maybe. But we won't be there for very long. See you in a little while, then."

Reid stared at the buzzing receiver for a full second after she hung up, wondering why he had the sneaking suspicion he was about to walk into a trap.

It was almost dark by the time she pulled into the parking space beside Reid's truck. Streetlights reflected eerily from slides and seesaws, and the wind shoved leather-seated swings, clanking their thick chains against hollow A-frame supports. She and Reid were the only two who'd braved the cold on this blustery November night.

He'd swapped his Stetson for a baseball cap, his denim jacket for one of thick down. When he walked toward her, she saw that he'd traded his pointy-toed cowboy boots for well-worn running shoes that left waffled footprints in the sand beneath the jungle gym.

"It's good to see you," he said when he reached her.

"Same here." And it was true. Which would only make what she had to say all the harder.

He stuffed his hands into his pockets and smiled nervously. If she didn't know better, Cammi would have said someone had tipped him off, because it seemed he sensed why she'd asked him to meet her here.

"How're you holding up?"

Reid stared at the toes of his sneakers, nodding. "Fine, fine." He looked up. "House seems strange without them. I didn't realize how quiet the place could be until…" He went back to staring at his feet. "How 'bout you?" he said. "Is everything okay?"

He referred to the miscarriage, of course. "Fine, fine," she echoed. How sad that it had come to this awkward perfunctory conversation, like they were strangers who'd ended up in the same line at the grocery store. Especially sad when she considered how warm things had been between them before Billy's ordeal.

She saw him lift his shoulders and pull his coat collar up around his ears. "Let's sit in my car," she suggested. "At least we'll be out of the wind."

His eyes locked on hers. "I—"

Reid clamped his lips together, a hint that he'd decided against saying whatever had been on his mind. Cammi got into her car and sat behind the wheel. Almost immediately, Reid slid into the passenger seat.

"All right, so let's have it," he said, his voice flat and emotionless.

"Have what?"

He turned slightly to face her, one brow up, one side of his mouth down. "I think it's safe to say you didn't ask me here on a night like this to invite me to the prom."

Blinking, Cammi bit her lower lip. "You're right. I asked you here to say…" But she couldn't say. Not just yet, anyway.

"…that you missed me?" he finished on a bitter chuckle.

Cammi sighed. "Reid."

He looked at the car's ceiling. "I've thought about you almost nonstop since Billy and Martina left." Eyes on her again, he said, "I know it sounds crazy, considering we've only known one another a few weeks, but I want—"

It wouldn't be fair to let him say it, considering what she'd have to say next. To protect his feelings, his ego, she held up a hand to stop him. "I've been doing a lot of thinking. I agree with you, about how fast things have progressed between us—I mean, because I feel the same way."

The sadness lifted like a curtain of smoke, and his face brightened, his eyes glittered. Smiling, Reid said, "I was hoping you'd say that." He took her hand in his. "Whew," he said on a laugh. "You really had me going there for a minute!"

He'd misunderstood her, completely. The point she'd been trying to make was that *despite* how she felt about him after such a short time—or maybe *because* it had been such a short time—she'd done some serious thinking. And it wasn't just that. It was the dreams and images, the pictures that flashed in her mind every time she saw him.

She hadn't made her decision in haste, the way she'd made so many others. Because this time, she needed to be right, for Reid's sake more than her own.

"You deserve so much better than the likes of me, Reid. You ought to have a woman in your life who will love and cherish—"

"Look me in the eye and tell me you don't love me."

His voice was hard, his eyes mere slits. He was hurting, and it showed, in the taut line of his mouth, in the furrows on his brow. She couldn't tell him she didn't love him, though she'd rehearsed it a hundred times. Couldn't say the words because…because she *did* love him, more than life itself!

Unfortunately, that didn't change the ugly facts.

"This is the hardest thing I've ever had to do in my life," she admitted, slowly, deliberately, "because in all honesty…" Yes, she loved him. Loved him with all her heart. Because he was the kind of man she'd been dreaming about since junior high school, the kind who was strong and capable, yet tender at the same time. If only *that* image overshadowed the others….

"You deserve better than a woman who sees what I see when I'm with you." She shook her head. "It just wouldn't be fair."

He sat quietly for some moments, shaking his head, shrugging, as if replaying the whole scene over and over in his head. "So what you're saying, then, is that when you look at me, you see your poor mama, the way she was that night. And since it's my fault she's dead, you're telling me we're over before we began…but it's all for *my* sake."

There was no mistaking the sarcasm in his voice, and frankly, Cammi couldn't blame him. Because it did sound ridiculous when he put it that way. Unfortunately, that didn't change things. He'd carried the burden of guilt for her mother's death all these many years. She wouldn't add to it now by letting him think such a thing.

She laid a hand on his forearm, felt him stiffen when she touched him, as if trying to prevent himself from recoiling. But she ignored it, gave his forearm a gentle squeeze. "It isn't you, Reid, it's me. Call me a fickle female, an overly sensitive idiot, a weak-kneed little brat. But I need time, that's all—time to sort things out." She shrugged. "So much has happened, to both of us, in these past few weeks. If only you'd give me some time."

He faced forward, staring through the windshield, nodding. "Time," he told the darkness enshrouding them. "She needs time."

Cammi could fix it all, could straighten out this misunderstanding by telling the truth, by saying three little words. But *if* she said them, he'd never let her go, because he believed he loved her. But did he? Or had he confused being her hero for the real thing?

Reid was a good man, a decent man, and he deserved the chance to find out for sure. Deserved a chance to share his life with a woman who'd saved herself just for him, who'd never been married or carried another man's child, who wasn't forever letting her "act first, think later" mind-set get her into trouble!

"Guess I'd better go, then," he said. He started to get out of the car, then got back in and closed the door again. "Will you do me one favor before I leave?"

"Sure," she said. "Anything."

Smiling a sad little smile, he said, "One more for the road?"

It's what he'd said that night in her kitchen, before taking her in his arms. Cammi's heart fluttered, just remembering it.

Reid leaned forward, tenderly held her face in his hands, studying her eyes, her cheeks, her forehead. He stroked her hair, then buried his face in it, as if trying to imprint every detail in his memory. Then he shifted and, closing his own eyes, he kissed her. Soft. Sweet.

Filled with so much tenderness and meaning that she almost forgot the message she'd come here to deliver.

"Take care, Cammi."

Before she could object, or change her mind, or agree, he was gone, and she knew the chilly wind wasn't the only reason she shivered.

Cammi leaned her forehead on the steering wheel, and prayed she hadn't just made the biggest mistake of her life.

Reid paced the darkened ranch house till long past midnight, reliving those moments in the front seat of Cammi's car. When he had taken her face in his hands and looked into her eyes, and challenged her to say she didn't love him, he had expected her to bend like a cheap spoon. *Good thing you're not a betting man,* he thought, frowning.

He'd stayed away these past weeks more for her sake than his own. Saying goodbye to Martina and Billy had taken a lot out of him, but his distress paled by comparison to what Cammi had gone through these past few months.

She sure had him convinced she loved him, looking at him with those soulful eyes, sighing each time their lips met—and standing beside him at the hospital when Billy struggled to live. Then, with no warning or explanation, she'd backed away, emotionally and physically.

She'd been straightforward about her reasons, he had to give her that. She'd been hurt and humiliated by Rusty—added to the pain of losing a baby, well, was it any wonder she wanted to be careful this time, to protect herself from repeating the same mistakes?

She needed time, he'd decided, to salt things out, to figure out this…what was happening between them. Knowing she was too big-hearted to ask for it, Reid gave her time, and plenty of space, too. Which hadn't been easy, what with the phone always in easy reach and River Valley on the way to or from just about every place he'd driven these long, tormenting weeks.

It had been missing her that weakened him enough to cut his "keep your distance for a couple of months" plan by weeks. When he called to ask her to dinner, Cammi had sounded…peculiar, not at all her usual spunky, live-wire self. Maybe she was miffed, he'd told himself, *because* he'd waited so long to call. All he needed was a few minutes, face-to-face, to explain that he'd stayed away for her own good….

Looking back on it, Reid had to admit that it seemed more than a little strange when she asked him to meet her at the park. But what he knew about women you could put in one eye; maybe she thought meeting there would be romantic! Then, when he first saw Cammi, slender shoulders hunched into the wind and dark hair fluttering, his heart thumped so hard he wondered if a man had ever died of longing, 'cause he sure had wanted to make her his own, right then and there!

Had Cammi truly been cold, he wondered now, when she suggested they sit in her car? Or was she simply guaranteeing a quick getaway once she'd delivered her speech?

Reid stopped pacing, stood in the middle of the living

room between Martina's easy chair and Billy's favorite recliner. He could almost picture them—Martina knitting, Billy working on a fishing lure—chatting amiably about the TV news, ranch business, the weather. They'd always sounded more like lifelong pals to him than a couple who'd been married more than half their lives.

The Stones had taught him a lot, right here in this room, important life lessons about always giving his all-out best to any job he might tackle, about doing the right thing, even when it hurt. He'd learned something else from them, too—something they might not have realized they'd taught him.

Not *all* marriages are rife with anger and accusation, like his mother's had been; some—like Martina and Billy's—were rooted in trust and respect, brimming with warmth and affection. Adversity and strife only strengthened the bonds of their love, and made Reid believe that someday, with the right woman, he, too, could have a marriage like that.

The right woman, he believed, was Cammi. Or could have been.

Driving his fingers through his hair, Reid groaned, feeling caught between the proverbial rock and a hard place. He wanted a life with Cammi more than he'd ever wanted anything. But he'd never have it. Why? Because one look at him and she would always be reminded of that terrible night….

He slammed a fist into his palm, knowing even as he did so that the fit of temper was pointless. He had no one but himself to blame for the sorry state of his life. If he hadn't always avoided commitment—and who was he

kidding?—hadn't always avoided *love,* he might already
have a wife and kids. If he'd had a family of his own on
the night Cammi Carlisle crashed into his life…

That idea only frustrated him more, since Cammi
was the only woman he'd ever considered sharing his
life with. Her carefully rehearsed speech had cut deep,
hurt worse than anything old Ruthless had done that
day in the bullring. He'd spend the rest of his days as
a hermit before he'd put himself in the line of fire that
way again.

Still…living out the rest of his life alone…

Confused, frustrated, angry, heartbroken… Until
Cammi, Reid hadn't known a man could experience so
many emotions, all at the same time!

He stepped onto the porch, hoping a few minutes in
the crisp cool air would clear his head, help him come
up with a solution for his problem.

And the dilemma, as he saw it, was whether to stay at
the Rockin' C, or leave Amarillo, this time for good. It
would be the toughest decision he'd ever make, because
the ranch had been the only real home he'd ever known,
Billy and Martina the only real family. This was his
land now, to do with as he saw fit. Selling it was not an
option, not after all the sweat and tears Billy had put
into it.

The distant notes of a coyote's cry pierced the omi-
nous black silence. Instinctively, Reid narrowed his eyes.
Every nerve end prickled, every muscle tensed as he
scanned the horizon. The critter was out there somewhere, probably perched high atop a mesa and silhouetted by the crescent moon. He had good reason to fear

the mangy thief, for coyotes were cunning—costly, too, in the damage they caused to livestock.

But this night, the mournful wail touched something in Reid, a long-forgotten primal chord that rang with the most basic of truths. Over the centuries, man and beast had come to see one another as the enemy. Yet despite eons-long battles over territory, the two had one thing, at least, in common. The stealthy hunter's cries were rooted in the most primitive of needs; he yearned for a life mate, for the comfort that is best satisfied by the bonds of companionship. Understanding that, Reid said a quick hopeful prayer that the sad-songed animal would find what it was searching for. "One of us oughta get some happiness in this lifetime," he said into the wind.

He headed back inside with more questions than answers. Should he re-up with the rodeo? If his shoulder gave out during a hard ride, he'd lose his balance and end up eating dust, end up permanently crippled… or worse.

Or should he stay?

A picture flashed in his mind: Cammi, on the arm of another man…one who wouldn't be a constant reminder of a sad and painful part of her past…smiling and happy with her new life. Nothing a saddle bronc or a bull could do to him would hurt anywhere near as much as that. And sooner or later, that life was bound to happen to her, because if ever a woman was born to be a wife and mother, it was Cammi!

So it was decided, then: Come first light, he'd have a long talk with Hank, best ranch hand Reid ever had the pleasure of working with, bar none. He'd promise a bigger paycheck and permission to move into the house in exchange for acting as overseer of the Rockin' C. That way, years from now, when time and distance dulled the pain of losing her, Reid would have a place to call home.

Meanwhile, he'd pull the old cab out of the shed and reattach it to the bed of his pickup. Sure, he had enough money for hotel rooms, but what more did he need than a bedroll for himself and oats for his horse? Till the day came when he could think of Cammi and not want to weep like a child, it would do just fine.

Chapter Twelve

Cammi couldn't believe her ears. "What do you mean, he's gone?"

"I mean, he left here more'n six months ago," said the man who'd answered Reid's phone.

She'd asked him for time that night in the park, and as the calendar pages turned, Cammi thanked him in her prayers for giving it to her. She'd made this phone call, hoping against hope that he still felt the way he had the last time she saw him.

"But I—I don't understand."

"Sorry, lady. Don't know what else t'tell you."

Surely Reid wouldn't have walked away from the Rockin' C. Not after what Billy had put into it. "Who's running the ranch?"

"That'd be me. Name's Jefford, Hank Jefford."

Cammi couldn't bear to ask the question, for fear of the answer. "Reid…sold you the Rockin' C?"

A dry chuckle filtered into her ear. "No, ma'am. Hired me. I'm the overseer."

It simply didn't make sense. No sense at all. "Did he say where he was going?"

"Signed himself up with the rodeo."

The breath caught in her throat. Hadn't Martina said Reid's shoulder injury was severe? Damaged enough that another fall could cause permanent damage…or a fatality? "Why would he do such a thing?"

"Never asked, and he never said."

Stunned, Cammi couldn't speak.

"Looked to me like ol' Reid got his heart broke."

She swallowed. "What makes you say that?"

"Not just me that says it. Fellers 'round here claim to have seen him with a purty li'l dark-haired gal, and since she ain't been 'round of late, my guess is she's the reason he hightailed it out of town."

Cammi's heart knocked against her ribs. Had Reid left because she…because she'd broken his heart? But how could that be, she thought, frowning, when they'd only spent a short time together?

Then she remembered the way he'd taken care of her after the miscarriage. Remembered that night in her kitchen, and after the fall near the barn, and those electric-quiet moments in her car when she'd asked him for time….

"Do you have any idea how I might get in touch with him?"

"Well," Hank drawled, "he moves around a good bit."

Exasperated, Cammi blurted, "Surely he left a number, or calls from time to time to see how things are going." *Please, God,* she prayed, *let this man know where I can find Reid!*

"He was in Durango last time he checked in. Said somethin' 'bout movin' on to Butte."

Montana? "When?" For all she knew, Reid had already been killed in a fall, or stomped to death by a Brahman.

"Oh, 'bout a month or so ago, I reckon."

She thanked Hank and hung up, then hid behind her hands. What kind of hideous, horrible woman causes that kind of damage to a man's ego—and doesn't even know it! Cammi's cheeks burned with shame, her heart pounded with guilt. If she'd told Reid the truth that night when he'd taken her face in his hands…if she'd admitted right then how much she loved him…

These past months had changed things, and prayer had answered her questions. She loved Reid, there was no getting around that. She'd wasted so much precious time, sticking her head in the sand to hide from her fears, to hide from the self-imposed guilt at how being with Reid might hurt her family. Now, it was time to face life, head-on.

She'd called the Rockin' C to explain all this to Reid, to cite her ludicrous reasons for avoiding him, to beg his forgiveness, to tell him how long and hard she'd prayed that he'd at least think about picking up where they left off.

She hadn't expected to find out he'd given up everything rather than face life without her. The notion humbled Cammi, because she didn't deserve to be loved that strongly, that deeply, especially not after the immature, self-centered way she'd behaved!

She had to find him—the sooner the better!—and try to make him understand.

But *if* she managed to find him, would he still feel the same way? Or had loneliness made him replace her with one of the willing females who followed the rodeo, hoping to win a trophy of their own?

There was only one way to find out.

Spring break would begin on Monday, so there'd be no need to ask for time off from school.

Retracing Reid's steps would be easy compared to explaining her plans to her father. Somehow, she had to make Lamont understand that she owed it to Reid to make things right. There was a chance the cowboy would send her packing—but maybe a miracle would happen.

Cammi headed upstairs to throw some things into a suitcase. She packed enough to last a good long while, because she didn't intend to come back until she'd found Reid and made her peace with him.

God willing, he'd still be healthy enough to hear it.

Bareback riding, Reid thought, standing near the bucking chute, was like trying to ride a twelve-hundred-pound jackhammer, holding on with only one hand.

Sheer strength alone wouldn't keep him on the horse. He had to spur just enough, turn his toes outward at exactly the right degree, make an educated guess how far down the animal's shoulders his feet should hang— until those pounding front hooves hit the ground after exploding from the chute. After that, he could only grab tight to the rigging, lean back and take whatever punishment the brute decided to dish out.

Spectators had jam-packed the arena, whooping and hollering as the announcer's booming baritone echoed through the stands: *"Ladies and gentlemen, I'd like to draw your attention to Chute Number Two, where Gold Buckle award-winner Reid Alexander is going for another All-Around win on the back of Malicious, one of the meanest, orneriest, buckin'-est equines on four legs...."*

The crowd stood, applauding and whistling in support of their favorite rodeo cowboy. "Get 'im, Reid!" shouted one fan. "Show 'im who's boss!" bellowed another. Their cheers woke the showman in Reid, and he gave them what they wanted—waving his hat in the air with one hand, throwing a punch with the other.

"The last rodeo cowboy who rode Malicious," the announcer continued, *"got himself freight-trained. Let's hope this animal won't run over Reid that a-way in this go-round!"*

Privately, Reid hoped the same thing. He'd seen this horse at work—definitely not a scooter, content to pivot without bucking. No such luck! Malicious liked to suck back, changing direction in a split second. He liked to crow-hop, too—jumping stiff-legged that way guaranteed the fans would see daylight between Reid's rear end and the horse's back. If that wasn't bad enough, Malicious was a star gazer, too. Every cowboy knew it spelled disaster, because it was near impossible to keep the slack out of the reins when a horse bucked with its

head up that way. Yep, Malicious was a good bucker, all
right. If Reid could hold his own here, maybe he really
could pick up where he'd left off.

He didn't want to admit, not even to himself, that
he was bone-tired, that his shoulder ached almost as
much as it had when he'd first left the hospital. But
what did he expect, after testing its limits by entering
the Keyhole Race, the Straight-Away Barrels, and the
Mad Mouse…for starters. Entering the Bareback event
in this condition was as good as asking for a stint in the
local hospital.

"Better hike up them shotguns," another cowboy
advised.

Nodding, Reid adjusted the belt of his step-in chaps,
then tugged at the hems of his leather gloves.

"You reckon ever'thing we hear 'bout this brute is a
windy?" the cowboy asked.

No, the tales spun about *this* horse were factual. He'd
seen the proof of it with his own eyes. Reid pressed the
Stetson tighter onto his head. "I ain't that lucky," he said,
only half joking.

Chuckling, the cowboy cuffed him on the back.
"Ready?"

Reid nodded again, grabbed the wall and threw one
leg over. "Ready as I'll ever—"

"Reid!"

He stopped so fast, the spur on his boot sang a whin-
ing, one-note tune as it spun round and round. Cammi?
But how could that be, way out here, after all these
months? *You're losin' it, old man*—he thought as he
continued to lever himself above the chute.

"How'd that li'l gal get in here?" the annoyed cowboy asked, as Reid hovered above the snorting, frenzied animal. "Lady, you ain't allowed down—"

"Reid, don't do it!"

It was Cammi, all right. But how she got here—and why—were questions he couldn't afford to ask himself right now. He had to concentrate on the ride…concentrate on the ride…on the ride….

She shoved past the cowboy and peered over the wall. "Why are you doing this, Reid?" she demanded. "Your shoulder! The rodeo can't be paying you enough to risk—"

He didn't hear the rest, because down there in the chute it was more obvious than ever how Malicious had come by his name. The horse wheezed and huffed, hard muscles rippling in a desperate bid to get out into the open, to get Reid off his back.

Cammi's voice echoed in his mind. She sounded scared, real scared, but that didn't surprise him; a born-and-bred rancher's daughter had seen enough rodeos to know what he was risking, tackling a horse like this in his condition. Reid wanted to tell her to go home, to quit worrying about his shoulder. But the clock was ticking now. Too late to change his mind, even if he wanted to. And he didn't want to. Because he hadn't come back to the rodeo just for the day money.

She'd been so glad to see him that it was all Cammi could do to contain herself. She wanted to scream his name, burst through the crowd of cowboys standing around him, wrap her arms around him and give him a kiss he'd never forget.

He looked so handsome standing there, dusty boot tips poking out from the hem of his flare-bottomed brown chaps. He'd fastened all but the top snap of his green plaid western shirt, and the tails of the white bandanna wrapped around his throat rested on one shoulder. His biceps bulged as he tugged at worn leather gloves, flexed again as he adjusted the black Stetson so that it shaded his deeply tanned face.

Thank you, God! she prayed, grateful she'd found him, thankful to see him looking hearty and all in one piece. "Reid!"

It seemed he hadn't heard her, so she moved closer, called to him again. This time, he locked onto her eyes with that so-green gaze of his. She smiled, waved again, expecting him to look at least slightly happy to see her.

Instead, Reid's brows drew together in the center of his forehead, one side of his mouth turning down before he returned his attention to the bucking beast in the chute.

Bareback riding was one of the most dangerous events of the rodeo, even for cowboys without injuries. For Reid…

She couldn't let him do it. Couldn't understand why he'd *want* to! Cammi shoved past the cowboys assigned to keep the horse under control until the gate opened, and called to him again, demanded to know what he thought he was doing down there.

If he heard her, he gave no sign. Reid clenched his jaw

and lowered himself onto the horse's back, got himself into position.

"Ready?" one cowboy asked. Reid gave a quick nod, and with his knees pressing into the animal's flanks and nothing to hold on to but the suitcase handle near the animal's neck, he threw his free hand in the air, gloved forefinger pointing toward the heavens—and gave the signal.

The wooden doors flew open…

…and Malicious charged forward, bound and determined to get rid of his rider. He was a beautiful animal, charcoal gray with a long black tail and a sleek black mane. He was grace and power personified, with glistening muscles that strained with every kick, twisting and turning with eyeblink speed.

The next seconds ticked by in a blur, a flurry of rib-racking noise and heart-pounding danger. She squinted through the fog of dust churned up by the horse's hooves, praying Reid would make it safely through this event.

"Uh-oh," the announcer yelled through the P.A. system, *"looks like Malicious is provin' how he got his name, again. Our boy Reid is down."*

Cammi scrambled past the cowboys and rodeo clowns, past the on-call doctor, and knelt in the dirt beside him. "Reid," she said, cradling his head in her lap. Blood oozed from a deep gash in his forehead, and his left leg lay twisted at an odd angle.

He looked into her face and smiled slightly, opened his bloodied lips and tried to say something before pain made him squeeze his eyes shut.

"Shh," Cammi said, smoothing the hair back from

his brow. "Just rest easy, 'cause the ambulance is on its way."

"Doesn't look good," she heard the doctor tell one of the barrel men. "Better have the announcer get something else going until we can get him off the field."

Please, God... she prayed, blinking back stinging tears. *Watch over him. Keep him safe. Let him be all right!*

The E.R. docs had rushed Reid straight to surgery, where he spent the next six hours. Two hours later, they wheeled him from recovery and assigned him a room on the fifth floor. Cammi spent the night curled up in the high-backed vinyl chair beside his hospital bed, waking every time he so much as flinched.

Warm sunshine, slanting through the narrow opening in the curtains, crossed the room like a buttery yardstick, measuring the distance from the window to where she dozed. Opening one eye, she yawned and stretched.

"How long have you been there?"

The suddenness of Reid's craggy voice startled her. Both palms pressed to her chest, she smiled. "You're awake!" Inching closer, she leaned on the mattress and gently took his bandaged hand in hers. "How're you feeling? Thirsty?" Grabbing the drinking glass from the nightstand, she held the bendable straw to his lips.

His eyes never left hers as he sipped. When he'd had his fill, Reid turned away. "How long have you been here?" he asked without looking at her.

"Oh," she said, smoothing his covers, "awhile."

"All night?"

She shrugged. "So what if I was?"

A raspy sigh hissed from him. "Go home, Cammi."

He sounded tired, sad, defeated all at the same time. Just the aftereffects of hours in the operating room, she thought. Just the pain medications. "I'm not going home or anywhere else until I know you're all right." And she meant it, too.

"Suit yourself," he said, still looking at the window.

"You never answered my question."

He closed his eyes and said a sleepy "What question?"

"How're you feeling? Does anything hurt? I can call your doctor."

Another sigh. "Still have one good hand," he told her, moving the fingers of his left hand. "If I need anything, I'll buzz a nurse."

He had a right to be angry with her. If it hadn't been for her self-centered remarks that night in the car, if she hadn't distracted him before he went into the arena this afternoon… It was Cammi's turn to sigh, because what had happened to him had been her fault.

The doctor said the fall had caused a concussion, a fractured shoulder blade, a broken thigh and shattered ankle, and a bad wrist sprain. And Malicious's hooves cracked three ribs—one of which had punctured a lung. "We'll keep him here for two or three days," the surgeon had said. "After that, he'll need bed rest for a couple of weeks."

And after that, Cammi knew, a wheelchair, followed by crutches, then a cane.

And she intended to nurse him right up until he felt like his old self again.

"Can't let you do that," Reid said when she announced her decision.

Using his good hand, he shoved himself upright in the bed. "Let me rephrase it, then." One brow high on his forehead, he said, "I don't *want* you to do that." He made a thin, taut line of his lips, as if to show her he meant business.

"Might as well get used to the idea." She plopped a stack of clean, fresh clothes on the foot of the bed.

"I won't get used to it!" He'd made the mistake of drumming his point home by punching his injured hand into the mattress. Wincing, he clenched his teeth. "Only way I'd move into Lamont London's house is in a pine box," he said once the pain dulled a bit. "I mean it, Cammi. I'm going home. To the Rockin' C. Got it?"

She folded both arms over her chest. "All right, then, I'll move a few of my things into *your* house, take care of you there until—"

"No."

He had every right to be angry with her, but had no right to abuse himself. "Hate me if you must," she said, narrowing her eyes, "but if Mohammad won't come to 'the London,' 'the London' will come to him!"

"Very funny."

He wasn't smiling, she noted. "Only way you can keep me outta there is by calling the sheriff." Grinning smugly, she shrugged. "Besides, it's all arranged. I've hired a man to drive your pickup back to the Rockin' C. He'll tow my car behind it. I tried to get a hold of Martina and Billy, but—"

"Leave them out of this. They've been through enough."

He'd been angry the night she ran the red light, and when Amanda foisted herself on him across from Georgia's Diner, and in her car, after she'd asked for time. But that had been a different kind of anger than what she was seeing now—a blend of resentment and frustration that turned his otherwise DJ-like voice cold, that changed his expression from welcoming to distant.

"I don't need your help," he tacked on, as if what he'd already said hadn't made his feelings clear enough.

His remark stung like a cold slap, but she hid it well, pretending to fuss with the clothes she'd laundered for him while waiting for his operation to end. How else *could* he react, when she knew as well as he did that it was her fault Reid lay flat on his back, broken and bruised in body and spirit!

It came to Cammi in a blinding, painful flash...

Every time Reid saw her face from this day forward, he'd be reminded of what his surgeon had said earlier: "I'm afraid your rodeo days are over, this time for good, son. One more fall like that and you'll spend the rest of your days in a wheelchair—if you have any days to spend."

The bitter irony throbbed and ached inside her, raising a sob in her throat, bringing tears to her eyes.

Cammi hoped and prayed she'd be able to make it up to him—and prayed Reid would give her the time to do it.

Chapter Thirteen

Reid was beginning to feel guilty about his grumpy attitude. True, he hurt in places he didn't even know he had, but that was no reason to take it out on Cammi. She'd worked tirelessly and cheerfully these past few weeks and he hadn't exactly been appreciative.

Just as she'd vowed on the day his surgeon signed the release forms, Cammi hadn't budged from his side. She had hired an ambulance to drive him from New Mexico to Amarillo, and when the driver had explained civilians weren't allowed in the back with patients, she had huffed and climbed inside anyway. "What're you gonna do," she spat when he repeated the rules, "call the cops?" Reid had sympathized with the driver, who gave up without a fight, shrugging as he closed the doors.

Every time they had hit a bump in the road, she'd patted his hand. "I'll bet that hurt!" she'd said, or "They need to do something about these roads!"

From the moment she set foot into the house, she'd taken charge, instructing Hank and the hands to rearrange the living room furniture so the hospital bed she'd rented would fit. "Put it beside the windows," she told the hands, "so he can watch what's going on outside." She made it up with velvet-soft flannel sheets "so bed sores won't develop," and smoothed out every wrinkle with her tiny, hardworking hands.

She stood there, wincing as the men moved Reid from the ambulance gurney to the bed. "Careful," she kept saying. "Be gentle with him!" And when she dismissed them, Cammi shoved the big old console TV across the room—grunting quietly, her face a knot of stubborn determination as she struggled with it—so he wouldn't even have to turn his head to see the screen.

Each morning, when he opened his eyes, the first thing he saw was Cammi, dozing in the big easy chair beside his bed. And she was there, pretending to be engrossed in a novel, when he settled in for the night.

She'd left him from time to time, but only long enough to cook a meal or get a fresh glass of water to wash down his pain medication. She was in the kitchen now, fixing his supper. The delicious scents of something Italian wafted through the house, and Reid's stomach grumbled with anticipation.

The front door opened, then closed with a *bang*. "Evenin'," Lamont said. He took off his hat, laid it atop the floor lamp's shade. "Feelin' better?"

Reid nodded. "She lets me up a couple of times a day now, puts me in that contraption for an hour or two at a spell." He pointed at the wheelchair that stood near the entry.

"I should've warned you it wouldn't be a picnic. Not with my Cammi in charge."

Another nod. Reid's feelings toward the older man had changed, from grudging acceptance to quiet admiration. Though he had said it in plain English, Lamont was now trying to show Reid how sorry he was for the way he'd behaved in the E.R. all those years ago. For his own part, Reid had said in a roundabout way, months earlier when they'd met at the diner, that all was forgiven.

"Hi, Dad," Cammi sang as she entered the room. "I didn't hear you come in."

"Just got here," he admitted, grinning. "Whatever you're cookin' invited me all the way from River Valley." He nodded at Reid. "What's the boy's incentive to get back on his feet when you're treatin' him like a king every minute of the day!"

Cammi blushed so deeply that Reid could see it from across the room, despite the low lighting. "Just doing my job," she said, tidying Lamont's collar. "Will you join us for supper?"

Chuckling, her father said, "You'd have to hogtie me to keep me away from the table."

"Everything is ready. I'll set a place for you as soon as I help Reid into his…into the…" Shaking her head, she sighed.

Reid hated how uncomfortable she seemed, just saying the word *wheelchair.* He'd pretty much stopped taking the big white pain capsules prescribed by his surgeon, and as the drug-induced fog lifted, he saw a lot of things more clearly.

Those first days home from the hospital, he'd secretly

blamed Cammi for the accident—and that was wrong, just plain wrong. Because down deep, he knew full well that what happened had been his own fault. He never should have entered the Bareback event in the first place, let alone after a long, hard day of competing in every contest offered. And the way she'd been behaving—fussing over him, doting on him, even when he barked at her, even when he behaved like a low-down ingrate—proved that she held herself far more accountable for his condition than he could in a month of Sundays.

It was high time the two of them laid their cards on the table. He'd decided, just this afternoon, to put it to her plain at supper tonight: He had nobody to blame but himself for the shape he was in. But since Lamont had agreed to share the meal, his announcement would have to wait.

Cammi rolled the wheelchair alongside the bed, exactly as she'd been doing for more than a week now. "I read up on this online," she'd announced that first day. "There's a system to getting this done with the least amount of strain on the patient." Then she proceeded to teach him "the system," step by step. First, Cammi cranked the bed's backrest to its full upright position and instructed him to sit up as straight as he could. Next, she helped him swing his legs over the edge of the mattress, and sat beside him, waiting till he draped an arm over her shoulders. Last, she stood slowly and easily, until his feet hit the floor. Cammi let him set the pace, acting as his support and his guide, until he could lower himself into the wheelchair's seat.

"Looks like the pair of you have that down to a fine science," Lamont said, grinning.

Reid chuckled. "Took some getting used to."

"Isn't that the truth!" Cammi draped a blanket over his lap. "He hates being waited on. Hates feeling helpless even more."

He'd never said that. Had tried not to complain about anything, as a matter of fact. So how had she known?

Dinner conversation was quietly pleasant, and Cammi sent Lamont home with the leftover half of a home-baked apple pie. He kissed her cheek, then shook Reid's good hand.

"When you get outta that contraption," he said, grinning, "you and I are gonna have a talk about your intentions toward my daughter—"

Cammi blushed again, even deeper than before. "Drive safely, Dad," she interrupted. Taking his hand, she led him to the door. "Sorry you had to eat and run, but…"

"…but here's your hat, what's your hurry," Lamont finished, laughing.

She stood there several seconds after closing the door, simply staring at the floor, as if trying to summon the courage to face Reid after what Lamont had said. Finally, she said, "I'm so sorry about that." She turned toward him. "I don't know what gets into him sometimes."

Reid only smiled.

"Want some help getting back into bed?"

He shook his head. "No." Pointing at the easy chair, he said, "Set a spell with me."

"I should really get busy on those dishes. That mozzarella cheese is like concrete once it hardens."

"The dishes are fine, soaking in the sink." He pointed at the chair again.

Cammi eased onto the seat and folded her hands on the knees of her jeans. "So," she began, "you okay? Need anything for pain?"

Chuckling, he took her hand. "I'm fine. Well, I will be once I get this off my chest."

She bit her lip, blinking and staring at him as if she expected him to light into her. Had he been *that* difficult to take care of?

"I owe you an apology," he said, reminding himself of the night they'd met, when he'd found himself saying he was sorry for bellowing. The accident had reminded him so much of the night that had changed the course of his life.

"An apology!" Cammi giggled nervously. "If anyone owes anyone an apology, it's—"

"Cammi, hush."

"But you don't have a thing to—"

"Humor me, will ya?" He'd said that before, too, the night that he'd carried her from the barn path to the house.

Her shoulders sagged slightly, and the expression on her pretty face said, "Okay, shoot."

"You've been great, Cammi. Everything you've done these past weeks…I wouldn't have gotten care like this from a full-time nurse. And don't think I don't know it!"

"It's the least I could do" was her quiet response, "since it's my—"

"Cammi, hush, remember?"

She clamped her lips together and raised her eyebrows. He could've kissed her for sitting there, looking for all the world like a penitent teenage girl. Maybe later, he thought; right now what he had to say was far more important.

He told her the fall from Malicious had been his own stupid fault, that he'd pushed himself too hard for too long, that his tired old body had simply seen hitting the dirt that day as the last and final straw. He admitted that, because he'd been mad at himself for making so many foolish choices—including the one that put him back on the rodeo circuit—he'd taken things out on her. "I should've done this a long time ago," he concluded, "because it isn't fair, letting you believe you're responsible."

"You wouldn't have left the Rockin' C in the first place if I hadn't said what I did to you."

"Hush," he said yet again. "You can't take the blame for that, either, pretty lady. I've had a lot of time to think on things, holed up in here the way I've been since my fall. Truth is, I'd been chompin' at the bit, lookin' for any excuse to get back to rodeoing. Something in me said if I'd just give it one more try, I'd find out the shoulder was strong enough, after all, that I could win a few more gold buckles before I hung up my spurs." He rolled the wheelchair closer to where she sat and gently chucked her chin. "Your li'l 'time' speech gave me just the excuse I needed."

Her dark eyes filled with tears and her lower lip began to quiver.

"Aww, Cammi," he said, palm to her cheek. "What is it? Why're you cryin'?"

She pressed into his touch, like a feral cat that, starved for affection, leans into the first person to show it some kindness.

"You're such a big-hearted guy," she said, sniffing. "What a nice thing to do—taking the blame on your own shoulders to spare me carrying the burden." She turned her face slightly, kissed his palm. "I love you for that."

Had he heard right? Heart pounding, Reid smiled. He hadn't felt as pleased or relieved in… He couldn't remember feeling happier! It started a chain reaction of words, and unable to stop himself, he said, "This is gonna sound like a line from a B-grade movie, but I've loved you from the minute I first set eyes on you. Every second we're together, the more sure I am that you're the girl God wants me to spend the rest of my days with."

Using the corner of the blanket that covered his legs, she wiped her eyes. "God? I must be hearing things."

"Like I said, I've had a lot of time to think these past couple of weeks. Figured a few things out, one of 'em being that God's been pretty good to me." He tugged on her hand, pulled her closer still. "He put us together. I'll be thankful for that the rest of my days."

Cammi snuggled as close as the wheelchair would allow. She buried her face in the crook of his neck and sighed.

He took her face in his hands, forced her to look

at him. "Look me in the eye and tell me you don't love me."

"Can't do that," she said, eyes sparkling with unshed tears. "They wrote some pretty good lines into those old B-movies, and I loved you at first sight, too."

Relief surged through him, thumping in his chest, at every pulse point. The future would be as rosy as her cheeks, brighter than the love-light gleaming in her eyes. "I think after we're married, I'll get me a dog like Obnoxious."

She kissed him long and hard.

"Is that a 'yes'?"

"Was that a proposal?"

"Yeah," he said, grinning, "I reckon it was."

"You 'reckon'?"

"Never been more sure of anything in my life."

Cammi got to her feet and pushed the wheelchair into the kitchen. After parking it beside the table, she stripped the tablecloth and walked toward him, twisting it into a rope, and tied one end to her belt loop, the other to his wrist.

"You tryin' to tell me something?" Reid said, chuckling.

"That's as far out of my sight as you'll ever get again." She winked. "Think you can stand it?"

He broke a piece of crust from the pie she'd baked and popped it into his mouth. "Somethin' tells me I'll muddle through…as long as the vittles are this tasty."

* * * * *

Dear Reader,

Even the strongest of us have moments of weakness, when we need to be saved…from the pain caused by the death of a close family member or friend, the illness of a child, unwanted career changes, the loss of a precious keepsake. We need to be saved from the pain of being let down by someone for whom we care deeply. For a reason I've never understood, that pain is never as punishing as admitting *we* have transgressed.

Why, then, is it easier for us to forgive others than to forgive ourselves? Maybe it's because, having suffered at the hands of others, we know exactly how it feels, and "knowing" makes us ashamed to have caused that kind of pain in another. Or maybe it's because we can't imagine *God* forgiving our offense.

But that's where we're wrong; throughout the Bible, we read examples of the Father's tender mercy. So the real trick is convincing ourselves *we* are as worthy of His perfect love as any other sinner, from Eve to King David to Mary Magdalene!

"Wherefore I say to thee, your sins, which are many, are forgiven." (*Luke* 7:47–8)

That's the promise I cling to when self-doubt darkens my heart, and that's the lesson Reid and Cammi needed to learn—individually *and* together.…

If you enjoyed *An Accidental Hero,* drop me a note c/o Love Inspired Books, 233 Broadway, New York, NY 10279. (I love hearing from my readers and try to answer every letter personally!)

All my best,

Loree Lough

AN ACCIDENTAL MOM

I will sing the mercies of the Lord forever;
with my mouth I will make known thy faithfulness
to all generations.
—*Psalms* 89:1

To Larry, without whose patience and
understanding my writing wouldn't be possible;
to Elice and Valerie, my daughters and best friends.

Chapter One

The four-year-old wrapped an arm around his father's leg. "Daddy," he said, tugging at the pocket of his father's sports coat, "why do people come to the simmy-terry?"

The day was as gray as Max Sheridan's mood, and Nate's questions did nothing to improve it. He looked into the innocent, brown eyes and smiled despite himself. Oh, but he loved this kid! "To visit loved ones, Nate. To pay our respects to people who have died."

Nate knelt in the damp grass. One by one, he placed the white roses he'd chosen at the flower mart at the feet of the marble angel guarding his mother's grave. "Mommy isn't in there." He spoke with conviction. "Only her bones. Her soul is in heaven with God."

He stood and pressed close to his father. "Right, Dad?"

Max inhaled deeply. "Yes, Nate." He'd told bedtime stories to soothe the boy to sleep; how different was *this* white lie? He'd tried believing in God, in miracles. Well, if God truly existed and He could perform miracles, he and Nate wouldn't be here at Melissa's grave, now would they?

For a long time, Nate merely stared at the tombstone. "She isn't cold, you know…."

Nate had been too young when Melissa died to have any real memory of her. He seemed to have no recollection of those bleak days in the funeral parlor, when friends and relatives speculated about why a beautiful woman with so much to live for would take her own life. If there had been a God to thank for that, Max would have prayed himself hoarse. Max had only brought Nate to Peaceful Gardens twice, and each visit inspired new curiosities—and childlike observations about death, dying and the afterlife—in his son.

"…because the tempa-chure in heaven is always a pleasant seventy-five degrees." Nate's beaming face told Max how proud he was to have remembered that tidbit of information.

Max chuckled. He was something else, this kid of his. "Where'd you hear that?"

"Gramma Georgia tol' me so, on the phone yesterday when I tol' her we were coming here to say goodbye to Mommy. She said Mommy will always be warm and happy, 'cause everything is *perfect* up in heaven."

If God didn't exist, then neither did heaven. But Max smiled. He saw no point in tarnishing the boy's image of…things.

Even Max didn't understand why, when in all other areas he'd been a no-nonsense, tell-it-like-it-is parent. Fairy tales were stories, nothing more. Santa and the

Easter Bunny were invented to put money into the pockets of the greeting card manufacturers. The tooth fairy? The lazy parents' way of coaxing their kids to brush and floss. Far better to extinguish his son's belief in fantasies like that than to let him grow up and find out how painful and unrelenting the real world could be.

Strangely, though, he was less rigid when it came to matters of religion, spirituality and faith. If Nate wanted to attend Sunday school with his school chums, fine. If he wanted to tag along when the neighbors attended services, so be it. Nate got so much out of the whole "church thing" that Max couldn't bring himself to put an end to it. Something, though, told him that the longer he waited to teach the boy the truth as he saw it, the more difficult it would be.

"Is Gramma full of beans?"

Laughing, Max took Nate's hand. Where did the kid come up with this stuff? "'Course not, son."

Nate's face crinkled with confusion. "But, Dad, you said so yourself, just last night, 'member?"

Yes, he remembered, only too well. He'd been on the phone with his mother, discussing the trip to Amarillo, when she started with her usual "bless this" and "pray for that" nonsense. Max's day had been bad enough to that point; being forced to listen to her spiritual malarkey was the proverbial straw on the camel's already overloaded back. "If your precious Lord is so merciful," he'd demanded, "why'd He allow Melissa to take her own life? Why'd He let you—a woman who devoted her whole life to Him—break your leg?"

"I didn't raise you to talk like that!" Georgia had

scolded. And when she started praying for his salvation, he'd put a hand over the phone and closed his eyes. "Mom," he'd muttered, "you're full of beans."

And that's when he'd noticed Nate, standing in the doorway.

"I was only teasing," Max had whispered past the phone's mouthpiece. "Besides, Gramma didn't hear me."

But Nate's doubting expression said he believed otherwise.

Now, Nate stood and brushed freshly mowed grass clippings from the knees of his jeans. "You gonna say goodbye to Mommy, Dad?"

Closing his eyes, Max held his breath and summoned the strength to go through the motions…for Nate. He'd tried to say goodbye to Melissa, for even as the EMTs struggled to save her, they'd known she was dying. Instead, he'd struggled to keep a lid on his temper. Max couldn't remember being more angry with her. He hadn't understood why she left Nate then, and he didn't understand it now…nearly three years later.

The very people who, when he was a boy, taught him that suicide was one of the most grievous sins a human could commit, also believed that God in His heaven had total control over things on earth, that He loved every last person. If that was true, why did some of His "children" die of starvation, while others became victims of genocide and war? Why did good people get cancer, while bad people robbed and raped and pillaged?

Despite all that, their simple faith seemed to bring them such joy, such solace. Nate—more than any of them, Max believed—deserved to grow up feeling that way. At least until life stepped in and taught him otherwise in its usual fist-to-jaw way.

"You gonna say a prayer for Mommy?"

Prayer. Of all the— Groaning inwardly, Max shaded his eyes. "Tell you what," he said from behind his hand, "why don't *you* say the prayer this time."

"Me?" Nate's brown eyes widened. "Thanks, Dad! I'll do a good job. I promise." He got down on his knees and bowed his head, then he closed his eyes and pressed both palms together, fingers pointing skyward. "God? It's me, Nathan Maxwell Sheridan. Um, me an' my dad won't be comin' to visit my mom here at the simmy-terry for a while, on accounta my gramma busted her leg an'—"

"Broke her leg," Max corrected gently. He didn't see much sense in correcting the "for a while" part.

"…on accounta Gramma broke her leg, an' we're going to Texas to take care of her 'til she can walk again. So, God? Could You do me a favor? I know my mom's soul is up there in heaven with You, so maybe You could tell her not to worry 'bout her bones an' her wedding ring an' stuff while we're gone, 'cause the men who work here take real good care of the place. Thanks." Nate started to get up, then changed his mind. Eyes squinted tight-shut again, he added, "And, God? Please send another wife for my dad…and a mom for me. We really, *really* need one. Amen."

On his feet again, Nate put his hand into Max's. "How was that, Dad? Did I do good?"

Max swallowed the hard lump that always formed

in his throat when Nate prayed for a new mom. It was only natural, he supposed, that even though Nate didn't remember Melissa, he'd yearn for a mother's love. But he was doing okay by the boy, wasn't he? Hadn't he learned to cook—a little? Hadn't he taught himself to do laundry—sort of? He'd figured out every gizmo on that fancy vacuum cleaner of Melissa's—hadn't he? And tough as it had been to go it alone, he hadn't missed a single Parents' Night at Nate's school. What did they need a woman for!

Max hoisted his son, held him close. "You did great with that prayer, kiddo, just great. Now what-say you and I head over to the burger joint. We have enough time for chicken fingers and curly fries before we head out."

Nate kissed Max's cheek. "You're the best, Dad. Almost as good as havin' a mom *and* a dad!"

Almost as good, Max thought, *but not quite.* Sad fact was, Nate would never have it "as good"—at least, not in the mom department, because Max had made a promise to himself when Melissa died.

And he aimed to keep it.

"Well, as I live and breathe," Georgia said, slapping the arm of her wheelchair. "If it isn't Lily London!"

"Oh, my!" Lily said, pointing at the woman's cast. "What have you done to yourself?"

The redhead smiled. "One leg too few in a three-legged race?"

"Don't let her pull *your* leg, Lily," the fry cook called over the counter. "Genius Georgia was changing lightbulbs…on a stool with wheels." He raised floured hands and shook his head. "Again!"

Georgia waved his comment away. "Oh, put a lid on it, Andy." As an aside to Lily, she added in a loud whisper, "That man doesn't know what he's talkin' about."

"I know what I saw," Andy argued.

Lily scooted a chrome and vinyl-padded chair nearer to Georgia's wheelchair. "Is that cast as uncomfortable as it looks?"

"Nah. Hardest part about wearin' this thing," she said, knocking on the toes-to-thigh plaster, "is not being able to get around like I'd like to."

"How long 'til you're back on your feet?"

"Ten weeks. Eight, if I'm very, very good." Georgia tucked a red curl behind her ear. "One good thing came of it, though."

"In other words," Andy tossed in, "ten weeks. Probably more!"

Georgia feigned a frown. "Funny man. Maybe we oughta get you a gig at the local comedy club."

Lily helped herself to a cup of coffee. "Can I get you some?"

"Had my quota for the day, thanks."

"So, what's the 'good thing' to come of your broken leg?"

"Max is coming home," Georgia said, beaming. "And he's bringing little Nate with him!"

Lily felt as though her heart had plummeted into her stomach. Max? Coming back to Amarillo? She put her coffee on the counter, afraid her trembling might cause her to spill it. "When…um…when will Max be here?"

Georgia glanced at her wristwatch. "They called from the road not half an hour ago, so they should roll in here any—"

The door burst open and a small boy with curly brown hair exploded into Georgia's diner. He was the spitting image of Max, right down to the adorable dimples bracketing his wide grin.

"Gramma!" he squealed, arms outstretched as he ran toward Georgia. "Gramma, we're finally here!"

Georgia hugged him tight, then held his rosy-cheeked face in her hands. "Lemme have a look at my favorite grandson," she said, pressing a noisy kiss to his chin.

Giggling, Nate said, "How can I be your favorite grandson when I'm your *only* grandson?" He swiped at the spot his grandmother had kissed. "And second, how can you have a look at me while you're *kissin'* me!"

His grandmother hugged him again. "Four-year-old genius," she told Lily, "just like his daddy. Yes'm. That's my boy!"

She glanced toward the door. "Speaking of which, where *is* your daddy?"

"Parking the car." Nate's eyes widened. "You should see all the squished bugs on the front bumper. Must be a million of 'em!"

As Georgia laughed, Lily smiled self-consciously. She had to get out of here, fast, because it would be only a matter of seconds before the genius's father followed him into the diner. And she had no desire to see Max Sheridan again, not after—

"Actually," Nate added, "it isn't 'zactly a car. It's an Ess Yoo Vee. It's big and red, like a fire truck. He bought it right before you busted your leg."

"*Broke* my leg," Georgia corrected. "I still think you and your dad should have flown into town, saved all those hours on the road. Especially considering there's a perfectly good car in the garage that he could've—"

"I'm a pencil pusher, not Mr. America," interrupted a teasing baritone. "What makes you think I could steer that boat of yours?"

It was Max, looking more gorgeous than Lily remembered. Tall and broad-shouldered, he seemed more at ease with himself than when she'd last seen him, more manly and mature. Marriage had done that to him, she supposed. Marriage and fatherhood.

Lily swallowed the lump of jealousy that formed in her throat and asked God to forgive her pettiness, because much as she'd wanted to be the one at his side when those things happened, he'd chosen someone else.

"Max!" Georgia waved him over. "C'mere and give your old fat mama a great big hug!"

He crossed the room in three long strides and bent to wrap his mother in a warm embrace. "First... you're not fat."

"I hope you're gonna say 'Second...you're not old.'" She gave him a playful poke in the ribs.

"Do you see 'Fool' tattooed to my forehead?" He assumed a serious stance and a pious expression.

They enjoyed a laugh, then Georgia said, "You know my motto."

"'God and Nature have decreed that I will age,'" Max quoted, "'…but I refuse to get *old!*'"

He crouched beside the footrest of her chair. "So, let's have a look at this leg of yours."

While Max inspected his mother's cast, Lily did her best to sneak out of the diner unnoticed.

"Stop right there!" Georgia hollered.

Lily froze in her tracks, only too aware that all eyes were now on her. Caught in the act!

"Where d'you think you're going, young lady? You can't leave 'til you put your John Hancock on my leg!"

Feeling the heat of a blush creep into her cheeks, Lily moved woodenly toward the wheelchair. "Sorry," she said, accepting Georgia's felt-tipped pen. "Where would you like me to—"

"Daddy," interrupted Nate's hoarse whisper. He tugged at his father's hand. "She's *bee-yoo-tee-ful!*"

Lily chanced a quick glance in Max's direction. Now he was blushing. Her heartbeat doubled when he met her eyes and smiled that oh-so-tantalizing half grin that had captivated her years ago. She'd changed a lot since he left for Chicago; she hoped he wouldn't recognize her.

He got to his feet. "Lily? Lily London?"

Yeah, she thought bitterly, *it's me. The silly little twit who used to tag along behind you like a well-trained puppy, hoping for a pat on the head.* She plastered what she hoped was a sophisticated smile on her face and tried to sound composed.

"How are you, Max?"

How long had it been since she last saw him? Five years? No, six…if she didn't count the tens of thousands of times she'd pictured him in her dreams. Six long years since he'd left Amarillo—with his blushing bride on his arm.

"Wow. Look at you! I hardly recognized you. It's great to see you."

If he'd given her a thought at all in all these years—which was doubtful—he'd probably pictured her in braces and a ponytail, and carrying an armload of books. Surely the change hadn't been *that* drastic, so why was he staring at her as if she had a third eye in the middle of her forehead?

Lily broke the intense eye contact by pretending to recap the pen, but ended up stabbing her palm with the point, instead.

She stifled an *ouch,* as Georgia said, "Who'da thunk that skinny freckle-faced li'l gal would grow up to be such a knockout!"

Nate took a step closer and smiled up at her. She'd heard through the grapevine that Max and Melissa had had a son. Mostly, she'd tried not to think about the fact that Max had started a life with someone other than her, because she'd loved him almost from the first moment they'd met—when she was a knobby-kneed seventh grader and he'd been Centennial High School's star quarterback.

"Hi," the boy said. "My name is Nathan Maxwell Sheridan. Max, here, is my dad. I'm very pleased to make your awk-a-ah…"

"Acquaintance," his father helped.

"That's it," Nate said, nodding, "'acquaintance.'" He looked up into Lily's face. "What's your name?"

"Her name is Lily," Georgia said. "Lily London."

"Sounds like a movie star's name." He furrowed his brow. "But I thought a lily was a flower."

"It is," Lily said, shrugging. "My mother's name was Rose, see, so I guess she thought it would be neat to name my sisters and me after flowers."

Nate giggled. "That's pretty funny." He giggled again. "What're your sisters' names?"

"The twins are Ivy and Violet, and there's Cammi… which is short for Camellia."

He narrowed his big, black-lashed eyes. "They're nice names, but I like Lily best."

A person would have to be made of stone not to warm to this child, she admitted, mirroring his friendly grin. "Well, thanks, Nate," she said, shaking his extended hand. "And I'm pleased to make your acquaintance, too."

He jerked a thumb over his shoulder. "My dad here could sure use a wife. See, my mom died when I was a baby. He does pretty good, considering he's not a lady, but he sure could use some help. So…are you married?"

Georgia chuckled under her breath as Max slapped a hand over his eyes and gave a loud sigh.

Lily found herself enjoying his discomfort, perhaps a little too much. "I'm afraid I'm a little too busy to… help your dad out. I have a job. Two, in fact."

His brows nearly met in the center of his forehead.

"Wow. *Two* jobs?" he said, stuffing both hands into his pants pockets.

As if on cue, Max did the same thing, Lily noticed. It was obvious the two spent a lot of time together, because Nate had also picked up Max's tendency to say "first" this and "second" that. Maybe Nate hadn't been too far from the mark when he'd said Max was an okay parent.

"I'm an animal rehabilitator," she told the boy. "And I manage my father's ranch."

Nate's brow furrowed. "What's that?"

"She nurses sick and injured animals back to health," Max explained, "then takes them back where they came from." To Lily, he added, "Sorry. He's a great kid, but sometimes he talks too much."

She was about to agree that Nate was a great kid and add that Max had nothing to apologize for, when Nate said, "Your dad has a ranch? With horses and cows and stuff?"

Lily smiled again. "He sure does."

"Man, I've never been on a real-live ranch before. They don't have 'em in Chicago, y'know."

She glanced at Max. He'd grown up in cattle country; why hadn't he taken the boy to see his buddies' homes during visits to his mother?

"Are you a vettin-air-yun?"

"No, Nate, but I do work very closely with one."

He crossed both arms over his chest. "I'm gonna be a vettin-air-yun when I grow up, 'cause I like animals."

"Do you, now? Do you have a cat or a dog?"

Nate shot his father a less-than-friendly look. "Dad says I'm not old enough to be }sponsible for a pet."

"Well, maybe you'd like to come out to our ranch sometime, see my animals."

Nate gasped. "Really? I could do that? Cool! What kind of animals!"

"Oh, a raccoon and a wolf cub, an eagle, some hawks, three monkeys and—"

"Monkeys! *Way* cool! Dad, I wanna—"

One look into his father's stern face was enough to silence the boy. Lily couldn't help but wonder why Max would have a problem with Nate visiting River Valley. It was the most natural thing in the world for a city boy to get enthused about the prospect of seeing animals up close, especially if his only prior contact had been at Chicago's Brookfield Zoo!

Lily knew that if she didn't get out of there fast, she'd likely say something she'd regret. "Where should I sign?" she asked Georgia, pen poised above the cast.

Georgia pointed, and Lily scribbled *Get Well Quick!* above her signature. "I'd love to stay and chat," she fibbed, handing Georgia her pen, "but I have a million things to do."

"You got any kids?" Nate asked.

"No," Lily told him. "But with two jobs, I don't have time to properly take care of children." She didn't tell him that not being able to make her "wife and mommy" dream come true was one of the most disappointing and heartbreaking facts of her life. The lump that formed in her throat surprised her.

And before any of them could say another word, she

headed for the door. "Bye," she called over her shoulder. "See you all later."

Not! she tacked on as the door hissed shut behind her. At least, not if she had anything to say about it!

During the drive back to the ranch, Lily's cell phone rang. "There's a dog doing its best to keep from drowning in Lake Meredith," her sister said. "I heard two small-craft pilots talking about it, listening to my CB radio. They've been hovering overhead for a couple minutes. Don't know how long the poor thing has been down there. If someone doesn't do something for it soon, one of 'em is gonna put it out of its misery—with a rifle!"

The mental picture of a dog paddling like mad to stay afloat, while sharpshooters zeroed in on it, made Lily's heart flinch. Ordinarily, she didn't specialize in household pets but this was hardly an ordinary circumstance. "Okay, all right, calm down before you fall down," Lily said, making a quick U-turn on Route 40. "I'm on my way. Meanwhile, get back on that CB of yours and see if you can reach those guys. Tell the trigger-happy one to keep the safety on his weapon. I'll be there in less than an hour."

She'd witnessed situations like this before, and knew that unless the dog had been injured, it could stay afloat for an amazingly long time. Over the years, people had taken to calling her Snow White because of her talent for communicating with animals. She hoped the gift would help her coax this poor pup to the shore before…

Taking the exit onto Route 136 and heading north to the small town of Fritch, Lily forced the horrifying image from her mind. *Lord, get me there fast,* she prayed. "Say, Vi…"

"Hmm?"

"I've always wondered…why do you have a CB radio in your shop?"

Violet laughed. "Well, originally I got it to keep track of deliveries. If a deliveryman called to say he was stuck in traffic, I'd know within minutes if he was telling the truth or feeding me a line of baloney. Didn't take long to weed the dishonest ones from those I could trust."

Grinning, Lily waited for the "other" reasons.

"I realized pretty quick it's also a great place to catch up on local gossip. *And* I find out when a busload of tourists is rolling in at Georgia's. One quick trip to the diner, one quiet mention of all the good deals across the street at my boutique, and I have all the business I can handle 'til the bus rolls out again."

Lily couldn't help but smile. "So much for the 'dumb blonde' adage. You're one of the savviest businesswomen I've ever known."

She listened to the heavy silence for a few seconds before saying, "Vi? You there?"

"Yeah. I was just thinking about that poor dog."

Nodding, Lily said, "Me, too. But don't worry. I'll do everything I can to save it."

"'Course you will. Why do you think I called you as soon as I heard about it!"

"I only hope the mutt is wearing tags, so I can reunite him with his owner fast as I can. This whole ordeal will be traumatic enough without being separated from loved ones."

"Well, a customer just walked in. Call me later, let me know how things turned out."

Lily hung up, hoping that when "later" came, she wouldn't have to tell her sister she'd been forced to take the dog home. It wouldn't be the first time she'd taken in a lost dog or cat, and experience had taught her it wouldn't be the last. Whether bringing the animal back to its former healthy state took months or days, every situation lasted only long enough to roust out a good family to adopt the pet. But regardless of how much or how little time and energy she invested in the creatures, Lily always experienced a period of mourning while she adjusted to life without the furry critter.

Nate Sheridan came to mind, with his big brown eyes and mop of dark curls. If she managed to save the dog and couldn't find its owner, maybe…

Of course, that would require direct contact with Max. Lily's heart beat double time at the mere thought. Clucking her tongue, she whispered through clenched teeth, "Get a grip, girl." Because, really, what could happen between them in the few minutes it would take to get his permission to introduce Nate to the rescued dog?

"You're getting way ahead of yourself, Lily." She had no idea what kind of dog was splashing around for its life, no clue what condition it might be in by the time she reached it. A glance at her dashboard clock told her she'd been on the road less than fifteen minutes; it was nearly an hour's drive to the entrance gate at Lake Meredith.

It dawned on her suddenly that she hadn't asked

Violet *where* the pilots had seen the dog. Acres of water made up this stretch of the park.

She reached for her cell phone, punched in her sister's code. "Hey, kiddo…it's me," she said when her sister answered. "I didn't think to ask earlier, but did those pilots mention where they spotted the dog?"

"I remember something about the boat dock. They thought maybe the dog had fallen off a sailboat or something."

"But who'd go boating at this time of year?"

"I know I wouldn't want to waste a nice day like this if I'd sunk a hundred grand into a sailboat."

Violet made a good point, Lily admitted. The weather had been remarkably balmy for October, these past few weeks. "Did you manage to raise either of them on your CB?"

"No. We must be on a weird frequency. I'm hearing them fine, but they didn't respond to me at all."

Just great! Lily thought. Chances were pretty good that the sharpshooter who'd talked himself into believing he'd be doing a good deed by "putting the dog out of its misery" might actually take aim…and pull the trigger!

"Thanks, Vi. I'd better step on it. I'm still forty-five minutes away. I'll call soon as I know something," she said, and hung up.

"Please, God," she said aloud, "watch over that pup. Give him the strength he needs to hang on 'til I get there."

Maybe she should phone Georgia, so she and Nate could join in her prayer. No, the kid would get his hopes up. And knowing how much danger the dog was in would only worry him. Besides, if she didn't reach the lake in time, his little heart would break, and for what? Lily knew only too well how much it hurt to lose an animal, any animal.

"Help me, Lord...."

What if she phoned ahead, told the rangers at the gate who she was! If she described her car and explained the urgency of her mission, they'd let her through without stopping.

Lily said a quick thank you to the Almighty for the idea and grabbed the phone again, dialed the number she'd memorized ages ago—and stomped on the gas.

Chapter Two

"Here's our very own TV star!" Georgia said when Lily walked into the diner. "Does your dad know what got you on the evening news *this* time?"

"No, thankfully." Lily plopped onto a stool at the counter and sighed. "But I'll have to keep him away from television, at least 'til this whole 'daring rescue' nonsense is old news."

Georgia clucked her tongue. "In all fairness to the reporters, from what I saw, you *did* risk your life to save that mutt."

Shrugging, Lily rolled her eyes. "I borrowed a rowboat and paddled to the middle of Lake Meredith. Hardly what I'd call life-threatening."

"Yeah. Right. Without knowing if the dog was vicious, or diseased." She punctuated her opinion with a haughty *harrumph*. The redhead aimed a bony forefinger at Lily. "You can't fool an old fool, so quit tryin', girlie!"

Then Georgia's brow furrowed. "How'd the soggy

ol' fleabag get out in the middle of the lake in the first place?"

Grinning, Lily shrugged again. Leave it to Georgia to put a brand-new spin on things. "Near as anyone can figure, she fell off a boat. When her leash got tangled in a buoy wire, she couldn't get loose." She frowned. "Guess her collar fell off in the struggle. Weird thing is, none of the boaters on the lake claimed her."

"Maybe she didn't fall. Maybe somebody tossed her overboard."

Lily gasped. "Why would anyone do such a horrible thing! Especially considering she's a beautiful, well-behaved, intelligent golden retriever."

"Maybe she has the mange."

"There isn't a single solitary thing wrong with her. She's positively perfect."

Georgia leaned closer and whispered beside a cupped palm. "Maybe she witnessed a murder and the killer had to get rid of her so she couldn't identify him."

Lily laughed. "That would be pretty spectacular, even for a dog as smart as Missy."

"Oh, ho! Don't be so quick to judge. I read a novel where a dog could communicate by spelling stuff, using Scrabble tiles. Now *that* was one brilliant canine." She narrowed her eyes. "Hey, wait just a minute. Did you call her 'Missy'?"

Lily nodded.

"I thought she didn't have a collar."

Another shrug. "She didn't. But, how she got into the lake, who owns her, her medical history—it's all a mystery. So I called her Miss-Terry."

"Miss-Terry, I get it," Georgia said. "Missy for short." Then she added, "Not the smartest move you've ever made."

Lily held up one hand. "I know, I know. If I do find her family, it'll be harder to give her up now, because I named her." But then, it always was hard to give up an animal once she'd rehabilitated it. Eagles and hawks, lizards and snakes, fawns…it didn't matter what species; Lily inevitably went through a period of mourning when her work with the animal was done.

She glanced at Georgia's cast. "What's this I hear about your leg not healing properly, about your needing surgery?"

"Where'd you hear that?"

"One of the park rangers is married to your doctor's receptionist. She called on his cell phone while we were debating how to save Missy. He mentioned my name, and she wanted to know if I was the girl who used to waitress at Georgia's Diner. I said no, that was my sister, Cammi. And she asked if he'd heard about your leg."

Georgia stared in silence for a moment. "Well, I guess it's true what they say."

"Bad news travels like wildfire?"

"'Zactly."

"So," Lily pressed, "what does the doctor hope to accomplish with an operation?"

It was Georgia's turn to shrug. "Oh, who knows? Robert probably wants to do it so he can pay off that fancy sports car of his." Chuckling, she added, "Either that, or he wasn't kidding when he said the bone isn't knitting like it's supposed to." She shook her head. "Says he'll have to put a pin or two in there, hold things in place."

Lily patted her hand. "I'll add you to my prayer list. That'll get the job done." She gave Georgia a look. "'Robert'?"

Georgia blushed but ignored the question. "So tell me, what brings you to town? It isn't like you to stay away from your menagerie so long."

"Well," Lily began, looking left and right, "I wanted to run an idea by you. If you agree, maybe I can solicit your help."

"Oooh," the woman said, rubbing both hands together. "Sounds like a conspiracy. Count me in!"

"Hear me out, first. You might decide it's the worst idea since Custer took his last stand."

"Then, time's a-wastin', girl. Spit it out!"

Lily told Georgia about her plan to unite the golden retriever with Nate. "Missy has such a sweet-natured temperament. If Max will allow it, she'd be great company for Nate."

Georgia pursed her lips, chin resting on a bent forefinger, considering the idea. "Y'know, I think you're right." She met Lily's eyes. "There's plenty of space in my apartment, even for a dog Missy's size. It's just the three of us, after all, rattling around in six big rooms." She nodded. "I think it's a terrific idea. That poor li'l guy hasn't had it easy, being alone with Max since his mama died."

The mere mention of Max's wife made Lily bristle, waking feelings of jealousy. She felt petty and silly, too, because Max had never so much as given her the time of day. "If I'm not being too personal, how did his…" She struggled to get the word out. "How did his wife die?"

"Killed herself. Pills."

Georgia said it so matter-of-factly, Lily didn't know how to react. "Suicide? But, why?" With a man like Max for a husband, and a son as great as Nate, why would any woman in her right mind—

"She never was wrapped too tight," Georgia said as if she'd read Lily's mind. "A bubble off plumb, as my daddy used to say." She gave a dismissive wave of her hand. "I told Max she'd be trouble, but would he listen? Nooo. He had to be the big brave hero, try and rescue her."

"From what?"

"That's just it. The girl was born with a silver spoon in her mouth. Her mama took her to New York every summer, to outfit her for school. She'd do just about anything to be the center of attention. Guess when li'l Nate came along and stole her thunder, she just plain couldn't handle it." Crossing both arms over her chest, Georgia shook her head. "Spoiled brat, if you ask me."

"Did she…did she leave a note?"

"But, of *course*." Sarcasm rang loud in Georgia's voice. "How better to command center stage again, even if it had to be from the grave! She made good and sure Max would spend the rest of his life blaming himself for her death. And so far, she's succeeded."

"What do you mean, she succeeded?"

"First, he hasn't been out on a date since before he met her. And second, he won't go anywhere or do anything that might even *hint* at having fun. As if that's not bad enough, he's totally given up on God."

Well, that explained the ever-so-serious expression on his handsome face. Explained his stern attitude toward Nate, too. "Sad," Lily said. "He used to be so goofy, such fun, the life of every party."

"Which is *exactly* why I think you had a doggone good idea, if you'll pardon the pun."

Lily forced herself to grin. "You really think Max will go for it?"

"You 'n' me will see that he does!"

"Just so he doesn't see it as interfering…"

"How could he see you matching his son up with a great dog like Missy as interference?" Georgia laughed. "You add my leg to your prayer list, I'll add Max's answer to mine."

"Deal!" Lily said, shaking the woman's hand.

Neither of them noticed the three-foot tall shadow standing near the bottom of the stairs….

Nate's dad had scolded him enough times for thundering down the steps. This time, he was determined to get to the first floor as quietly as possible. So he pretended to be an Indian brave, stalking a deer in the forest. "Heap big bunch of meat," he whispered, remembering the Daniel Boone movie he'd seen earlier. "Take home to squaw." He raised the plastic shovel-turned-tomahawk just as he reached the bottom step…just in time to hear Lily and his grandmother talking about getting a dog!

He snuck back up to the second floor and slipped into his room. *A dog!* he thought as his sneakered foot hit the top step. A dog named Missy. Nate didn't give a thought to the color of her fur, her age, the loudness of her bark. His only thought was a dog that he would soon have of his very own!

Flopping onto his back on the twin bed that was his here in Amarillo, he kicked both feet into the air and punched the mattress. "Yippee!" he whispered.

"Gramma, how old does a person have to be to use the telephone?"

"Old enough to talk, I guess," she said distractedly.

Nate watched as she filed her fingernails. "What if a person wants to talk to somebody, but he doesn't know their number?"

"He could look the number up in the phone book…."

Slapping a hand to his forehead, Nate did his best not to appear impatient. "But what if the person can't read?"

"Then, I guess he'd have to call Information."

"Information?"

His grandmother nodded. "He'd have to dial four-one-one and tell the nice lady what city and state the person he wants to call lives in."

"We're in Amarillo, Texas, right?"

"Right."

Now he watched as Georgia shook a tiny bottle of fingernail polish. "You gonna paint your nails, Gramma?"

"Mmm-hmm."

"Why? 'Cause that nice man is coming over again

tonight?" Nate thought she looked right pretty, not at all like a grandmother, when she smiled like that.

He was about to tell her so, when she said, "He's going to load me into his car and take me out to eat. And then we're going to the movies."

"Cool. Whatcha gonna see?"

"Who knows? Something funny, I expect. Robert loves comedies."

Nate nodded, mirroring Georgia's frown as she concentrated on layering each fingernail with a coat of pearly white polish. "So Gramma…"

"Hmm?"

"After this person tells the nice lady what city and state, then what?"

"Then he tells her the name of the person who lives in that city and state, and she recites the phone number. Unless it's unlisted."

"'Recites'?"

"Tells," Georgia clarified. "She tells him the person's phone number."

Nate could read better than most four-year-olds, but not nearly well enough, he knew, to look someone up in the telephone directory. He could write his numbers, though, because his dad had started teaching him as soon as he could hold on to a colored marker.

He was thankful that his grandmother's focus was still on *her* hand. And his dad was down the street, buying washers to repair the leaking kitchen faucet. If God had been listening when he'd asked for assistance, Nate could make the call before either of them could say their favorite word: *Whippersnapper.*

"What's for supper, Gramma?" he asked, heading for the stairs.

"I think your dad said something about fixing chicken fingers for the two of you." Suddenly, she tucked her tongue between her top and bottom lip. "What do you expect," she muttered to herself, "when you've only used nail polish twice in your entire life!"

"I *love* chicken fingers. 'Specially with honey-and-mustard dippin' sauce."

"Mmm-hmm…"

"God?" Nate whispered as he climbed the stairs. "Help me remember everything Gramma just said, okay?"

Closing the apartment door quietly behind him, the boy sat on the end of the couch nearest the telephone. Holding the handset to his head, he pressed *four-one-one*.

"And, God?" he continued, waiting for the numbers to connect him to the nice lady. "Let Dad say yes about Missy the dog!"

Lily rather liked the way Missy followed her around. The dog sat quietly as Lily fed milk to a baby squirrel. And while she cleaned the eagle's cage, Missy lay quietly, head resting on her forepaws, cinnamon-brown eyes watching every move. It was as though the retriever understood that the barn was both shelter and hospital for birds with broken wings, for orphaned bunnies…for dogs who'd been separated from their families.

"You're a pretty cool mutt," she said, ruffling the golden fur. "Even Obnoxious thinks so!" Missy got along well with her dad's dog. Surprising in itself, because while Obnoxious had never been vicious, he'd never before befriended one of Lily's visiting canines.

Missy sat on her haunches and sent Lily a happy-doggy grin. She was about to admit that if Max said Nate couldn't have a dog, she'd keep Missy for herself—but the phone rang, forestalling her speech.

"Miss Lily?"

Nate? But why would he be phoning *her?* "Yes."

"It's me, Nathan Maxwell Sheridan. We met at my gramma's diner?"

Lily grinned. "Yes, I remember." How could she forget, when he'd plied her with compliments and practically asked her to be his mother! "How nice to hear from you, Nate."

"I just called to say thanks for saving that dog today. You're not just pretty, you're brave, too."

He was his father's son, all right, adept at flirting, even at the tender age of four. Max had made an art form of it in high school. Surely he'd only improved since—

Lily remembered what Georgia had said—that Max hadn't dated, had practically refused to do anything that involved a good time since his wife's death.

"I heard you, a little while ago, telling Gramma that you want me to have the dog. So I'm calling to make sure you know I'll take *very* good care of her. I'll be nice to her and I'll keep her clean and I'll feed her on time every day and I'll take her for walks. I *promise.*"

If it was possible to hug a person through the phone, Lily would have hugged Nate, just for being his adorable, sincere self. "I'm sure you'll be a wonderful master for Missy," Lily said. She was about to explain that the dog could only be his with his dad's approval, when Nate spoke.

"I'm very gentle, you know. I don't pull dogs' ears or tails, like some kids do. I don't tease them, either, because, well, teasing isn't nice! Oh, and I'll make sure she gets plenty of water, 'cause I know how 'portant it is—for a dog to drink plenty of water, I mean."

Lily repressed a giggle; she couldn't have Nate thinking she wasn't taking him seriously. "I'm sure you'd make a wonderful master," she said again, "but—"

"Who do you think you are," a deep male voice interrupted, "making decisions regarding my son without discussing them with me first?"

Blinking, Lily sat in stunned silence for a second. "Max, I—"

"If and when Nate gets a dog, *I'll* be the one who gives the go-ahead, not you!"

"I—I never intended to—"

"How do you expect me to deal with his disappointment, now that you've got his hopes up that he'll get a dog?"

"Max, if you'll just calm down for a minute, I can explai—"

"There's nothing to explain. Your 'find the mutt a home' scheme may have worked in the past, but it isn't going to work this time."

It was pretty obvious by the tone of his voice, by the heat in his words, that Max had no intention of listening to reason. She didn't understand the level of his anger. Especially with little Nate within earshot.

As Lily saw it, she had two choices: sit quietly as Max continued his tirade, or hang up.

If she hung up, Nate wouldn't have a chance in a million of adopting Missy. But if she stayed on the line, maybe she could slip a word in edgewise…if she was patient until Max spent the last of his wrath. *Lord,* she prayed, *give me the strength to know when to speak… and what to say when I do.*

"I've had it up to *here*," Max was saying, "with people who think they know better than I what's good for my boy. Especially people like you, who don't even have kids of their own!"

That hurt, Lily admitted silently. And it was unfair, to boot. Because she might have kids of her own, if loving Max hadn't made every man look so sad by comparison.

"Stick to what you know, Lily—animals. And let me raise my son in peace."

He seemed to have run out of steam. In the moment of silence that followed his last stinging remark, Lily debated whether or not to stand up for Nate. The boy clearly wanted—and as Georgia had pointed out, *needed*—something to occupy his lonely hours. Seemed to Lily he needed something to love, too—something that would love him in return, unconditionally.

"Are you finished?" she asked.

He cleared his throat. "Yes."

"May I have a moment, then, to explain?"

"There's nothing to explain," he shot back. "I'm—"

"I'm sure you don't *mean* to sound like an unreasonable bully, but..." She paused.

She listened to the silence and prayed he hadn't hung up. Then he coughed, and she added, "If you'll just be quiet for a minute, I'll be happy to tell you what's *really* going on here."

"Go on," Max said, his voice tight.

She sighed heavily. "Nate called just now to—"

"*He* called *you?*"

"Yes, he did, to thank me for rescuing Missy at—"

"I heard all about it on the news. 'Lily, the hero of Texas wildlife.'"

Lily ignored his caustic tone and continued. "He called to tell me he'd overheard Georgia and me talking earlier, in the diner. I'd stopped by to ask her if she'd mind having a dog underfoot...*if* you gave Nate permission to have a dog, that is." Not the whole truth, but not exactly a lie, either. But what was she to do, faced with his irrational ire? It didn't seem fair for Nate to suffer because his father was a loudmouthed know-it-all! "Mind you, I'm no expert when it comes to what's good for kids, but it isn't Nate's fault that he jumped to conclusions based on the small portion of the conversation he overheard, because, after all—" she narrowed her eyes and accentuated each word "—he's *only...four...years...old!*"

This time, Lily didn't much care if he hung up or not. Then again, if he actually was the stodgy old grouch he'd sounded like, he might make Nate pay for the scolding she'd just given him.

"Max," she began, tempering her voice, "I know it's

been a long time since you've spent any time in my company." Long time, she laughed to herself. What a joke! Max *never* had spent any time in her company, because he'd always preferred short-skirted cheerleader and prom-queen types—a far cry from what Lily had been—and from what she'd become! "But you need to know, I would never do anything so underhanded as to get Nate's hopes up about getting a dog—not without making sure it was okay with you first." This time, thankfully, the whole truth and nothing but.

When he didn't respond, she added, "So here's the lowdown. The dog is a golden retriever, one of the gentlest breeds God created. She's smart, well-trained and quiet. She'd make an excellent companion for Nate. Georgia says there's room for her in the apartment. I'm sorry the little guy overheard the conversation, but now that the cat's out of the bag, the ball's in your court." Lily groaned inwardly at the back-to-back clichés. "Think about it for a couple of days. I'll hold off finding a home for Missy 'til I hear from you."

And with that, she banged the receiver into its cradle.

"Take *that,* you bossy, swaggering—!"

"My, what was *that* all about!"

Lily turned toward the sound of the friendly voice. "Hey, Cammi." She slumped onto the nearest hay bale. Immediately, Missy curled up at her feet. "That was Max."

"Uh-oh," her older sister said. "I'd heard he was back in town, but I was hoping you could avoid a collision."

Lily only shrugged.

"So tell me, how's he look?" She wiggled her eyebrows and winked. "Handsome as ever?"

"Yeah, I guess."

Cammi ruffled Missy's thick golden fur. "Still stuck on the big galoot, eh?"

"Yeah, I guess," she said again.

"Didn't sound much like it when I walked in."

Lily filled Cammi in on what had happened, from their sister Violet's call to her hanging up on Max.

"Wow. Somebody put some starch into your spine, I think. Never thought I'd see the day you'd stand up to him, not knowing how you've always felt, anyway."

Cammi was the only person on earth who knew that Lily loved Max—that she'd loved him when she was twelve and he eighteen, that nothing had changed, not a whit, in the years since. She sighed.

"You really ought to see other guys," Cammi suggested. "Who knows? Maybe God has put your Mr. Right out there someplace, and He's just waiting for you two to bump into one another." She sat beside Lily, draped an arm over her shoulder. "How you gonna find your knight on a white steed if you never leave this barn?"

"I'm content, right here, doing what I do."

"Baloney. You were born to be a wife and mother. This—" Cammi waved a hand, indicating the cages and the critters in them "—this *stuff* you do is proof you're filled to overflowing with natural nurturing tendencies." She held up both hands to stall Lily's retort. "You're doing great work here, nobody could quibble with that. But be honest with yourself, kiddo. Wouldn't you rather be spending all that love and care on children of your own? On a husband?"

Yes, Lily thought. But only if Max were her husband and the father of those children.

"Well, I didn't come here to lecture you, so how 'bout we talk about the reason I *did* come?"

Lily forced a grin. "The wedding?"

"Yup. Did you get your dress yet?"

On a sigh, she said, "No. Not yet."

Cammi frowned. "What's the matter? You don't like the style?"

"It's fine. Gorgeous, in fact. We'll all look like fashion models. It's just…I haven't had time."

Her sister stood, put both hands on her hips. "You have three weeks to pick up that dress and have it altered. It isn't like you have a choice. You're the maid of honor, don't forget. How can I get married without you there by my side?"

Lily got to her feet and hugged Cammi. "I know. I'm sorry. You have enough on your mind with all the last-minute plans. I'll do it first thing tomorrow. I promise." She brightened to add, "Did you get all the presents put away yet?"

Cammi groaned. "Not yet. There were about a hundred women crowded into the living room. Must have taken you weeks to get the shower organized."

"Took longer to recuperate, once it was over!"

The sisters laughed, and Missy barked happily.

"Tell you what, since tomorrow's Saturday, how 'bout when you pick up the dress, we meet for lunch," Cammi suggested. "My treat. Least I can do for you throwing the biggest, bestest shower a bride ever had."

"It's a date."

"Let's meet at Georgia's. I have a ton of stuff to do in town, anyway."

Georgia's? And risk seeing Max there?

"If he's there," Cammi said knowingly, "we'll talk loud and fast about the new love of your life." She giggled and crouched to hug Missy's neck. "He doesn't have to know it's a dog!"

"Maybe I ought to borrow that sweater," she said, grinning as she plucked a shiny dog hair from Cammi's shoulder. "He'd think my new beau was a blond!" Lily walked her sister to the door. "On second thought, it would be a waste of perfectly good playacting. Max doesn't care who I see. Truth is, that scolding he gave me earlier was the most attention he's paid me, ever."

"Then, we'll do something better than try to make him jealous."

"What's that?"

"We'll ignore him." Cammi headed for the house. "See you at supper, kiddo?"

Smiling, Lily nodded. "Sure."

Ignore Max Sheridan? It would take more than a wedge of lasagna to give her the strength to accomplish a feat like that!

Chapter Three

"Lily?"

She recognized the deejay-type voice immediately: Max. Just what Lily needed—a run-in with him on the telephone just before bedtime. "Yes," she said cautiously.

"Sorry to call so late, but I wanted to wait until Nate was asleep."

Why, she asked silently, *so he won't get upset when you start browbeating me again?* "What can I do for you?"

Missy padded up, circled several times, and flopped at Lily's feet. She patted the dog's head as Max sighed heavily into her ear.

"I don't blame you for being mad. In fact, that's one of the reasons I'm calling…to apologize. I had no right chewing you out the way I did this afternoon. Especially since I didn't have all the facts. Nate and my mother explained things, and, well, I'm sorry."

"It's okay. I understand." She didn't, but if saying so made his apology easier…

"Do you? Understand, I mean?"

"You've got a lot on your mind these days, what with your mom needing surgery and all."

"Frankly, Mom's leg was the last thing on my mind when we spoke earlier. I just…"

She could picture him, running one hand through his hair and staring at the ceiling, the way he had as a teenager, when nervousness or frustration got the better of him.

"Max, really," she said, feeling an unexplainable need to rescue him, "it's okay. Water under the bridge." She frowned, wondering why she'd been speaking in clichés lately. Maybe, Lily thought, because the wisdom of each adage "fit" better than brand-new ideas?

"You don't have to go easy on me. I can take it on the chin. Especially when I deserve it." He hesitated. "And I deserve it."

She heard the smile in his voice, and grinned herself. "Okay then, next time I see you, I'll give you a good whack and we'll call it even."

Max chuckled. "You always were a good-natured little thing."

Always were? Meaning, he'd noticed something about her back then? Lily didn't quite know what to make of that. She'd always suspected he only saw her as incidental, as someone who stood on the fringes, as a girl who was never a real part of things. To find out he'd seen her, that he'd watched and listened closely enough to know she was good-natured…

She knew her heart had better quit beating double-time or it would jump clean out of her chest. "So, how did things go with Nate? Is he terribly disappointed?"

"Why would he be disappointed?"

Lily rolled her eyes. *Oh, no reason,* she thought, *except, maybe, that Nate wants a dog, and because his dad thinks he's master of the universe and wasn't properly consulted, the answer is no.* "Well, you're not going to let him have Missy, right?"

At the mention of her name, the retriever raised her head and met Lily's eyes. Funny how quickly the pup had adapted to her new moniker. If Lily were the type to read meaning into every little thing…

"Not necessarily. I explained to him that a dog is a big responsibility, especially one like Missy, who'd need regular brushing, *especially for a kid who's only four.* Besides, she hasn't been lost for more than a few hours. Her owners might claim her in the next day or two and…"

Lily didn't hear anything Max said after "owners." She'd put a half-baked effort into finding out who Missy belonged to, tacking Lost Dog posters on a few telephone poles, mentioning during the TV interviews that she'd keep the pup until it could be reunited with its family. But there was more she could have done, like running ads in the local papers, placing announcements on the radio. Lily had done it all so many times that "getting the word out" had become second nature.

So, why not this time?

"Nate understands we'll consider taking Missy— and I stressed the word *consider*—only if her owners can't be found." He paused. "How long does that usually take?"

Lily snapped back to attention. "If she fell off a boat, as the rangers suspect, it shouldn't take long at all. In fact, I'm surprised she hasn't been claimed already." It was true, after all. If Missy had been her dog, she'd have been frantic with worry. Which raised the question: If the dog *had* fallen from a boat, where was the boat?

"Well, I won't keep you. I just wanted you to know I didn't mean to come off sounding like—what was that you called me?—a bully." He chuckled. "You always did have a way with words."

And there it was again—"always."

"If I'd used that tone on the job, maybe I wouldn't have had so much trouble collecting fees from my clients!" he said.

Georgia had told Lily that Max had earned his CPA, then worked his way up the corporate ladder to a partnership at one of Chicago's most prestigious accounting firms.

He laughed again. "I can be a blockhead sometimes. I'll just thank my lucky stars you're the forgiving sort."

Lucky stars? This, from the boy who used to depend on the Lord's help by praying before every game, who sang solos in the church choir, who regularly talked his peers out of smoking and drinking because it wasn't the behavior of believers?

Georgia had said something else, too: Max had lost his faith after his wife's suicide.

"You are the forgiving sort, aren't you?"

"Sure," she said, "'course I am."

"Whew. All that silence made me think maybe you were looking through your phone book for the nearest knee cracker."

"Knee cracker?"

"You know, guys who take baseball bats and teach people—" He cleared his throat. "Never mind. Long as you're okay."

For the second time, Lily felt an overpowering need to reassure him. "It'd take more than a browbeating from you to do me any lasting harm." So far, that was the biggest whopper she'd told, because his reprimand had hurt her, far worse than it should have. "Guess it's only natural you'd assume the 'daddy' role," she added, grinning, "seeing as you're so much older than I am."

"You sure know how to hurt a guy. Guess I don't have to wait to see you to 'take it on the chin,' do I!"

Odd. He sounded serious. But how could that be, when she'd intended her remark as a joking reminder. Since Lily always tagged along with her older sisters and their friends, she'd frequently been their I-told-you-so target. Once, when a particularly humiliating comment put tears in her eyes, Max had slung an arm over her shoulders. "Aw, don't take 'em seriously," he'd said. "They don't mean anything by it. They're just practicing for when they're parents themselves one day."

"But I'm almost thirteen," she'd cried, "not *that* much younger than the rest of you!"

She remembered the peculiar look that had crossed his face. "Six years," he'd said, his voice trembling slightly as he withdrew his arm. "More than enough to make a guy—"

A cheerleader ran up and hugged him just then, preventing him from finishing the sentence. It was such a common occurrence—girls throwing themselves at him—that Lily didn't give it another thought. Until now.

"I'm not *that* much younger than you," she said, returning to their present conversation. Hopefully, he'd remember the scene from their past, too, and finish his sentence this time.

"Well, guess I'll let you go. I promised Mom I'd open the diner in the morning. Five o'clock rolls around faster than I'd like to admit."

"You slept late when you were a corporate big shot, eh?" she teased.

"Not really. Most days, I was up by six, out of the house by seven. Until—" He cleared his throat. "Slept later once it was my job to get Nate ready for the sitter."

Which used to be his wife's job, Lily surmised.

"So, you'll be on duty at lunchtime?"

"Yeah," Max said. "Why?"

"Cammi and I are meeting at the diner at noon." She told him about having to pick up her maid of honor dress and get it altered for Cammi's upcoming wedding—a stall tactic, because hadn't Max said he'd called for *two* reasons?

"Cool. Guess I'll see you then, then."

How long since she'd heard him say "then, then"? Lily wondered. *Too long.* And she'd missed it. Missed everything about him, from that way he had of bobbing his head when listening to others, to the way he looked deep into a person's eyes when he was the one doing the talking. She missed the delight he seemed to get from little things, like helping someone by picking up a dropped book or holding open a door. If schoolmates seemed down in the dumps, his antics were sure to raise their spirits. And then there were the adorable dimples that formed beside his sexy half grin.

"Yeah." *I'll see you then, then,* she added silently.

"If you're lucky, I'll pay for your dessert."

If she was truly lucky, he'd pay her a little one-on-one attention!

"What was the other thing you called about?"

"Other thing?"

"You said…" She didn't want to remind him of the apology; in her opinion, his discomfort had caused him to squirm long enough. "Never mind," she said, hoping the disappointment didn't ring too loudly in her voice. "I'll see you tomorrow."

"Who was that?" her dad asked when she hung up the phone.

"Max Sheridan." And now that she had a moment to think about it, had he been flirting with that "pay for dessert" comment? *Don't be silly, Lily.*

"Sherman Tank Sheridan?" Lamont whistled. "Man, could that boy throw a pass! If the Cowboys could get a couple guys like that on the team…" Her dad went silent and met Lily's eyes. "What's he doing calling you?"

The flirtation question died a quick death when she realized her dad was right; why would the handsome, former star quarterback be interested in Lily London? She bent to kiss her father good-night. Still, it sure sounded like Max had been flirting.

Lily couldn't concentrate on an answer. Not while looking at her father's puzzled expression. "Bacon and eggs in the morning?" she asked, heading for the stairs.

"Mmm," he grunted, flapping his newspaper. "Girls," he muttered. "Never could understand 'em."

It wasn't the first time she'd heard him say that. And with four daughters born in quick succession, he'd likely say it 'til he drew his last breath.

Maybe someday she'd tell her father what had come to mind every time he'd said it:

Boys are just as confusing!

"I understand congratulations are in order," Max said, when Cammi joined her sister in the booth. "When's the big day?"

"Three weeks from today. If I'd known you'd be in town, I would have sent you an invitation."

As they chatted, Lily sat back, smiling and thinking that Cammi had been looking particularly beautiful these days. She'd always been one of the prettiest girls in town, but since Reid had come along, she practically glowed. *Thank you, Lord,* she prayed, *for sending him into her life.* What were the chances He'd send a man like that into Lily's life?

Cammi dug around in her purse, pulled out an invitation. "This came in today's mail. One of Dad's friends can't make it." She handed the tiny envelope to Max.

"Why don't you come in their place, and bring your little boy!"

Lily's heart thumped so hard, she thought surely anyone in earshot could hear it. *Don't take it, Max,* she prayed. *Don't take it.* She didn't want him there. Because Cammi had hired a band to play forties music, and he'd always loved to dance. Lily didn't want to watch him move across the floor with another woman in his arms!

"Your mom already RSVP'd," Cammi was saying, "so I'll rearrange the tables so the three of you can sit together."

Max tucked the invitation into his shirt pocket. "Thanks. Maybe Nate'll meet some kids his own age, 'cause it looks like we'll be staying in Amarillo longer than we thought."

Cammi frowned. "I heard about your mom's leg. What a shame." She brightened to add, "But she's on every prayer list in Texas, so she'll come out of it better than new." As an aside, she said, "Besides, the way I hear it, her surgeon has more reason than most to succeed."

Max's expression darkened, and Lily wondered if it was because he didn't approve of his mom's relationship with her doctor, or because Cammi had mentioned prayer. The latter, probably, she decided, remembering what Georgia had said about his faith crisis.

"I didn't pack a suit for Nate, but we have three weeks to buy—"

"He doesn't need a suit," Lily cut in. "He's four years

old. No one's going to notice if he's not dressed up like a tuxedo advertisement."

Cammi pointed. "Oh, Max, is that li'l cutie over there Nate?"

He looked over his shoulder to where his son sat, deep in concentration as he colored on construction paper, and nodded. Lily couldn't help but notice how his entire demeanor changed at the mere sight of the boy. He stood taller and smiled. Not that half-baked grin he'd been tossing around since he'd come home, but a genuine, full-faced, two-dimpled smile. If anyone doubted Max's love for Nate, they need only see him now to believe how much his son meant to him.

Lily frowned. "He looks a little pale today. I hope he isn't coming down with something."

Max's wide grin faded. "His appetite has been off the past week or so. And he isn't sleeping well, either."

"Probably just having trouble adjusting to the climate," Cammi offered. "The Texas Panhandle is very different from Illinois."

"Yeah, maybe." But Max didn't seem convinced, as evidenced by his worried expression. He faced them suddenly and whipped out his order tablet. "So, what can I get you ladies?"

"What, no waitress today?" Lily asked, grinning.

"Flat tire or something," he said. "So I'm 'it' until she gets here."

Cammi was on her feet in no time. "You handle the cash register," she told him, tying an apron around her waist. "I remember from our high school days what happens when someone puts a food-laden tray in *your* hands." Closing her eyes, she looked at the ceiling. "Anyone wearing a white shirt when you walked by was in trouble!"

A quiet *thump* captured everyone's attention.

A woman got to her feet, knocking her plate on the floor when she did. "This little boy just fell out of his booth!" she shouted, pointing.

Max was beside his son in a heartbeat. "Nate?" He gave the semiconscious boy a gentle shake. "Nate, what's wrong?"

Lily stood behind him, one hand on his shoulder. Nate's brown eyes looked even darker in his ashen face. Hearing his long, ragged breaths, she said, "We need to get him to the hospital, now." She gave Max's shoulder a squeeze. "I'll bring my car around and meet you out front in a minute."

Max's worried eyes met hers briefly before he turned his attention back to Nate.

Lily grabbed her purse from the table and raced for the door, dialing her cell phone as she went.

"Don't you worry," Cammi told Max. "Andy and I will handle things here." She met the cook's eyes. "Right, Andy?"

"You bet," he said with a jerk of his spatula.

Cammi held open the diner's door while Max hurried to Lily's waiting car. "I've already called ahead," she said, buckling the seat belt over him and Nate. "They'll have someone waiting at the E.R. entrance."

"Thanks," he said, as she got behind the wheel.

It didn't escape her notice that there were tears in his eyes when he said it.

Tires squealing, she pealed away from the curb.

Lily glanced at Max, who held his son close. Worry creased his handsome brow and made his jaw muscles bulge as he stared through the windshield. She reached across the seat to pat his hand. "Don't worry," she said. "Everything will be fine. He's in the Lord's capable hands."

Max grunted, then pressed a kiss to Nate's temple.

Pay him no mind, Lord, she prayed. *He's just had a rough go of things lately.* But even as the thought formed, Lily knew better; Max had been nursing his grudge against the Almighty for a long, long time. But she didn't have to worry. The God she had come to know had a great capacity for love, infinite patience, boundless mercy; He wouldn't hold Max's anger against him.

Now, if only she could convince Max of that.

"Don't worry, Mrs. Sheridan," the nurse said, "your little boy is in good hands. Dr. Prentice is the best pediatric cardiologist in the area."

Lily started to correct the woman. "I'm not—"

"Thanks," Max said, sliding an arm around her waist. "That's good to know." And once the nurse left Nate's E.R. cubicle, he added, "We can set her straight once Nate's out of harm's way. Right now, I'd rather she put her full concentration on doing her job."

Lily nodded, feeling an odd mix of confusion and gratitude. For years, she'd dreamed of being Mrs. Maxwell Sheridan…but this wasn't the way she'd pictured it happening.

Dr. Prentice blasted through the pastel-striped curtains, clipboard in one hand, stethoscope in the other. "So who do we have here?" he said, wiggling Nate's toes. He draped his stethoscope around his shoulders and slid a pair of black-framed half-glasses from his lab coat pocket. "Says here your name is Nathan," he said, squinting at the chart. "Okay if I call you Nate?"

Smiling feebly, the boy nodded.

Dr. Prentice balanced the glasses atop his balding dome. "Well, Nate, we're gonna run a few tests, see what put you in here. And once we find out, we'll do everything we can to make sure it never happens again. Whaddaya say to that?"

The smile broadened slightly as Nate gave another nod.

The doctor faced Max, held out a hand. "I see you've already signed the necessary consent forms, so there's no reason to keep him waiting." He winked at Nate. "We'll get you home fast as we can, okay?" Waving Lily and Max nearer, he perched on the corner of the gurney and addressed his comments to Nate. "Here's what we're gonna do: First, we're gonna show you all sorts of neat machines. X-ray, electrocardiogram, echocardiogram. Nate, m'boy, you're gonna feel like you're the star of a science-fiction movie!" He wiggled the boy's toes again. "Now, I know you've seen all this stuff on TV, so I really don't need to tell you that not one of these tests is gonna hurt, not even a little bit—right?"

A look of wide-eyed fascination brightened Nate's pale face.

"After we're finished with the big gizmos, we'll do

a couple of blood tests. Ever stick yourself with a pin, kiddo?"

"Yessir. And once, when my dad and me were fishing, I got a fishhook stuck in my thumb." He showed the doctor a tiny crescent-shaped scar.

"Man," Dr. Prentice said. "How'd you ever get the hook out?"

"Dad cut the sharp part off with pliers."

"Wow. Bet you cried buckets."

"I didn't cry at all, did I, Dad."

Max grabbed Nate's hand. "Not a single tear. You were tough as nails."

"I'm impressed," the surgeon said. "And that run-in with the fishhook? I can absolutely guarantee the blood tests won't hurt *nearly* as much! Just a teeny tiny pinprick, one for each test. You think you can handle that?"

Nate lifted his chin. "Sure. No sweat," he said, grinning to prove his bravery.

"Well, we might as well get busy, then. Sooner we get started, sooner you can go home." He stuck his head out into the hall and summoned a tall, lanky orderly. "George, drive my friend Nate here to the X-ray department, will ya?"

"Can…can my dad come, too?"

Hearing the tremor in Nate's voice, Lily grabbed his hand, gave it a gentle squeeze. He squeezed back.

"The more the merrier," Dr. Prentice said. With that, he strode from the cubicle, white lab coat flapping behind him.

"Gotta oil these wheels," George said as the gurney

squeaked down the hall. "Sounds like somebody ridin' over and over a mouse's tail, don't it!"

Nate grinned. "Yeah. A mouse's tail." He giggled softly.

"You'll like Doc Prentice. He's the best."

When Lily let go of Nate so George could steer the gurney into the elevator, Max grabbed her hand. "Thanks," he whispered.

"For what?" she whispered back.

He only shrugged. "Just...thanks." And as his son had done moments before, Max squeezed her hand.

She wanted Max to be happy, the way he was back in high school. Wanted Nate to be safe and healthy, too. Lily stared at the toes of her white sneakers. *Everything's going to be all right,* she said to herself. *The Lord will see to it. He makes miracles happen every day, right?*

But she knew only too well, having lost her mother when she was barely Nate's age, that not every story has a miracle ending. She closed her eyes tight. *If anyone needs to witness a miracle, Lord,* she prayed, *it's Max.*

"I know I neglected to tell Nate about the catheterization earlier, but I honestly didn't think we'd need one. The test results make it necessary." Dr. Prentice leaned against a wall in the small waiting room as Max and Lily sat woodenly on orange and blue upholstered chairs.

"Sounds painful," Max said.

"I won't lie to you...it's not comfortable. But I'll give him a local anesthetic, and a mild sedative, as well. He'll be loose as a goose by the time we do the procedure—probably be asleep through the whole test."

Lily leaned forward. "Will we be able to stay with him the whole time?"

"I don't have a problem with that, long as you don't mind gowning and masking up." The doctor pulled a chair around to face them and sat down. "That kid is a real trouper, all right." A look of genuine admiration crossed his face. "He's seen half a dozen technicians this afternoon alone, who introduced him to some weird-lookin' gizmos. Most kids don't come through it the way Nate did. He's brave, that boy of yours."

Lily bit her lower lip, wondering if now was the time to 'fess up, admit she wasn't Nate's mother. Max slid an arm behind her, as he had in the E.R. cubicle.

"He's truly a gift from God," she said instead.

The words were no sooner out than Max withdrew, sat forward and leaned both elbows on his knees. "How'd this happen?" he asked. "I mean, what caused Nate's fainting spell?"

"Well, I won't know for sure until all the rest of the test results are in," Dr. Prentice said, mimicking Max's pose, "but from everything I've seen so far, it looks to me like he has an atrial septal defect…a hole in his heart."

Max swallowed so hard that Lily heard it from where she sat.

"A hole in his heart? Why hasn't he shown symptoms before now?"

"I wish I had some concrete answers for you, Mr. Sheridan, but the fact is, we don't know for sure. Some kids are born with it. In other cases, a bacterial or viral infection is the cause. The thing to remember is, we can usually repair things, and most kids grow up to live perfectly normal lives."

Max hung his head. "Should I have known? I mean..." He ran both hands through his hair. "If I'd been on the ball, would I have noticed something, and maybe headed this off?"

"Absolutely not. Kids get fevers and colds, and most of the time, the stuff clears up and goes away. Other times, some damage gets done. There's no reason to beat yourself up because there's absolutely no way you could have predicted this."

Dr. Prentice faced Lily. "I must say, Mrs. Sheridan, you're awfully calm and quiet." He smiled. "Now I see where your boy gets his stoicism. Can I answer any questions about your boy?"

"Much as I wish it were true, Nate isn't my boy," she blurted. "I'm just a friend of the family."

"Not *just* a friend," Max put in. "I don't know what we'd have done without you today."

The doctor continued his explanation. "The catheterization isn't as gruesome as it sounds. We'll insert a small plastic tube in through Nate's groin, moving it slowly until it reaches his heart. Then we'll take some blood samples and measure blood pressure through the catheter. We'll inject some blue fluid through the tube into a blood vessel in his heart. The fancy word for the process is *angiocardiography*. But in plain language, it's an X-ray that'll let us see what's wrong with Nate's li'l ticker."

"How long will it take?" Lily asked.

"Oh, an hour, maybe two, usually."

"And how long before we can talk to him?"

"Takes a few hours for the sedative to wear off. He might wake up with a slight fever, an upset stomach, so don't be concerned. That'll all pass in a couple of hours, too. And by that time, I should have the rest of the test results back, and we can talk about treatment."

"Treatment?" Max's voice was thick with emotion.

"Could be we'll find it's not a large enough hole to require anything further. Or, he might just need surgery. But let's not put the cart ahead of the horse, okay?" He grabbed one of Max's wrists with his right hand, one of Lily's with his left. "No sense getting all worried and upset until there's a good reason for it. And I see no reason for it at this juncture."

Max inhaled a deep breath and held it, while Lily rubbed soothing circles on his back. Dr. Prentice got to his feet. "Get some rest," the doctor said. "Hopefully, you won't need it."

But his "just in case" warning was clear, all the same.

He walked backward down the hall, talking as he went. "See you bright and early. I've scheduled the procedure for 8:00 a.m." He saluted, then rounded a corner and disappeared.

Lily and Max sat in stunned silence. "You want to get back to Nate?" she finally asked.

"Yeah," he said, nodding. "Poor kid's probably wondering what's going on." He turned to face her. "You don't have to stay. I know you have a ton of stuff to do, what with your animals and all."

She didn't want to leave him, not for a minute, not even for her beloved animals. And from the look on his face, Max didn't want her to go, either.

Lily rested a hand on his forearm. "Cammi has helped out more times than I can count. She knows what needs to be done."

He rubbed his eyes. "You sure? 'Cause I can hitch a ride with—"

She flipped open her cell phone. "I'll only be a minute."

He stood slowly. "Thanks. You're—"

"—dialing Cammi. Now go," she said, shooing him with her free hand.

Max grabbed her fingertips, pulled her into a one-armed hug. "Aw, Lily, why can't life be simple?" He breathed into her hair. When he stepped back, there were tears in his eyes. He swiped at them, then shook his head. "Go on. Make your call. I'll meet you in Nate's room."

She watched him walk down the hall, head low, hands pocketed. Her heart ached for him…and throbbed with love for him, as well.

Chapter Four

Lily made the call to Cammi as she headed for the hospital chapel. With her sister's promise to "pinch hit" for as long as need be echoing in her ears, she knelt in the front row and recalled the way Max had looked, sitting in front of Dr. Prentice. Someday, maybe she'd understand what had turned him from happy-go-lucky boy into a serious, no-nonsense man.

"Lord," she prayed, "help me know how to comfort Max. Give me the words to reach him, and guide me in knowing when to speak those words." For now, she'd simply be his friend.

Invigorated by her decision, she hurried back to Nate's room. The four-year-old was sleeping peacefully when she peeked in, so Lily tiptoed inside and stood beside Max. "How's he doing?" she whispered.

"Fine," he said softly, "all things considered."

"Any news from the doctor?"

He shook his head.

She looked at Nate. "Natural sleep, or drug-induced?"

Max pointed at the plastic tubing connected to the bag hanging above Nate's bed. "Sedative. Nurse told me he'd be out most of the night."

"Let's go to the cafeteria, then—get you a sandwich and something to wash it down with." She took his hand. "You haven't had a bite all day."

"How do you know that?"

"Well, have you?"

"I had breakfast…."

His usually strong voice sounded forlorn. "Remember what Dr. Prentice said."

"What?"

"He said you needed to rest because you might need it later."

"Oh, that," Max said. "I'm not tired. Besides, he said *we,* not me."

"Anyone would be tired after six hours in a hospital," she said, tugging his arm. "Especially when you've spent most of them pacing."

When he got to his feet, she added, "Dr. Prentice was right, you know. No matter what those tests tell us, Nate is going to need you at one hundred percent."

He glanced at the boy, whose small chest rose and fell with each soft breath. "He still looks so pale."

Sandwiching Max's hands between her own, Lily forced him to meet her eyes. "You have to believe he'll be fine, have faith that everything will turn out all right!"

She watched as his dark, long-lashed eyes bore into

hers. If she didn't know better, Lily would have said it was love beaming back at her. But, of course, it wasn't, she told herself. Gratitude, maybe. Exhaustion, even. But love? Who was she kidding!

His stomach growled just then, making them both grin.

"I hate to say 'I told you so,' but..." She laughed. "Let's get something into you before you have everyone thinking there's a grizzly bear loose in Pediatrics."

A sad smile was his answer. He looked at Nate again. "I don't want to leave him. What if he wakes up?"

She could have hugged him right then. "Okay, I'll go to the cafeteria, bring you a sandwich and a soft drink." Lily headed for the door. "Or would you prefer coffee?"

"Doesn't matter." Then he said, "Thanks, Lily."

"You're beginning to sound like a broken record," she teased. "Really, there's nothing to thank me for. What are friends for, after all!"

He slouched back into the chair beside his sleeping son's bed. "You're way past being a friend. Way past."

How *far* past friend? she wondered as she walked toward the elevator. Dare she hope?

No. Especially not now. Max was worried, confused. It simply wasn't fair to expect him to talk rationally under such stressful circumstances. Wasn't fair to expect him to talk about *anything* but his son. Maybe when all this ended and Nate was home again, safe and sound, *then* she'd hope. Maybe. Meanwhile, she'd support Max in any way possible, do anything for him she could.

How could she help him most right now?

First, by getting some nourishment into him, and when he'd had his fill, she'd suggest a much-needed nap. And while he slept, she'd pray.

The image of Nate, melting to the floor at Georgia's, flashed in her mind. No flu bug had caused his collapse.

Yes, she'd pray, because she had a feeling Max was going to need all the God-given strength he could get these next few days.

Max alternated between pacing the gray-tiled waiting room floor and fidgeting in the itchy upholstered chairs. Lily, on the other hand, sat beside him, calm and quiet, leafing through her Bible.

He found it hard to believe she'd brought the thing along. Did she always carry it with her? Well, he was glad if she found comfort in its gilt-edged pages. Hadn't been so long ago he found solace there himself. No, it had been years ago, before life taught him that consolation—what little the world had to offer—came by dint of his own determination and the sweat of his own brow.

He leaned back in the chair, one leg bent at the knee, the other stretched out in front of him. This waiting would drive him nuts, if Lily hadn't decided to stay with him. He peeked over at her, watched how intently she focused on God's Word. Maybe she'd be spared the hard lessons that had taught him prayer was an exercise in futility.

It hadn't saved his dad, who'd devoted himself to the church and spent every spare moment in prayer, hadn't saved his brother, who'd joined the seminary, intent on becoming a missionary—and died when the Africa-bound plane crashed. Didn't protect Georgia from being widowed at a young age, though she'd devoted her life to the church.

And it hadn't saved his marriage.

Max leaned his head against the wall and closed his eyes. If he believed in prayer, he'd say one now, to silence the memories whispering at the corners of his mind.

Long before she'd started to threaten suicide, and had been under psychiatric care for her depression, Melissa had tested the limits of his patience, spending more than they could afford, disappearing for days on end, then bringing unwholesome types home with her. They had no place else to stay, she'd insist. "We can't call ourselves Christians if we turn our backs on the needy!"

The "needy" kept her too busy to cook or do laundry. If any cleaning got done around the house, it was Max who did it—after a long, hard day at the office. Mostly, he took it on the chin and prayed for patience... until Nate was born. Then he prayed motherhood would change her.

It did not.

His prayer life ended that awful evening when he came home from work and found her, lounging on the family room sofa with her latest needy person...while Nate stood crying in his playpen, soiled diaper hanging loose from his pudgy body and a bent cigarette in his dimpled hand.

Max prayed for forbearance as he cleaned tobacco bits from his son's weeping face and chubby fingers.

Prayed for strength as he tucked the baby into his crib. Prayed for self-control, so he wouldn't do more than boot her latest long-haired friend out of the house.

As he tossed the man's guitar case and duffel bag onto the lawn, Melissa said, "You've embarrassed and humiliated me for the last time, Max Sheridan." She tossed the musician's rumpled T-shirts and tattered jeans into a brown paper bag. "If I can't even choose my own friends, then tell me, what do I have to live for!" Tucking the sack under her arm, she stormed out of the house.

Max flung open the door and followed her onto the porch. "What about Nate?" he'd called after her. "You leaving him, too?"

She had turned halfway down the walk to face him. "Yes, I guess I am."

She'd made him angry before in their five-year marriage, a hundred times, but never like that. "You don't deserve a kid as great as Nate."

"Maybe not, but he's stuck with me, thanks to your insistence that we make a baby!"

White-hot rage burned in him as she climbed into the front seat of her ruddy-faced visitor's pickup. "Maybe you're right, Melissa. Maybe you *don't* have anything to live for." Then he'd slammed the front door so hard that the impact cracked both narrow windows beside it.

Always before, prayer had helped him find the strength to tolerate her erratic behavior—to forgive it, even. Not that night! He hoped that in the morning, he'd find it in himself to forgive her, yet again, for her indiscretions, for neglecting Nate, for disrespecting *him*.

The baby fell asleep in the queen-size bed, sucking

his thumb and cuddled in the crook of his daddy's arm. When the sun woke Max the following morning, he laid Nate in his crib, then padded on black-socked feet to the kitchen to brew a pot of coffee.

He'd decided halfway through his fitful near-sleepless night that first thing in the morning, he'd find a full-time sitter for Nate. Melissa had proven once and for all that she couldn't be trusted to care for him. And while Max waited for the coffee to perk, he'd make a few calls. Plenty of folks at his office enrolled their kids in day care; surely one would have an opening.

But he never made a single phone call, never started that pot of coffee, because the instant he'd set foot on the cool white tiles, he saw Melissa...slumped in a ladder-back chair, long, tangled blond hair splayed across the tabletop. "What're you doin' *this*—"

The next five or ten seconds seemed like hours.

First, he saw the note, crumpled beside her right hand. The pen with which she'd written lay on the floor near the fridge, its cap half hidden under the dishwasher. "You're right," Melissa had scribbled on the back of an overdue bill, "I have nothing to live for. Please don't teach Nate to hate me." She'd underlined *please* three times, and hadn't bothered to sign her name.

The amber-colored pill bottle lay open and empty beside the note, its white cap tucked in her left hand. She was breathing, but just barely, so he'd grabbed the phone and—

"Max."

Someone was shaking his shoulder. A soft voice said, "Max? You're white as a sheet."

He looked into big green eyes. Eyes that shimmered with worried tears. Eyes fringed by thick black lashes. Beautiful eyes. Loving eyes. *Lily's eyes.* For that moment, at least, his upside-down world was right side up again.

Then Max remembered where he was, and why.

His heart thumped and his pulse pounded. If anything happened to that kid…

"Max," Lily repeated, a hand on either side of his face. "You're shaking like a leaf. What's wrong? Talk to me or I'm going to start hollering for a doctor."

She gave his face a gentle shake, much as he'd shaken Melissa that night. The way he'd shaken Nate on the floor of the diner. If anything happened to that kid…

"Shouldn't be hard to find one. We're in a hospital, you know."

He blanketed her hands with his. "Sorry. Didn't mean to scare you." But he knew that he had; fear was written all over her face. All over her pretty, loving face.

She knelt on the floor in front of his chair and grabbed his wrists. "What on earth were you thinking about just now? You were a million miles away. Why, if I believed in ghosts, I'd say you saw one just now!"

He had, in a way…but Max couldn't tell Lily that, now, could he? At least, not without admitting he believed he felt partly responsible for Melissa's suicide. He'd never said as much, not to anyone, and sure couldn't confess the awful truth to Lily! Not here. Not now, with Nate going through who knows what in the O.R.

"I'm told I'm a pretty good listener," she said, smiling softly.

He'd known since she was a knobby-kneed sixth grader and he was a junior at Centennial High that Lily London had a crush on him. But because they were separated by six years—an important six years—Max never allowed her to face it. Hadn't faced it himself... until today.

He kept telling himself that someday, she'd grow up, find a man who'd love her as she deserved to be loved. Then Max would become a dim memory and she'd wonder why she'd wasted so many years dogging his heels, waiting, hoping.

She'd grown up, all right. But she hadn't found her Mr. Right. Because she was still waiting, and hoping? "Your heart is as big as your head," he said, chucking her chin.

Lily laughed. "My, but you do know how to turn a girl's head, don't you?"

He tucked a dark curl behind her ear. He'd always wondered what her hair might feel like. It was shinier than his mother's favorite satin bathrobe. He imagined it would be softer than the mink stole his grandma wore. And he'd been right. His fingers seemed to have a mind of their own as they combed through her luxurious waves.

Long, lush lashes dusted her cheeks as she pressed a light kiss to the heel of his hand. "Don't worry, Max. You're going to be all right," she whispered. "And so is Nate."

He drew her closer, his thumbs tracing slow circles on the smooth contour of her jaw. "You're sure of that, are you?"

When she nodded, a curl fell across one eye. At that

moment, she didn't look anything like the freckle-faced girl she'd been. Lily was a full-grown woman, and the six years between them didn't mean diddly anymore.

"Yeah," she sighed. "I'm sure."

His forefinger drew the outline of her full, pink lips. Lips that had spoken kind, comforting words. Lips that had smiled reassuringly. Sweet lips…

Max stood, pulled her to her feet and kissed her.

She returned it, he couldn't help but notice. Wrapped her arms around him and held on as if finally, at long last, she had what she'd waited her lifetime for. If only he could tell her it's what *he'd* wanted, too.

Guilt surged through him at the admission. He'd married Melissa because he couldn't have Lily. She'd been too young, he'd been too impatient. Too impatient to wait until she was old enough.

So he'd leaped into a full-blown relationship.

With the wrong woman.

For all the wrong reasons.

Melissa was dead now, in part because he hadn't been the husband he should have been. Oh, he'd tried to love her, had tried to build a life with her, raise a family. But the ugly truth was, he'd done it all…to forget Lily.

Marrying Melissa had been a mistake. A terrible, tragic mistake. One he'd regret—and pay for—the rest of his days.

His son lay unconscious in the next room, with a hole in his little heart. Would the surgeon be able to repair it? Or would Nate continue to weaken?

Lily snuggled closer still, blurring the lines where she ended and he began. He ended the comforting kiss but didn't let her go. Couldn't let her go...not just yet. She felt good in his arms, so good, pressed close to his heart. It felt right, holding her, kissing her, and yet...

So much time had passed since he'd left for Chicago, yet nothing had changed.

He still yearned for Lily, and she still deserved better than the likes of him.

"Nate will be fine," she said again, leaning her cheek against his chest. "You'll see."

She'd misread his mood, he realized. Big-hearted, see-the-good-in-everyone Lily had convinced herself that the entire cause of his misery was concern for his son. Well, there was more to it! It was also about believing Lily would never be part of his life.

Max kissed the top of her head and heaved a sad sigh. "I hope so." *Hard to believe a man could mess up his life as badly as you have in just thirty years.*

"And *you'll* be all right, too."

Maybe. But he sure didn't deserve to be all right. Physically healthy, yes, because Nate needed him, more now than ever. But emotionally? Nah. He didn't deserve that, not one whit.

"Thirsty?" she asked.

He wasn't, but nodded anyway.

"You stay here, in case Dr. Prentice comes out to talk to you about Nate. I'll find a vending machine, get us something cold to drink."

He nodded again. My, but she was beautiful, especially looking up at him that way, her enormous green eyes brimming and shimmering with full-out affection. She looked at Nate that way, too—proof she'd be a loving, devoted mother. If only…

No point torturing yourself, he thought. Dreams like that were for schoolgirls, not grown men who'd botched up their lives.

"Back in a jiff," Lily said, popping a tiny kiss to his chin. "Don't pace a path in the floor while I'm gone, okay?" she called over her shoulder.

He smiled despite himself. *And don't you be gone too long,* he thought. Because if Dr. Prentice came through the O.R. doors and the news wasn't good, well, Max knew he couldn't face it without her standing beside him. He didn't want to face anything, not even *good* news, without her beside him!

Max watched her walk down the hall. When she disappeared around the corner, he flopped onto a tweedy-seated waiting room chair and knuckled his eyes. "Shouldn't have kissed her, Sheridan. Should've kept your big dumb lips to yourself."

Because now that he knew it was everything he'd dreamed it would be, he was a goner. Her helpful nature, her nurturing tendencies, her adorable gestures—they'd all plucked a chord in him that he hadn't even known existed, putting music and harmony and balance into his dreary, lonely life. But that kiss…

She deserved better, and if only she'd give herself half a chance, Lily could find happiness with another man.

Another man? The mere thought made his heart ache, made his stomach lurch, made his ears hot. The picture of her, smiling that *smile* of hers for some other guy, kissing some other guy the way she'd just kissed him…

Max drove his fingers through his hair. Why was the stupid procedure Dr. Prentice was giving Nate taking so *long?*

On his feet again, he walked the length of the hall and back again. All right, so Lily would marry someday, have a couple of kids, live the rest of her days fulfilled and satisfied and, yes, happy. And he'd make himself be happy *for* her.

Because, to put it simply, she deserved it…and he didn't.

"What we're going to have to do," Dr. Prentice said, tugging off his surgical mask, "is called a keyhole bypass." He sat across from Max and leaned his elbows on his knees. "I've done dozens of 'em, and it's usually the last step in cases like Nate's. Minimally invasive— doesn't require me to crack the sternum."

Max nodded while Lily patted his hand. If only she could do something to fix everything wrong in his life! That power, she knew, was God's and God's alone, and she prayed that when this was over, Max's faith in the Almighty would be back, and stronger than ever.

Dr. Prentice, meanwhile, grabbed one of the paper napkins she'd brought back from the cafeteria. Clicking his ballpoint pen, he began drawing a diagram of the human heart.

"See, Nate has a hole, here, in the top chamber of his heart, called a secundum atrial septal defect. Fortunately, there's an adequate rim around the hole to allow us to implant a device to close it."

Prentice scribbled, while Lily watched Max trying to take it all in.

"My team and I are gonna close that hole up," the doctor continued, "using an Amplatzer occlusion device. Basically, it's nothing but a wire mesh disk that's about the size of a dime."

"How long will it last?" Max asked.

"It's made of nickel and titanium, and filled with polyester fabric, so I'd have to say forever. In a few months, it'll be completely covered by heart tissue, which means it'll be a permanent part of Nate's heart wall."

Max put the drawing down and hung his head.

"Sounds scarier than it is," Dr. Prentice said.

"So, how does it work, exactly?"

"We'll insert it into a catheter that we'll run through the femoral vein in Nate's groin to his heart. When the disk comes out the other end, it'll deploy—open up kind of like a tiny umbrella against the inner and outer walls of the heart, directly over the hole."

"Sounds dangerous," Max said, staring at the drawing. "What are the risks?"

Dr. Prentice shrugged one shoulder. "The whole process is far less formidable than open-heart surgery. But it's surgery, nonetheless, which means there's a small chance of bleeding, infection, perforation of the heart, device embolization—"

"Embolization?" Max picked up the napkin, turned it this way and that.

"An obstruction, like with a blood clot. But that's rare, very rare. Once we get the thing in place, we'll watch for leaks, and—"

"Leaks?" Max's head snapped up.

"Again," Dr. Prentice stressed, hands up to forestall Max's fears, "that's the exception rather than the rule. Couple months back, I performed the procedure on a little girl with a condition similar to Nate's. Took less than two hours, and she was sitting up in bed, playing with her little brothers soon after the anesthesia wore off—and home again the next morning."

Relief softened Max's features. "How's she doing now?"

Prentice winked. "According to her mom, she's running the pants off her brothers."

"Will he be in much pain?"

"For the first few days he might experience some slight discomfort, but that'll pass quickly."

"Will he be able to feel it?" Max winced. "I mean, when he moves around, will it—"

"Not one of my patients has indicated they're aware of its presence at all."

"So he'll be a normal, active kid again afterward?"

The doctor laughed. "I didn't have a chance to spend much time with Nate, but it didn't take long to figure out he's the kind of kid who isn't gonna let anything slow him down much." He stood, patted Max's shoulder, then headed back to the O.R. "He'll be fishing and swimming and chasing down pop-flies in no time. Don't worry," he said over his shoulder.

"Easy for you to say," Max muttered as the doctor left. "Nate's not your son."

Lily stood beside him, leaned her head on his shoulder. "Easy, now. He'll take good care of Nate. The nurses say he's the best in Texas, and I say he's a good man."

He brought her into the circle of his arms. "I understand how his reputation as a surgeon precedes him, but you just met him. How could you possibly know what kind of man he is?"

"I looked into his eyes," she said, blinking up at him. "And you know the old saying…"

One side of Max's mouth lifted in a wry grin. "Well, if he slips up, even a little—" he shook his fist "—I'm gonna shatter both of those windows to his soul."

Lily giggled and wrapped her hands around his fist. "C'mon, tough guy. Let's go see your kid."

The next days passed in a flurry, with Lily staying at Georgia's apartment with Nate while Max waited outside the O.R. during Georgia's leg surgery. Lily fully expected that once his son and mother were home again, Max would relax.

But he didn't.

After interviewing a dozen nurses, he hired a pleasant, middle-aged woman to look after Georgia and Nate while he worked in the diner. And he worked from dawn 'til dark, filling in wherever he saw the need—bussing tables, washing dishes, mopping floors. When he wasn't busy with patrons and staff, he pored over the ledger books in the cramped, cluttered office space behind the kitchen.

If she didn't know better, Lily would have said he was intentionally avoiding any contact with people—herself in particular. Because every time she'd called to ask how his mom and little boy were progressing, he'd answered with one-word replies. The first few times, she blamed his tone on stress, but by the sixth or seventh call, Lily felt she had no choice but to assume Max didn't want to talk to her.

His attitude answered her *unasked* questions, too, things she'd been asking herself ever since that wonderful moment when Max had tenderly held her close: What had his breathtaking kiss *meant?* Was it proof he cared for her, too? Dare she hope their relationship could begin to shift, gradually, from friendship to…more? Or had it been simply the result of Max's mounting worries about his little boy's condition. Had she mistaken his reaching out to her for comfort and reassurance for blossoming love?

Lily decided she wouldn't make a fool of herself, not even for Max Sheridan, not even if she'd loved him since junior high. She'd always been close to Georgia, and almost from the instant he burst into the diner, Lily had adored little Nate. Max's chilly conduct couldn't change that. So she'd call when he was working in the diner, ask the nurse to put Georgia on the phone, find out what she needed to know about Georgia and Nate without the grumpy, distant middleman!

She'd done well with her new "be cool" attitude, balancing the ranch checkbook and caring for her winged and furred charges with visits to Georgia and Nate, real well. Until the church social.

How Georgia managed to get Max to attend was anybody's guess. But there he stood in the food line, filling a plate for Georgia, another for Nate. She knew neither plate was his; Max had never liked chicken wings, and a healthy portion of the golden-fried stuff lay on the foam dish. Blue jeans clung to his muscular thighs, and he'd rolled back the cuffs of his white shirt, exposing brawny, slightly hairy forearms. He'd gotten a haircut; she knew because when he'd kissed her outside the O.R. that day, her fingers had played in the dark waves caressing the back of his neck….

Stop it! Lily scolded herself. Remembering that moment, and how it left her weak-kneed and dizzy, accomplished nothing. Well, that wasn't exactly true—memories of that sweet slice of time made her yearn for him all the more, because she'd so wanted to believe it meant as much to him as it had meant to her.

"Hey, Snow White!" Georgia hollered from across the room.

Smiling, Lily crossed the green-tiled floor of the church basement and grabbed a chair. "Nice to see you're getting around without that wheeled contraption of yours," she said, kissing the redhead's cheek.

"Couple more weeks of physical therapy," she said, thumping the rubber-tipped end of her cane on the floor, "and I'll be rid of this, too!"

"I imagine you're chompin' at the bit to get back to work."

"Are you kidding? I've loved every minute away from that greasy spoon of mine." She looked around, waved Lily closer. "I'll let you in on a little secret, if you promise to keep it to yourself."

Nodding, Lily pulled an imaginary zipper shut across her mouth. "Mmmm's the wrrrd," she said through tight lips.

One last scan of the room told Georgia no one else could hear. "Robert asked me to marry him," she whispered.

Lily's eyes widened as she leaned back and gasped. "That's wonderful news! Why do you want to keep it a secret?"

"He hasn't told his kids yet, and I haven't had a chance to tell Max and Nate, either."

Lily frowned. "You don't look very happy about it. Don't tell me you said no."

Georgia made an are-you-kidding face and said, "Don't be ridiculous! He's a wonderful, loving man. I'd be crazy to let him slip through my fingers."

"Then, why the long face?"

"I have another bit of news, and I'm not too sure Max is gonna like it."

Lily giggled nervously. "You're not pregnant, are you?"

Georgia laughed. "'Course not, you silly nut!" When the moment passed, she said, "I'm going to retire. Permanently. Robert, too. We're going to take a world cruise for our honeymoon."

"Why would Max object to that? You've worked hard in that diner all your life."

"Because I want to hand the deed to that diner over

to him. It's been in the family for generations. I don't want it going to strangers."

Lily thought about that. He'd pulled hundreds of shifts in the diner as a boy, and although she'd never heard him complain, exactly, if his expression and body language were any indicator, he hadn't liked the work one bit.

And he'd spent the past six years in the big city, no doubt working at a big fancy desk in an air-conditioned, mahogany-paneled office. Probably lived in a ritzy Chicago suburb, too, in a too-big-for-him house on a street with other snooty accountants.

"What scheme are you two cooking up?"

Lily lurched and Georgia gasped.

"Oh!" Georgia exclaimed. "You just shaved ten years off my life, sneaking up on us that way!"

Max chuckled. "I didn't sneak. It's just that you two were so deep in discussion, you didn't hear me." He raised an eyebrow. "So, what gives?"

"None of your beeswax, boy," Georgia said, chin in the air. "Honestly, how old does a mother have to be to get a little privacy?" She sniffed.

Max held up his hands in mock surrender. "*Excuse* me for interrupting. I only came over to deliver your plate." He put the dish on the table, then handed her a paper napkin and plastic utensils.

"Kids," she said to Lily, "never get too old to lay a guilt trip on you." Rolling her eyes, she sighed. "Sorry for snapping your head off, son."

"Yeah," he said, laughing, "*that* sounded sincere!"

"Where's Nate?" she asked, changing the subject.

He pointed. "Over there, with the pastor's kids. He's lovin' it here."

Georgia nodded. "It's good to see him so happy."

"And healthy," Lily put in.

He looked at her then, as if seeing her for the first time. "Right," he agreed, smiling sheepishly. Pocketing both hands, he said, "So, how have you been?"

"Fine." She squirmed on her chair. "You?"

Max nodded, lips pressed tightly together. "Fine. Fine."

"You look a little tired," she admitted, "here, around the eyes."

He ran a hand through his hair. "Nah. It's eyestrain. I've been getting Mom's books in order." Max shot Georgia a feigned stern glance. "It's been a while since she balanced the checkbook."

"Honestly," she huffed, "do you have to air *all* my bad habits?"

The three of them grinned nervously for a moment before Max broke the silence. "Lemonade, ladies?"

"None for me, thanks," Lily said, standing. She didn't know how much longer she could remain this close to him without crying. Because, like it or not, she loved him still; admitting he didn't feel the same way—and never would—hurt. Cut deep. Time healed all wounds, as the sages promised, but Lily had a feeling she needed distance every bit as much as she needed time. She headed for the card table that held bottles of soda, lemonade and iced tea. "Take it easy, Georgia," she said, waving.

"Wait," Max said, grabbing her elbow when he caught up with her. "What's your hurry?"

Lily lifted her chin a notch. "I'm not in a hurry. I just saw—" she picked someone out of the crowd at random "—Cammi over there. I forgot to ask her something earlier."

"Really?" he said, a suspicious smile on his face. "What?"

Pursing her lips, she said, "Something to do with the wedding. Girl stuff." He hadn't let go of her elbow, she noticed; the warmth of his big hand spread all the way to her fingertips. He stood so close she could inhale the crisp manly scent of his aftershave. She missed him desperately, though they'd never been anything but friends. But that didn't stop her from wanting more, from dreaming and praying for more. Knowing she'd never have it was enough to break her heart.

Lord, she prayed, *save me or I'll fall apart right here in front of him!*

Lily tugged free of his grasp and hurried to where Cammi stood, arm in arm with her fiancé.

"Hey, kiddo," Reid said when she walked up. "What's wrong?"

"Nothing," she snapped. "What makes you ask a question like that?"

"Oh, I don't know," her future brother-in-law replied. "Maybe that 'I just lost my best friend' look on your face?"

She'd never been a crybaby, had never been one to give in to tears. For a reason she couldn't explain, Lily felt a sob aching in her throat. It wasn't likely she'd actually *cry,* but just in case, before the dam burst, she ran to the ladies' room.

"What did I say?" she heard Reid ask Cammi.

"I'll find out what's wrong," her sister said as the door swung shut.

Lily locked herself in a stall and pressed her forehead to the cool, pink-metal wall. What was *wrong* with her? She'd had years to get used to the idea that Max would never be part of her future. Nothing had changed, so why the tears?

"Lily? Are you okay in there?"

She nodded, and then, realizing Cammi couldn't see it, said, "Yeah. I'm okay."

"You want to talk about it?"

She shook her head. "No. Not really."

"It's about Max, isn't it. I saw you two talking earlier. You want me to sic Reid on him? He can fix it so the lout wears black eyes and a swollen lip for weeks."

Lily snickered. "Thanks, but I'd hate for Reid's fingers to be too swollen next week to wear his wedding band." She opened the stall door and stepped into the comforting circle of her sister's open arms. "Oh, Cammi," she sighed, biting back tears. "What's wrong with me?"

Cammi held her at arm's length. "Not a thing. It's *Max* who has the problem."

She wrinkled her forehead. "Max? But—"

"He could have the sweetest, prettiest girl in Texas for his own, if he'd just open up his eyes and see what's right in front of his face."

"His very handsome face," Lily said, grinning.

"Okay, so he's cute. I'll give him that much." Cammi walked to the sink, jerked a brown paper towel from the dispenser. "But he isn't as smart as I thought he was." She dampened the towel, then pressed it to Lily's cheeks. "He's got some silly notion that life is a ledger book where everything is black and white."

She took the towel, dried her eyes with a corner of it. "I don't get it."

"You don't fit nice and neat in a column, and until he can find a way to make things between you add up…"

Lily gave a deep sigh. "You're giving me a headache," she teased. "You know I never was any good at math."

Cammi laughed and draped an arm over her sister's shoulder. "Yeah, right. The gal who has kept dad's ranch running for a decade, all by herself, isn't good at math."

"That's different. It's—"

"Black and white. I know." She opened the door and led Lily back into the church hall. "Look around you, kiddo," she said, a bent forefinger guiding Lily's chin. "There are other fish in the sea, as they say." She kissed her sister's cheek. "Your problem is, you have an aversion to worms. Can't bait the ol' hook if—"

Lily laughed. "I feel that headache coming on again."

"Well, if you're okay, I'm going to get a slice of peach pie for Reid, before it's all gone. It's his favorite, you know."

Nodding, Lily winked. "I'm fine. Go 'do' for your man." She gave her a playful shove. She had no idea what kind of pie Max preferred, or whether he preferred it to cake, or how he voted in the last election, or if he liked classical music. She didn't know his favorite color, or if he wore glasses to watch TV. She knew he liked fishing, but only because she'd overheard Nate telling Dr. Prentice about the fishhook in his thumb.

So what are you blubbering about? Lily asked herself. It seemed ridiculous, getting all teary-eyed and heartbroken over a guy she knew so little about, a guy who barely had given her the time of day. The concept brightened her mood.

Until she saw him, laughing at something Reid had said. She might not know if peach was his favorite pie, but she knew this:

She loved him. Always had.

And always would.

Chapter Five

Lily sat at the head table, pretending to enjoy the filet mignon and caramelized potatoes on the gold-rimmed china dinner plate in front of her. Lamont had gone all out, a string quartet playing "The Wedding March" in the church balcony, biggest banquet hall in the hotel, Amarillo's best chef. Everything looked wonderful, right down to the fluted vases where colorful Japanese fighting fish swam in the center of each table. The bride looked like a fantasy princess in her designer gown and veil, and the groom, her storybook prince.

If happiness could be measured by looks alone, the newly married Mr. and Mrs. Reid Alexander would live in bliss from this day forth. Lily knew the union would be rock solid, forever, and not because of gauzy veils, satin-lapeled tuxedos and thousands of white roses. Cammi and her new husband had been the perfect love match, from the moment they crashed into one another outside of Georgia's Diner. Why perfect? For starters, both loved the Lord with all their hearts.

Lily wanted a love like that—a marriage like her sister's would surely be. She sighed and sipped ice water from a crystal goblet. Fat chance of that happening if she couldn't get over this thing for Max Sheridan. She'd been compiling a "Reasons It Won't Work Out" list, and at the very top, wrote, "'Yoke ye not to unbelievers….'"

Had Cammi deliberately seated Max so that he faced the head table? Or had it been a ridiculous coincidence? She tried not to look at him, at his dark, shiny curls—her image of male perfection in his tidy gray suit and blood-red tie, smiling as he cut his son's steak into bite-size pieces. He loved that kid more than anything in his life, and it showed. Didn't he realize Nate had been God's greatest gift to him? That alone should give him more than enough reason to believe!

The photographer dashed past, blocking her view of the Sheridan table. She watched the balding, potbellied fellow hurry from table to table, leaning and crouching and kneeling, cameras clicking as he captured guests laughing, dancing, waving and shouting to friends across the banquet hall. The waitstaff bustled in and out, delivering coffee, hustling dirty dishes into the kitchen. The maître d' pointed the way to the rest rooms as the band-leader announced the title of the next song.

Controlled chaos, Lily thought, grinning wryly. The scene reminded her of a wedding she'd attended last summer. Cammi had scowled at the groom's drunken uncle. "When *I* get married," she'd steamed, "there had better not be anything like that frozen on film in *my* wedding album!"

The photographer snapped Lily's picture just then,

startling her so badly that she actually said "Eek!" Who said that, she wondered, besides cartoon mice! She blinked past the blue dots floating before her eyes, feeling suddenly self-conscious. Hopefully, when that picture was developed, it wouldn't upset Cammi.

Lily wasn't accustomed to wearing her hair this way. Every time she'd tried an updo, unruly wisps escaped, no matter how carefully she secured them. Squinting into the bowl of a sterling soupspoon, she tucked in a wayward curl and checked her lipstick. *Well, you won't win any beauty contests,* she thought, putting the spoon beside her plate, *but hopefully, you won't make anyone lose their lunch, either.* Smiling at her little joke, Lily glanced up…directly into Max's smiling brown eyes.

He'd caught her primping! And his teasing, all-knowing expression told her he'd lumped her in with every other prissy, vain female he'd ever met. Lily groaned inwardly. She'd been watching him from the corner of her eye all during the meal. Why had he picked *that* moment to look up! If only he would take the time to get to know her, he'd realize that fussing with her hair and makeup had never been high on her priority list.

Forcing a grin, Lily returned Max's snappy little salute and turned to the groomsman seated beside her. "Would you mind passing the salt, please?" she said, though nothing on her plate needed salting. Really, what did it matter *what* Max Sheridan thought of her, she fumed, absently thanking the tuxedoed gent when he handed her the shaker. It wasn't as though Max's opinion of her would enhance their relationship, such as it was.

She forced herself to focus on the conversation at the opposite end of the head table: "We've had such unseasonably icy weather for November," said a bridesmaid. "Plays right into my plans to go skiing over the Thanksgiving holiday," said another. "Do you have a bandage?" the skier asked. "These newly dyed shoes gave me a blister the size of my nose!" Better to listen to the chitchat than admit that there *was* no relationship between her and Max…and that there likely never would be.

It took all the willpower she could muster to avoid looking toward his table. She knew he was watching her; it seemed his big dark eyes were boring holes into the side of her head. But why would he watch *her,* when at least a dozen eligible bachelorettes had come to the wedding, sans beaus?

"May I have this dance?"

Lily looked into the grizzled face of Hank Gardner, one of her brother-in-law's ranch hands. It was no secret the man was sweet on her; he'd made sure she knew, every chance he got.

"Oh, go on," Cammi insisted, giving Lily's shoulder a gentle nudge. She leaned in close to whisper, "Guess who is watching. Give him an eyeful!"

The sound of butter knives clinking against water goblets interrupted the sisters' secret conversation. "Ah," Cammi sighed, feigning boredom, "a woman's work is never done." Then she faced her new husband and gave her guests exactly what they'd asked for.

Hank pulled out Lily's chair. "C'mon, Lil," he said, grinning good-naturedly, "song's half over already!"

Lily let him lead her to the dance floor, where the band was playing an old Patti Page ballad.

"You look gorgeous," he said, taking her in his arms. "Don't tell anybody, but I think you're prettier than the bride."

"When was the last time you had your eyes checked?" she teased. Leaning back slightly, she wiggled the knot of his silk tie. "I must say, you clean up real good yourself!"

Hank blushed. "Had to borrow it from Reid. Must be eatin' too many biscuits with supper, 'cause the shirt collar's a mite snug." He looked into her eyes as the female singer crooned.

"Nice song," he said.

"Very nice." Lily had hummed it dozens of times when trying to soothe an injured animal. "It's one of my favorites—"

"May I cut in?"

Hank's brows knitted in the center of his forehead. "I reckon." But it was obvious to anyone within earshot that he wasn't any too happy to hand over his dance partner. The cowboy stepped away but held tightly to Lily's hand. "Be gentle with her, bud," he told Max, "'cause this purty li'l gal is a genuine blue-ribbon prize."

Nodding, Max stepped into Hank's place. "He's right, you know," he said once the cowboy had walked away.

How would you know? she wondered. Max didn't know her well enough to testify to that.

"You're the most beautiful woman in the room, bar none."

Lily felt her face go hot. Heart hammering, she wanted to protest, because in the first place, Cammi was the bride, and in the second...

She was quoting him, Lily realized, with her "first" this and "second" that. Absurd, especially considering how little time she'd spent with him. "You look nice, too." But the compliment paled against the truth. Max truly *was* the best-looking guy in the room.

She couldn't seem to get her mind off the warmth of his hand, pressed gently against her lower back as he guided her across the parquet tiles. That, and the way the fingers of his other hand linked almost possessively with hers.

"Nate looks adorable," she said, mostly to distract herself. "How's he doing?"

"Pretty well, all things considered." He paused, touched her chin with a bent forefinger. "I've never seen you with your hair up before. Looks gorgeous. Very sophisticated."

She grinned self-consciously. "You've seen it up, plenty of times. Ponytails, braids—remember?"

He pulled her a little closer, ran a fingertip down the bridge of her nose. *"This,"* Max whispered, his nose a mere fraction of an inch from hers, "is not the girl I remember at all. *This,*" he said, bringing her closer still, "is all woman."

Lily licked her lips and swallowed. If she didn't know better, she'd say Max was gearing up to kiss her—right here in the middle of the crowded dance floor, with her father and sisters and the pastor watching.

"Don't worry," he said on a chuckle. "You're safe. There's a time and a place for everything."

How could he have known what she'd been thinking? Nothing was making sense, especially considering the way he'd snubbed her these past weeks. What kind of head game was he playing? she asked herself. She ought to walk away, leave him standing there alone.

The song ended, and she admitted she'd never have done anything of the kind. He brushed her cheek with a gentle kiss. "Thanks for the dance," he whispered into her ear. "It was a real treat."

She grinned as he headed back to his table.

Strange how, throughout the remainder of the reception, Max managed to find her, no matter what maid of honor duties she was performing. He was there when the best man gave a long-winded toast to the bride and groom. During the father-daughter dance, he surprised her by sliding an arm around her waist. He stood shoulder to shoulder with her, watching as Cammi and Reid cut the wedding cake. And when she joined the unmarried females to compete for the bridal bouquet, Max caught her eye from the other side of the dance floor.

She'd only stepped into line to be a good sport… and because the photographer literally dragged her there. Lily had no intention of reaching up, of actually trying to catch the flowers. It was a silly superstition, a fun tradition, nothing more.

Was she seeing things, or had Max mouthed *Good luck!* from his side of the floor? Lily never had time to answer, because on the bandleader's count of three, she reached up without even thinking…and caught the bouquet in one hand.

When her gaze met Max's, he winked, gave her two thumbs up. It would be interesting to see the wedding album a week or two from now. Would the photograph of her catching the bouquet show a starry-eyed young woman in love…or the look of stunned disbelief she truly felt?

No time to answer that question, either, for it was time to help the bride change into her going-away outfit. Lily had packed her sister's suitcase, making sure to include the lovely white nightgown a neighbor had given Cammi at the bridal shower.

How long before her dad and their longtime neighbor Nadine would announce *their* plans to wed? Lily wondered as she unfastened dozens of tiny satin-covered buttons on the back of Cammi's dress. Had she been the only one who'd noticed the way they'd sat all through the reception, staring lovingly into one another's eyes?

She considered the question as the dwindling number of wedding guests gathered in the lobby of Amarillo's Grand Hotel to say goodbye to Cammi and Reid. First thing in the morning, the couple would board a Florida-bound jetliner that would take them to Miami, and from there, they'd cruise the Caribbean. While the band packed up and the last well-wishers finished up the remaining hors d'oeuvres and pastries, Lily began loading beautifully wrapped presents onto a wheeled cart.

A commotion in the lobby captured her attention. Lily ran toward the hotel's main entrance and stood on tiptoe to see what all the ruckus was about. When she spotted Max on all fours beside his unconscious son, Lily elbowed through the crowd and knelt beside him.

"What happened?"

"Dunno," he muttered. "He just…collapsed."

She put a hand on his shoulder. "Where's your cell phone?"

Hands trembling, he gave it to her. She flipped it open. "Is Dr. Prentice's number programmed into this thing?"

"No. Uh, I think so. Yeah, under *P.*"

When the phone's highlighter bar illuminated the doctor's name, she pressed "Send" and got to her feet. "Don't you worry, Max," she said, grabbing her car keys from the tiny purse that matched her gown. "Meet me out front." She held up two fingers. "Two minutes. I'll call ahead to the E.R., tell them to expect us."

Bolting across the parking lot, Lily thanked God that the hospital was only a few blocks from the hotel. "Lord," she said, revving the motor, "get us there fast, and watch over little Nate in the meantime."

She pictured the boy's face…so much paler than when he'd fainted in his grandmother's diner weeks ago. Something was wrong, terribly wrong. Had the patch Dr. Prentice placed over the hole in Nate's heart come loose? The surgeon had said it could happen. Extremely unlikely, but possible.

She parked beside the curb, ran around to the passenger's side and flung open the door. Max held Nate close as he climbed into the bucket seat.

And hadn't Dr. Prentice said Nate could bleed to

death if that should happen? Lily tried to look confident and smiled bravely as she clicked the seat belt into place across them.

"We really have to stop meeting this way," he said as she slid behind the steering wheel.

Despite his half grin, she could see that Max was terrified, far more afraid this time than he'd been when they made their last trip to the E.R.

No surprise, Lily thought, because Max had heard Dr. Prentice's warning, too.

"Sorry, Mr. Sheridan, but you're not a compatible donor."

Max looked grim as the doctor added, "It's fairly common—a parent having a different blood type than his child."

"Spare me the lesson in hematology, Doc. Just tell me what you're gonna do to save my son."

Dr. Prentice took a deep breath, as if summoning patience. "We're searching the blood bank now. Hard to find AB negative, and that multi-car pileup on the Interstate cost us our last unit of O positive. We've put the word out that we need donations. Might take a couple hours."

"He could *bleed* to death in a couple hours!" Max shouted. Hands fisted beside him, he said, "Where's the nearest supply? I'll drive there myself and get it, bring it back here!"

"Max," Lily said, laying a hand on his forearm, "I'm O positive. I'll give Nate whatever he needs."

He looked at her, blinking as if she'd spoken in a foreign language. "You…you'd do that?"

How could he even ask such a question! "Of course I will." She faced Prentice. "What's the procedure? You have to draw some blood, test it—then what?"

The doctor patted her biceps and then headed down the hall. "Right this way," he said, ushering her into an E.R. cubicle. "I'll have a nurse get you started."

Lily was about to follow the surgeon when Max grabbed her hand. "I…I don't know how to thank you."

"Have faith, Max—faith that everything is going to be all right," she said, meaning it. "That'll be thanks enough for me."

Max was young when his father died—barely sixteen.

His dad had taught him how to parallel park, safely merge and change lanes on the Baltimore Beltway, but didn't live to see his son get his driver's license.

He'd taught Max how to catch a pop-up fly ball, how to keep score during a football game, how to bait a fishing hook. But there'd been countless other lessons he'd learned at his father's knee, too. To defend himself against the schoolyard bully…without becoming one himself. To behave like a gentleman, even if the girl he was with hadn't earned it. To do his level best, no matter how menial or trivial the task.

And the most important lesson of all—to stand up to the responsibilities and obligations that went hand in hand with being a man.

He wanted to teach Nate those lessons, wanted to show his boy, by example, as his father had taught him, the fruits of hard work and determination.

Would he get that chance?

Or would *God,* in His so-called infinite wisdom, decide to take Nate, as He'd taken Max's father, his brother, and in a roundabout way, Melissa.

Icy fear pricked at his soul, chilled him to the bone. Max shivered unconsciously. The very thought of losing Nate made his heart beat like a parade drum, made his pulse pound like a jackhammer.

He'd gladly gone to work every day, built a house in a safe Chicago suburb, where his kid could attend the best schools the state could offer. To accomplish all that, he'd had to give up his reckless bachelor ways—no more sky-diving, no more river rafting. It hadn't been a sacrifice. Quite the opposite! Max quickly adapted to fatherhood, and happily looked forward to every moment with his sweet-tempered little boy.

They'd developed quite a bond, Max and his boy.

To lose that now, to lose it *ever...*

Hands linked behind his back, Max paced the hall-way outside Nate's E.R. cubicle. *Pull yourself together, Sheridan. You're useless to him this way.* Knuckling his eyes, he took a deep breath, then pushed through the curtains. "Hey, bud," he said, feigning bravery as he kissed his son's forehead. "How you feelin'?"

Nate's sleepy eyes fluttered open. "Better," he rasped, one side of his mouth lifting in a weak grin.

He hated seeing his boy this way—connected to machines and tubes and bags of glucose and medication.

If he could lie there in Nate's place, he'd do it in a minute. Had there ever been a time when he'd been this afraid? If there had, Max couldn't remember it.

"In no time at all, you'll be better still." Thanks in no small part to Lily, he admitted.

The boy's lower lip trembled slightly. "I'm scared, Dad."

Max eased his arms under the boy's upper body, hugged him gingerly. "I know, pal, I know." He kissed Nate's temple. "But you're gonna be okay."

"Why does it hurt so bad, Dad?"

Slowly, he released Nate back onto the pillow. "I don't know," he said. "That's what Dr. Prentice wants to find out." He ruffled his son's hair. "Any minute now, he'll take you to the operating room, and before you know it—"

"Will you be in there with me?"

"No, that wouldn't be safe." He winked. "Germs, y'know." He took Nate's hand in his, stroked each small, dimpled finger. "I'll be right outside, I promise."

Dr. Prentice burst into the cubicle and announced, "We'll get that patch put back on your li'l ol' heart in no time, kiddo." He pinched Nate's big toe, then added, "Can I borrow your dad for a minute?"

When the boy nodded, the doctor waved Max outside. He took several steps away from Nate's bed before saying, "Your girlfriend is a champ."

Girlfriend. The word echoed in Max's head for a second.

"She's already given a pint of blood, and insisted on staying in there—" he threw a thumb over his shoulder to indicate the room down the hall "—until we're sure Nate's out of the woods."

Max's heart thumped with gratitude…and more. "'Champ' doesn't even begin to describe her." Then he added, "She'll be okay, won't she? I mean, she's barely bigger than a minute herself."

Dr. Prentice dropped a hand on Max's shoulder. "Relax. She's petite but strong as an ox." He headed toward the O.R. at the opposite end of the hall. "You can go as far as those stainless-steel doors. There's a nice waiting room right across the way. I'll send a nurse to update you from time to time, and I'll be out to talk to you as soon as we're finished."

The surgeon had already given Max a detailed explanation of what would happen once those stainless-steel doors closed. If all went well, he'd said, Nate would be in the recovery room in an hour—two, tops.

When he'd learned about the hole in his boy's heart, Max thought the world would surely end; a four-year-old, enduring major surgery! Though the first operation had been a success, he'd always wondered when the other boot would drop, as his mom was so fond of saying. Now it had. "It had better go well this time," he said to himself.

Because if it didn't…

Max couldn't finish the thought. Life without Nate was simply unthinkable.

Lily held the velvety petals of a long-stemmed red rose to her cheek and, smiling, closed her eyes to inhale its delicate fragrance. This latest delivery had arrived shortly after breakfast, and now stood among other gifts she'd received in the week since Nate's operation.

She tucked the flower into the cut-glass vase nestled among shiny brass pots and colorful ceramic containers overflowing with the deep-green leaves of English Ivy, philodendron, and dumb cane blended with assorted mini-palms, and vases of chrysanthemums that filled the window seat in her room. Rooting through empty brown-pleated wrappers in the bottom of the candy box that had come with the roses, she searched for a chocolate-covered cherry. Finding none, Lily settled for a chewy caramel.

Sitting cross-legged on the plush Persian rug blanketing the hardwood floor, she fingered the lovely bracelet glistening on her wrist. A series of *X*s and *O*s, each golden link caught and reflected the sun, flecking the carpet with sparks of amber and shards of bronze.

Every gift arrived by special courier, each messenger bearing a pastel-enveloped card. None of those preprinted verses for Max Sheridan! He preferred the blank-inside kind, so he could spell out his sentiments in strong, bold pen strokes.

Lily read what had accompanied the bracelet: "Your friendship is more valuable to me than all the gold on earth," he'd written. The one that came with the last box of candy said, "You are sweeter than any candy a confectioner could dream up." Asked to choose her favorite, Lily would probably grow dizzy trying to decide!

She called after opening each gift, to thank him, to tell him how unnecessary the gifts were, but always got the answering machine instead of Max. Probably at the hospital, she'd told herself, keeping Nate company. Still, it hadn't been easy, swallowing her disappointment. She missed him, more than she'd imagined it possible to miss another human being.

She thought of the way he'd held her, there in the hospital waiting room, of the way he had eased her into a gentle kiss. Nothing in the thousands of dreams she'd had over the years could begin to compare with the real thing. For the first time since they'd met, Lily felt at peace, felt as though the Lord had heard and answered her prayers. Because surely that loving, tender kiss was proof that Max felt more than mere friendship toward her.

Lily sighed moonily as something drew her back to the card she'd found among crisp sheets of green tissue in the box of roses: "Red, like the lifesaving blood you shared with Nate." Her smile vanished like smoke as hot tears welled in her eyes. Why hadn't she realized it before: The hug, the kiss, every one of these gifts had been inspired by gratitude, and nothing more!

What a fool she'd been, reading more into his actions and his words than he'd intended. Hands trembling, she stuffed the card back into its pink envelope and tossed it onto the pile with other rainbow-hued cards and thanked God that she hadn't been able to reach Max directly. Because wouldn't she look like a silly little twit if she admitted her feelings, and put Max on the spot!

Wiping her eyes with the backs of her hands, she got to her feet and hurried to the barn. She'd encounter no heartbreaking realizations there, no dashed hopes or misguided conceptions. Just the natural appreciation that came when she fed a hungry baby bird or changed a horse's soiled bandage. Her animals didn't expect kindness or generosity. Though some had experienced the pain and horror of neglect or abuse, they'd learned the hard way that disappointment was the other side of the coin.

Over time, she'd taught them that the sound of water bubbling into a stainless-steel bucket meant a fresh drink, that the sight of her big red-plastic grain scoop meant a full feed bag. Wouldn't hurt to take a lesson from *them* for a change, Lily told herself.

Long ago, she'd adopted a strict mind-set, and never allowed herself to deviate from it: Expect the worst; if it happens, you can say 'I told you so!', and if it doesn't, you'll be pleasantly surprised.

Missy trotted beside her from the house to the outbuilding, russet ears keeping time to every paw-beat. Lily crouched beside her, scritch-scratched the thick neck fur. "Starting right now," she said, kissing the bridge of Missy's nose, "we go back to base zero."

First, because Max had more than enough on his mind, with Nate and Georgia so soon out of the hospital, without having to worry or feel guilty about whatever harebrained idea she'd gleaned from his actions.

And second, she was tired of hoping and praying for something that, experience had taught her, simply wasn't going to happen.

Chapter Six

Since donating blood for Nate's surgery, Lily hadn't felt like her usual energetic self. But she'd promised to bake brownies for the church bazaar, and gave the pastor's wife her word to man the "goodies booth" from noon 'til three.

"I'm surprised to see you here," Lily said stiffly.

"Mom wanted to come and she isn't ready to go out on her own just yet." Max put a plate of chocolate chip cookies on the table. "She's plenty ready for baking, though," he said, smiling.

Of course you wouldn't set foot in a church without being forced to! Lily thought. "Where's Nate?"

"Outside, on the playground."

His furrowed brow told Lily she hadn't done a very good job of hiding her feelings. Instinctively, she wanted to ease his discomfort.

"And Georgia?" She glanced around again.

He nodded toward the curtained stage in the church basement, where his mom and her beau sat, holding hands as they chatted with friends. "Robert offered to bring her, but since Nate wanted to come, too, I didn't see any point making the man go out of his way."

"Robert, eh?" She quirked an eyebrow. "Things are pretty cozy between them, I take it."

Max shrugged. "I expect to hear any day now that the ol' boy has popped the question." He punctuated the statement with a ragged sigh.

Frowning, Lily clucked her tongue. "You make it sound like he's about to be escorted to a prison camp!"

"Well, he's been footloose and fancy-free for a couple of decades." Another shrug. "Guess the 'grass is greener' adage fits."

She crossed both arms over her chest. "Oh, really. And why is that?"

"He thinks married life will be better than bachelorhood." Max chuckled bitterly. "I thought so, too…a lifetime ago. If I had an ounce of decency in me, I'd take him aside, tell him some stories that'd make him think twice."

Lily lifted her chin a notch. "If I know your mom, she'll spoil him rotten," she snapped. Just because Max's experience with marriage had been miserable didn't mean every married man would end up miserable. But what did she care about his opinion on husbands and wives and matrimony?

"There's my dad and Nadine," she said, pointing. "Think I'll go over and say hi."

Max wiggled his eyebrows and said from the corner

of his mouth, "Speaking of cozy couples, the pair of them look mighty cozy themselves."

They did, at that—she had to agree. All right, so maybe they were in love. Last she heard, there was no law against a widower and a widow linking up romantically. Especially when the couple in question had been neighbors for decades…had become close friends after sharing the pain of losing their spouses.

Narrowing her eyes, she glared at him. "*Some* people believe in happy endings. Just because you have no faith doesn't mean everyone else—"

Brows raised, he held up both hands. "Whoa," he drawled, laughing uneasily, "easy there, li'l lady. Didn't mean to rile you." He looked apprehensive. "Are you angry with me for some reason? You haven't exactly been your warm, cheery self."

Shaking her head, Lily looked at the ceiling. She'd promised herself not to behave like a starry-eyed teenybopper if she ever saw Max again…and had intended to avoid him whenever possible. So much for that! But she knew Max didn't deserve to be on the receiving end of her short temper. He had enough to contend with.

Simulating a mischievous grin, Lily said, "It'd take a lot more than the likes of you to rile me. Sorry if I've been biting your head off. It's just been one of those days." Then she winked and spun on her heel and left him standing alone near the enormous stainless-steel coffee urn.

From here on out, she'd have to be a lot more careful, she decided, heading for her dad's table. If Max got wind of her true feelings…

"Hey, cutie," Lamont's date said as she patted his shoulder. "Look who's here!" Nadine reached for Lily's hand. "Haven't seen you since Cammi's wedding. My, but you look pretty in that color."

She'd chosen the ruby-red sheath, hoping it would brighten her mood. It had not. No matter how colorful, clothing couldn't hide the fact that Max's interest was rooted in gratitude and friendship, and that's all it ever would be. She bent to kiss Nadine's cheek. "How are you?"

She flicked a quick, flirty glance at Lamont. "Never better." Then, blue eyes on Lily, Nadine tucked a blond curl behind her ear. "And how're *you,* darlin'?"

"Great." But she wasn't. Night after night of never-come-true dreams involving Max had made her weary... and brokenhearted. Lily knew exactly what the problem was: she hadn't taken her own good advice and put the matter at the foot of the Cross. Not really, anyway. Starting now, she'd try harder to do just that.

Lily stood behind her dad and patted his shoulders. "So, what're you two up to?" she asked, popping a kiss to the top of his gray-haired head.

He turned to face her. "Up to our Adam's apples in artery-cloggin' food," Lamont joked, pointing at his plate. "Do yourself a favor and grab a slice of Nadine's coconut pie, 'cause it's goin' fast."

"So much has been going on, I haven't had a chance to ask, how was Abilene?"

Lamont told her about the hearty young bulls he'd bought there, using his hands and animated expressions to highlight the story. He'd always been a handsome man—tall, broad-shouldered and barrel-chested, with brawny arms and manly hands that belied the thick fringe of dark lashes surrounding his big gray eyes. When he looked at Nadine, those eyes sparkled and he smiled like he meant it. He'd known her since her now-deceased husband had bought the land beside River Valley Ranch, and over the years, they'd become friends. It was obvious something else had come from that friendship, and that "something else" made Lamont look much younger than his fifty-five years.

Ten years younger and happier than she'd seen him in decades. *If that's what love can do,* she thought, *maybe Cammi's right.* Maybe she should give up this Max Sheridan dream and find a guy who could return her feelings.

"Oh, by the way," Nadine was saying, "Elmer says hi."

Lily grinned, remembering that a few months ago, she'd nursed the woman's orphaned calf back to health. "I've really enjoyed having him follow me around the ranch, but I hope I didn't ruin him for you like a puppy. He must be huge by now."

"Already twice the size he was when you sent him home. You were wonderful with him, darlin'. I thought sure I'd have to put him down before he mourned himself to death. You're a lifesaver!"

"Lifesaver? I thought her nickname was Snow White," Max chimed in.

When had *he* walked up? And how long had he been standing there?

"Actually, 'lifesaver' *is* more accurate."

Lily tried to ignore the heat in her cheeks, hoped he wouldn't tell them—

"Did she tell you she saved Nate's life?"

Groaning inwardly, Lily held her breath.

Lamont and Nadine exchanged puzzled glances. "I'd heard your boy had a heart problem…." Lamont said to Max.

"But how did Lily save him?" Nadine finished.

"I didn't save him," she insisted. "Dr. Prentice did."

Max harrumphed. "After Nate was out of danger, the doc told me in plain English that if it hadn't been for you, stepping in when you did, he—"

Lily waved his comment away. "Nurses and doctors donate blood all the time. They'd have found someone else."

He shrugged. "Maybe. But none of them was wearing a pretty blue bridesmaid gown—"

"Maid of honor," Nadine corrected with a playful wink.

"None of them was wearing a maid of honor gown, or those pointy-toed, high-heeled matching shoes."

She didn't know what her outfit had to do with anything, but she knew this: Max had an enormous capacity for love and he had proved it that night when he came into the E.R. cubicle to hold her hand while Nate was being prepped for the O.R. He had noticed how cold her hands were and had hunted down a nurse to get a blanket. Such a big heart!

So why couldn't he find room in it for God?

"It was no big deal," she said. "I just happened to be in the right place at the right time."

"Uh-huh." He turned to Lamont and Nadine. "The patch they'd put on Nate's heart had worked its way loose, see, and he was bleeding internally. Hemorrhaging is more like it. I'm not a match, and the hospital had some kind of emergency that made them run out of his blood type." He looked at Lily, a sweet, lopsided grin on his face. "She volunteered to give him as much as he needed, right then and there."

"Doesn't surprise me," Lamont said. "My girl has a heart as big as her head." He sandwiched her hand between his own. "No wonder you've been lookin' a mite pasty-faced these past couple of days. Why didn't you tell me?"

Because you'd have made a big fuss, she thought. "Really, it was no big deal."

"Well, it was a big deal for us," Georgia said.

Lily had barely had time to adjust to Georgia's presence when her boyfriend added, "You're the Sheridan family hero, girl!"

"Dr. Prentice says you saved my life," Nate put in.

Why hadn't she noticed that they'd joined the group?

She'd never been comfortable with compliments, whether about her work, her face and figure, or her so-called good deeds. Lily wanted to bolt from the church basement, go straight home and hide in the barn, where she could do what needed doing and not have to deal with this awkwardness. In their own way, her animals appreciated what she did, too. The difference was, they accepted her nurturing quietly and without question—and didn't embarrass her with a lot of unnecessary thank-yous afterward.

"I'm glad you like the bracelet," Nate said, touching his small forefinger to a golden *X*. "I helped Dad pick it out."

Pride beamed from his big brown eyes, making Lily want to hug him.

So she did.

"I love the bracelet. Haven't taken it off since it was delivered last week." She held him at arm's length to say, "But how did you help your dad pick it out? You were so sick in the hospital!"

"There was a picture of it," the boy said, "in a magazine one of the nurses brought me. I showed it to Dad, and he said, '*X*s for kisses and *O*s for hugs. Perfect for Lily.'"

Lily met Max's eyes. Kisses and hugs. Did he mean…?

He nodded in response, telling her with those big brown eyes of his that Nate might have pointed it out, but *he* wanted her to wear it. Unconsciously, she wrapped her hand around the bracelet, stomach fluttering, her heart clenching. Dare she hope he felt some of what she felt?

Stop it! she scolded herself. *Remember your promise.*

She stood quickly. "Well, I'd really better be going. I haven't fed the animals yet, and I'm sure they're kicking up a fuss."

"The animals? Oh, Lily! Could I come over and

watch you feed them? I won't make any noise or touch anything, I promise. I'll be like a statue."

To prove it, Nathan stood, stone-still, and stared straight ahead, reminding Lily of the stiff-backed soldiers in the *Nutcracker* ballet. She'd like nothing more, and would have said so, but didn't want to risk a misunderstanding like the one she and Max had had the night she found Missy.

The boy faced his father, folded his hands as if in prayer, and in a soft, sweet voice said, "Can I, Dad? Please? If you'll take me, you can give me a chore, any chore, and I promise to do it without complaining."

"C'mon, Max," Georgia said, "take him to Lily's. He'd have a ball!"

"Yes," Nadine agreed, rumpling his hair, "let the kid go, Max."

Max continued to gaze into Lily's eyes, one corner of his mouth twitching slightly. Lily didn't know if he intended to lash out at the lot of them, as he had that night on the phone, or say yes. She was about to say something along the lines of *This isn't a good time, but maybe another day,* when Max's mouth broadened in a rascally grin.

"Do you have time for gawkers and interlopers?"

Lily looked from his dark eyes to his son's, and sighed. "No, I don't," she began, matching his grin, "but I have time for you and Nate." She had a lifetime, in fact.

Nate jumped up and down, clapping his hands and yelling "Yippee!" as Georgia and Nadine made the "shush" sign with fingers to their lips.

"I'd say let's all go in my car," Max said. "But how would you get yours home?"

She had opened her mouth to say *Let's meet at the barn,* when Nadine pulled Nate into a grandmotherly hug. "I rode over here with your dad," she told Lily. "Have to go back to River Valley to get my car, anyway, so I can drive your car."

She winked at Lily. Winked! What if Max thought it was a sign that they'd succeeded in pulling off a well-planned plot to get her and Max together?

She chanced a glance at him. If he suspected anything of the kind, it didn't show on his face. He stood, feet shoulder width apart and hands in his pockets, waiting for her to make a decision: drive home in her car, or ride over with him and Nate.

Lily dug her car keys out of her purse, handed them to Nadine. "Thanks, Nadine," she said, hoping she wouldn't regret her choice.

"Only too happy to help out." Another playful wink at Lily before turning back to Lamont. "Well, handsome, you ready to hit the road, or do you want me to fetch you another slab of pie?"

Blushing, Lily's dad grinned and patted his stomach. "Couldn't eat another bite."

"Follow me, then," she said, crooking her finger and wiggling her eyebrows.

Grinning like a schoolboy, he got to his feet. "I'm right behind you." Eyes on his prize, he added offhandedly, "See you at home, Lil."

It was so *good,* seeing him this happy! After Rose

died, he'd sacrificed his whole life for his daughters; if this woman could make him happy, Lily was all for it.

It seemed odd that romance was blooming all around her—Georgia had Robert, newlyweds Cammi and Reid had only recently returned from their honeymoon, even her father had found his match with the widow who lived next door. She didn't begrudge any of them their joy. Quite the opposite! It was just…why couldn't *she* have a slice of that kind of happiness?

She suddenly remembered what he'd said earlier, about Robert's freedom. *Because, you big idiot, you went and fell in love with this big galoot, and he thinks of marriage as a prison!*

"Ready?" Max said, offering her his arm.

Timidly, she took it, and walked beside him.

Beside him.

If she had her way, it's where she'd spend the rest of her days.

"Thank you, God!" Nate said, climbing into the back seat.

God.

Max was no longer a "follower," Lily recalled. What would it take to bring him back to the Lord? Prayer and faith had been responsible for Nate's now-healthy condition, and it was the reason Georgia's surgery had been such a success, too. Lily believed that with all her heart, so why couldn't Max see it!

During the drive to River Valley Ranch, Max pointed out landmarks to his son. Funny, touching, when-I-was-a-kid stories that made Lily smile. But her mind wasn't really on the old movie theater or the corner drugstore.

It was on the future—one that she still couldn't imagine without Max in it.

Maybe finding someone who shared that rose-covered-cottage dream *and* her love of the Lord wouldn't be so hard, if only she'd let Max go. Maybe she ought to take Cammi's advice and move ahead without him.

Without him?

The very idea stung like a slap. Still, she couldn't— *wouldn't*—share her life with a man so stubbornly and deliberately separated from the Almighty.

"You're awfully quiet," Max said, reaching over the console to pat her hand. "You feelin' okay?"

"'Course I am." She'd answered too fast. Even she could hear the tension in her voice. "Why wouldn't I be?"

"Well, it's been a pretty hectic couple of weeks."

True. There'd been Cammi's wedding, Georgia's surgery and therapy, Nate's brush with death…and the new critters she'd added to her collection. She realized suddenly that this was a perfect time to express her faith. "Nothing I can't handle. It's all at the foot of the Cross."

One brow rose high on his forehead, one side of his mouth turned down slightly. His nonverbal message was clear: "Believe what you want. I don't fall for that nonsense anymore."

"My teacher at Sunday school in Chicago said that," Nate announced from the back seat. "She said if you give your troubles to God, He will help you through them."

Lily smiled over her shoulder. "She's absolutely right, Nate."

His adorable face crinkled with uncertainty. "Maybe. But I dunno."

Sensing he had more to say, she turned to see him better.

"I've been asking God for a mom for*ever,*" he said, hands extended in helpless supplication. "And when you found that dog? I talked to Him about that, too." Frowning, Nate slapped his hands on blue-jeaned thighs. "No mom, no dog. 'Nuff said."

"God doesn't always answer with a yes, Nate, but He always answers. *Always.*"

He thought about that for a minute. "So His answer is no?"

He looked so sad and disappointed. Lily didn't know what to say. *Help me, Lord. Speak through me so this little boy will grow in faith!* "I don't think He's saying yes or no. I think maybe He's saying 'wait.' When the time's right, if it's His will—"

"His will? What's that?"

What had she gotten herself in to? *Lord, don't fail me now!* she prayed. "Well, 'will' is…it's like a plan. Long before you were born, God knew you, knew what was best for you, too. And for as long as you live, He'll do everything in His power to see that you have what you need."

"What I need is a mom." And he added under his breath, "A dog would be nice, too."

Oh, if only *she* could fill the role of mom! He was adorable, big-hearted, and smarter than any four-year-old she'd ever met. And he was part of *Max*. No wonder she'd gone nuts over him!

She chanced a peek at Max, who stared stonily through the windshield. It dawned on her that Nate's remark had hurt his feelings, because he was trying his best to fill both roles. "Your dad does okay in the parent department, don't you think?"

Nate shrugged. "Yeah, I guess."

Max chuckled. "Careful, you two. My head gets any bigger from this onslaught of praise, I'll have to buy a convertible."

Lily faced front, discouraged with herself. Why hadn't she been able to tell Nate what he needed to hear? Perhaps because she wasn't cut out to be a mother, after all. Because if, as Cammi was always saying, she was a born nurturer, wouldn't the words have been there, on the tip of her tongue?

"So what kind of animals do you have in the barn?" Nate asked.

She said a quick prayer of thanks for the change of subject. "One hawk with a broken wing, an owl that's blind in one eye, a billy goat and a squirrel and a couple of monkeys…" She put a finger to her chin and squinted. "Hmm, seems I'm forgetting something."

"What about the dog?"

She couldn't help but notice how carefully he'd chosen his words. For an instant, she felt angry with Max for being so stubborn about a dog for his boy. But then, he'd been a dad for four years. Nate was living proof that he'd done a fine job, especially considering he'd done it alone. So who was she to question his parenting tactics!

No, clearly it had been her misconception—this idea that 'good mommy genes' flowed in her veins. Faced with cogent evidence that she didn't possess natural-born skills, after all, Lily was torn. On the one hand, this new revelation freed her to move in a different direction with her life; on the other, it required her to give up her dream. Not an easy undertaking, because, frankly, she'd grown pretty comfortable with it.

"That dog you found in the lake, I mean."

She forced a giggle. "Of course! How could I forget Missy?"

"Why'd you name her that?"

"Because we don't know how she got here, or where her owners are. She's a mystery. So I started calling her Miss Terry, Missy for short."

As his mother had when Lily explained the reasons behind the name choice, Max groaned. "I get it. 'Mystery.'" He shook his head. "That's reachin', Lil," he teased. "*Really* reachin'."

He pulled into the long, ribboning lane that connected the highway to the house. "Place looks just as I remember it," Max said, parking in the circular drive.

"Wow," Nate said. "It's as big as the castle at Disney World!" He popped out of the car, sneakered feet thudding across the bridge's wide planks. "Look, Dad. A river!" he said, pointing.

"And Lily's dad put it there, with his own two hands," Max said. "Amazing, isn't it?"

Nate's voice was filled with amazement. "Yeah. I'll say."

Lily led the way to the barn, with Nate skipping on ahead and Max walking on her left. "Dad has never done anything halfway."

Max nodded. "My pop was the same way. He never built a river, mind you," he teased, "but he always said, 'Do your best or don't bother.' Didn't matter if I was cleaning my room or doing homework or mowing the lawn. 'It's a test of a man's character,' he'd tell me, 'to see what kind of work he'll put out when he thinks nobody's watching.'" Using his chin as a pointer, he nodded at Nate. "I'm trying to do for him what my dad did for me."

"You're doing a terrific job. Nate's a great kid, and he didn't get that way with smoke and mirrors."

"I'm trying," he said again. "But they're big shoes to fill," he said. "Real big."

"Your dad was a wonderful man," Lily agreed. She remembered Max's father from Youth Group at church. He'd volunteered one evening a week to run the program that allowed parish teens to gather for basketball or board games, movies in town, or just sit around, talking. He'd organized fund-raisers, picnics, collections for the needy, and taught "his kids" the importance of sharing not only their time, but themselves.

"My biggest regret," he said, "is that Nate will never meet him."

"And I'll bet he regrets not getting to know Nate. Hard not to love that kid."

Max stepped in front of her, blocking her path. She

didn't know what to make of the intense eye contact, didn't know how to read the silent message he sent on the invisible cable connecting their gazes.

"Dad! Lily!" Nate called. "I can hear 'em in there!"

The boy stood, ear pressed to the barn door, waving them forward. It was enough to get Lily's feet moving. "We'll have to be very quiet," she whispered, opening the door, "and move very slowly once we get inside, so we don't startle anybody."

Nate nodded, dark eyes bright with anticipation. Max looked pretty excited himself, Lily thought, smiling. As the threesome walked among the cages and stalls, Lily introduced them to her "patients."

Missy loped up, long golden fur rippling with each happy stride. She stopped just feet away from Nate, rear end in the air and tail wagging as she lowered her shoulders, an invitation to play.

His grin made it clear that he was more than happy to oblige. "Hi, girl," he said, kneeling on the straw-covered floor.

The dog nuzzled the crook of his neck. "Hey, that tickles!" he said, laughing so hard he lost his balance and rolled onto his side. "And your nose is cold!" he added. On his knees again, he hugged her. "I like you, Missy. You're fun!"

Max leaned his forearm on a stall door and shook his head. "Gonna be hard, makin' a clean getaway from here after *that* introduction."

So he'd made the decision, had he, that Nate couldn't have the dog? It was a shame…for Nate. But good for her, because she'd become very attached to the retriever.

Lamont's pup, Obnoxious, joined them, his quiet, breathy barks starting up a whole new fit of giggles in Nate. "Do *all* your dogs have cold noses?"

"These are the only dogs we have," Lily said. "And yes, most dogs have cold, wet snouts."

"Snouts," Nate giggled. "That's funny, Lily." He jumped up, grabbed Max's hand and asked, "Dad, Dad! Are we having ham for Thanksgiving dinner like we did last year?"

"Where did *that* come from?" Max said.

"Well, Lily said snouts, and pigs have snouts, and— I dunno. I just thought of it." He went back to playing with the dogs.

Lily frowned slightly. "Ham, instead of the traditional turkey dinner and all the trimmings?"

Max blushed guiltily. "Never learned how to roast a turkey, but ham I can do."

"Dad calls it our Canned Holiday feast, 'cause everything comes out of a can. 'Cept the gravy. That comes in a jar." He hid his grin behind both hands. "'Member how you forgot to thaw out the pun-kin pie last year?" A merry giggle punctuated the question. "And we had to slice it with the 'lectric knife? And how it crunched when we ate it? That was really funny, huh, Dad."

Max's blush deepened. "Yeah. A real memory-maker, all right." He lifted both shoulders and extended his hands, palm up. "I never claimed to be a French chef."

"Well, sounds to me like you did just fine, cooking for two." Lily hoped, even as she said it, that Max would correct her, that he'd disagree and point out how many others had joined them at their holiday table. When he remained silent, she realized they'd spent the day alone.

Had they eaten *all* their holiday dinners that way?

The picture of the pair of them, huddled over a Formica table at Georgia's Diner, eating TV dinners or canned ham, upset her more than she could bear. And Georgia wasn't well enough yet to stand all day, basting the turkey, mixing up the stuffing, whipping potatoes....

"We always have a huge feast on Thanksgiving," Lily said, opening a can of dog food. "You and Nate are more than welcome. Georgia and Robert, too, of course." She plopped the meat into a bowl near the one-eyed owl.

Nate looked up at her as if he believed she'd hung the moon. "You mean a *real* turkey, with gravy and stuffing...and *everything?*"

Lily laughed. "Yep. And a whole table full of desserts, too." To Max she said, "Nadine always joins us, and she's bringing one of her sons and his family this year. It'll be great. A big old-fashioned fiesta!"

The boy wiggled his pointer finger, summoning his dad closer. "Can we go, Dad?"

Max looked hesitant. "You're sure it'll be all right with your dad?"

"Absolutely. 'The more, the merrier,' he always says." She spooned dog food into another container in the hawk's cage. "Eat up, now," she crooned to it. "You have a long way to go before your wing is healed well enough for you to fly home."

The bird cocked its head, watching Lily first with one gleaming eye, then the other. As she scrubbed her hands,

Lily said, "Maybe after dinner on Thursday, all you fellas can have yourselves a rousing game of football."

Father and son followed her around the barn, looking over her shoulder as she changed bandages, fed and watered every creature, and gave each one a moment of affection and one-on-one attention. Nate stared, open-mouthed, as she petted the one-eyed owl. "Aren't you scared he'll bite you? He has a very sharp beak."

"No," Lily said, stroking the feathered hunter's head, "because I've gotten to know him very well." To the owl, she said, "You would *never* bite me, would you?" In response, it merely blinked its golden eye.

Lily washed up again, and as she dried her hands she said, "How 'bout some hot chocolate, Nate? I make mine from scratch."

"Scratch? What's that?"

"It means 'not from a mix,'" Max offered.

"Is it better than the stuff in the little envelopes?"

"Way better." He chuckled. "What a great way to top off a cold Sunday evening."

Missy pranced alongside her as she led them down the flagstone path connecting the barn to the back porch, wondering as they went what they'd find to talk about while she prepared the cocoa, while they sipped it.

"I like Lily, Dad…."

Lily knew she wasn't supposed to have heard that; the boy had done his four-year-old best to whisper.

"…and not just 'cause she's pretty, either."

It was all she could do to keep from turning around to see how Max had reacted to *that*.

"Ditto," he said.

"Ditto? What's 'ditto,' Dad?"

"It means 'I feel the same way.'"

He hadn't lowered his voice, hadn't even attempted to keep her from hearing him, Lily noticed.

For the moment, she forgot the promise she'd made to herself. Dismissed the possibility that Max was just being "nice." Why not enjoy the possibility that he had feelings for her that went beyond the boundaries of friendship—just for the moment, of course.

"Is Missy allowed in the house?"

"Sure," Lily said over her shoulder.

"My friend in Chicago had a dog but it wasn't allowed inside. Which was weird, 'cause he had a big ol' green lizard with pointy things on his back, and his mom let him keep *that* in his bedroom!"

What would they talk about?

Something told her that with Nate around, topics of conversation wouldn't be a problem.

Max's quiet, masculine laughter floated on the chilly November breeze as Lily bit her lower lip to keep from saying *Thank you, Lord!* out loud.

Chapter Seven

The kitchen was warm with the scents and sounds of festive Thanksgiving preparation. On the stove, lids danced atop steaming pots, while on the counter, loaves of home-baked bread, rolls and biscuits, blanketed with blue-striped towels, sat in orderly rows. The timer *ding*ed, and Lily put down the potato peeler to grab an oven mitt.

Max had intended to join her here, and offer to help if he could. But in the minute or so since he'd rounded the corner, he'd stood, mesmerized. It surprised him to see Lily alone in the room, handling each womanly chore with deft precision; he'd expected to find all three of the London girls in there with her, laughing and talking as they put the finishing touches on the Thanksgiving banquet. Surprised, but relieved, because this way, he could watch her unnoticed.

She'd piled her long, thick hair atop her head with a green plastic band that matched her shirt. Wisps of hair that had escaped the upsweep curled in the hollow at the back of her neck; a few more formed bouncy ringlets beside her ears. He'd give anything to press a gentle kiss to those lovely lobes.

After painting the turkey with a thick coat of melted butter, she covered it with a tent made of aluminum foil and closed the oven door. The bracelet he'd given her caught a beam of light, forcing his attention to her slender wrist. Max wouldn't mind placing a soft kiss there, either.

Suddenly, she began humming a tune he hadn't heard since boyhood. Smiling, he pocketed his hands and leaned on the door frame. He'd forgotten what a beautiful voice she had. Crossing one booted ankle in front of the other, he listened, captivated by her voice, her movements. She was a vision, a dream come to life.

"'Over the river and through the woods,'" she sang. Then, without looking up, she said, "You remember the words, Max, feel free to sing along."

Chuckling, he shook his head. "How long have you known I was here?"

When she met his eyes, his heart thumped and his stomach lurched. She was ravishing, what with her heat-pinked cheeks and big green eyes. And that smile... She could charm the leaves from the trees with that smile, Max thought.

"Not long," she said.

Something told him she'd seen him the instant he'd appeared in the doorway, and she'd only said "not long" to spare him any embarrassment. Even as a kid, Lily had gone out of her way to make others feel good, even if it meant taking it on the chin herself. And he'd always loved her for that.

Loved? No, Max admitted. Nothing past tense about it.

He took a few steps closer. "Anything I can do to help?"

She cocked her head, gave it a moment's thought. "As a matter of fact, there is."

"Your wish is my command," he said. He bowed, more to keep her from reading his emotions than to emulate a gentleman. Because there was no getting around it: Max didn't think he could deny her anything, ever. *Just part of the problem,* he admitted. Years ago, love for Lily had made him feel guilty, because even at eighteen, he'd known how inappropriate his feelings for her were because of their age difference. He'd been too young, too immature back then to understand what motivated his reaction to her. But he understood it now. Her father had been right when he'd said her heart was as big as her head. Even as a callow youth, Max had sensed that she was good—that she'd be good for *him*.

"You can go into the dining room, see how Cammi and Violet and Ivy are doing. They swore they could fit all twenty-six of us at the table, and I'm dying to find out how they did it…if they did it!"

Much as he wanted to do what she'd asked, Max couldn't leave the kitchen. It felt good in here, cozy and comfortable. "Why don't we just wait 'til it's time to put stuff on the table. Let it be a surprise."

"I've never been too keen on surprises." She held up

the paring knife, used it as a pointer and grinned. "You can peel potatoes, instead, if you'd rather."

Laughing, Max held up his hands and ducked out the door, saying, "I'll be back in a second."

"Thank you!" he heard her say as he stepped into the dining room.

Immediately, he could see that her sisters had been busy. The already-long dining room table where he'd shared many a Sunday dinner as a boy had been lengthened even more by the addition of two card tables at each end. Their thin brown-painted legs looked weak and flimsy by comparison to the sturdy light oak that supported the main table. China, crystal and silver glinted in the light of the ornate chandelier overhead. Mismatched chairs, mixed among those that matched the table, lent a casual warmth to the elegance.

Lily was whipping potatoes when he returned to the kitchen. "Couldn't find them," he reported, stepping up beside her. "But the job's done and it looks great. Only thing missing is food."

She spooned a dollop of sour cream into the mashed spuds. "Mmm, perfect," she said over the *whir* of the electric mixer. "Would you do me one more favor—ask the girls to come help me put the food on the buffet?"

"You bet."

"Thanks, Max."

He tucked a tendril of hair behind her ear, allowed his crooked finger to graze her lightly freckled cheek. Max leaned close and kissed it, lingering for an instant because she smelled like flowers and line-dried sheets and sweet butter.

Lily stiffened slightly at first, and just when he thought she'd tell him to back off, she faced him and, closing her eyes, invited him to kiss her again—for real this time.

It was an offer he couldn't refuse.

The moment pulsed and crackled, like the energy that surged through the cord, powering the mixer. She must have felt it, too, for she sighed and leaned closer, lifting the appliance from the deep pot as she did.

Egg-size blobs of mashed potatoes spun loose from the beaters and landed *splat,* on Max's shoulder, on her cheek, on his forehead, on the back of her hand. Lips still pressed to his, she began to giggle. "Maybe we should share some of this with the rest of them."

"No way," he said, a forefinger to her full lower lip. "This is mine. All mine."

Her smile vanished like smoke as she blinked up at him. What was going on in that pretty head of hers? he wondered. One thing was certain, the magic of the moment had disappeared. "Well, guess I'll round up the relatives and herd them into the dining room."

One delicate brow rose slightly as the hint of a grin lifted the corners of her lovely lips. "I'll turn you loose, then," she said, though one hand still held the mixer, the other the pot handle.

She had it all—a big heart, looks, brains, too many talents to list, and a sense of humor, too. "If I have the sense God gave a goose, I wouldn't let you get away this time."

He saw her swallow, heard her quick intake of air

as she looked left, right…anywhere but into his eyes. "Well," she started, "I, um…"

Difficult as it was to let her go, Max pocketed his hands and headed for the door. "How long 'til soup's on?" he said from the hall.

She cleared her throat. Touched fingertips to her lips. "Five minutes." She looked away, then met his eyes to add, "Ten at most."

Nodding, he walked away smiling to himself. His kiss had rattled her. Because she hadn't expected it? Because she had enjoyed it every bit as much as he had? A frown replaced the smile at his last thought: Because she'd finally figured out he wasn't right for her?

His heart had pounded during that kiss, but not half as hard as it hammered at *that* possibility. He walked into the family room, saw his son frolicking with Missy as the adults discussed the weather, politics, who'd win today's football game.

"London girls," he said, standing at attention and saluting, "report for kitchen duty."

When the laughter ended, Cammi, Violet and Ivy hurried to the kitchen. "You're such a nut!" Cammi said as she passed him.

"Y'gotta love a guy with a sense of humor," Ivy chimed in.

His practiced smile hid the truth. He'd spent the past six years pretending to look happy. Obviously, since no one ever gave a hint they suspected his joviality was an act, he'd gotten pretty good at it.

What would it take, he asked himself as the ladies filed by, to make him happy…*truly* happy?

Lily stuck her head out the kitchen door and smiled, waving her sisters into the room. "I thought you'd abandoned ship!" she teased. "Everything's ready—just needs to be put on the buffet."

"You're terrific, Lil," Ivy said.

"But really, you should have let us help more," Vi agreed. "I don't know why you insisted on doing it all yourself."

"I know why," Cammi singsonged. "To show a certain…"

Her voice trailed off as she ducked into the kitchen, preventing Max from hearing the end of Cammi's sentence. But it didn't take a genius to figure out who Lily was trying to impress. So, had he misread her reaction when he'd cracked the "I wouldn't let you get away" remark?

He hoped so. Because he knew exactly what would make him happy, now and until he breathed his last.

Being with Lily, that's what.

"Dinner was great, Lily," Georgia said. "If I'd known you could cook like that, Andy's job would have been in jeopardy!"

Lily blushed and rolled her eyes. "Please. You never would have agreed to let me put paper doilies under the pies and cakes…too fancy for your truck driver clientele."

Laughing, Georgia said, "You make a good point." She turned to Robert and said, "Now?"

Grinning like a schoolboy, the doctor got to his feet, clinked the handle of his butter knife on his water goblet. "Excuse me. Ahem. May I have your attention, please?"

One by one, they stopped talking to look his way.

"I have an announcement to make. Or rather," he said, one hand on Georgia's shoulder, "*we* have an announcement."

Max leaned toward Lily. "Here it comes," he whispered, "the moment we've all been waiting for."

"Robert asked me to marry him," his mother said, fanning her face with her napkin, "and I said yes."

The instant of silence was broken when Lily applauded. "Congratulations, you two!" she said, hurrying to their side of the table. She gave each of them a hug, a kiss on the cheek. "What wonderful, wonderful news!"

"I agree," Max said, joining them. "It's about time, *Dad*," he added, jacking Robert's arm up and down like a pump handle.

"Does that mean you're my grandpa?" Nate asked.

Robert said, "Yep, it sure does."

Lily and Max returned to their seats as Lamont stood. "Time for the traditional London family thank-you list." He looked from Robert to Max, from Georgia to Nadine's son and his family. "For those of you who've never joined us for Thanksgiving dinner, we have this ritual. Nobody gets dessert 'til they've shared one thing they're thankful for." He faced Lily. "Sweetie, why don't you show 'em how it's done."

She sat back, hands folded primly in her lap, and said, "I'm thankful that every one of you is part of my life." She faced Lamont. "Your turn, Dad."

When it was Cammi's turn, she grabbed Reid's hand.

"I'm grateful to have the husband of my dreams to wake up to every morning."

Nate said, "I'm thankful for having Lily's blood in me, 'cause maybe it'll make me into a good vettin-air-yun when I grow up."

So much for "save the best for last," Max thought, because now it was his turn. He'd never been much good at public speaking, and this came close enough. It made him nervous, made his voice waver, his hands shake and his ears hot—and an icy sensation snaked down his back. "Truth is, I have a lot to be thankful for," he said. But if he had to single out one thing, as everyone else had, what would it be?

I rediscovered Lily, he thought.

"How utterly romantic!" Ivy gushed.

"That's one of the sweetest things I've ever heard," Vi agreed.

Ivy and Vi had been confusing him since high school. Now, their identical faces lit up as if they were still teenagers! Until the twins spoke up, Max hadn't realized he'd said aloud what he'd been thinking. How was he going to dig himself out of *this* one!

His mouth was suddenly bone dry, his palms damp. He reached for his water glass and missed, spilling it across the tabletop and into Lily's lap. "Aw, man. I'm such a clod," he said, attempting to blot it with his napkin.

But she leaned forward at the same moment he had, and his chin connected with her eye.

Instantly, Lily's hand covered the spot. "Self-defense," he said, groaning inwardly. "Not that I blame you." He slid his chair closer to hers, put an arm around her. "I'm sorry, Lily. Man. I'm batting a thousand, aren't I. You okay? Lemme see."

"I have a hard head," she said, smiling good-naturedly. "I'm fine."

But she wasn't. A tiny trickle of blood had already started creeping toward her cheek. "You're not fine. You're bleeding!" He grabbed his napkin, dipped it into her glass and tried to daub the tiny cut. Nate chose that moment to get a closer look and bumped Max's elbow, causing him to poke Lily in the eye, instead.

"Good grief, Max," his mother said, "stop helping her before you *really* hurt her!"

"He didn't mean it, Georgia," Nadine said. "Men sometimes get clumsy around girls they're sweet on." She pointed at a bruise on her forearm. "Got this one when Lamont tried to help me out of the car the other day." She showed them a scratch on the opposite elbow. "And this is from when he boosted me into the saddle when we went riding the other day."

A smattering of laughter punctuated her story. "You know what they say—'love hurts,'" Lamont said, chuckling.

Their banter did little to ease Max's guilt. He sat back, shoulders sagging, as Lily excused herself.

"I'll just be a minute, guys. Help yourselves to dessert, why don't you!"

Max rose halfway, intending to pull out her chair. At the last second, he decided against it, for fear he'd trip her with one of its legs. Not until she was safely out of the room did he get up. The others were busy pointing to which dessert they'd like to cut into first; he hoped no one would notice he'd left the table.

He stepped outside, quietly closing the huge front door behind him, and took a deep breath. The sky mirrored his mood—cold and gray. He sat on the top step of the porch and leaned both elbows on his knees, staring across the vast expanse of lawn that made up the London front yard. Shaking his head, he ran a hand through his hair. "Klutz," he grumbled. "Bumbling idiot. Clumsy oaf."

"Don't be so hard on yourself."

Her sudden appearance on the porch startled him, and he lurched slightly. "How long have you been standing there?"

"Not long," she said, reminding them of their earlier conversation in the kitchen. She sat down beside him, held the hair back from her temple. "See? No big deal. It's just a teeny tiny little—"

He groaned, aloud this time. "Aw, man. You're gonna have a big ugly knot on your head by morning." Wincing, he added, "Sorry, Lil."

She nudged him with her shoulder. "Accidents happen, Max."

He looked into her face, saw that she'd meant every word. Max couldn't help but chuckle at the situation— he'd clocked her, not the other way around, yet Lily was comforting *him!* No doubt about it: Happiness could be his for the asking…if only he could figure out how to ask.

Max slid an arm around her, gave her a little sideways hug. "You're something else, you know that?"

He felt her shrug, heard her sigh.

"What?" he said.

But she only shook her head.

"Headache?"

"No."

He wasn't so sure. It would be just like her to hide any discomfort he'd caused her.

As if she'd read his mind, she looked at him just then. "Honest," she said, patting his thigh. "I'm fine."

She didn't take her hand back, he noticed, but let it lie there instead, warming not only the skin beneath it, but his entire being. Maybe he should just 'fess up. Tell her how he felt.

Then again, maybe he shouldn't; knowing Lily, she'd echo his words, if only to spare his feelings. Because, really, what did a gorgeous li'l gal like her want with a guy like him? A union between them, well, it was all in his favor. He'd get a pretty, big-hearted wife, Nate would get a loving mom—and what would Lily get? He glanced at her, saw that the spot where his chin had connected with her temple was already bruising. A lot of hard work, he thought, answering his own question— and contusions and abrasions.

She shivered.

"Let's go inside," he said, standing. And looking at the darkening sky, Max quoted Shakespeare: "'Something wicked this way comes…'" He held out his hand to help her up, and she willingly put hers into it. "You're a brave, trusting soul, aren't you," he teased.

"Either that," she shot back, "or a glutton for punishment."

He cringed. "Oooh. Cheap shot. But I guess I had it coming. That, and then some."

She stood in his path and, hands on her hips, said, "You have plenty coming, Max Sheridan, but it's all good stuff, 'cause you're a good man."

My, but she was gorgeous standing there, green eyes flashing, long dark hair billowing in the breeze.

"You're kind and hardworking and decent, right down to the very core of you!" She emphasized the point by jabbing a finger into his chest.

"You think so, huh?"

She tidied the collar of his shirt, in a gesture he could only call "wifely."

"No. I don't think so, I *know* so."

"Well," he said hoarsely, taking her in his arms, "if I'm so good and decent, why is it that every time I look at you, I want to kiss the daylights out of you?"

He heard her tiny gasp, saw her big eyes widen further as he slid his arms around her. She hadn't stiffened this time, he noticed, the way she had in the kitchen while she mashed potatoes, and his wild emotions flew about. Could it mean she felt the same way he did— that happiness, genuine happiness, could be found right here in one another's arms? Was that too much to ask for? If he was a praying man, he'd ask the Almighty to intervene, right now, on his behalf.

Instead, he buried his face in her hair and held her tight, so tightly that not even the frosty wind could have squeaked between them. *Ah, Lily,* he thought, eyes closed as he inhaled the sweetly feminine scents clinging to her soft tresses, *if only I could—*

She bracketed his face with her hands and forced him to meet her eyes. "They're eating up all the dessert without us, you know."

He smiled. What did he care? In his opinion, the sweetest thing ever made was standing right here in his arms. "Probably."

Hands on his shoulders now, she said, "We'll be lucky if there are even crumbs left for us."

"Maybe…"

"Funny, I'm not cold anymore."

"Me, neither." But then, he hadn't been cold to start with.

"Think they've even noticed we're gone?"

"No doubt in my mind. The room temperature likely dropped twenty degrees when you left, 'cause you're warm as the sun."

She batted her lashes and gave his chest a playful smack. "Cut it out. You're gonna make me blush."

Max studied her face for a quiet moment. He memorized every detail, from the perfectly arched feminine brows to the gently sloping freckled nose to the generous pink lips. Those wonderful, velvety soft lips…

"You planning to kiss me again, or just stand there, staring at my mouth?"

He almost laughed because, once again, she'd read his mind. There wasn't another woman like her, not in all the world.

"All right, then," she said, tucking in one corner of that tantalizing mouth, "I guess I'll have to take the bull by the horns."

She stood on tiptoe and, one hand on either side of

his face again, kissed him. Kissed him like she meant it, right down to her toes. It seemed like a fog had descended on him, blotting out rational thought, blocking common sense. He struggled to work his way out of it, so he could tell her *with words* that she was the answer to his every prayer.

Prayer? *That* brought him back to the Land of the Thinking, because Max hadn't prayed in years. He ended the dizzying contact, held her at arm's length. She looked so starry-eyed that he had to fight the impulse to kiss her again. "You just saved me a ton of empty calories," he said, his voice gravelly and gruff, even to his own ears. So he cleared his throat and smiled. "My waistline thanks you."

She only stood there, blinking, a faint smile shining in her eyes.

"Guess we'd better get back inside, before your father sends Obnoxious out here to tear my throat out."

Lily laughed. "Obnoxious is quite literally all bark and no bite. You're safe as a babe in his mother's arms with that pup."

Max stood beside her, draped an arm over her shoulders. "Looks like rain."

"Mmm…"

"Hope it won't be the thunder and lightning kind. Nate is terrified of storms."

She was quiet for a minute, and then she said, "Well, I have a feeling you handle that just as well as you handle everything else."

He opened the door, held it for her. *The girl sure is good for what ails a man,* Max thought as she stepped into the foyer. In the weeks he'd been back in Amarillo, she'd awakened emotions in him he'd forgotten existed. It amazed him that some good-lookin' dude hadn't come along, snapped her up, made her his bride.

He closed the door harder than he'd intended, bristling at the thought of Lily married to another man, having his kids, sharing his life.

"What's wrong?"

Max looked at her. "Wrong? Nothing. Why?"

"Well, you look so—" she frowned, searching for the right word "—a cross between horrified and furious."

That pretty well described it, all right. "Ate too much, that's all."

"So you really don't want dessert? Georgia told me your favorite sweet treat is Dutch apple pie."

Lily looked downright disappointed, which meant she'd baked one, just for him. Max's heart melted at the realization that she'd sought out yet another way to show him she cared. It wasn't her fault, was it, that all his life he'd pretended to love the stuff rather than hurt his mother's feelings? "Well," he said, holding his thumb and forefinger an inch apart, "maybe just a small slice." Max patted his stomach. "Any more and I'm liable to explode."

Her exquisite face brightened and her voice went back to its usual melodic tones. "Sounds like everyone has retreated to the family room. Go on in and make yourself comfy while I get it for you." She headed for the corner of dining room, where no fewer than a dozen delectable treats lined the sideboard. "Go on," she said, motioning him onward. "I'll be right in."

Just like that, she was out of sight. Max thought he knew how Noah must have felt when God turned off the sun and started the clouds to raining on the sinful earth, because she'd taken the warmth and brightness with her.

You must be crazy, Max told himself, *not snapping her up yourself, years ago.* Wasn't like he hadn't thought about it, dozens of times. All he needed to do was head back to Texas, make sure he ran into her, start up where they'd left off. So many times, he'd almost asked his mother how Lily was doing—if she'd fallen in love, married, started a family. Hearing that news would have cut like a saber, so he hadn't asked. Nothing could have surprised him more than learning none of those things had happened. Any man would consider himself blessed to have her as his wife!

Blessed? What was with him today, he wondered, remembering that minutes ago, he'd thought about prayer.

Not so surprising, really, that he'd have heavenly things on his mind. In his opinion, Lily was his own personal messenger from God.

Chapter Eight

Max took the only seat left in the family room, beside Lamont. The man was impressive in so many ways that he could be downright intimidating, and Max had never been sure—not as a boy and certainly not now—whether Lamont meant folks to read him that way.

Behind his back, people sometimes called Lamont "John Wayne," not for his rolling gait, but for his tough, no-nonsense way of communicating. That style had commanded the respect and admiration of bankers and cowboys alike—and had helped make Lamont London one of the wealthiest men in the Texas Panhandle.

Years ago, Max had walked into the barbershop just as Lamont was leaving. "Now, there's a man y'don't want to cross," said one man. "They don't call him The Griz for nothin'," said another. Months later, Max saw with his own eyes what they'd been talking about when Lamont lit into a cashier for shortchanging him and denying it.

Max wondered which of Lamont's daughters had

inherited his fiery temper. Definitely not Lily, and from what he could see, not Cammi, either. Left to decide between the twins, Max would choose Violet over Ivy. He looked at her now, perched on the arm of the sofa nearest her date, arms crossed over her chest, chin up and left eyebrow raised as she surveyed the goings-on in the room, while Cammi and Ivy giggled and chattered, like a couple of cartoon chipmunks.

Better watch it, bud, he warned himself. *These people could be your in-laws some day.*

Max almost laughed out loud at the thought. He'd shared, what, half a dozen kisses with Lamont's youngest girl? Even if Lily was, in his opinion, perfect, enchanting, a *gift,* they were a long way from marriage.

Right?

He did some surveying of his own in the London family room.

Max supposed Robert had felt the same unease before asking Georgia to marry him. Reid likely had experienced some angst before proposing to Cammi. Even Lamont appeared ready to take the plunge…but hadn't.

He may not yet have popped the question, but could that be far off? Because *something* major had changed about Lamont in the years Max had been away, and he suspected Nadine Greene had everything to do with it. Lamont laughed at Nadine's jokes, looked long into her eyes, clung to her every word—and she mirrored the loving, affectionate behavior. A far cry from the growly, grumpy man who'd earned the nickname "The Griz"!

If love could tame a man like Lamont, Max knew he didn't stand a chance.

But…did he *want* a chance?

He'd been thinking wacky, crazy thoughts since coming back to Amarillo, things like how great life would be with Lily, and what a terrific wife and mother she'd be.

Then again, when Lily had pointed out that Georgia and Robert would be happy together, he'd raised her hackles with his "grass is greener" remark.

So which was it? Did he want his freedom or didn't he?

It was a question he'd better think about, long and hard, and soon.

She came into the room carrying a pie plate in one hand, a cup of coffee in the other. "It's decaf," she said, putting them on the end table beside him. She pulled a napkin-wrapped fork out of her pocket, handed it to him.

"Looks terrific," he said. And it did, too—golden-brown crust, perfectly sliced cinnamony apple wedges. "Thanks."

She patted his shoulder. "I'll be in the kitchen if you need anything." And with that, she hurried off.

Her sisters soon joined her, followed by Nadine and her daughter-in-law and Max's cane-toting mother. A minute passed before Nadine's son said, "Amazing how much noise women can make, isn't it?"

Reid laughed. "Much as I hate to admit it, Adam, you make a good point."

"Why, I didn't even notice the racket, 'til the racketeers were gone," Robert joked.

Nate came over, sat on Max's knee and pointed tentatively at the pie. "You gonna eat that?"

"No," he said, sliding the plate toward him. "Help yourself."

"Thanks, Dad!" On his knees at the coffee table, Nate gobbled a few bites and smacked his lips. "Mmm. Delicious. Lily's a good cook, too."

Meaning, Max thought, in addition to her other qualities and talents. And there were plenty, all right. He glanced around the room again, at the faces of the contented, cheerful men whose lives had been made better because they'd chosen the right women. Must be nice, he thought, starting every day knowing there was someone beside them—a partner to share life's ups and downs, its joy and sadness.

When these guys left for work every morning, each took with him the knowledge that his toil had a purpose, that the responsibility of caring for his loved ones wasn't a burden, but a pleasure. And when he came home again at night, someone would be waiting, and she'd welcome him home with a warm hug and a warmer kiss.

But he wouldn't turn on the TV because he'd much rather sit in the kitchen pretending to read the newspaper, watching as she puttered, checked the doneness of things, hummed to herself, all while looking pretty in the gold *X*s and *O*s bracelet he'd bought her. And somewhere along the way she'd press her soft hands to his face and smile sweetly, and after another delicious kiss, tell him she'd baked his favorite pie for dessert.

And even though it wasn't *really* his favorite pie, he'd eat it, because—

Whoa. How had *he* gotten involved in the scene?

Max checked to make sure he hadn't drooled. Wouldn't have surprised him at all to find that he had! *You're losin' it, pal.* He'd better get a grip soon.

He wondered exactly what would happen if he *didn't* get a grip. Would he get down on one knee, take Lily's hand in his, slide a diamond on her finger? Or would he simply tell her, in plain English, that he thought they'd make a perfect pair? Nodding to himself, Max thought, Yeah, that was definitely more his style.

He sat back and stared at the TV screen, where two NFL teams were going at it on the field. At the moment, he couldn't remember who wore green and yellow and who wore purple, but he sure could identify with the guy who'd fumbled the ball!

Max couldn't remember feeling more confused. Couldn't think of a time when he'd felt this addle-brained. What was going on?

Who was he kidding? He knew what was going on. If love could do *this* to a man, he didn't know if he wanted any part of it.

Then again, that whole little kitchen scene he'd just dreamed up had been awfully nice….

"What's your problem?" Robert asked him. "You look kinda green around the gills."

Max tried to smile. "Ate too much, I guess."

Robert nodded at the pie plate. "Good thing Nate likes your mama's pie." He wrinkled his nose. "I love her more than life itself, but…"

Max shuddered. "I've been chokin' the stuff down since I was a boy. Maybe one of these days I'll screw up the courage to tell her I'd rather eat raw muskrat."

The men laughed, each sharing a similar story.

"Why do we do it?" Adam asked. "They're sure quick enough to find fault."

"Not Georgia," Robert said.

"Never heard a word of complaint from Cammi," Reid agreed.

Lamont shrugged. "Nadine's pretty good at takin' it on the chin. If she has a beef, she hasn't shared it with me."

They looked at Max. "Well?" Robert said.

He cleared his throat. "Well, what?"

Groaning and laughing, the men shot "cut it out" and "oh brother" his way. "You know what we're talkin' about," Robert said. He extended his hands, palm up, wiggled his fingertips. "Give."

Give what? Some concocted story that made him part of the group? He *wasn't* part of the group! He and Lily were friends.

Max remembered those kisses they'd shared on the front porch earlier. Okay, so they were *good* friends. That didn't mean they were a couple, that they'd spent enough time together, alone, to discover one another's faults, or lack of them.

"Yeah," Adam said, "give."

"I—I, uh, well…"

He felt like the stuff between the proverbial rock and the hard place: There sat Lily's father, looking his grizzly best. Her brother-in-law Reid mirrored the expression. Even his future stepfather sat on the edge of his seat. Max didn't know whether to be amused or angry, because why did any of them care one way or the other!

"Sorry," he said, shoulders up and hands out, "we just don't have that kind of relationship." For Lamont's benefit, he quickly added "Yet," though for the life of him he couldn't say why.

Before the night was over, he might just find himself in the middle of a "what are your intentions toward my daughter" conversation. And to be honest, Max didn't think he was ready for that. Didn't know if he'd ever be ready for that. If he was smart, he'd start looking for reasons Lily *wouldn't* be good for his life, instead of compiling a long, unwieldy list of reasons she would. But then, if he was smart, would he be here, feeling uncomfortable because he had no story to tell?

Nate looked up at him, licking the caramel-colored goo that holds apple pie together from his lips. The boy smiled, saying with his expression that he thought his dad was awesome. He could see himself having a couple more kids, just like this one, who'd look up to him that way…

"That pie was great, Dad. Thanks." Nate got to his feet and picked up the plate and fork. "I'm gonna take this to the kitchen, so Lily won't have to come back for it."

Suddenly, the others began collecting china and silver and heading for the kitchen. He only hoped the boy wouldn't tell Lily *he* had eaten the pie she'd baked especially for Max, because it might hurt her feelings. He winced. He didn't want that.

Now everyone gathered in the kitchen.

Everyone but Max, that is.

He sat, slumped in the chair that matched Lamont's, staring at a commercial geared more to humor than to selling a product. But he wasn't getting the intended joke. His mind was such a muddle, he wasn't getting much of *anything*. Resting his head on the chair's back cushion, he slapped both hands over his face.

"Not feeling well?"

Lily…

Max opened his eyes, tried a smile on for size. It didn't fit, but he kept it on, anyway. "Hey. I didn't hear you come in." Did his cheeriness sound as phony to her as it did to him? Max hoped not.

"It's a talent," she said, perching on the arm of his chair.

He noticed suddenly that she held a dessert plate in one hand, a silver fork in the other. *Uh-oh,* he thought, it was just as he had feared: *Nate spilled the beans.*

"I understand Dutch apple isn't your favorite pie, after all."

Funny, she didn't sound hurt.

"Seems a shame to go without dessert." She leaned across him to put the plate on the end table. "I want you to know," Lily added, smiling *exactly* the way he'd pictured her in that daydream a little while ago, "I think it's sweet, the way you've been eating something you don't like all these years, just to spare your mom's feelings." She leaned in again, pressed a kiss to his temple. "Do me a favor?"

He glanced at the plate. Chocolate cake. Looked homemade, too. He'd only picked at his dinner, and Nate had eaten his pie… Max licked his lips and forced himself to meet her eyes. "Favor? Sure. Anything." This time when he smiled, he meant it.

"Don't ever do that to me, okay?"

He frowned, shook his head. "I'm not following you."

"Don't ever pretend you like something, just to please me. I'd much rather *really* please you."

She tilted her head when she said it, flirty-like. And her smile went from sweet to kind of mischievous. Max didn't quite know what to make of that.

Mmm…so therein lies the rub, he thought. *She* thought of them as a couple, too. *That's what you get, idiot, for kissing her like you meant it.*

But he *had* meant it, hadn't he?

"Promise?"

Promise what? Promise he meant it? Or promise not to say he liked pie if he didn't? By now, he honestly didn't know for sure, but Max nodded, feeling like one of those back-car-window doggies. "Sure. I promise."

Earlier, he'd assessed the changes in Lamont, thought that if love could change a man that much, maybe he ought to try it. *Maybe you ought to think again,* he decided. Because this whole "love" thing was turning him into a bumbling, babbling, half-wit.

"Do you like chocolate cake?"

His gaze darted to the thick wedge beside him.

"Well, yeah!" He laughed and grabbed the plate. "Who doesn't?" His mouth began to water because now he could smell the delicious richness of it.

"You're not just saying that, to be nice...."

She tilted her head again, and suddenly he didn't know which sweet treat had started him salivating. "I'll be honest," he started, using the fork as a pointer, "I don't know if I want to jam this whole thing into my mouth at once, or kiss you."

Lily tipped her head back a bit and laughed. She gave his shoulder a playful shove. "The cake will get stale if you don't eat it soon, but there's plenty of time for—" she wiggled her eyebrows "—for the other." With that, she hopped off the chair arm and walked toward the door.

Max stuffed a forkful of cake into his mouth. "Aw, man," he said around it. "This is terrific."

She stopped long enough to say, "Glad you like it."

"Homemade?"

"Yup. My mama's recipe." And she disappeared around the corner.

"Max," he said to himself, slicing off another bite of the cake, "your boy's right...the girl can cook."

And she genuinely enjoyed cooking for *him*. If he told her how he felt, Lily would reciprocate. Max knew that, as well as he knew his own name. As the fudgy frosting melted on his tongue, he realized he'd better get his head together. It wasn't fair to Lily to string her along. She deserved the best, *only* the best. No doubt she'd be good for him, for Nate.

But Max had been on his own a long time, doing

things his way, in his own good time. Could he change? Could he open up and welcome her into his world?

Did he *want* to?

He ate another chunk of cake. Yeah, he did.

Those kisses on the porch echoed in his memory again. She was like no woman he'd ever met. Honest and straightforward, hardworking, with—how had Lamont put it again?—a heart as big as her head.

With a heart like that, she could put up with any nonsense he and Nate might dish out. But what about *her?* What could he and Nate offer Lily?

That's what he needed to ask. It was only fair, after all, to force her to peek over the legendary "fence," see that the grass might not be as green as it seemed, especially considering she'd been looking over there since junior high.

Did he love Lily?

Yeah, big time.

Was he *in love* with her?

Definitely. No doubt about it.

Enough to spend the rest of his life with her?

The question echoed in his mind, a moment, another…

Enough to spend the rest of my life with her?

That welcome-home kitchen scene he'd conjured earlier flashed in his head—beautiful, loving Lily at the stove, singing a tune under her breath, telling him "I've made your favorite."

Suddenly, the fantasy grew. Two more kids in the kitchen with Nate, laughing, running in circles around a high chair, where a baby squealed with delight, banging a big wooden spoon on the tray. In this version, Lily's stomach was swollen with child...*his* child. She wanted to name this one after his dad, if it was a boy. It's only fair, she was saying, since he'd let her name the last one Rose, for her mom.

It didn't have to be an illusion. It could be every bit as real as the cake crumbs on the plate in his hands.

Did he want that?

Max stood. Like his son, he'd take the plate to the kitchen, to spare Lily having to come fetch it. He saw her the minute he stepped into the family-crowded, brightly lit room, bent at the waist to wipe cake crumbs from Nate's mouth. She took the boy's face in both hands and rubbed her nose against his, then kissed his forehead. And the kid responded by wrapping his arms around her waist.

Yeah, he wanted that. Wanted *her,* more than anything.

Lessons his dad had taught him rang in Max's head. A man can't take his happiness at the expense of others. Do what's right, even if it hurts. *Earn* what you want.

That last bit of advice reverberated. Max nodded, realizing *that* had been the missing puzzle piece. Lily had loved him for what seemed like forever, but what had he done to earn it?

Nothing.

All the more reason to love her, because she'd handed over her heart, and would hand over her life if he asked her to, without so much as a hint of "what's in it for me?"

Well, there ought to be something in it for her. *Had* to be something for her.

He'd make a point of spending more time with her, let her get to know the *real* Max Sheridan—not the one she'd been looking at all these years over that legendary "fence."

Scary concept, he thought, because what if Lily discovered he wasn't anything like the Max she'd fantasized about since girlhood?

It was a risk he had to take, for her sake.

And if things worked out as he hoped they would, it was how he'd earn her love.

Chapter Nine

Lily loved spending time with Max and Nate. They'd been together a lot lately. Twice, sometimes three times a week, they'd drop by to watch her feed the animals. Nate warmed to the monkeys, and they to him, so she allowed him to feed them fruit and vegetables. She found herself drawn to Georgia's Diner, too, and not for the food!

Now, she sat at the counter while Max whistled off-key, flipping burgers as Andy watched over him like a mother hen. Did he like helping out in the diner as his mom recuperated? Or would he rather be back in Chicago, rubbing elbows with rich, powerful clients at the accounting firm?

It wasn't the first time the questions had come to mind, but things always seemed to prevent her asking them. Things like…did the Windy City remind him of his marriage to Melissa, her suicide?

Lily might have asked him now, if the phone hadn't rung.

His peaceful expression turned stony and stern when

he recognized the caller's voice. His tense tone told her the conversation wasn't going well; the abrupt way he hung up meant the news hadn't been good.

He slapped a hand to the back of his neck and kept his back to her for a moment. She heard his heavy sigh, saw his shoulders sag. "Max," she said quietly, "what's wrong?"

He turned slightly, but not enough so that she could see his face. "Nothing." Then he added, "Everything."

When he faced her, it seemed he'd aged ten years, right before her eyes. She wanted to comfort him, to ease his mind. But a hug didn't seem the medicine he needed right now.

She patted the stool beside her. "C'mere, tell Lily all about it."

For a second there, it looked like he might decline. But soon he was beside her, both elbows leaning on the red-speckled Formica counter. "I've been gone too long," he said, his voice a gruff whisper. "It's time to go back."

Lily's heart ached, just thinking of him being so far away. But hearing that would only add to his stress, so she laid a hand on his forearm.

"I took a leave of absence when Mom broke her leg. Extended it when she had the operation." He heaved a deep breath. "Truth is, I've stayed far longer than she needed me to. She's been up and around for weeks, now."

"Well, maybe she could handle the cash register, but that's about it."

Feeble excuse to keep him here? Lily asked herself. Probably, but if feeble was all she had, she'd use it.

"The other partners are demanding a decision. Soon."

She studied the lines of his strong, masculine profile, and it pained her to see the worry lines beside his mouth, beside his eyes. What had put them there? Dread at the thought of going back…or the thought of staying in Amarillo forever? Lily swallowed hard, terrified of the answer. "How soon?"

He folded his hands on the counter. "They want an answer by the end of the week."

"Saturday? That's awfully fast."

"I wish." He blew a silent whistle. "End of the *business* week." He looked into her eyes. "Tomorrow," he said, and stared straight ahead.

He may as well have said "The End." These few months had been the happiest of her life because Max had been a part of them.

Lily wished she knew what he needed to hear, what he needed her to do right now. Telling him to stay for her sake was out of the question, because this was a guy who'd forced down who knows how many slices of Dutch apple pie rather than hurt his mother's feelings. It would be just like him to quit the firm if she told him the truth—that it would break her heart if he went back to Chicago.

She wouldn't ask that of him. No, if he decided to make Amarillo his home again, it would have to be because *Max* wanted it—not to spare someone's feelings, not to please someone else, but for reasons of his very own.

"Do you...do you have any idea what you'll decide?"

"It's good money. No, *great* money. Nate could go to any college in the world. And the house...it's huge, with a big back yard and a swing set, and a place where he can ride his bike..."

Like her own father, Max was prepared to sacrifice, to suffer for his child. She admired that. Respected it. But she was living proof that no amount of money can buy happiness; she would much rather have seen her dad happy and at peace, than have had all the luxuries his money provided. And she told Max so.

"Nate's a great kid. He'll be happy if you're happy," she said.

Max nodded. "Part of me knows that, of course. And part of me feels he should never have to want for anything."

Customers' forks clinked against their plates as their quiet banter echoed through the diner. The dishwasher clanged pots and pans against the deep stainless-steel sink while Andy's spatula scraped against the grill. It had never been clearer: Life goes on, no matter what. *Oh, Lord,* she prayed, *use me now to bring Max back to You.*

"You'll make the right decision," she said, patting his arm.

He swung to face her. "You're that sure of me, are you?"

Lily read the smile in his eyes. Instinct made her

comb through the hair behind his temple, then slide her fingertips across his manly jaw. "Yes, I'm that sure of you."

If he could read her heart, he'd know how far from the truth her answer had been. How could he even consider making a life-altering decision like this without consulting the Almighty!

"Have faith, Max," she blurted. "It'll take you much farther than worry."

His expression turned hard again. "Faith. Don't make me laugh. Name me one reason I should believe in *that*."

"It pulled you through after Melissa's suicide. Got you through Nate's illness and your mom's surgery."

"Faith had nothing to do with it," he insisted. Jabbing a thumb into his chest, Max added, "*I* got me through. God had nothing to do with it…as usual."

The way he tacked on the qualifier reminded Lily he'd once believed—strongly enough to ask God's help, to hope for miracles. "God can't control human beings. I'm sure He wishes He could, but He gave us free will. The best He can hope is we'll make the choices He'd make for us…if He *were* in control of us."

"Oh, don't give me that Bible-thumping, Sunday-go-to-meeting nonsense. I'd have better luck playing with an eight ball than I'd have with prayer."

Obviously, this was neither the time nor the place to try to change his mind about God. But something had better change it, because as much as she loved him, Lily couldn't envision herself spending decades defending her faith! "You have so much to be grateful for!" Lily said, sliding off the stool. "I'd say 'count your blessings' if it didn't sound so trite." She grabbed her purse. *I'd say you're acting like a spoiled, immature boy, too*—if she didn't think it would add fuel to his fire.

He looked miserable. But then, why wouldn't he? Max had convinced himself he was on his own, that there was no one he could turn to at times like these. Stubborn as he was, determined as he seemed to be to hold tight to his "If God exists, He doesn't care" mind-set, she loved him. Lily stood behind him, gave him a little hug and kissed the back of his neck. Lips beside his ear, she whispered, "Count your blessings, Max. You might be surprised how much God has given you."

Lily didn't give him a chance to argue the point. She was turning out of the parking lot when she wondered if he'd take her advice.

And if he did, would *she* be one of his blessings?

"I've got good news."

Lily sat on a hay bale and patted the space beside her. "It must be great news, sister dear, the way you're huffing and puffing."

Cammi sat beside her, biting her bottom lip. "I've just been to see Dr. Anderson," she said, and covered her mouth with both hands, trembling with excitement as she waited for Lily to say…

"Dr. Anderson…isn't he an obstetrician?"

Cammi hid behind her hands, peeked between two fingers.

"A baby?" Lily hugged her. "You and Reid are going to have a baby?"

"Isn't it wonderful?"

After Max's news a few hours earlier, it was more than wonderful. "I'll say." Lily held Cammi at arm's length. "When's the big day?"

"Fourth of July."

"Wow. Talk about a patriotic couple."

"Reid doesn't even know yet. You're so good with ideas, I thought I'd see what you'd come up with—some way I could surprise him."

"I'm flattered to be the first to know," Lily said. She furrowed her brow. "Hmmm…well, you could always wait for the annual pyrotechnics display out at Lake Meredith, tell him during the finale that there's a little firecracker on the way."

"Oh, Lily. Now you're just being silly. Really. Help me come up with something spectacular, something he'll never forget."

She pretended to be insulted. "If he doesn't think a fireworks display is spectacular, maybe I'm wrong," she teased. "Maybe Reid isn't so patriotic, after all."

"I was thinking dinner by candlelight, in the living room, in front of the fireplace. Soft music. A special meal. His favorite dessert." She clapped her hands. "What do you think?"

Cammi positively *glowed* with happy radiance, so much so that it warmed Lily's heart, too. For the moment, she forgot about the possibility that Max might move back to Chicago, that she might never see him again.

"What do I think? I think you wasted your time

coming over here to get my ideas. Sounds like you cooked up the perfect evening all by yourself."

Cammi nodded. "Then, it's settled. I'll go to the grocery store on my way back to the Rockin' C."

"Guess the *C* can stand for 'cradle' now, eh?"

Cammi giggled.

"What *does* that *C* stand for, anyway?"

"Reid inherited the ranch from his adoptive parents, Billy and Martina. He told me once that Billy named the place after an old army buddy, Calvin. He was a rock and roll musician before he joined up. See, Cal loaned him the money for the down payment."

"Rockin' C. Now I *see*," Lily said, laughing.

Cammi frowned suddenly.

"What? A pain? You okay?"

"'Course I am. Are *you* okay? You look like you just lost your best friend."

"Man. Talk about hitting the old nail on the head."

"Uh-oh. This is Max-related, isn't it."

Lily nodded.

Cammi got to her feet and held out her hand. "Let's go up to the house and talk about it over a cup of tea."

Over teacups and chocolate chip cookies, Lily filled Cammi in on the state of her relationship with Max. "...and now he isn't sure if he should go or stay."

"I remember how awful it was for me when Reid left town to re-up with the rodeo. I feel for ya, kid, honest I do."

"I've always wondered—if you hadn't followed him, do you think you'd be together today?"

"Nope. He's more stubborn than those bulls he used

to ride. He probably would have sentenced us both to life apart rather than admit how he felt."

Lily sighed. "What is it about men? What's so hard about those three little words?"

Cammi grinned. "Have *you* said 'I love you'?"

She flicked a cookie crumb onto the floor. "Well, no. I haven't."

"Why not?"

"Because…because what if he doesn't feel the same way? What if he says—" Lily assumed the deepest voice she could muster "—'Sorry, Lil ol' girl, I think you're a great kid and all that, but…'" She rolled her eyes. "I'd just about die!"

"Have you ever considered that maybe he feels the same way?"

Lily stared into Cammi's bright eyes. "No. Guess I haven't. But how frustrating is *that?* I mean, how are two people supposed to get together if they're both scared stiff of admitting their feelings!"

"They get together," Cammi said, "because one of them thinks it's worth risking rejection in the hope he or she will hear those three magic words echoed right back at them."

Lily took a sip of tea, then grinned. "I can't wait 'til I'm as old and wise as you."

"Neither can I," Cammi teased. She got up and grabbed her purse from where she'd hung it on the chair back. "Well, I'm off to the store." She checked items off an imaginary list, written on her palm. "One romantic evening, one joyful husband, one spectacular celebration…"

Walking beside her to the back door, Lily added, "Can't wait 'til I'm as happy as you are, either."

Cammi hugged her tight. "Aw, Lil...that day will come. I know it will. Where's your faith?"

Lily waved as her sister headed toward her car. Ironic, she thought, that Cammi would pose that particular question. Especially considering the lecture she'd laid on Max a few hours earlier.

"'Judge not lest ye be judged,'" she quoted, because Cammi was right. If she believed things would work out between her and Max, they would.

Right?

Common sense prevailed: They'd work out if God saw it as part of His plan.

Let it be part of Your plan! Lily prayed.

"Hardly seems fair," Georgia said when Max broke the news to her that day. "I mean, you're not taking more than your share of the profits, right?"

Max shook his head. "No, but the partners have had to divide my clients among them. They want full percentages if things are going to stay this way."

"What did you tell them?"

"The truth," he said.

"Which is?"

"I don't know."

His mother sighed. "Seems a shame for you to go back to that rat race. You've seemed so calm and rested here." She glanced over at her grandson, who was filling a paint-by-numbers canvas with primary colors as

Robert looked on. "And Nate took to Amarillo like a born Texan!"

"I know, I know."

She waved Robert over. "Well, here's something that might make your decision a little easier." Once her fiancé joined her in the booth, Georgia said, "We've decided to retire after we get married."

That surprised Max, and he said so.

"There's a big wide wonderful world out there," his future stepfather said, "and we've both worked so hard, we've only seen a small slice of it. And we want to see it, together."

His mother had worked hard all her life. Max couldn't remember her ever taking more than a day or two away from the diner. "What about this place?" he asked. "Andy's a great guy, a terrific fry cook, but I've seen him make change. You don't want him keeping the books."

"You're right. He means well, but his math skills sure leave a lot to be desired." Georgia leaned forward, waved Max closer. "But I have it all figured out," she whispered. "Piece of cake."

"Easy as pie," Robert added.

"Simple as—"

Hands up in mock surrender, Max laughed. "Okay, okay. I get it. So out with it, already. What's this idea of yours?"

Robert slid a fat brown envelope from his inside jacket pocket. "Open it."

The envelope contained the deed to Georgia's Diner, a topographical map of the lot, a license to operate an

Amarillo business, and an inventory of the restaurant's equipment. Max was more than happy to provide them with a little free tax advice. He leafed through the documents and then, folding them up again, nodded. "Everything appears to be in order." He held out the folder. "You planning to hire a live-in manager?"

Georgia and Robert exchanged a glance. "Sort of," she said without taking the envelope.

Max donned his most professional pose—elbows on the table, hands clasped atop the paperwork. "You aren't planning to leave on your world tour tomorrow, so it isn't like there's any big rush. You have plenty of time to find someone trustworthy to run the place while you're gone." Grinning, he shrugged. "Who knows? You might miss the place."

Georgia wrapped a hand around her beau's arm. "Not a chance. I've given this place my all. Rarely spent a dime of my tip money, put most of the profits back into the business."

Max said, "Which is why it's the busiest eatery in town."

"Which is *also* why I'm the tiredest diner owner in town. I have some zip in my step…or soon will, thanks to ol' Robert, here, so—"

"Hey," the man teased, "who you callin' old?"

"I want to enjoy what's left of my life. No more getting up at 3:00 a.m. to drive to the markets for vegetables and meats. No more baking pies 'til all hours of the night. No more smiling when some trucker complains that his burger wasn't cooked enough…or that it was overcooked. No more soups to stir, or chili pots to scrub."

"Mom," Max said, blanketing her hands with his, "no one is saying you don't deserve some freedom from this place. You've been a slave to it most of your life!"

He'd seen expressions of anger, weariness, joy and disgust on her face, but Max had never seen *that* look before. She continued to sit there, blinking and silent, refusing to take back the diner's paperwork.

When Georgia looked down, turned her engagement ring around and around, Max thought he'd figured it out.

"Mom, it's been in your family since Great-Grandma Georgia first moved to Amarillo. You can't be seriously considering selling the place...."

Her head snapped up. "'Course not," she said. "I want you to have it. Lock, stock and griddle brick."

Max laughed nervously. "Me? You're kidding, right?"

He glanced from Georgia's serious face to Robert's and back again. "You're *not* kidding." The documents suddenly seemed too hot to touch, so he sat back and crossed both arms over his chest.

"Even if I was interested, I can't afford it right now. Everything I have is tied up in the house in Chicago, in the firm. It'd take weeks to liquidate."

"Maxwell Sheridan, don't you insult your mama that way! I wouldn't dream of taking a dime from you. Why, you wouldn't let me pay a penny of your college tuition. And when you went into that business out there in Chicago, you wouldn't let me help you."

She turned to Robert. "Do you realize that every time things got tough around here, money-wise, this boy bailed me out? Why, there were times I'd have gone belly-up for sure if he hadn't come to the rescue."

She faced Max again. "And you refused to let me pay those loans back. You've bought and paid for this place twice over, way I see it!"

"Mom…"

"Son, you love this place every bit as much as I do. You'd hate seeing it go to strangers."

She was right on both counts. "But, Mom, I'm a lousy cook, and—"

"Andy has agreed to stay on."

Max frowned. "—and I'm clumsy as they come. I don't think I've ever delivered a meal without spilling something."

"Vera will stay, and so will Betty. They're two of the finest waitresses in all of Texas." Georgia winked. "I oughta know, I trained 'em myself!"

True again. But he didn't say so.

"Think of yourself as the overseer," Robert suggested. "Someone who balances the books, orders the food, counts the cash."

Georgia nodded. "Right! And you wouldn't even have to set foot in the kitchen if you didn't want to." She hesitated. "'Til the health department did its annual inspection, that is." Another pause. "And of course you'd pass, 'cause, like I said, I trained Betty and Vera my very own self."

It was definitely something to think about. Because he didn't relish the idea of going back to Chicago, picking up where he'd left off, even if the money he earned out there did guarantee Nate could attend the Ivy League college of his choice.

His mother had been right about something else, too: he *had* felt good, real good, since coming home. And Nate had taken to the place like a fish to water.

Then there was the matter of Lily….

"Like you said," Robert said, "we're not going anywhere tomorrow, or even the next day. Take some time, bounce the idea around a bit."

Max didn't have time; he had promised Donald Wilkes he'd have an answer by tomorrow. But he nodded anyway. "I'll give it some thought." Then he added, "When do you need to know?"

Georgia looked suddenly guilty, like a little girl caught with her fingers in the cookie jar. "Just take your time, son."

But she hadn't meant a word of it; the tension in her voice told Max she had something up her sleeve. If experience hadn't long ago taught him it would be a waste of time and energy to ask *what,* he'd nag it out of her.

Still, she hadn't had to write it on the menu board: they needed to know ASAP.

So now he faced *two* deadlines. Three, if he counted the self-imposed restriction he'd put on himself where his future with Lily was concerned.

"Pray on it, son," Georgia said, patting his hand. "The Good Lord will let you know what's best for you and Nate."

Not a chance, he thought, echoing his mom's earlier

quote. "Mind if I take these with me?" he asked, pointing to the papers.

"If you make the right choice, they're yours." Georgia slid them to the edge of the table. "So be my guest."

"I'm going up to bed now," he said, bussing her cheek. And reaching across her, he shook Robert's hand. "Drive safe goin' home."

He was halfway up the back stairs when he heard his mother holler, "Pray on it, son!"

Max took a deep breath. "Okay, Mom." Maybe prayer was his only way out.

It never had worked before, no reason to believe it would work now.

But he was pretty much out of options…so what could it hurt?

Max tossed and turned until his sheets were in a knot. Since it was obvious sleep would elude him, he got up and headed for the living room.

He stood for a long time, just looking around at the tables and chairs, at flea-market paintings on the walls, at the place he'd called home as a boy, as a young man.

This was a good room, filled with plain colors and plainer furnishings, where on Sunday mornings his father sat in the big easy chair, giving the newspaper a hearty *flap* every time he turned a page. "You'll put me in the loony bin with your paper-snapping," his mother would say.

But it hadn't been a scolding, not really; their eyes would meet, and his dad's wry grin and his mom's merry wink were proof that, different as they are, man and woman could share…life.

Shortly after her husband's death, Georgia began turning on his desk lamp every night before going to bed. "He needs the light to guide him," she'd say as she twisted the tiny brass button on its base 'til one *click* echoed in the quiet night. "Not much light, just enough, so he won't trip or stub his toe on his way to our room." She wound his pocket watch every night, too, and gently laid it atop the blotter, arranging the fob in an *S* pattern…*S* for Steven. Then her fingertips would graze the top rung of his desk chair, lingering.

Max was grateful for having grown up in a house filled with love like that. It had surrounded him as a boy, like warm tidal waters and fresh, sunny air. No wonder it had been so easy to recognize love when he saw it for himself.

His mother didn't look at her new fiancé in quite the same way she'd looked at Max's dad. But then, Robert probably didn't look at Georgia as he'd looked at his first wife, either. They'd met each other in time, and that was all that mattered. Max was grateful for that, too.

He heard Nate in the next room, muttering in his sleep. Max closed his eyes and reveled in the sound. He'd almost lost the boy, twice. He was thankful that he'd been an eyewitness to back-to-back miracles, and now his one and only son grew more healthy and robust with each passing day.

Lily had been right…he had needed to count his blessings.

He sat on the hard wooden chair that matched his

father's desk and adjusted the lamp's goose-neck until its dim beam illuminated the documents his mother had given him. Should he run the diner so it could remain in the family? Or go back to Chicago, where a big house and a corner office in a fancy skyscraper waited for him?

The steady *tick-tick-tick* of his dad's pocket watch seemed to be telling him, *"Stay, stay, stay..."*

Max padded into the kitchen on socked feet, turned on the flame under the teakettle. It was all the light he needed to see his favorite cup, resting upside down in the drainboard. When the water was hot, he'd make himself some hot chocolate. Wouldn't be as tasty as the stuff Lily whipped up, but maybe it would make him drowsy.

He needed a good night's sleep, because tomorrow, first thing, he'd book a flight to the O'Hare airport, take a cab to Wilkes Towers and start the "I'm outta here" ball rolling. Max wasn't sure exactly when he'd made the decision. He only knew that he couldn't go back to that life, or that world. Not when everything he'd ever wanted was already here.

He'd keep things to himself for a while, at least until his house was on the market and he'd discussed a fair and reasonable settlement with the Wilkes partners.

It felt good, knowing he was home again—home to stay. So good that he turned off the teapot before the water even began to simmer. What did he need with store-bought cocoa when he'd found the girl who would make it for him from scratch!

Max tidied his sheets and climbed back into bed. On

his back, with fingers linked behind his neck, he stared at the ceiling. Was God really up there, someplace far beyond his boyhood toys in the attic and abandoned birds' nests still tucked among the eaves? Could He truly hear the voices of nondescript humans calling through the clouds and the stars for help from on high? And if He heard, why had He so often turned a deaf ear to *this* human? Max wondered.

He remembered Lily's words in the car that day, when Nate asked a similar question. "Maybe He isn't saying yes or no," she'd said. "Maybe He's saying 'wait.'"

Wait.

The silence was interrupted only by the tire-*hiss* of the occasional passing car. It was easy to wait, when the world was at rest, when life was so quiet. Not so easy in the bright light of day. At least, not without practice.

He'd waited a lifetime for Lily. He could wait a few more days, until he could turn the last page on the Chicago chapter of his life.

Chapter Ten

"Hey, Lil…I have to go to Chicago. Sure would be nice if you could come, too—"

Lily listened to the message three times before throwing her purse across the room. What had cut off the end of his message?

She dialed the diner, hoping Georgia would be there.

"Geor-gia's," the redhead sang into the phone.

"Hi, Georgia. It's Lily."

"Howdy, kiddo!"

"How's the leg?"

"Still attached, last time I checked." She chuckled. "Robert says if I stick with my physical therapy, I might be able to throw this nasty cane away by Valentine's Day."

"That's wonderful news. I'll keep you on my prayer list. Make sure you keep doing your exercises."

Another chuckle. "Thanks. I think." Georgia paused. "So what can I do for you, kiddo?"

"When I got back from Lake Meredith, there was a strange message from Max on my answering machine. I was just wondering if—"

"What were you doing up there *this* time?"

"Oh, some goofy hikers left a bunch of twine at their campsite, and a spike buck got tangled in it. Ended up pinned to a tree trunk. Boy Scouts troop leader called me from his cell phone."

Georgia clucked her tongue. "Those addle-brained fools. Is the li'l guy all right?"

"Will be, once his cuts and scrapes heal. I just got him settled in a stall."

"So, about this message from Max…"

"He said he was on his way to Chicago." Lily's heart pounded at the thought. "When did he leave, exactly?"

"Day before yesterday. But don't worry, he'll be back."

"He will?"

"Has to. He left Nate with me." Georgia's laughter filtered through the phone line.

"You wouldn't have his phone number handy, would you?"

"Home, office, fax or cell?" Georgia asked.

"I'll try all of them." Her hand trembled as she wrote down the numbers Georgia dictated. "Just one more question. Is he…is he coming back for good?"

"I sure hope so."

Georgia didn't sound as jovial, as sure of herself, suddenly, and it made Lily's blood run cold. "Well, thanks. Take care of yourself."

If the woman had more to say, Lily didn't hear it. Dazed by the news that Max had left town, she hung up without another word.

Suddenly, she was reminded of her conversation with Cammi the other day. Her sister had followed Reid all the way to Montana or Idaho or…Lily couldn't remember where. The only thing that really mattered was that the trip had a happy ending—Cammi and Reid wound up together.

And they were married.

And now they were going to have a baby.

Lily raced up the stairs, dialing Cammi's number as she went. "Hey, can you do me a huge favor?" she asked when her sister answered the phone.

"If I can, 'course I will."

"I'll need you to feed the animals for a couple of days. Do you think Reid will mind helping?"

"I've done it all before. I don't need his help."

"I just brought home a spike buck. Nothing serious wrong with him, but he's strong as a bull elephant. Reid will need to hold him while you change the bandage on his leg."

"What happened to him?"

"Long story. Mind if I tell you when I get back?"

"Mind telling me where you're going?"

"Chicago."

"Ah, I should have known." Cammi sighed. "When are you leaving?"

"I'm packing as we speak," she said, throwing her suitcase onto the bed. "Hopefully, I can get a flight out of Amarillo International today."

"I'll pray that you get your flight, that you arrive safely, that you find that knucklehead when you get there…and drag him home!"

"Thanks, Cam. I owe you big time for this one."

"Tell me something I don't know," Cammi said, snickering.

Lily put jeans and sweaters, a business suit and a simple black dress into the suitcase as she asked how Cammi was feeling. She prayed her sister wouldn't miscarry this child, as she had her last. Satisfied Cammi was doing well, Lily hung up and ran downstairs to write her father a note: "Going to Chicago. Explain later. Call you when I get there. Take care! All my love, Lily."

All the way to the airport, she prayed.

Prayed there'd be a seat for her on a standby flight, that she wouldn't get lost in the maze of terminals that made up Chicago's O'Hare.

Prayed she'd be able to find her way to a hotel in the city, that there'd be a room available.

Because wasn't Chicago known as "Convention City"?

Or was that New York?

Lily prayed that once she got hold of Max, he'd sound genuinely happy to hear from her.

But most of all, she prayed he wouldn't tell her he intended to stay in Chicago permanently.

Because if he said that, Lily would have to pray for the strength to return to Amarillo without him.

Lily sat on the edge of her hotel room bed and used her cell phone to call Max's. On the third ring, she began rehearsing what she'd record on his voice mail; on the fourth, he said, "Sheridan."

"Max. Hi. It's Lily."

"Hey, there! Good to hear from you. Did you get my message?"

"Part of it. Something cut you off after your invitation to Chicago."

"No way. Man. Well, no wonder you never called me back, then."

"That's only half the reason. I had an emergency."

"Everybody's okay back there, I hope."

She smiled. How like him to worry about the people she loved. "Everyone's fine. It was an animal rescue kind of thing. I was at Lake Meredith all weekend. And like a ninny, I forgot my cell phone."

"So, how are ya?" he asked.

"Cold." And it was true. "I could probably have lived my entire life without knowing why they call Chicago the Windy City. I don't know how people stand it!"

"Whoa. You're in town?"

Maybe she shouldn't have come. Maybe politeness had made him invite her. *Maybe you should answer his question.* "Yes. I'm staying at the Sheraton Towers."

"No kidding? When did you get here?"

"About an hour ago."

"You here 'cause of my message?"

Why else would she have traveled nearly nine hundred miles, enduring a luggage search and being frisked at both ends of the line! "I was just curious to see how the other half lives."

Max laughed. "You're in for a major disappointment,

then. I'm glad you decided to come, though, whatever the reason."

He was the one and only reason!

"Say…have you had anything to eat yet?"

"Not since this morning."

"I have a few loose ends to tie up here. How 'bout when I'm finished, I pick you up and buy you some dinner?"

"Sounds great. What time should I be ready?"

"I'll give you a call as soon as I finish up. What's your room number?"

She told him, then hung up, immediately wishing she'd asked what kind of dinner he had in mind. Because Lily would hate to show up in blue jeans if he had something fancier in mind—

The phone interrupted her reverie.

"Hey, Lil," he said when she answered. "How would you feel about joining me for dinner at one of the partners' homes? The firm's senior partner is throwing a shindig to show off his new house. Mansion is more like it," he said, laughing. "The thing has ten bedrooms, eight bathrooms and five fireplaces! We'll leave there with full bellies, 'cause his wife, Brandy, really knows how to put on a banquet!"

Brandy? Lily had a feeling she was going to put the proverbial bull in a china shop to shame. Already, her hands had begun to shake. "Sure. Why not?"

She agreed to meet him in the lobby, seven o'clock sharp. The alarm on her night table said 3:04 p.m. More than enough time for a nap before she showered and dressed for the…*banquet.* Lily opened her suitcase and had started putting clothes on hangers when the phone rang again.

"Make it six," Max said. "I want to show you my office before we head over to Donald's house."

He sounded so businesslike, so matter-of-fact. Maybe the icy temperatures had that effect on his vocal cords. Had he missed her as much as she'd missed him? Had he thought about her nonstop, dreamed about her, pictured her during idle moments?

"Lily?"

"Yes?"

"Thought we'd been disconnected for a minute there. So, what do you say? Okay if we meet at six instead of seven?"

"Sure," she said again. "Why not?"

This time when the call ended, Lily lay down on the thick quilt covering the massive bed. How would she wear her hair? Was the little black dress she'd brought elegant enough for a banquet in a mansion? Max would be introducing her to the other partners in his accounting firm. Because he intended to ask her to stay here with him? Or simply because he didn't want to attend the function alone?

The clock said 3:45 p.m. now. She'd left the house at eight in the morning, managed to snag a seat on a standby direct flight from the Amarillo airport to O'Hare. Stretching, Lily yawned. "Guess you'll find out soon enough," she said, closing her eyes.

From Max's office, tucked in a corner on the penthouse floor of one of the city's tallest skyscrapers, Lily could see most of Chicago. She didn't know much about commercial real estate, but she knew the price rose with the elevator.

"I'm impressed," she said.

"Don't be. I'm not."

There it was again—that incredible nonchalance that had led her to believe the firm was made up of a couple of college buddies, that maybe they'd rented the ground floor of a house-turned-office on a busy side street.

"You have every right to be proud of what you've accomplished," she insisted, running a fingertip along the arm of his desk chair. Its buttery brown leather matched the sofa and love seat that faced one another along a mahogany wall lined with hardcover books.

"Didn't say I wasn't proud." He shrugged and pocketed his hands. "I'm just not impressed."

"That's okay. I'm impressed enough for the both of us."

He sat in the enormous chair and pulled out a desk drawer. "Mind waiting while I make a quick call to Nate?"

"Take your time," she said, taking a seat in one of the beige upholstered wing chairs facing his desk. "Tell him I said hi."

She watched him chat with his son, laughing and nodding in response to something the boy had said. If Max didn't love that kid with everything in him, Lily thought, he'd missed his calling as an actor. He seemed to have infinite patience with Nate, whether the boy was recounting a movie he'd just seen, word for word, or singing a song he'd just learned.

"I miss you, too, kiddo. Kiss Gramma good-night for me." He paused, listening, and Lily knew even before he responded what Nate had said, for Max's face lit up brighter than the Christmas tree in Rockefeller Center.

"I love you, too. I'll call you tomorrow, okay?"

"He's some kid," she said when he hung up.

Max stared at the phone for a moment. "You can say that again." He met her eyes. "I want you to know, I took your advice."

Brows raised, she asked, "What advice?"

Max stood, shoved the chair under the desk. "You were right. I have plenty to be thankful for."

She got to her feet, too, and followed him to the massive double doors.

"You gave me a lot to think about, which is why I'm here in Chicago. Had some tough decisions to make, and your 'count your blessings' advice made me decide to—"

The many-buttoned black phone on his desk buzzed, cutting off the rest of his sentence.

His shiny shoes thudded softly as he crossed the Persian carpeted floor. "Sheridan," he said into the mouthpiece. He listened a moment, then said, "Why don't you just take a cab?" Another moment of silence. "All right. I'll be there in—" he checked his watch "—give us fifteen minutes. What? Oh, 'us.'" He glanced at Lily. "Nobody you'd know. Friend of mine from Amarillo."

Whoever was on the other end of that call made him nervous. Max ran a hand through his hair even before he hung up. And when he met her eyes this time, she got the feeling Max wasn't really seeing her at all.

"You ready?" he said, opening the door.

Lily nodded and stepped into the enormous, well-appointed waiting suite. Here, as in his office, the furnishings were rich in texture, subtle in color. Wood tones and earthy hues were in abundance, from the recessed light fixtures in the ceiling to the plush carpeting underfoot.

Max Sheridan was a wealthy man, perhaps more so than her father. And like her dad, he'd never gloated or boasted about it. In fact, to look at him, to talk to him, a person would think he was barely making ends meet!

He walked ahead to push the elevator button. "Ritzy digs, eh?" he teased. "Rent around here is sky-high, so I talked the guys into buying the space. Best investment we ever made."

She couldn't help but notice that he held his head higher here, spoke with a quiet authority that hadn't been necessary back in Amarillo. There, he'd donned blue jeans and cotton shirts; here, he wore a suit that screamed "made in Italy!"

"It's a beautiful office," she said.

As the brass-doored elevator hissed shut, Max jutted out his chin and folded his hands behind his back. "It'll do."

If he could be that casual about opulence like this, what must his home look like!

"If we get out of Wilkes's early enough, maybe I'll drive you over to my house—see what you think of the place."

In the months since his return to Texas, Lily had learned he'd been blessed with many gifts. 'Til now, she hadn't realized mind reading was one of them.

But wait… Why would he care what she thought of his house—unless he planned to ask her to share it with him?

He'd lived there with his wife. In fact, Melissa had died at that address. Lily seemed to be moving farther and farther from her "rose-covered cottage" dream….

"Have I told you that you look gorgeous tonight?"

Lily blushed. "Only about a dozen times."

"Yep," he said in his thickest Texas drawl. "Y'clean up purty good…fer a li'l farm girl."

Wink or no wink, his teasing comment made Lily bristle. No one had ever called her a *farm girl,* not even in jest. She'd been born and bred a rancher's daughter, and grew up to be proud of it!

"It's pretty brisk out there," he said once the elevator reached the lobby. "Why don't you wait here while I bring my car around?"

"Your car?"

He chuckled. "Let me guess…you thought because of the fancy-schmancy office, I have a chauffeured limousine waiting at the curb?" An out-and-out laugh this time. "Sweetheart, you think far too highly of me!"

Lily hid her frustration behind a pleasant smile. But while he was out getting the car, she couldn't help but think he was a different Max out here. "I mean, really…*'sweetheart'*?"

"What's that, ma'am?" the doorman said.

"Don't mind me," she told him with an exaggerated

southern accent. "I'm just a crazy little farmer from Texas who doesn't know what to make of the tall buildings y'all have out here!"

The man tipped his black-billed hat and went back to standing by the door.

He probably believes you, she thought.

Before she knew it, the huge thick-glass door swung open. "Your ride is here, ma'am," said the uniformed gent.

"Why, thank y'all," she said, smiling her biggest, brightest smile. "Y'all just have the *nicest* manners 'roun' these parts. Wait 'til I git home an' tell mah daddy." She leaned close to whisper, "Here he was, thinkin' all you big-city folk were mean an' nasty. Ain't he gonna be surprised!"

Max opened the passenger door of a low-slung silver convertible. The doorman handed Lily off as if he were only too glad to be getting rid of her. Not that she blamed him. It hadn't been fair to make him pay for Max's remark.

She saw Max tuck paper money into his gloved hand and hoped it had been a generous tip. *The man earned it tonight,* she thought, grinning slightly.

Lily continued with the overdone drawl. "This is a right-fine car you've got yourself here, if I do say so myself."

He cut her a quick, puzzled glance. "Uh…thanks."

"Bet this baby ain't no gas guzzler. Bet she parks like a dream, too, don't she?"

Max braked at a red light. "Lily, what…?" His confused expression smoothed to one of comprehension.

"Okay, I get it. You took offense at that 'farm girl' reference, didn't you?"

She stiffened. "Of course not. Don't be silly."

"Seems to me *you're* the one being silly. You should know I'd never say anything to deliberately hurt your feelings or insult you. If I did, I'm sorry."

Lily felt like a selfish, spoiled brat. She sighed. "Let's just blame it on the long trip. I really hate to fly these days."

He patted her hand. "Okay…"

He'd left his sentence unfinished. Curiosity ate at her until she said, "Okay *what?*"

"Okay, Silly Lily."

She had to hand it to him. Max sure knew how to calm a tense moment. But then, he'd had four years of practice, thanks to Nate. The knowledge didn't do much to erase her mind-set.

He fiddled with the radio dials, stuffed a couple of CDs into the changer, adjusted the knobs on the dash. It wasn't until Max used his coat sleeve to dust the top of the steering column that Lily thought he was taking tidiness a bit too far.

Yes, he was definitely different out here. In Amarillo, he drove with the windows down and didn't even seem to notice how much dust and grit accumulated on the car's interior! But then, Georgia's old boat probably hadn't cost one-tenth what Max had paid for *this* piece of machinery. And obviously, he was very pleased and proud of his purchase.

It was a nice car, to be sure. But really, Lily thought

as he used his sleeve again, this time to buff the steering wheel, it's *a car!*

He pulled into a driveway, put the sports car into "park" and tooted the horn.

"Sounds like a roadrunner," she teased.

"Which is precisely why I bought it," he shot back, grinning. "Reminds me of home."

He climbed out of the car and walked around to the passenger side as a tall, leggy blonde sashayed toward them.

Chapter Eleven

She had the walk of a runway model, the wave of a British royal. Max was out of the car in a heartbeat, taking her elbow and escorting her to the passenger door. *This* was the partner Max had agreed to drive to the banquet? Lily's heart all but ceased beating.

"Lily London, this is Susan Fisher. Lily and I go way back."

"So you said on the phone…an old Texas chum." She laughed.

"I hate to make you stand in the cold, Lil," Max said, "but would you mind, just long enough for Susan, here, to climb in."

The blonde tucked her chin into her neck. "You have *got* to be kidding! No way these legs of mine would fit back there!" As if to prove it, she stuck one out for Max and Lily to see. She looked imploringly at Lily. "You have shorter legs." And wrinkling her nose, she added, "Would you mind terribly much if I rode up front?"

Lily got out of the car, then got right back in and settled down in the back.

"Thanks," Susan said, taking Lily's place. "You're a doll." She struggled with the seat belt for a moment, then grunted with frustration. "Maxie, be a dear and fasten it for me, will you?" Over her shoulder she added for Lily's benefit, "This thing has *always* given me fits!"

Max leaned in, headfirst, and snapped the buckle into place. "All tucked in?"

When she nodded, he closed the door.

"Doll," indeed, Lily grumbled to herself. It was pretty apparent by things Susan had said that she and Max were more than business associates. But how much more? And for how long? If they were more than friends, why had he invited Lily here?

Maybe what he'd said on the answering machine had only *sounded* like an invitation. Maybe the half of the message that she hadn't received said something entirely different.

"You okay back there?" Max asked her, down-shifting.

"Fine and dandy."

Susan laid a long-taloned hand atop his. "Isn't she the cutest little thing?"

"Yeah," he said. "Cute."

Lily didn't know what to make of his tone. She knew this: Coming to Chicago had been a mistake. A *big* mistake.

Well, she told herself, *you're in it up to your earlobes now.* What choice did she have but to go along for the ride, literally and figuratively?

As they headed for the Wilkes's mansion, Susan told Max about the cellist who'd played a solo at the symphony the night before, about the way she'd cried at the end of the ballet last week. She'd heard the most talented new tenor singing at the opera. Her techno-stock had risen in value by *two whole points!* And the latest client to sign on with the firm was sure to send their profits through the roof this year. "But really, Max," Susan said, one long, red fingernail drawing circles on the back of his hand, "if it hadn't been for your securing the Vanemier account, I don't know where we'd be. Why, the Vanemiers recommended so many of their contemporaries that…"

Lily put her hands over her ears. If she had to listen to another word of this drivel, her head might just explode.

"You sure you're okay back there?"

She met Max's eyes in the rearview mirror and quickly put her hands in her lap. "Yup. Right as rain."

"Rain…that reminds me," Susan said, "I'm going to my cabin in Wisconsin this weekend, and the weather man says it's going to be great ski weather. Care to join me?"

"Nah. Thanks, though."

"But, Maxie, you love to ski!"

"I have to pass."

"Remember last time we went skiing? When you tried the 'expert' slope? Oh, if only I had a picture of your face when you came down that hill." Susan threw her head back and laughed.

Everything about her was sultry, from her deep, husky

voice to her shapely legs to her waist-long golden hair. No wonder Max was attracted to her.

Lily winced.

Evidently, she'd taken the quiet moments she and Max had experienced, the warm kisses, the caring conversation, far more seriously than he had. He'd been right to call her Silly Lily earlier, but not because she'd teased a doorman! It had been absurd to read so much into what he'd said, into what they'd shared.

Correction: into what she'd *thought* they shared.

"Have you fallen asleep back there?" Susan asked. "I haven't heard a peep out of you since we left my house."

If only sleep *could* rescue her from this moment! "Oh, I'm awake. Just mesmerized by the scintillating conversation going on up there."

It was too dark to read Max's eyes in the rearview mirror. But something told Lily that her remark had not amused him. *Tough beans, Maxie,* Lily thought. She knew exactly what Cammi would say to that: "Tough beans? Such language!" The thought made her smile. Which reminded her that, no matter what happened between her and Max—between Max and Susan—Lily would always have her family to love and protect her.

The thought of family made her think of Nate. Had Susan met the boy? And if she had, had she liked him? "Say, *Maxie,*" Lily said over the seat, "when's Nate's bedtime? Eight o'clock, right?"

Max nodded. "Uh-huh."

"He'd probably love it if you called, sang him a lullaby over the phone."

"A squeaking door hinge can hold a tune better than I can."

"Oh, I dunno," Lily insisted. "I've heard you humming around the diner. You're not so bad."

"Diner?"

Susan's voice wasn't so honeyed now, Lily noted.

"Would anybody mind if I made a quick stop at my place?" he said quickly. "I seem to have forgotten my wallet."

Nice save, Max, Lily thought. But "I don't mind" is what she said.

"We'll be late," Susan protested. "You know how Donald hates tardiness."

"We'll make it on time. My house is five minutes from the Wilkes's."

Max lived that close to a neighborhood full of mansions? What other things would she learn about him during this short visit to Illinois?

"Max," Susan said dully, "why must you always push the envelope? Honestly, sometimes I don't know what to think of you."

What would she think of Max the short-order cook, Lily wondered, or Max the waiter? Would she draw pictures on the backs of his hands if she'd seen them buried deep in a tub of sudsy water, washing greasy dishes? How would she feel about Max the doting son, who'd carried his injured mother up and down the stairs for weeks, who'd lovingly changed the dressing on her incision every morning? And what of the Max who'd nearly worn the speckles off the hospital's linoleum, pacing while his little boy was in surgery? Would she find his paternal concern attractive?

Something told Lily that Susan had no idea such a Max existed.

The car stopped in front of his house. "I'll leave the car running," he said, opening the driver's door. "Won't be but a minute."

"Mind if I use your little girls' room, as long as we're here?" Lily asked. Seeing inside the place would tell her still more about him. And she wanted to learn every detail, no matter how small.

He huffed a bit, then shoved his seat forward, extending a hand to help her out of the car. Lily pretended not to see it. No sense stirring up memories of times when he'd sandwiched her hands between his own; that would only remind her of happier moments.

"You know, I think I might just join you," Susan said. "My nose could use a little powdering."

Max walked ahead to unlock the door.

"Maybe you can give me a tour, Susan."

"Tour?" Susan stopped suddenly, as though someone had nailed her shoes to the redbrick driveway. "I… well…" She brightened, gathering her composure. "Of course. I'd be happy to."

Without knowing it, she'd given Lily the answer to a question she hadn't even asked: Susan had never been to Max's house. Lily's heartbeat doubled with relief.

He flipped a switch in the foyer, ushered his guests inside. "Powder room is the third door on your left, down that hall, there," he told Lily. And to Susan he said, "Wallet's on the dresser. Be down in no time. If you don't want to wait for the powder room, there's another bathroom one floor down, end of the hall."

Lily and Susan stood side by side, watching as he took the stairs two at a time. They glanced around, taking in the polished hardwood floor, the curved staircase with its mahogany railing, the enormous oil paintings hanging on the walls of the two-storied room. A grandfather clock chimed in the distance, counting out the seven o'clock hour.

"Uh-oh," Lily said. "'We're late, we're late...'"

Surprisingly, Susan laughed. "'...for a very important date,'" she finished.

Okay, so the big blonde wasn't *all* bad. Her only flaw, really, was a colossal interest in Max, and Lily could hardly blame her for that.

They walked through the darkened, quiet rooms, peering into doorways, looking around corners. It was a big house, bigger than he'd made it sound. Tastefully furnished with overstuffed sofas and chairs upholstered in muted plaids and elegant stripes. Had Melissa done the decorating? Or had Max had the place done over after the suicide, to hurry the healing along?

"So, have you two had your fill yet?"

Susan squealed and Lily gasped.

"Maxie! You scared me out of ten years of my life."

"Don't give it another thought," Lily told her. "From what I hear, those last ten years are the hardest, anyway."

Again, Susan laughed at Lily's joke. If not for their common interest in Max, maybe they could be friends....

The instant her shock at his sudden appearance wore off, Susan struck a pose: one high heel in front of the other, knee bent and hip thrust out slightly, right shoulder a tad higher than the left, head tilted *just* enough.

On second thought, Lily admitted, maybe they couldn't be friends, after all. "Beautiful house, Max," Lily said. "Your decorator has exquisite taste."

Leading them back to the foyer, he laughed. "Decorator?"

Susan lowered her head and looked up at him through mascara-rimmed eyes. "Don't tell me you did this all by yourself?"

He opened the front door. "Okay, I won't tell you."

Lily wasn't surprised. He had a certain masculine sensitivity about him, an eye for detail. She gave him a playful shot to the arm on her way by. "Nice job, pal. I'm impressed. Again."

"Don't be impressed. I'm not."

The look he gave her, when he said it, was reminiscent of those marvelous, magical moments on her front porch on Thanksgiving Day.

But Lily couldn't afford to put any stock in her memories.

During dinner, Lily laughed quietly at Donald Wilkes's knock-knock jokes. But her attention wasn't on the senior partner or his corny riddles, his elegant silk gabardine suit or his thousand-dollar-per-place-setting china. Fingers drumming lightly on the base of an intricately carved crystal goblet, she watched from the corner of her eye the couple who'd been seated directly across from her.

Susan had gradually slid her dinnerware nearer to Max's, allowing her to sit closer, to touch his hand each time she apologized for bumping his elbow or leaning into his shoulder. Much to Lily's dismay, Max didn't seem to mind a bit. If he'd figured out Susan's little scheme, it sure didn't show on his face. In fact, it looked to her as if he was flattered by the blonde's blatant flirtations!

They seemed to have much in common, much more than just their work. There was opera and ballet, the symphony, stocks and bonds… But Susan didn't seem the type who'd warm to children. Didn't look like the kind of woman Nate could relate to.

He'd lived in that quiescently dignified house for years, yet hadn't invited Susan to it. If they had so much in common, if he thought so highly of her, why hadn't she been a guest before?

"Who hasn't seen the house?" Wilkes asked. He picked up his wineglass, sloshing a bit of the red stuff on the white linen tablecloth. "Follow me, people, and we'll take the grand tour!"

"Donald," his wife scolded, "look what you're doing!"

He blotted the stain with a matching napkin. "Not to worry, darling. I'll buy you a new one. I'll buy you *ten* new ones!" His bawdy laughter bounced off the faux-suede painted walls. "Thanks to Sheridan, here, we'll have plenty of money come bonus time." He raised his glass. "A toast to Maxwell, for bringing us the biggest account in all of the Midwest!"

Quiet murmurs of appreciation and a smattering of applause resounded in the room. But no one patted him on the back, no one shook his hand, Lily noticed. What a difference between this crowd and her father's cronies!

One by one, the guests followed Donald and his wife for the "grand tour." Max, however, lingered in the library. "Been there, done that," he explained when Susan waved at him to come along. "Bought the T-shirt and outgrew it."

"C'mon, Lily," Donald slurred, grabbing her elbow. "Lesh go shee the resht of my place. I tol' the architect to make a copy of the stairs in *Gone with the Wind*," he said. "Whaddaya think? Doesh it look like Scarlett's staircase?"

The last thing Lily heard before he guided her toward the second story was Susan's musical laughter.

"All right, then," Susan told Max, "I'll keep you company...."

"I can't stay," Max said a few minutes later.

"Aw, Maxie," she sighed, "you can't leave. Chicago just wouldn't be the same without you!"

He wondered if Susan would pout that way if she knew it had absolutely no effect on him. She was a nice enough gal; he didn't want to hurt her feelings, but the woman simply couldn't take no for an answer. Even before Melissa died, Susan had put her antennae up, sending signals...hoping Max had received them.

He'd picked up on them, all right, but no matter how he tried to tell her he wasn't interested, she hadn't read *his* signals.

"Let me put it another way," he said. "I don't want to stay. Everything and everyone I care about is in Texas."

She pressed close, tilted her head, fluttered her lashes. "Everyone?"

He looked into frosty blue eyes. Pretty eyes, to be sure, but they didn't sparkle with love for him the way Lily's did. "Yeah." He nodded. "Everyone."

Susan lifted her head. "Do you mind if I ask who?"

Max tried to disengage himself from her, but she'd wrapped her arms around him so tightly, he couldn't budge. "Well, my son, for starters. And my mother. She's getting married one of these days—so my stepfather, too." He hesitated, wanting to say "Lily" but worried what Susan's reaction might be.

"And Lily?"

Well, there it was, out in the open. So why not admit it? "Yes, Susan. *Especially* Lily."

He thought she looked haughty when her brows went up like that, when she tipped her head and stared at him from the corner of her eye. A little arrogant and a whole lot mean.

"She doesn't have a clue, Max." Susan fiddled with his lapel, tucked the silk handkerchief keeper into his breast pocket. "Don't get me wrong…I'm sure she's *lovely*. But, really, she couldn't be a day over nineteen!"

Leave it to Susan to hit an almost-forgotten sour note.

"Lily is twenty-four," he said, hoping he didn't sound as defensive to Susan as he'd sounded to himself.

She laughed softly. "A very young, very naive twenty-four, then."

Without warning, she was stone serious. He'd seen that expression during meetings. The partners rarely left the conference room with a win in their pockets once she'd plastered that look on her pretty face.

Max steeled himself, waiting.

She drew close, even closer than before. "What you need, Maxwell Sheridan," Susan breathed, "isn't a starry-eyed girl, but a woman, a *real* woman who knows how to take care of a man."

He considered reciting the "you'll make some lucky guy a great wife someday" speech, but changed his mind. Because then he'd be forced to tell her *he* was not that man—not now, not ever. Knowing Susan, she'd force him to tell her why. And there simply were no words to explain it—at least, none that wouldn't hurt her.

She combed fingernails through his hair until her hands rested, one on his neck, the other pressed against the back of his head. If a wind had blown through the room right then, Max thought, not a trace of it could have slipped between them. Even if he didn't have a chance with Lily—and would she be here if he didn't?—the situation would have made him uncomfortable. Because his whole life was bottom lines. The bottom line here?

Susan was not his type.

She rested her head on his shoulder, began swaying

to and fro, as if to an imaginary waltz. *Enough of this, already!* Max decided. What if someone walked in here and saw them like this?

What if that someone was Lily?

Given the choice between hurting Susan and hurting Lily, well, that wasn't really a choice at all.

He gripped her upper arms, forcing her to take a step back. He hardened his expression and looked into her eyes. "Susan," he said, his voice more stern than it ever had been when scolding Nate, "what do I have to do to make you listen to reason? As soon as I get my house on the market and settle the partnership deal, I'm outta here. Gone. Vamoose. Done with Chicago. For good. Period." He gave her a gentle shake. "Got it?"

Eyes gleaming with challenge, she gave him a half smile. "My, but you're handsome when you're all riled up."

She wrapped a leg around his; if he moved either of his feet, they'd both hit the floor like felled trees.

Max had never backed down from a challenge in his life.

Why start now?

He narrowed his eyes. "So, what's your plan, kid? Keep me standing here 'til Lily comes down those stairs, make sure she gets a good eyeful of you and me like this?"

Susan's eyes filled with tears and she made no attempt to wipe or blink them away. One silvery drop slid down, leaving a white path on her rouged cheek. "You've never even given us a *chance,* Max. How do you know there's nothing here in Chicago for you? *I* could be something. But how will you know if you won't even try?"

She had no way of knowing that Melissa had mastered the art of Crying on Demand. Max had learned to harden his heart to her pseudo-sadness—that, or spend his entire life bending to her every whim, just to keep her quiet.

"I care for you, Max. Very deeply." Using one red-polished fingertip, she traced the outline of his upper lip. "I think you already know that, don't you?" She looked at him through tear-clumped lashes. "I think you've always known that."

"Stop it, Susan," he all but growled. "Stop it right now. You're making a fool of yourself."

The little-girl-wounded look was gone in a snap. Eyes glittering with anger, she said through clenched teeth, "No one talks to me that way. *No one.*"

Someone just did, he thought. He gave her a moment to figure that out, then said, "I'm leaving, so—"

She crooked her leg tighter around his.

Max glared at her. "You don't honestly think you're gonna change my mind, do you?"

"And you don't think that little girl is gonna make you happy, do you?"

The anger left him, just like that. Max almost thanked her.

"Yeah," he said matter-of-factly, "I do. I love her. More than I've ever loved anyone. And if she'll have me, I want to marry her."

"Marry her!" She released his leg, loosened her hug. "Well, you can't blame a girl for trying, can you?"

Max relaxed. Finally, he'd made her see reason! He made a move to walk away, but she threw herself into his arms and locked her lips to his. Seemed to Max it took a full minute to peel her off him. When at last he succeeded, he didn't look at her, didn't say a word. Instead, he wiped his lips with the back of his hand and stormed from the room.

He'd search every inch of Wilkes's mansion until he found Lily. And when he did, he'd take her in his arms and tell her that he loved her…had from the minute he'd first set eyes on her…would 'til the day he died. Didn't much matter who heard his confession, and he didn't care who saw him get down onto one knee to beg her to be his wife, either.

A few minutes earlier, Lily had been enduring the tour. She had seen some big houses in her day. Her own father's six-thousand-foot rancher boasted six bedrooms, six bathrooms… But this?

The only time she'd seen anything more opulent than Donald Wilkes's home was as a kid, when she and her classmates took a field trip to the state house. That place had four floors, servants' quarters…more rooms than she could count back then. *Give me a simple two-story Victorian any day of the week!* she thought, escaping and half running down the stairs. She hoped that when she found Max, he'd be ready to find the car.

One of the guests, upon learning it was her first visit to Chicago, had said, "You have to visit Navy Pier while you're here, ride the mile-high Ferris wheel. You can see half the city from up there!"

Going around and around on a hundred-fifty-foot tall ride in Chicago in December sounded like a fun and romantic thing to do. *Great excuse for cuddling!*

She'd had time to think about the whole Max-Susan thing as she traipsed from room to well-appointed room. His roots were in Texas, and so was his heart. She couldn't have been wrong about that. He'd seemed so happy there, so calm and contented. Like all those years ago, when they were just kids and the biggest worry in their lives was whether or not Centennial would win the championships.

He'd been fine-looking then, in his padded red and white uniform. But not nearly as handsome as now.

She had to admit he looked charming in his well-cut suit, looked professional and successful and important, all rolled into one. Lily knew she should have told him so earlier, but she would now...if she could find him again in this labyrinth of rooms and hallways they called a house!

Lily couldn't help remembering the little place across the road from River Valley Ranch. Just a farmette, no more than ten acres. The drive wasn't a twisting, turning black ribbon, like the one her father had built to bring folks from the highway to the house. Instead, it was a straight shot with two narrow lanes of pea gravel that led from the curb to the garage.

It had always been her favorite house. Nowhere in Amarillo had she seen one better. Not too small, but not big enough to get lost in, either. Tall, narrow windows flanked the front door, and Victorian gingerbread decorated the wraparound porch.

Every day, while waiting for the school bus, she had stared at that house, memorized every board and every brick. Of course she loved the house her father had built, stone upon stone. But *this* house, with its quaint little nooks and crannies, well, it had long been a dream to raise her children in such a house!

Someday, if the Good Lord answered all her prayers, maybe she *would* have a place like that. And maybe the kids who'd leave tricycles and jump ropes on that gorgeous covered porch would be Max's.

Ah, yes…if Lily's memory hadn't failed her, the staircase wound down and down, ending at the library door. And she'd left Max in the—

Lily's heart stopped and her mouth went dry as a bed of cotton. She felt the slick perspiration between her palm and the gleaming oak railing. She tried to move, wanted to move, because the last thing on earth she wanted to do right now was stand here and watch.

Max had both arms wrapped around Susan and was kissing her every bit as earnestly as he had kissed Lily back in Amarillo.

She ran toward the foyer, where a maid had hung her coat and purse. Once she'd stepped outside, where she could think, she'd call for a taxi to take her back to the hotel.

There would be no romantic Ferris-wheel-in-December ride tonight. Or ever.

Chapter Twelve

"Have you seen Lily?" Max asked the senior partner a while later.

"Is she the blonde or the brunette you came in with? I forget." He laughed. "You amaze me, Maxwell. I mean, who else could come in here with bookend beauties!"

If he'd had his way, Max would have walked into the room with only Lily on his arm. Because they'd seen him with women like Susan before, dozens of times. Lily was one of a kind: petite, pretty, with a smile that put the sun's warmth to shame and big green eyes that sparkled brighter than any emerald he'd ever seen. She looked classy in her elegant long-sleeved black dress. Its neckline exposed no more than her collarbones, its hem skimmed the tops of her knees. She'd chosen a single strand of pearls, dangly earrings to match, and piled her hair atop her head so that it looked like a mink-and-satin crown.

"Lily is the brunette."

"Hmm," the man said, nodding. "She's a looker, all

right, that one. And she didn't get that way with makeup. No siree. That one was born gorgeous."

Donald stared off into space. Picturing Lily, no doubt, Max thought. A buzz of jealousy coursed through him, and he had a notion to snap his fingers in front of Wilkes's face.

"Um…Lily?" he said instead.

That brought Donald around. "We had quite a pleasant conversation during our little tour. That's some special young woman, your Lily. Pretty as she is on the outside, she's even prettier on the inside."

His Lily. What Max wouldn't give to truly make her his. "Have you seen her?"

Wilkes gave him an "are you kidding?" look. "Last time I saw her, she was headed back to the library. Said that's where she'd left you."

The library, where until a short time ago, he'd been preoccupied with a certain blonde octopus….

Then Max's heartbeat sped up. Surely he hadn't been *that* preoccupied. He'd have noticed, wouldn't he, if Lily had come into the room while Susan was—

"Mr. Sheridan, sir?"

The partners faced a middle-aged woman in a gray uniform. She smoothed her white apron with one hand, held a gold key ring in the other. "A young woman asked me to give this to you."

Lily had volunteered to stow his car keys in her purse, so he wouldn't have to lug them around all night. How like her to make an offer like that, Max thought, slipping them into his trousers pocket. "Where is the, uh, young lady now?"

"Oh, she left, sir. About half an hour ago."

Now his heart thundered. "Left? But she came with me."

The woman shrugged. "Taxi came for her, like I said, 'bout half an hour ago."

No doubt about it. Lily had seen him with Susan. Why else would she have run off like that?

"Lovers' quarrel?" Donald teased, elbowing Max in the ribs.

"We've never had so much as a cross word," he said, mostly to himself. Then he remembered the time he'd read her the riot act over that whole golden retriever fiasco. "I have to go—see if I can get to the bottom of this."

"Right, before it gets any deeper," Donald agreed. "It's been my experience that diamonds are great smoothing-over tools. My advice to you is, wait until the jewelers open up in the morning before you confront her. If you're going to poke at a hibernating grizzly, be prepared with a tasty treat, I always say."

"Great advice, Don. Thanks for nothing."

Wilkes frowned. "No need to take that tone, Max. Let's not forget who's the senior partner."

"I remember. But I'm outta here, officially, tomorrow. Let's not forget *that*."

Max followed the maid to the door. "Was she very upset when she left?"

"I probably shouldn't say anything, Mr. Sheridan, sir. It's none of my business, after all."

"I'm making it your business."

The woman sighed. "Well, there were tears in her eyes when she walked out that door."

Wincing, Max grabbed his coat from the hall tree and stepped onto the granite porch. He hesitated, remembering he'd driven Susan to the party. He looked back inside. "See that blond woman over there by the piano?"

The maid nodded. "Miss Fisher." She all but scowled. "Yes?"

"I want you to tell her that Max Sheridan said she can hike home or ride on the back of an elephant, for all I care. Don't clean it up—use those words, exactly." He peeled a twenty-dollar bill from his wallet and held it out to her. "I can count on you, right?"

She looked at the money but didn't take it. "Mr. Wilkes doesn't allow us to accept tips from his guests."

"Mr. Wilkes is too pie-eyed to know who's doing what." Max shoved the bill into her apron pocket. "Those words exactly, okay?"

The woman smiled. "It'll be my pleasure, sir."

One more bridge burned, he thought as he started the car.

It was all Max could do to keep his mind on the road during the drive from Wilkes's house to Lily's hotel. He hadn't needed to see her face to imagine how she must have looked, if indeed she'd witnessed the kiss. He cringed, picturing her, green eyes wide with disbelief, lips slightly parted in shock, one delicate hand pressed to her pearl-draped throat. She'd have stood there a second or two, if he knew her, blinking to make sure she hadn't been seeing things. And when she realized the scene was all too real, Lily no doubt had lifted her chin, thrown back her shoulders and marched resolutely toward the nearest exit.

She'd always been a tough little thing. It seemed to Max she'd rather have the earth swallow her whole than allow anyone to see they had enough control over her to make her cry.

He pounded the steering wheel. "Idiot!" he said through his teeth. "What kind of man are you?"

Not the kind she deserved. The guy Lily deserved would have been far more concerned with *her* feelings than with a woman he barely knew. He'd put up with Susan's shenanigans because he hadn't wanted to embarrass her. But it would take a lot more than being brushed off by the likes of him to hurt a woman like that. He'd behaved like the stereotypical ladies' man, believing he was attractive enough, sexy enough to have that kind of power over a woman.

But he *did* have the power to hurt. He'd wounded Lily deeply, cut her to the quick. If he hadn't, she never would have run off like that. Not his take-it-on-the-chin Lily!

He'd never felt more like a heel. When he got right down to it, his own ego had been in control of the situation, not Susan. He hadn't tried hard enough to get rid of her. Who would he be kidding if he said he'd done everything humanly possible?

Certainly not him.

Definitely not Lily.

Max braked hard in her hotel's parking lot and ran from the car to the lobby. He stood, toe tapping nervously on the beige marble floor, waiting for the elevator. When finally it arrived, he got in, punched the button for the fifth floor, drummed his fingers on the brass rail that followed three walls of the car.

The doors opened with a high-pitched *ding* and he stepped into the hall, his hurried footsteps muffled by the plush carpeting. Max found her room, took a deep breath and knocked on the door. He'd make her understand, somehow, that what she'd seen had been a horrible yet meaningless mistake, that nothing like it had ever happened before or would ever happen again.

No answer.

He knocked again, then steeled himself, because if she opened that door and she stood there, eyes red-rimmed from crying…

Still no answer.

Max pressed an ear to the door, knuckles banging a third time. "Lily?" he called quietly. "You in there?"

A bellhop walked by, shoving a cart laden with soiled dishes. "If you're lookin' for the lady who was in that room, I think she checked out."

Max stiffened. "Checked out?"

"Saw her pulling one of those wheely suitcases down the hall." He thought about it a moment. "Must've been ten, fifteen minutes ago, when I delivered room service at the other end of the hall."

"Are you sure she checked out?" He'd floored the sports car, risking a speeding ticket or an accident to get here as fast as he could. How could she have had time to pack and—

"I remember her," the young man said, "because she

nearly bumped into me." He tugged the sleeve of his white jacket. "Looked like maybe she'd been cryin'."

"Thanks," Max said, slipping the kid a five.

"Hope you catch up with her," he called, as Max raced toward the bank of elevators.

"So do I," he said under his breath. "So do I...."

Lily decided enough was enough. No more tears. Period. She sat woodenly on the black vinyl chairs at gate nine, hands folded primly in her lap, waiting to board the plane.

She'd been lucky today—catching a standby flight coming into O'Hare, getting another going out.

But luck had nothing to do with it, and she knew it. The Good Lord had orchestrated things.

She learned the hard way, and God had made sure she'd get to Chicago so she could see for herself that things could never work out between her and Max Sheridan. And He'd arranged quick passage home so she could lick her wounds in the bosom of her loving family.

She should have known better. Because, really, what more could she expect from a man who'd abandoned his faith...who, despite his many blessings, questioned the Almighty more often than he questioned local politicians. If he couldn't trust the Lord, how could he be trusted himself?

He can't, she admitted, remembering the sight of him with Susan.

Lily closed her eyes, hoping to block the image from

her mind. But it seemed just as vivid, just as painful behind that curtain of darkness.

She focused on the young couple seated across from her. Newlyweds, no doubt. She could tell by the way the girl kept holding her hand up, trying to catch a beam of light in her diamond wedding band. By the way they sat, shoulders touching.

She looked away, unable to watch a moment more of their bliss, because the truth was, she'd never have a moment of it for herself.

True as that was, she couldn't put all the blame on Max's shoulders. Half belonged to her, for convincing herself he cared for her, that maybe he was falling in love with her. He had never said anything of the kind, had never made a single promise, had not so much as hinted at a commitment.

She'd read far more into those kisses than he'd intended. From Max's point of view, they'd probably just been for sport. Trivial. To give meaning to them had been a mistake. One of the biggest she'd made. Ever.

She inhaled a gulp of air, exhaled slowly.

Life was pretty good, right?

She had her dad, her sisters, her animals, right?

Lily remembered a day from long ago…

"Where'd you get that black eye?" her dad had asked, pulling her onto his lap.

"Jimmy Peters dumped my book bag on the school bus floor. And when I was crawling around picking them up, he kicked me. So I socked him. I hate him!" she had said, burying her face in the soft flannel of his plaid shirt.

"Now, now," he said, drying her tears with the pads of his thumbs. "Let me tell you a story. It's about an old Navajo and his young grandson. 'There is a great battle going in within me, a war of two wolves,' he told the boy. 'The first wolf is evil, and symbolizes worry, hatred, bitterness, anger, superiority, laziness—all the worst of human emotions.

"'The second wolf is good, representing kindness and love, hope, faith, trust, helpfulness—the best things man can be.'

"The grandson thought about this for a long, long time, and then he said, 'Grandfather? Which wolf wins?'"

Lamont had taken Lily's face in his big callused hands at that moment, had looked deep into her eyes and finished the story: "'Whichever wolf I feed,' said the grandfather. 'Whichever wolf I feed....'"

Lily hadn't fully understood the moral, not as a ten-year-old.

But she knew its meaning now, and held it close to her heart.

God had blessed her with free will, had given her the ability to choose how she would react to things that happened to her, throughout her life.

She would have to choose now, between feeling disappointed and angry with Max, or forgiving and forgetting. She knew which decision the Lord expected her to make.

So she'd pray, hard, for the strength to get through this quickly, quietly, without complaint.

"Good evening, ladies and gentlemen. Flight number

three-five-seven is now boarding at gate nine. If you'll have your boarding pass ready, please…"

Lily stood, grabbed her carry-on bag, and got into line with her fellow passengers. As she shuffled, one slow step at a time closer to the airliner's entrance ramp, she decided to pray, too, for the wisdom to remember that Max hadn't guaranteed anything but friendship. In that regard, he hadn't let her down at all.

That was the truth she'd hold on to until the pain lessened.

And it would only subside, for it would never leave her.

Max wished he'd left his coat in the car, because as he ran through the terminal, he could feel the sweat running down his back. He checked the monitors, looking for any flight bound for Amarillo International, and saw one, scheduled for takeoff in less than fifteen minutes.

Maybe it would be late and he'd reach her in time, stop her from getting on that plane. He couldn't have her thinking there was any truth in what she'd seen in Wilkes's library.

He tried her cell phone again, hoping she'd finally turned it on. But it rang and rang before a pleasant-voiced woman instructed him to leave a message after the beep. "Lily," he said, breathing hard as he ran toward gate nine, "don't get on that plane. Please. You have to let me explain—"

His cell phone cut out on him. Max slapped the mouthpiece shut. "No-good piece of worthless trash," he grumped, shoving it into his shirt pocket. "Of all the times for it to die on me…"

He encountered a throng of people, milling through the security check-in point. Max hadn't thought of this. He'd never make it through the system without a boarding pass. Even if he'd managed to book a last-minute flight, he couldn't leave Chicago. Not with all the paperwork he'd put into motion before Wilkes's party. There was no turning back. Not that he wanted to. But if he didn't stay, scribble his John Hancock at the bottom of every document, he'd have to start the whole process over again. No…better to stay put, clean things up, and then put the Windy City behind him, once and for all.

Then he had an idea.

He backtracked a few yards, until he found an available agent at a ticket counter. "Miss," he said, "I need to have a passenger paged. It's an emergency."

Seconds later, the woman's voice echoed throughout the terminal: "Will a Miss Lily London please pick up the nearest airport telephone. Miss Lily London…"

Max waited, pacing back and forth near the security area. There was no other exit from the airport; she'd have to come this way.

The plane was scheduled for takeoff within minutes. Surely she'd already boarded. And, in that case, no way would she have heard the message.

In the unlikely event that she'd arrived moments ago, Lily would be passing through the final leg of security right about now. If she figured out who'd inspired the announcement, would she pick up the phone?

Max rubbed his eyes. No, she wouldn't. And he could hardly blame her.

He walked to the wide wall of windows in time to see an east-west jet taxiing toward the runway. Somehow, Max knew Lily was on that plane.

The best he could hope for now was to redouble his efforts, get the real estate papers signed and get the partnership documents filed. Making a profit was the last thing on his mind.

He took his time heading for the parking lot. No need to hurry now. Just as he stepped into the biting night air, a jetliner screamed overhead, its nose pointed toward the sky. A departing flight, Max thought. Lily's?

"Keep her safe," he whispered sadly into the blackness, "always."

Chapter Thirteen

Lily felt like a silly schoolgirl, avoiding Max's calls this way. Better that, she thought, than to answer the phone and let him hear her bawling on the other end like a starving calf. He'd been tying up loose ends in Chicago for the past few days now. Would he ever tire of leaving messages that never got returned?

She'd learned from Georgia that Max had sold his house in Chicago, that he'd let the partners buy him out of the accounting firm. Which meant that this time, he was coming home for good. According to Georgia he was flying in to Amarillo today.

Lily had to get a handle on her emotions before she talked to him again, because now that he was a full-time Amarillo resident, she'd likely run into him often. When that happened, she wanted to conduct herself with an air of dignity and pride…instead of running off to blubber over unrequited love.

It was as she'd spooned the last of a can of dog food into the one-eyed owl's bowl that the phone rang.

"Lily, Cammi's asking for you. Can you come to the hospital, quick?"

Hospital? Why was Reid at the hospital?

"She lost the baby, kiddo, and she needs you."

Oh, Lord, Lily prayed, *please let it be a mistake!*

"I'm on my way," she told Reid, banging down the phone. "Missy," she told the dog, "you stay here and guard the rest of the guys, okay? I'll be back as soon as I can."

The golden retriever smiled and wagged her tail as if in agreement.

Lily began backing out of the driveway when the biggest pickup truck she'd ever seen pulled in behind her, blocking her in. A tall, lean man got out of the driver's side, strolled up to her car. "You Lily London?"

"Yes," she said tentatively.

"Rangers at Lake Meredith told me you're the gal who's got my dog."

Her heart felt as though it had dropped into her stomach. *No,* she thought, *it can't be. Not after all these months.*

"Come to fetch her," he said, when Lily didn't respond.

She turned off the car, stepped onto the blacktop. "I posted signs, placed ads, even advertised on the radio. But that was months ago."

The man shrugged one bony shoulder. "Been busy."

Lily looked at the truck. A woman sat in the passenger seat, looking every bit as grim-faced and stubborn as the man.

Missy came bounding toward them, stopping several

yards away when she spotted the visitor. She wasn't "smiling" now, Lily noticed.

"She never did cotton to me," he said, rolling a toothpick from one side of his mouth to the other. With his thumb, he gestured toward the truck. "Belongs to my wife."

"I've grown very fond of Missy...."

At the sound of her name, the retriever's ears perked. Still, she remained a safe distance from the man.

"Missy? Her name ain't Missy. It's Yella Gold—Goldie for short." He inspected grimy fingernails. "Tell you what," he said, chomping on the toothpick, "since you're so smitten with the mutt, I'll sell her to you."

Lily had her checkbook, right there on the front seat of her car. She reached over the console to grab it. "Name your price," she said, opening it up and clicking the ballpoint she kept inside its case.

"Ten thousand dollars."

Her mouth dropped open. "Ten thousand..." She looked at Missy and knew that if she had that kind of money, she'd gladly pay it. But Lily poured every penny of what she earned managing River Valley Ranch into the care and feeding of her animals. "I...I don't have that much." She glanced at the register, saw the dismal total on the bottom line.

She narrowed her eyes, suddenly suspicious. "How do I know she's your dog?"

He smirked, pulled a sheet of folded paper from his shirt pocket. "Kinda thought you might ask that," he said, handing it to her. "That's her pedigree you're holdin'."

She glanced at it, tried to hand it back. "This is still no proof that you're her owner."

He wouldn't accept the paper. "So, it's proof you want, is it?" The man faced Missy and snapped his fingers. Her fur bristled as she bared her teeth. A low, ferocious growl echoed from deep in her chest as she lowered her head. "Goldie," he ordered, "come!"

Missy's snarling intensified. She hadn't shown any signs of being vicious, not once in the months since Lily had pulled her out of Lake Meredith. "Where'd you lose her?" she demanded.

"Me an' the missus was fishin' on Lake Meredith. She fell in the water." He shrugged again. "We thought she drowned. Then I found this."

The paper he handed her this time was one of the Lost Dog posters she'd hung on every telephone pole in Amarillo. "I still haven't seen any proof that you're her owners."

"Kinda thought you'd say that, too," he said, "bein' that you're Lamont London's baby girl and all. Here's the check I wrote to the kennel, and the one I wrote to the American Kennel Club. See? The numbers jibe. She's my dog."

Now Lily understood. They'd heard that her father was one of the wealthiest men in the Texas Panhandle; they'd put two and two together, and come up with ten thousand.

Well, she couldn't ask her dad for the money. Lamont had always been generous to a fault. But he'd been born and raised a rancher, with a practical, down-to-earth mind-set about money. To him, animals were a family's bread and butter. No dog, not even his beloved Obnoxious, would be worth ten thousand dollars.

"I can give you five hundred now, five hundred more if—"

"Nope. Ten grand. Take it or leave it."

It made sense, suddenly, that they'd named her Goldie. Who knows how many times they'd pulled this scam?

Maybe if she could buy some time… "Could you give me a few days?"

He glanced at his wife, who gave one slow nod.

"You have a week." He checked his watch, then climbed into the driver's seat of his truck. "Ten grand," he repeated, "or the mutt goes home with us."

With that, he backed down the drive and headed north.

Trembling, heart hammering, Lily hugged Missy. "Those terrible people!" she said, kissing the dog's head. "What have they done to you?" Ruffling the retriever's long, shiny ears, she added, "Don't you worry, girl. I'll find a way to keep you." She kissed her again, this time on her snout.

Lily got back into the car and headed south, toward the hospital. "When it rains, it pours," she muttered. With Cammi in the hospital and Missy's future in jeopardy, she'd have plenty to worry about….

Her father's wolf story came to mind.

Which wolf are you going to feed? she asked herself.

Cammi had always been Lily's rock. Since they lost their mother when Lily was four and Cammi twelve, her sister had been more like a mom. Now it was Lily's turn to be the supportive, nurturing one.

Cammi would need her to be strong. So would Reid, for that matter. Could she do it?

She could…if she fed the right wolf.

Home. Max had thought about it as he signed the real estate papers, as he scribbled the bottom line on the documents that would free him from the partnership, as he read the in-flight magazine during the trip home.

It sure would be good to unpack in Amarillo, never to live anywhere else again.

But there were more important things to consider than his suitcase. He had to straighten things out with Lily—the sooner, the better.

He must have called her fifty times since she left Chicago the other night, must have left half that many messages. But she hadn't answered one. Maybe he'd been wrong on Thanksgiving when he'd speculated which of Lamont's daughters had inherited his fiery temper. Maybe it *was* Lily, not Violet, after all. Because if she wasn't mad at him, what kept her from answering the phone!

Hurt feelings, that's what. In her shoes, he'd have been humiliated, witnessing what looked like a passionate love scene. But unlike Lily, Max would have confronted things, head-on.

Wouldn't he?

He'd driven straight from the airport to River Valley Ranch, fully expecting to find Lily in the barn, mothering her animals.

He'd been wrong.

Missy had been there and, strange as it seemed, hadn't acted like her usual happy self. "What's wrong, girl?" he asked, ruffling her soft fur. "You missin' your mama?"

The dog whined, broke free of his hug and began pacing. Something had agitated her, and Max couldn't help but wonder what. Missy was the most laid-back dog he'd ever met.

He knocked on the back door of Lamont's ranch house.

No answer.

He tried the front door.

Same result.

That was almost as weird as Missy's behavior, because not once in all the years he'd come here as a boy had the place been deserted.

It was like a ghost town. No Lamont. No Lily. Not even a ranch hand he could quiz.

Puzzled and worried, Max left.

"I don't get it," Max said, a short while later in Georgia's diner. "What do you mean, someone wants ten grand for Missy?"

Georgia shrugged. "I'm only repeating what I heard in town. Strangers showed up, put papers under Lily's nose to prove they're the dog's rightful owners. She has a week to come up with the money or Missy goes with them next time they leave." She pointed to the bulletin board near the phone. "That's their number."

"How'd *you* get it?"

"They came here first, looking for her, while she was out visiting you in Chicago. Told me if I heard from her, I should have her call them." She paused. "How'd things go out there, anyway?"

"Don't ask."

"Max Sheridan, you can't say a thing like that to a woman and get away with it!"

He knew it was true. Particularly with *this* woman. Max told her all about it—about how surprised he'd been when she called to say she'd taken him up on his invitation, about the dinner party…about Susan.

"Good grief, Max. What were you thinking!"

"That's just the trouble. I wasn't."

"Well, what're you going to do?"

He shrugged. "Mom, I honestly don't know."

"You love her, don't you?"

"Big time," he said without hesitation.

"Then, you have to set her straight, as soon as possible."

"She'll probably never speak to me again."

"'Course she will. She loves you, too."

"Wish I could be sure of that."

"Trust me. I've been people-watching my whole adult life. This place gives me plenty of opportunity to hone up on it. I know the difference between infatuation and 'til-death-do-you-part love. That girl's got a bad case of the 'I Love Max' blues."

He met her eyes. "Y'think?" he asked hopefully.

"I *know*." She took a sip of coffee. "Trouble is, she's as stubborn as that bear of a father of hers. If she's got it in her head to stay away from you, that's exactly what she'll do."

He frowned. "Man. I hope not."

"I remember years back, when you were off at college, she was working for me part time. One of the young truckers who came in a couple of times a week did something to rile her. She'd walk *way* around his table here in the diner." Using her chin as a pointer, she indicated the street. "Out there, she'd go clean across the street to avoid him."

"Whew. What did he do to get her that mad?"

"Never did find out. But I can promise you this—if that fella walked in here right now, and Lily saw him, she'd head straight out the door."

Talk like this wasn't helping build his confidence any. Max said, "So, is she going to give the money to Missy's owners?"

"Don't see how she can. She puts every dime she gets her hands on into those animals of hers."

"What about Lamont? Surely he'd help her."

She gave him a hard stare. "You're joking, right?"

Max sighed. "I guess that is pretty ridiculous." He'd lived in cattle country most of his life. Dogs were for protection, for herding cows. Sure, folks got attached to them, but not ten thousand dollars' worth of attachment. It just wasn't practical. "She must be brokenhearted," he said. "She loves that dog almost as much as I love Nate."

"Shame it had to happen right now, too. She's already got enough on her shoulders, considering what's going on with Cammi and Reid."

"What's going on?"

Georgia sighed. "That poor girl…she came back to town a year or so ago. Did you hear she'd gone to Hollywood, tried to become an actress?"

"Doesn't surprise me. Cammi always did love the stage. And she's the spitting image of her mom."

"Rose could have been a big star if she hadn't married Lamont. She'd gotten top billing in a dozen or so movies before they met."

"Think she regretted giving it up?"

"Not a chance. She was born to be by his side."

Max understood that only too well. He'd loved Lily for just about as long as he could remember.

"Cammi got married out there, some stuntman."

"I hadn't heard that."

"It's true. The young fool took risks all day long on the movie sets, and would you believe he died when he crashed his car into a tree?"

Max shook his head as he poured himself a cup of coffee.

"Poor kid tried her best out there, but she couldn't make ends meet. Told me that on the very afternoon she buried her husband, the doctor called to tell her she was gonna have a baby."

"But…"

"She lost that one, too."

"What do you mean, 'too'?"

"What do you think it means?"

Max winced. "Man. That's rough."

Nodding, Georgia sighed again. "The whole family is at the hospital, lending moral support. I imagine it's hardest for Lily, because she and Cammi have always been closer than sisters."

He should go over there, lend moral support to *her*. But what if his presence only upset her more?

"If you had the sense God gave a goose, you'd go over there, hold her hand."

"She'd probably slug me."

"So, let her. You've got it coming."

"Hey. Whose side are you on?"

"I'll tell you whose. If this cane reached farther, I'd smack you upside your head. What were you thinking, letting that hussy—"

"I already told you. I wasn't thinking."

Not clearly, anyway. But he was thinking rationally now. He downed the coffee in one gulp, then headed for the door, stopping near the corkboard. He snapped the slip of paper bearing the name and number of Missy's owners from under its peg, shoved it into his shirt pocket.

Georgia smiled. "Careful, son."

"Why?"

"People are gonna get the idea you have a heart, after all."

Truth was, he didn't care what people thought. Aside from his mother and son, the only opinion of him that really mattered was Lily's.

And he intended to do everything in his power to prove it to her, starting now.

When he'd left River Valley before his trip to Chicago, Max had seen Hank's sister at the house across the road, carrying a For Sale sign to the front porch. He'd heard that Gladys and George were thinking of moving to Florida; evidently, they'd made their decision.

Now Max had more than enough time to check things out. Nate was playing happily with Georgia's old baking pans when he left his mom's apartment. Georgia's plan, she'd told Max, was to "teach that boy to make his *own* chocolate-chip cookies, since he eats them by the dozen!" As he pulled into the driveway, he remembered that when others commented on Lamont London's regal ranch house, Lily always shrugged. "I'd rather live in a house like the Morgans'," she'd say. "It's my dream house." If he'd heard that once, he'd heard it a hundred times.

He fully intended to keep the diner, but Max didn't want to live in the apartment upstairs anymore. He yearned for a lush green lawn, a yard for Nate to play in, a vegetable garden, a garage where he could putter with his woodworking tools. If he bought the Morgan place…

He'd gone to high school with Pat; maybe she could help him cut through some red tape.

"It needs some work," she admitted, showing him around inside. "But it's a good, solid house. I'd bet it'll still be standing here when both of us are six feet under."

"Now, there's a cheery thought," he teased. He walked outside, grabbed the For Sale sign. He handed it to her. "I want it."

Laughing, she said, "You don't even know the asking price."

"Doesn't matter. I'll take it." He handed her a business card, scratched out his Chicago information and scribbled in his new numbers. "Call me when you've drawn up the paperwork."

"Max, don't you want an inspector's report?"

"Yeah, but whatever is wrong can be fixed. You said yourself it's a good solid house."

"Well…"

"How long will it take?"

"Couple of hours, if the Morgans take your offer."

"Make them an offer they can't refuse. Top their asking price by five grand."

"Max!" Pat said, fanning herself with his business card. "You're supposed to talk them *down,* not jack the price *up!*"

He glanced at the wrought-iron archway across the road. If Lily said no the first time he proposed, he'd be nice and close; it would be real easy to show up unannounced and pop the question again and again 'til he wore down her resistance and she said yes, if only to shut him up.

"I want it," he said again. "I'll pay cash."

She opened her mouth to protest, but he held up a hand to stop her. "Have the papers ready by morning and I'll double your percentage."

Pat didn't need to think about it. "Done!" she said, grinning.

Now, as he pulled into a space in the hospital parking lot, he smiled to himself. He wasn't going to let Lily get away this time. He'd waited twelve years to make her his own. If it took another twelve before she said "I do," so be it. And in the meantime, he wouldn't have to wake up to the smell of frying bacon every morning of his life!

He stopped at the desk, asked where he might find Reid and Cammi and the rest of the Londons. Third floor, Maternity Ward, the lady in the striped smock told him. That seemed cruel, Max thought, putting a woman who'd just lost her baby among new mothers and newborns....

On his way to the elevator, he spied the gift shop. Inside, he bought two bouquets of flowers: pink roses for Cammi, red ones for Lily. He bought chocolates, too, and a card that said "My thoughts are with you." He signed it while the cashier rang up his order, tucked it into Cammi's blooms. "If you need anything," he wrote, "just say the word." Max drew a line under *anything,* and signed his name.

What does a man say in a situation like this? he wondered as the elevator took him up two floors. "I'm sorry," while sincere, seemed weak and inadequate. Might be best to say nothing, shake Reid's hand, hand Cammi the roses—tell them how he felt, just by being there. Maybe something profoundly genuine would strike him once he was in their presence.

Lamont and Nadine, Violet and Ivy had gathered in the waiting room. Max studied their joyless faces and waited for something wise and comforting to come to mind. When it didn't, he sat in the nearest empty chair. "Sorry to hear what happened. Is Cammi okay?"

"Physically, she's fine," Nadine said.

No one needed to spell out how she was doing emotionally.

"Nice of you to come," Vi said. "Are the flowers for Cammi?"

He nodded, shoved the vase of pink roses closer to her. "You can take them to her. I don't want to intrude."

"We appreciate your being here, son," Lamont said.

His deep voice was foggy with grief, something Max understood only too well. Watching a child of your blood suffer was hard and painful, especially if there wasn't a blessed thing you could do about it. Parents were supposed to protect their kids from harm, dads in particular....

"Lily is in the chapel," Ivy said. She smiled sadly. "I take it the other bunch is for her?"

Max nodded.

"Well, go on," Lamont instructed. "Take 'em to her before they wilt. And don't forget the chocolates. Lily has loved the stuff since before she cut her first tooth."

He got to his feet, hesitated.

"Chapel is one floor up, end of the hall," Ivy told him.

"Thanks," he said, and headed for the elevator.

"Lord," he whispered, "get me through this."

He couldn't believe his own ears. Had a *prayer* really just come out of his mouth? No wonder, he thought as the elevator doors closed, with all the tragedy and trauma that had been going on lately.

What would he say when he found Lily?

Would words even be necessary?

He'd get down on his hands and knees if that's what it took, because he wanted her to be a permanent part of his life—the sooner the better.

When he peered through the arched window carved into the door, the chapel appeared to be empty. But then he saw her, seated in front, her head bowed.

Easing the door open, Max stepped inside, the blood-red carpet dulling his footfalls. He walked up the center aisle and stopped beside her. *Hi, Lil,* he wanted to say. Instead, he tucked the box of candy under his arm and laid a hand on her shoulder.

She didn't move, save for the slightest intake of air. For a moment Lily merely sat, staring straight ahead. Then she placed her warm hand atop his, gave it a gentle *pat, pat, pat,* and slid over in the pew to make room for him.

"Peace offering?" she whispered, pointing to the candy on his lap, the roses in his hand.

He tucked in one side of his mouth. She had a knack for reading his mind, and he said so.

"What you saw in Chicago," he started.

She held up a hand to silence him.

"It wasn't what you think," he continued.

Lily met his eyes and he read the hopeful expectation there.

"I was explaining to Susan that…" He coughed. "I was…"

"…telling her goodbye?" she finished for him.

Max smiled. "That, and then some."

He watched her left brow rise slightly, as if the

unasked question was too much to bear. This wasn't the time or the place for romantic admissions. He'd tell her the "and then some" when the time *was* right. He gently changed the subject.

"I'm sorry, Lily, about Cammi's baby, about…" He blew a stream of air through his lips. "About a lot of things."

Lily opened the box of candy, popped a vanilla cream into her mouth. "So am I," she said around it.

"You?" He turned slightly in the seat, draping an arm along the pew back behind her. "What could you possibly have to be sorry for!"

"Just…things." She held out the box, offered him a piece. When he shook his head, she bit into a solid chocolate.

"What things?"

She met his eyes. "Does it matter?"

He could see that she'd been crying, that she was struggling to staunch tears, even now. Max wanted to wrap her in his arms, protect her from pain of any kind. Instead, he grazed his knuckles across her satiny cheek.

"No," he whispered. "It doesn't matter."

She tilted her head, hugging his fingertips to her shoulder. Such a sweet gesture. So sweet that he shifted, intending to hold her close, to start the litany of excuses for his awful behavior.

But she lifted the flowers to her face, closed her eyes and inhaled. "Amazing, aren't they?"

"Amazing?" Max sat back. *All in good time,* he thought. "How so?"

"Well, they're so delicate. Soft as velvet. You could crush one with your bare hands. And yet…" She sighed, drew in their perfume again. "And yet they're tough enough to slice through denim. I know, because it's happened to my blue jeans when I hiked in the—" She looked up at him again. "I'm boring you."

"You couldn't bore me, not even if you tried. Now go on. You were hiking…"

"The point is, nothing is what it seems."

When she looked at him this time, he read the challenge in her eyes. So many things she could be referring to… But Max didn't dare ask what, for fear he'd mention the wrong one, give her a whole new reason to avoid him.

"Get your cell phone fixed?" he asked, changing the subject.

Lily blinked. "It isn't broken." Then a slow smile broadened her mouth as she realized what he was getting at. "I've been…busy."

"So I take it." He stroked her cheek again. "I'm sorry about Cammi's baby."

Lily nodded. "Me, too."

He took his arm from the pew, rested it across her shoulders. "Is there anything I can do?"

When she smiled up at him, his heart lurched.

"You're already doing it, Max."

"How's she doing?"

"Pretty good, all things considered. They'll be sending her home in the morning. Nothing more the doctor can really do."

"I guess she's taking it pretty hard?"

"No harder than would be expected. But she's been through it before. She'll be okay, in time."

Max faced forward, pressed the pads of his fingertips together to form a spider that squatted and stood, squatted and stood. "Doesn't seem fair."

"What doesn't?"

"With a world of wicked, evil people to pick on, why did God choose Cammi to do this to? She's as good as gold."

"He isn't picking on her," Lily corrected. "It just…" She shrugged again. "It just happened. It isn't God's fault."

"Then, whose fault is it?"

"I guess if we need to name a culprit, we can choose life."

He shook his head. "I'll never understand you people."

"'You people'?"

"Believers. Followers. Born-again, saved, baptized, in-the-spirit Christians—whatever you're calling yourselves these days."

She pursed her lips, tilted her head. "I like to think we're the faithful."

"See, that's where you lose me."

"Where faith comes in, you mean?"

He nodded.

"You can't have faith by taking a pill, Max. It doesn't magically show up in some people, skip over others. It's something that develops, over time. Something that you learn to *do* as much as you learn to *feel*…."

"Through suffering?"

"Not necessarily, but that's one road."

"Thanks, but I think that's one road I'll stay off of. Too many potholes."

"You put them there. You should be able to avoid them."

He turned to her. "What?"

"Well, you did." She replaced the top on the candy box. "Every time you feel doubt, or fear, or worry, you're digging a new hole. See, that's where I was going before, with all that 'rose' talk. We're a lot like those flowers. We sometimes look weak and fragile, but we're really not.

"Because God made us of strong stuff, gave us what we need to fend off things like doubt and fear and worry. You have all the tools you need to avoid those potholes—right here." She laid her hand over his heart. "*That's* where faith is born, Max. You can't get it simply by showing up at church, or by reading the Bible. You won't find it by donating money to charity or doing good deeds."

She patted his chest. "You'll find it *here,* within yourself." A last shrug. "If you choose not to look, then you have no one to blame but yourself when your tires go flat."

"Tires?"

"Well, the potholes metaphor was yours…."

He chuckled. Leave it to her to make him laugh, even at a time like this. Max put his arm around her again. "So you're really okay with what happened to Cammi's baby?"

"I didn't say that. I'm heartbroken. I'm sad. Angry. It shouldn't have happened. She'd make a wonderful mother." She took his hands in hers, gave them a gentle shake. "Don't you get it? I have faith that things will turn out all right in the end. I have no idea *how* they'll turn out, mind you, but I know everything will be all right."

"And that's faith."

"My version of it, anyway."

He pulled her into a sideways hug. "How'd you get so smart?" he asked, kissing her temple.

"Not smart…"

"Faithful," they said together.

"I'm not sure I get it," he admitted, "but I promise you this—I'm going to give what you said a lot of thought."

"Why the sudden change of heart?"

He could almost feel the warmth of her little hand against his chest, above his heart. "Truth?"

Eyes wide, she pointed to the cross up front. "You're in a church," she said, grinning. "I strongly advise it."

He'd been beating himself up over Melissa's death for far too long. Logic and common sense told him it wasn't his fault that the poor girl had overdosed. Still…

But Lily had a point. Maybe. If she was right about this whole faith thing, maybe he could let go of the past.

No maybes about it, Max thought; if Lily was at his side, he could overcome *anything*.

"I don't want to lose you again, Lily. If learning how to have faith will keep you in my life, it's as good as done."

"We go too far back for you to worry about anything like that."

She'd misunderstood, thought he meant he didn't want to lose her *friendship*. Sure, he wanted that, because what kind of marriage would it be without it? But he wanted more. All of it. The whole ball of wax. Fireworks, hearts and flowers, bells and whistles, the whole nine romantic yards.

Max grabbed her shoulders, forced her to meet his eyes, gave her a gentle shake. He wanted to say, *I love you and I want to spend the rest of my life with you!* But that look in her eyes—that spark of suspicion, that glint of mistrust—choked off the words.

He pressed a tender kiss to her forehead, then gathered her near. "Ah, Lily," he sighed into her hair. Soon, he'd tell her everything she needed to hear—and a few things she hadn't even considered yet.

But not here, not now. He had a lot of work to do first, to earn her trust, to smother her suspicion.

"Want to go back to Cammi's room?"

She nodded.

He gathered up the flowers and the chocolate, then slid an arm around her and led her into the hall.

Yes, he had a lot of work to do. But he had time. And when he had finished, things would be all right.

Funny, but suddenly he believed that. *Really* believed it.

Smiling, Max understood why.

He'd found the meaning of faith.

Chapter Fourteen

After the Christmas Eve service, parishioners gathered on the church steps, laughing and talking, sharing holiday plans. Max hadn't felt this welcomed or at ease, anywhere, in a long time.

"Your mom did *what?*"

"Eloped. Left a note and everything."

Lamont chuckled. "No foolin'?"

Max pretended to read it: "'Dear Son, Running off to get married. Take care of my cane.'"

Laughing, Lamont said, "Well, she spared you the fuss and bother of a wedding. Count your blessings."

He found himself doing that a lot lately, thanks to Lily.

A week or so before Christmas, she'd introduced him to the writings of Henry Van Dyke. Max hadn't expected to like the poems and essays, but read them because he had promised Lily he would. No one was more surprised than Max when the simple yet beautiful words reminded him of God's awesome power. As a result, he'd gone back to church—not because Georgia needed a ride or Nate wanted to attend a social, but because his rediscovered sense of peace had drawn him into the fellowship.

"Speaking of marriage," Max said, taking Lamont aside, "there's something I'd like to talk to you about."

Backs to the rest of the crowd, the men stood just around the corner of the church.

"I'm sure you know how I feel about Lily…."

Lamont smiled. "I've known since you were both still in school."

Nodding, Max said, "I figured as much. So I was wondering…what would you say if I asked her to marry me?"

As the awkward moment of silence ticked by, Max realized he hadn't considered what he'd do if Lamont didn't give his consent. He wouldn't go against the man's wishes.

Or would he?

He loved Lily, more than he'd ever imagined it was possible to love another human being. But without her father's blessing, life might prove to be difficult at best.

Lamont gave Max a fatherly slap on the back. "I'd say it's about time, that's what!"

Overwhelmed with gratitude and relief, Max threw his arms around his father-in-law to be. "Thanks, Lamont." He stepped back, ran both hands through his hair. "I'll be good to her. You've got my word on it."

He looked at the older, wiser face, read the mischievous expression and prepared for a "you will if you know what's good for you" speech.

"I don't doubt it for a minute," Lamont said instead. Abruptly, he turned, guided Max back toward the church entrance. "Tell you what," he said. "There's no sense in your going home, spending Christmas Eve alone. You're coming to dinner anyway, so why don't you and Nate stay in the guest room tonight." He paused, then added, "I think it would do us all a lot of good, having a child in the house on Christmas morning."

Cammi and Reid hadn't been out of the house until tonight's service. He'd half expected they'd be sullen and withdrawn, burdened by their grief. They'd been anything but! The newlyweds looked genuinely happy. Surely there would still be private moments of mourning, but it was clear that their faith had pulled them through.

"Thanks, Lamont," Max said. "Nate would love that...and so would I."

Lily's dad grinned. "Once there's a ring on her finger, feel free to call me 'Dad.'"

He'd noticed that's how Reid referred to the man; Max was touched to be so easily included into the London family. "Thanks," he said again, meaning it.

One more blessing to be counted....

"This is really nice of you," Max said at the London house later that evening. "If I wrapped them, Nate's presents would look like a gorilla had done it."

Lily pointed to the one gift Max *had* wrapped and

grinned. "I see what you mean." Then she added, "Don't think I'm doing it for nothing."

He took a step closer. "So there's a price tag on the gesture?"

"Mmm-hmm," she said around a length of curly ribbon, "big one. You have to help me decorate the cookies."

"You're joking. Knowing what a klutz I am, you'd—"

"The cookies need to look festive, not store-bought. Your touch is exactly what the job calls for."

"Okay, if you say so...."

"This is my favorite night of the year."

"Why's that?"

"Well, listen to the house, all hushed and peaceful. I wonder if it sounded like this in the manger, the night Christ was born?"

Max took her in his arms. "Not likely, with all those cows and donkeys. And let's not forget that kid with his drum."

Lily laughed. "And you call *me* silly!"

He glanced at the tree. "Your dad tells me you decorated the tree all by yourself."

She nodded.

"Decorated the whole house."

Another nod. "And your point is?"

"Answer me something..."

"Yes?"

"How'd you get the angel up there? That tree must be twenty feet tall."

"Fifteen. But only because we're limited by the ceiling. And to answer your question, I got the angel up there with the aid of a handy little invention known as the stepladder. Amazing contraption. Every house oughta have one."

"Nut," he said. He drew her closer. "What if this was your standard eight-foot ceiling?"

"Then, I guess we'd have a seven-foot tree." Grinning as her brow furrowed, Lily said, "Why do you ask?"

A smug little grin turned up one corner of his mouth. "Oh, nothing. Just wondering, that's all." Max glanced around the room. "Where's Missy?"

"Upstairs in the guest room…on the foot of Nate's bed."

Max chuckled. "I should have known. That kid loves her."

"She loves him, too."

Another all-knowing little grin. Then he said, "Yeah, she does."

Lily grabbed his wrist, started rolling up his shirt-sleeve.

"What're you doing?"

"Just checking to see what's up there." She gave him a wary glance. "You've been acting like the cat that swallowed the canary all evening. What's up?"

He let go of her, headed for the tree. Down on one knee, he wiggled his eyebrows. "What-say we open one present tonight?"

"Max! We can't do that! It's—"

"It's past midnight. Technically, it's Christmas morning. C'mon. What do you say?"

He looked so much like an innocent boy at that

moment, with the colorful lights reflecting in his big dark eyes, that Lily didn't know how she could refuse. "All right," she said, joining him on the floor, "but just one."

"One'll do it," he said, grabbing the package he'd wrapped.

Lily slid one of his presents from a small stack; if he opened this one tonight, he'd be able to wear it tomorrow.

He took her hand, led her to the couch. "You first," he said, patting the cushion beside him.

"No…*you* first."

"But what about the old rule— Ladies First?"

"I like to shake things up once in a while. Gentlemen can be at the front of the line…sometimes." She nodded toward his gift. "Go ahead. Open it."

She'd spent half an hour getting the foil paper tucked over the corners—just right; arranging the wide bow— just so. Max tore into it in less than a second, it seemed. Laughing as he lifted the lid, she said, "What took you so long!"

He dug through the tissue paper and pulled out the sweater. "It's great," he said. "I hope it's big enough." He looked inside the collar. "Hey, there's no label."

"That's because I made it."

Max stared at her, blinking as the information sunk in.

"A homemade sweater?" He held it up to his chest. "You *made* this?"

She nodded.

"When did you have time?"

"I had hours and hours, in the barn. If one of the animals is bad-off, I spend the night out there, to keep an eye on things. Can't risk dozing off, so I do stuff like that to keep myself awake."

"You spent hours and hours on *me?*"

Smiling, she said, "You're worth it."

Max studied the intricate cabling that decorated the sweater's front. "It's beautiful." He met her eyes. "I'm impressed."

"Don't be," she said. "I'm not."

"That's exactly what I said to you in Chicago, when you saw my office."

He was right, and it touched her that he remembered something so seemingly trivial. Maybe he'd been telling the truth that day in the hospital chapel, when he'd said he had much to prove to her.

"Your turn," he said, pointing to the box on her lap.

Lily deliberately took her time peeling off the stick-on bow, picking at the cellophane tape that held the Christmas-stockings paper in place. The waiting was driving him crazy, and she knew it. Smiling, she slowed her pace even more.

"You have exactly ten seconds," he said, his voice quiet and deep, "to open that box. After that, *I'm* gonna do it for you." He pulled back his shirtsleeve to expose his watch, and started counting. "Ten, nine, eight…"

"All right, spoilsport, have it your way." Lily lifted off the lid and pulled back the crinkled white tissue paper. "It's…it's a…" She met his eyes. "A dog leash?"

"Uh-huh. But there's more. Keep digging."

She found an envelope buried in the bottom and slid

out its contents. Missy's pedigree! "Max," she sighed, heart thumping with relief and joy and love. "How did you… When did you? I can't believe it!" She threw her arms around him, kissed him soundly on the cheek. "So she's mine? For real?"

"That's what the papers say."

"Maxwell Sheridan, I love you!"

"Yeah, yeah," he said, pushing her away. "Quit stalling. There's more in that envelope."

Lily couldn't help but notice…he hadn't said he loved her, too.

Sighing, she focused on his instructions. When she shook the envelope, a key fell into her upturned palm. The key to his heart? *Fat chance,* Lily thought.

"What does it open?"

"A door."

"A door," she echoed. "*What* door?"

"To a house."

"A house," she said, her voice a dull monotone as the frustration built. "*What* house?"

"The one across the road."

She looked toward the front door. "The Morgan place?" Frowning, Lily said, "Max, what on earth are you doing with their house key!"

"Isn't theirs," he said calmly. And poking a finger into her chest, he added, "It's yours."

"Mine? But…" She didn't understand.

"Okay. All right." He leaned forward, balancing elbows on knees, and clasped his hands in the space between. "Maybe this will clear things up…." He held her left hand in his and looked deep into her eyes. "What would you say if I told you Missy and the house across the road are yours to keep?"

"I'd say, 'Will you marry me?'" she blurted. Instantly, her fingertips went to her lips. Too late—the words were already out. In the space of two minutes, she'd succeeded in saying *everything* guaranteed to scare a confirmed bachelor into the next county.

He huffed. "You're not even gonna get down on one knee?"

Lily blinked. "I'm not— *What?*"

"And here I thought you were an old-fashioned girl, one who treasured tradition. Boy—" he shook his head "—was I wrong."

"Max, I—"

"When you ask a guy to marry you, you're supposed to get down on one knee. Take his hand in yours. Look longingly into his eyes. *Then* you say, 'Will you do me the honor of becoming my husband'?"

Lily's breathing was coming in short, soft gasps, her heart pounding like a parade drum. "And if I did all that," she began, not even caring that her voice trembled, that her hands quaked, "what would you say?"

He answered by taking her face in his hands. "I'd say, 'I love you, with all my heart. Always have, always will. And I could kick myself for not realizing it years ago, so we could be married by now!'" He paused, smiled. "*Then* I'd say, 'What took you so long to ask!'" He kissed the tip of her nose.

"So…is that a yes?"

"Say yes, Dad!" Nate said, jumping up and down in the doorway. "Say yes!"

Missy joined the three-way hug, tail wagging and doggy lips grinning.

"Well," Nate said, frowning at his father. "What are you waiting for?" He smacked the heel of his hand to his forehead.

"Say it!"

"Yes," he breathed.

"Hooray!" Nate hollered.

"Shh." Lily rustled his dark curls. "You'll wake everyone up."

"Sorry…Mom."

Tears sprang to her eyes as she looked into the merry little face.

"Get a load o' *that*," Max said. "One minute you're footloose and fancy free, the next…"

The answers to every prayer she'd prayed for herself were right here in this room. Lily had a feeling this would be the most memorable Christmas ever.

"Mom," she whispered. "Accidentally, sort of, but, *Mom!*"

* * * * *

Dear Reader,

Some of my all-time favorite poems and stories were composed by Henry van Dyke (1852–1933). The words of this gentle Pennsylvania-born man who spent his life pastoring in New York and teaching English literature at Princeton have been touching readers' hearts since his first works were published.

I wish Max Sheridan, my hero in *An Accidental Mom,* had discovered van Dyke's writings earlier; maybe then he wouldn't have slipped so far from his Father's guiding hand....

For the poet's guileless words remind us how simple it is to invite God into our lives, how very eager He is to accept our invitation. Perhaps a word, a phrase from the quiet, thought-provoking verses would have spared Max years of cold, lonely searching.

If you, like Max, find yourself a little lost, a little too far from the restful solace of the Almighty's embrace, do yourself a favor and read as many of Henry van Dyke's poems and stories as you can get your hands on. I promise, you won't regret it!

If you enjoyed *An Accidental Mom,* drop me a note c/o Love Inspired Books, 233 Broadway, Suite 1001, New York, NY 10279. I love hearing from my readers, and try to answer every letter personally.

All my best,

Loree Lough

REQUEST YOUR FREE BOOKS!

2 FREE INSPIRATIONAL NOVELS
PLUS 2
FREE
MYSTERY GIFTS

LIREG11

Love Inspired.
HISTORICAL

INSPIRATIONAL HISTORICAL ROMANCE

Wedding bells will ring in these two romantic
Regency stories from two favorite
Love Inspired Historical authors.
'Tis the season for falling in love!

The Wedding Season

by DEBORAH HALE *and* LOUISE M. GOUGE

Available June wherever books are sold.